FORGED BY MALICE

BEASTS OF THE BRIAR
BOOK THREE

ELIZABETH HELEN

LUNA FOX
PRESS

Published by Luna Fox Press

First Edition published December 2023

Interior Design © 2023 by Elizabeth Helen

Cover Design and Illustration © 2023 by saintjupit3rgr4phic

Proofread by Andra Kapule of sinfulalohaediting.com

Identifiers

ISBN: 978-1-998945-01-6 (eBook)

ISBN: 978-1-998945-00-9 (paperback)

ISBN: 9978-1-998945-02-3 (audio)

To Felix, a loyal friend, wonderful writing partner, and a true prince among men.

TRIGGER WARNINGS

Forged by Malice is the third book in the multi-book Beasts of the Briar series. It is a why-choose romance. Book 3 ends on a not-happily-ever-after cliffhanger. It contains mature themes, explicit sexual content, and is intended for audiences 18+. The following paragraph contains trigger warnings. **Please note these warnings do include a spoiler for the book.**

Trigger Warnings: Fantasy violence and gore, on-page death of a parent, mentions of physical and emotional abuse in a previous relationship, physical and emotional abuse by a parent against their adult children, the attempted sexual assault of a main character, body mutilation of a main character

PART ONE
ABSOLUTION

PROLOGUE

I sidora knew the monsters were coming. It wasn't the sight of the smoke curling over the fog, the felled trees, or even the wails that bounced off the mountain's path.

No, it was the smell. A horrendous stench belched from the bowels of the Below. Something akin to rotten waterlogged crops. The monsters' presence seeped over Mount Lumidor in a cloud of rot. Isidora knew wherever the wretched creatures traversed, no more plants would grow.

She pulled her scarf up over her mouth and inhaled through the fabric, masking some of the odor. The scarf still smelled like her mother, who had wrapped it hastily around her shoulders as Isidora had left. "We've asked for help before, as did many others. There is nothing they can do."

Isidora had gone anyway because she had to do something. Had to try. Try for her village, and her mother, and her little brother. Because surely this time the High Clerics would listen. Listen as she explained there were monsters on her doorstep.

One step in front of the other, she dared not look back to see if there was smoke rising from her village.

Smooth rocks slipped beneath her mud-caked boots; the ground was wet from last night's rain. A damp mist settled through the trees as night drew closer. Isidora kept moving. The scent of decay diminished, and she inhaled deeply, air growing thinner as she ascended.

Then there it was, piercing through the haze like the tip of a sword: Queen's Reach Monastery. It was so much bigger up close. Black metal arches seemed to pierce the sky itself. But here, in front of it, she was shadowed by the massive door, over five times her own height, and inlaid with iron bolts.

But she had not climbed all the way here to cower before a door. Isidora drew in a deep breath and knocked. It sounded so quiet to her, but a moment later, the door slid open.

There stood a woman dressed in robes of white and gold, a hood shadowing her gaze.

"I need to see the High Clerics." Isidora made her voice loud. "I need their help."

The robed woman ushered her inside. "Follow me."

Isidora thought that entering this place was not unlike stepping inside the maw of a terrible beast. One made of metal and glass instead of flesh and bone.

Two members of the Queen's Army flanked the door, spears held in tight grasps. But they were facing inward toward the stairs and a strange contraption was in the center of the chamber. Several other fae dressed in the same gold and white robes as the woman paced the entrance hall.

"This way," the woman said, sliding open a strange metal gate.

Isidora followed her into a small cyclical room, like a cage made of twisting metal. The woman closed the door, then tapped the side of her nose, a bemused smile on her face. "Well, you don't want to take the stairs, do you?"

The woman traced a rune on the door, and the whole cage rattled, then shot upward. Isidora's stomach lurched, and she grasped for purchase on the sides.

With a musical laugh, the woman said, "I believe my expression was the same as yours the first time I rode this. I wasn't much older than you."

Isidora struggled to catch her breath. Outside, polished metal whizzed by, then a blast of air on one side as half of the cage was exposed to the world. Isidora saw the mountain, and the bright spot of the capital carved into the side of it. Florendel …

"It's quite the sight," the woman said, removing her hood.

She was beautiful. Young, with short brown hair curled behind the most delicately pointed ears. But it was her eyes that made Isidora stare, as blue as the river at midnight. "Are you a princess?"

The woman laughed again. "No, I'm one of the Golden Acolytes. We worship the light of the Above."

"Oh, yes." Because of course she was. There were no more princesses left in the Spring Realm.

"What's your name?"

"Isidora."

"Beautiful," the acolyte replied. "A very regal name."

"I was named after the late High Princess." Isidora made herself unclench her hands from her skirt. High Princess Isidora wouldn't have clutched her skirts in fear. "What's your name?"

"Wrenley."

"I like your name, too," Isidora said. Wrenley reached down and clutched her trembling hand.

The cold air on one side vanished, and metal again enclosed their cage as they slowly rose higher and higher. A small lantern dangled from the ceiling, waving back and forth, casting a ring of buttery orange light. Something glittered on the acolyte's neck.

Wrenley caught her gaze. "We are each allowed one thing from our life before we decide to dedicate ourselves to the Above." She gestured to the string of seashells around her neck.

"It's lovely," Isidora said, letting her finger trail over the most beautiful one, a golden nautilus shell.

"My father was a flower merchant and used to bring me a shell every time he returned home from trading in the Summer Realm."

Cold air blew Wrenley's hair back from her brow, and Isidora turned to see nothing but clouds on one side of the cage. They were so high. Pressure grew in her ears.

"We're almost there." Wrenley stood.

Something flashed in Isidora's vision, a streak outside. She gasped, stumbling back into Wrenley's legs. What was that? A bird …

But birds didn't scream.

Wrenley only said, "I believe fate has brought you on this day for a reason." The cage clattered to a stop. "Step back."

Isidora did. A thick, glistening liquid pooled into the cage before dripping through the grates. Wrenley covered her hair with her hood, then pulled back the gate. She stepped wide over the wetness.

It was blood, more black than red, and Isidora couldn't help but follow the trail to a corner of this new room, to where a broken body lay, a body in golden robes.

The golden robes of the High Cleric. Fear tightened in Isidora's chest. Those who she had come to seek help from could not even help themselves.

"There is someone here to see you," Wrenley said.

Wrenley's words drew Isidora inside. And she knew they were at the highest point of the monastery. Windows of stained glass rimmed the circular room, except for one that was shattered. Red, blue, and green shards littered the ground.

That streak falling outside the cage … That had been a High Cleric as well.

White- and gold-robed acolytes bowed before the center of the room, where three shadows stood. Shadows of dark metal and wavering black robes.

Wrenley squeezed Isidora's shoulder and took an empty place around the circle before the shattered window, becoming as anonymous as all the other Golden Acolytes orbiting the shadows.

And Isidora was very much alone.

Her eyes darted from the lifeless High Cleric on the ground to the shattered window. There had been five High Clerics ruling this monastery for as long as she could remember. As long as anyone could remember …

But now they were dead.

She stepped forward, unable to avoid the blood, and felt its wetness seep into her worn boots. "I've come to ask for help. Goblins are coming to my village."

The shadows rippled, and one detached itself from the rest: a full set of beautifully crafted armor, pitch black like the cape he wore, the helmet eerily avian.

Isidora was a child of the Enchanted Vale. She knew of magic. But magic to her was Elder Miguel healing the scrape on her knee, or Mother singing to the harvest to encourage growth. Magic was a flower she righted after her little brother accidentally snapped the stem.

Isidora had never felt magic like this. It flooded the room, pricking her skin and ringing in her ears. She gasped for air she couldn't take in.

The figure marched forward, gloved hands tight on a massive hammer. Then he knelt before her, and it felt like night descending as she was shrouded by his shadow.

"You need not worry any longer, child." His voice was deep, reverberating beneath his helm. "The age of stasis is at an end. No longer will those with the power to protect squander and hide away while the citizens of Spring cower in terror."

His helmet was crafted in the shape of an owl, and she said: "You're a prince." This time, it wasn't a question. She recognized the helm. He was the second-born Prince of Spring. Suddenly, Isidora was no longer afraid.

"First, we will liberate the mountain villages from the wayward creatures." Prince Kairyn stood and quirked his helm toward the shattered window, in a move oddly reminiscent of the animal his mask resembled. The sharp, quick motions of an owl. "Then it's long past time I visited my father, the steward, and his princeguard."

"You're really going to save us?" Isidora asked.

"I will save all of Spring. But to do that, I'm going to need a little help." He kept his gaze fixed on the shattered window, on the capital. "Tell me, child, have you ever heard a nightingale sing?

I

ROSALINA

"**M**arigold! The teapot!" I cry, my hands full of falling cups, plates, and saucers.

Marigold gives a flying leap across the kitchen, floral apron flapping. She snags the teapot right before it shatters on the stone floor.

I have only a second to sigh and gently place the saved tableware in a drawer before the castle starts to shake again.

This isn't the first time, but it's certainly the worst.

"I need a bucket!" Astrid cries, running into Castletree's kitchen. "A piece of the roof's given out in the entrance hall, and the rain's pouring in!"

A vein throbs in my head. "Where are the princes? They were supposed to be back today."

It's been six weeks since we left the Autumn Realm, and I almost think fighting ice zombies, nearly getting eaten by my mate, and discovering I'm actually a magical faerie was a lot easier than trying to manage Castletree.

Farron has been back and forth between Castletree and Autumn. He's been helping his father assume the role of steward after the tragic death of his mother, Princess Niamh. With Perth Quellos's betrayal—and the foreboding news that he escaped from prison—Kel was forced to return to Winter. I know he's been avoiding any true leadership of his home realm since the curse over twenty-five years ago, but it didn't seem like he was going back only out of necessity. No … There's been a change in him, a determination instead of his usual apathy.

Though, the Sword of the Protector is still lying discarded under his bed. But returning to his realm is a good start.

Astrid snatches the bucket, and Marigold follows her into the entrance. I sigh, then take off after them.

Gray light filters in through the windows—and rain pours through the broken ones. If it's not pieces of the wall crumbling, it's windows cracking, doors falling from their hinges, book stacks falling over in the library, or rocks shattering to dust in the hot springs.

It's only been me and the staff here in Castletree. Perhaps influenced by Farron and Kel, Dayton took the opportunity to return to his realm and check in with his little sister, the steward.

And despite Ezryn's worry about the lack of communication from Spring, he didn't go back. Instead, he claimed we'd been away from Castletree for too long and the Briar would be out of control with goblins.

He was supposed to be checking on Castletree—on me—in the other princes' absence, but I haven't seen him once.

I can't help but wonder if he's avoiding going back to his home.

Or maybe he's avoiding me. Maybe Dayton is, too.

After all, Farron and Kel have found their mates.

Found me.

Briars fill the entrance hall—a familiar torment from the Prince of Thorns. It's his magic that's sapping Castletree of its strength. But even Caspian's briars seem brittle, frail. I choose to create more from my bracelets instead to help patch the holes. The thorns lace from floor to ceiling, trapping the crumbling pieces of bark and stone back into the wall frame.

Angry briars fly from my wrists. "The princes were supposed to be back today!"

As soon as the words leave my mouth, something sparks inside my chest. A warmth like fire, a feeling that glows and shimmers all at once. The door to Castletree opens, and a crisp breeze blows through, bringing with it the scent of maple leaves and an apple orchard.

And standing there is Farron, High Prince of Autumn. My mate.

His name leaves my mouth in a reverent breath, and I rush forward, only for a crack to sound. A fissure splits the stone beneath my feet and I stumble.

But Farron is there, catching me in his arms, spinning us both until I'm upright and wrapped in his arms. I take one moment to lose myself in the soft amber of his eyes, the way his face lights up as he looks at me, before grabbing him into a kiss.

Our kiss is hungry, urgent. My fingernails scrape down the back of his neck as I try to get closer. The taste of him both comforts and electrifies me. For a second, I think I'd be okay if the entire castle crumbled around us, as long as I can stay in his arms.

But then he jerks up and shoots out a hand, a gale holding back a chunk of ceiling that tumbles toward us. He pulls me out of the way. "And here I was, thinking you'd be bored with us gone."

"Oh, you know, just been doing a little redecorating." I trace his jaw with my fingers, hoping my touch can convey the need for him my words will never be able to. "I really thought the castle would look nice with huge chunks torn out of it."

With that, rain pours through the latest hole. "Astrid, we need more buckets," I call.

Farron runs a hand along the sharp point of my ear. It's so sensitive, I can't help but shiver. "I'm sorry I've been gone so long." He looks around. "Where's Ezryn? I thought he was supposed to be keeping an eye on things here while the rest of us were away."

The mirror beside the door shimmers with iridescent light, and another shiver laces through me. "You know Ez," I say as I turn to see who's coming through the mirror. "Once he's out in the Briar, he forgets about us entirely."

Just then, the castle groans again. A large candelabrum attached to the wall breaks free from its sconce and plummets toward us. The iridescent shape emerging from the mirror leaps forward and tackles Farron and me to the ground, throwing us out of the way.

I take in a heavy breath, staring at Farron wide-eyed beside me. We both look up to see Dayton on top of us. His skin is golden, hair wavey and smelling of sea and salt.

He grins down at us. "How could anyone forget about you two?"

My mouth is suddenly dry, eyes blinking and unblinking as if he may disappear from my sight. *Gorgeous.* That's the only word my mind seems capable of right now. A single day hasn't gone by when I don't think about the night the three of us spent together, on the eve of battle …

A night we haven't repeated since.

"Bucket! I've got the bucket!" Astrid cries and runs in, swinging the metal pail.

Dayton pulls Farron and me to our feet and takes the bucket from Astrid, positioning it under the leak.

"You haven't arrived a moment too soon," Marigold says, crossing her arms. "The castle's falling to bits and poor Rosalina's been left to manage it all on her own!"

Astrid steps up beside Marigold and mimics her movement, arms crossed, and hip popped. "But she's done just fine by herself, thank you very much."

As much as I wanted the princes back at Castletree, I know how important it is for them to spend time in their own realms, helping their people. Especially Dayton. Unless he finds his mate, he'll never break his curse and unlock the true potential of his magic. And that … That's what's most important.

"I thought Ez was—" Dayton begins, then jerks back. "We're going to need a bigger bucket!"

Already, the rain pouring in from the ceiling has filled this one. I could shoot thorns from my bracelets to patch the roof, but the princes don't know about my bargain with Caspian. They think these bracelets are nothing more than jewelry.

Caspian. The Prince of Thorns. I was certain he'd show his traitorous, perfect-haired head around Castletree while the princes were away, especially once he discovered I took back the book he stole from Farron. But even he's avoided me. And the briars he's laced through every crevasse of Castletree look as sick as the castle does.

I hope he's all right.

The thought comes unbidden, and immediately I give my head a shake. It's his briars that are causing this ...

But if that's the case, why are they dying, too?

I stare up at the hole in the ceiling. Rain pelts my face and runs down the tip of my nose. I've been trying to summon my own briars: not using Caspian's bracelets or even the briars he's placed around the castle, but my very own, grown from nothing but my magic. It's been to no avail. I've only been able to do it twice: first in the Below, then when I created golden briars that helped me rescue my princes and defeat the monster Lucas became.

The power that helped me realize what I truly am. Fae.

A crackle of magic sings through the air, and suddenly the rain fuses together into a deadly rod of ice.

Out of the mirror steps Keldarion, blue eyes flashing as he takes in the state of the castle. His ice rod smacks to the ground, toppling the bucket.

"Is that what you were going for, Kel?" Dayton raises a brow. "Because if I wanted water all over the floor, I wouldn't have put the bucket there."

Kel only sneers in his direction before turning to me. My breath catches in my throat. That feeling in my heart when I saw Farron bursts to life again, but it's different: not a fire, but the glow of the moon off a frozen lake, the twinkle of stars fighting against a storm-covered sky. The phantom of a feeling, now that I know the true depths of what I'm missing.

As always, I have to fight the urge to run to him, to ask him if he missed me as I missed him. But I do—I fight it. I offer him a tight smile and a nod, and his own expression turns stoic.

"What in the seven realms is going on here?" he growls.

The seven realms flicker through my mind: Winter, Spring,

Summer, Autumn, the Below, the Above, and of course, our home here in the Briar.

Farron's got his ear pressed to the stair banister, fingers knocking against the wood. "It's been too long since we pooled our magic. Castletree can't stand without us."

Keldarion's voice is a raspy growl. "Where is Ezryn?"

At that moment, the door flings open. Not to another realm, but the true world outside of Castletree: the Briar. Ezryn stands like a shadow, cape snapping in the harsh wind, metal armor shining with water. His mud-caked boots echo off the floor as he strides in.

He tilts his helm, taking in the castle and all of us the same way Keldarion did. Then his dark visor lands on me. It's so strange—it's been almost a year since the first time I met Ezryn, and now I can read the helmet as clearly as any expression.

Or more so, I can feel it. Apprehension.

Guilt.

I've been fine on my own, I think, though I know he can't hear me.

And it's true.

But it doesn't mean I didn't think of him, out alone, in the Briar with only the goblins for company. Doesn't mean I didn't wonder what he was looking for out there when he could have stayed here in his home, with the staff who adore him, with me who would have …

Who would have treasured that time to learn even one more thing about the High Prince of Spring.

My hands graze the smooth flesh of my wrist, a piece of me that used to bear a hideous scar.

Ezryn tears away from my gaze and looks at each of the princes. "I felt a disturbance. I came as soon as—"

"A disturbance?" Dayton laughs. "Yeah, the bloody castle falling to pieces is a bit of a disturbance."

Kel storms over to Ezryn. "You were supposed to be checking on the castle. On Rosalina."

"The Briar was festering. I knew Rosalina could handle herself," Ezryn responds in a low growl.

"And I did," I say. "But now that you're here, can we please do something?"

Kel turns away and storms up the stairs. "To High Tower."

The breath is heavy in my throat as I follow the four princes. I know they must channel their magic into Castletree. I know it drains them.

And I know I can help.

I did it before, the night I first learned of the Enchantress's curse. But Kel had become so angry, I hadn't dared try again when they were gone.

Instead, I've been using my thorn bracelets to reinforce the different areas of the castle. As we walk up the stairs, I bet the princes can't even tell which thorns are mine and which are Caspian's.

The thought unsettles me.

Farron pushes ahead into High Tower. The roses bloom in the middle, Farron's bursting with color, the other three wilted and drooping. Golden thorns grow around Farron's rose, while the rest of the room is covered in dark purple ones. "We have to give as much as we can," Farron urges, sinking to his knees by the flowers. "Hold nothing back!"

The castle gives a great shudder as the others drop beside Farron. Dust and bits of stone shower to the ground. Unlike the last time I saw them do this, this time I can *feel* it. My fae blood sings through my veins, my body lighting up like dry grass caught to flame.

The princes' bodies glow. The flowers perk a little, the stems fighting to straighten. More magic ... They need more magic.

Slowly, I kneel and touch one of the golden roses. "Help them," I whisper to the rose, to myself. "Give them strength."

I close my eyes, feeling that rush through my chest. But it's more than magic. The castle may crumble, the briars may fall, but for now, for this moment, we're together. All five of us. The thought gives my heart strength. And I pass it to them.

I don't know if we stay like this for a minute or an hour, but when my eyes blink open, I see Kel, Ez, Day, and Fare leaning against the stone, bodies clearly exhausted.

But the castle's stopped shaking, and the flowers stand at full attention.

How many more times will we be able to bring Castletree back to life?

I stumble forward, my own legs trembling and weak. Farron pulls me down to his side.

"See?" Dayton smiles, sweat dripping down his brow. "Nothing to worry about."

Kel snorts. "Of course the Prince of Summer would say that."

"He's right." I take a moment to look at each of them. "We fixed it. And we're together now." My heart brightens at the thought. "We're all back home."

An awkward silence passes through High Tower, and I realize everyone's eyes are darting away.

"What?" I snap.

"I'm sorry, Rosie," Farron mumbles, dropping his lips to my shoulder. "I only came back for a short visit. I have to return to Autumn to be with my father for a little while longer."

Pain stabs into my ribs. I turn to Kel. His ice fire eyes are staring at the ground. "Winter is still without a new steward. I must see that preparations are in place. Frostfang expects my return in two days' time."

"Oh," I whisper. I look up at Ez, but he's staring out a window. I don't bother asking—like Kel always says, Ezryn hates to stay.

"Guess it'll be up to us to keep Marigold out of trouble." Dayton flashes me a signature grin, but I can see the pain in his eyes.

I know he should return to Summer, too.

Because it doesn't matter how much I try to fool myself into thinking we all belong together; it can never be this way.

Like Castletree, my heart is shattering. Except there's no magic in all the realms that can put it back together.

2

ROSALINA

The library finally feels like home again now that Farron's returned. I peer over at my mate as he goes over the notes I've made in his absence. Beneath the table, I rub his leg with my foot. From the little quirk in his lip, I can tell he's trying hard to ignore me.

"How was your trip to Autumn?" I ask.

He peers up from the notes. "It was fine. My father's really settling into his role as steward." Farron still bears a great pain from losing his mother in our fight to protect Autumn. He's keeping busy. We both are. When we first returned to Castletree, before he was ready to return to his realm, we spent many long nights here in the library. At first, we allowed ourselves to rest, to read until midnight and get lost in stories without trying to decipher each word. We'd fall asleep in front of the fire with no worry of him transforming into a beast.

Then we transitioned to making a memory book for his mother, something small and personal, writing down every little detail he could remember of his time with her. But with the continued decay of Castletree, Dayton and Ezryn's curses unbroken—and Kel refusing to break his—there's an unspoken urgency for us to get back to work.

"There's hope in the people," Farron continues, snagging my ankle beneath the table. "Everyone at home is talking about you."

"About me?"

"You saved the Autumn Realm, Rosalina." He draws my foot into his lap, tugging off my slipper to massage my foot. "Not me, not Kel, not Ez or Day. *You* saved us all."

My eyes flutter closed, and the memory plays in my mind's eye: the four princes overtaken by vile magic of green flame as I explode in a burst of golden roses and thorns.

"My whole realm knows what you did," Farron says. "They call you *the Golden Rose.*"

"The Golden Rose," I repeat, my hand instinctively going to my necklace.

"How about you?" Farron pulls my other leg into his lap. "How's your research going?"

"Remember that book I found? It's no ordinary text. It has snippets of the Queen's own writing." A pang of guilt washes over me. I left out the fact that this new book I found was actually the book Caspian stole from the Autumn Realm's sacred alder tree … which I then stole from Caspian.

I will tell Farron. I just haven't found the right moment yet.

"The Queen was really fascinated with humans," I continue, trying not to get distracted by how amazing it feels to be this close to him again.

"I was really fascinated with a certain human." Farron reaches across the table and glides his finger over the tip of my pointed ear.

Because I'm not human. At least not fully.

"How's the magic practice going?"

"Flame comes easily. I've only set two dresses on fire!"

Farron had explained that a mate bond amplifies what magic you have. I discovered in my battle with Lucas that I can summon white flames. And of course, there's the strange case of me being able to manipulate the thorns, both Caspian's and the ones from my bracelets.

"Glad it wasn't this dress." Farron's gaze drops noticeably to my chest.

"Hey, we're supposed to be researching." I knock him in the stomach with my foot.

He gives me a devious grin and slides a hand up my thigh. "Sure, Sweetheart. That's why you've been giving me *that* look since we got in here."

"I don't have the slightest idea what you're talking about." I blink innocently at him.

But when his hand caresses over my thigh, then higher, and his fingers brush my slick entrance covered by absolutely nothing, he knows the truth.

He gives a throaty chuckle that gets my stomach fluttering. Then he pounces with all the speed and strength of a fae prince and gathers me into his arms. I kiss him hard, devouring his mouth as I push my tongue between his lips.

I'm allowed only a moment before he throws me on my back on the table. The Autumn Prince places a hand on either side of my head, leaning over me, a tousle of auburn hair across his brow, and the yellow glint of the predatory wolf behind his gaze. "If you wanted to be fucked so badly, you should have just asked."

I practically melt from his words, writhing on the table, desperate to feel him between my legs. "Maybe this is just my *Wilde Courtship* taking over."

Farron laughs, undoing his belt with one hand and reaching beneath my skirts with his other, beginning to massage my clit. "We've only found two references to that, and it's scared me both times."

The muscles in my core tighten. I'm so eager for him. *Wilde courtship* … During our research, we've found few mentions of this mating phenomenon: a brief seasonal state of uncontrollable desire. A frenzy that takes over mated pairs if they haven't consummated their bond in some time. It might be a myth, because thankfully, it hasn't seemed to affect anything between Kel and me. It's possible that it's only for couples who have accepted their mate bond.

"I think we're managing to keep it at bay," I smirk, moving my hips up against the wonderful friction of his palm.

"It's only been six weeks of not turning into a monstrous wolf at night," Farron smirks, "and I am going to take full advantage of it."

With him back and forth between his realm and Castletree, we've spent every moment he's home together, sometimes in his room and sometimes mine. I can't get enough of him.

And it seems he can't get enough of me either.

My mate drops his pants, not even bothering to remove his shirt, and spreads my legs, slipping his long cock deep inside.

A wave of ecstasy crashes over me, and Farron pumps in and out with agonizing slowness. I descend into whimpering bliss. Papers fly around us with our movement, fluttering off the table.

"Farron!" I cry out my mate's name, grasping for purchase on the wooden table as he thrusts into me. The Autumn Wing's library spins above in a glorious twirl of orange and red leaves.

"Stars, I missed you." Farron leans over and kisses me. I sigh into him, breathing in his delicious scent of wood smoke and apples. "I'll never get enough of you."

Running my fingers through his hair, I say, "I know what you mean. But I did really want to show you my notes."

"Later, Sweetheart." Farron grins, unlacing my corset and running his hands over my aching breasts, before straightening and thrusting again, filling me so deeply I cry out. "Gods, you feel so good."

A tingling sensation glides over my skin and warmth blooms in my belly. I tilt my head and see Ezryn. By his stance, leaning on the bookcase, legs crossed, I don't think he's just arrived.

What is his perception of us, with me splayed on this table, skirts up, breasts out and bouncing, and Farron, half-naked, thrusting into me like a wild animal? But the thought doesn't embarrass me. No, my whole body ignites with a desperate need, giddy at the idea of him watching us. Farron follows my gaze, and through our bond, I know he feels the same.

"Isn't she absolutely perfect, Ez?" Farron gasps. "Just look at her."

"I am," Ezryn says. "Put her legs over your shoulders."

"What—" I begin, but my voice cuts off as Ezryn moves toward us with swift, deliberate steps.

"You'll be able to get even deeper," he growls.

Farron takes my legs and lifts them over his shoulders, dragging me to the edge of the table. My cry turns into a moan as Farron's cock sinks deep.

"Rosie, yes," Farron groans, and I swear I hear a matching one from Ezryn.

I desperately search for words through the euphoric sensation. "How do you know that, Tin Man? You're always covered in metal."

"It's my helm I can't remove," he says flatly. "Not everything else."

My eyes shoot open, and jealousy spikes through me at the thought of him with anyone else. Though of course I know he has been. I give an involuntary yelp as this new position slides me closer to the edge of the table.

Ezryn grabs my shoulders, holding me steady, his gloved hands rough and so close to my exposed breasts.

I know he's not mine, not the way Farron is, or even Kel. I can't keep the Prince of Spring, but still I cry out, "Ezryn, touch me."

His grip tightens, and he's silent for a devastating moment.

"Fuck," he swears under his breath. Then he rips off his gloves, and I see a flash of his large, tawny hands. One seizes my breast, clutching firmly, before tugging on my nipple with his forefinger and thumb. His other hand runs almost reverently up the side of my neck before grasping my hair.

"Gods." Farron bites his lip, watching us. He keeps my legs tight to his chest. "Like this, Ez?"

Ezryn tilts his head up. "I've got her. You don't have to hold back."

"You've been holding back?" I gasp.

"Only a little." He gives a rueful smile. "I don't want to hurt you."

"She's not a delicate human." Ezryn gives a sharp tug on my hair, as if to prove a point. "She's a powerful fae. She's shown us that much."

"What do you think, Rosie? Ready?" Farron asks.

"Yes. Yes, Farron."

Farron pulls out of me completely before slamming deep. And his speed—I can barely comprehend it, almost a blur as it sends my body into a new high.

I scream, not caring if anyone hears, and grasp out behind me, my sweaty palms sliding down Ezryn's armor.

"Do you like that, Petal?" Ezryn lets out a growl, pulling my back against his chest, so I'm a V between them. "Do you enjoy having your pussy ravaged?"

Tears of pleasure run down my cheeks, my core tightening, tightening, tightening.

"Use your words," Farron says, the commanding voice of a High Prince. He pounds deeply into places I didn't even know could be touched. I feel my inner walls clenching around his long cock.

"Yes, yes, I do," I babble. "Farron, Ez, I'm—"

"Come for us, Baby Girl." Ezryn lowers his head to my shoulder, and I feel the cool press of his helmet against my cheek.

My orgasm crashes through me, vibrating my entire body from my face to my toes. I sense Farron's own hot release, emptying deep.

Ezryn holds my shaking form as I come down from the high. He lowers me gently to the table and brushes loose pieces of hair away from my brow.

"Aren't you glad you came to check on us?" I ask dreamily.

"Very," he says.

"Why were you here, Ez?" Farron says, pulling up his pants. "Not that I'm complaining."

"I'm leaving for Spring tomorrow," Ezryn says. He turns to Farron and ruffles his hair. "Meet me in the training grounds this afternoon. We've got time for one more lesson. Let's see if you can be as quick a learner at magic as you are at pleasuring our girl."

3

KELDARION

ow, this is the last place I expected to find you. I take a deep breath. The air in the Queen's Sanctum is stale and musty. The small chapel lies at the very back of Castletree and has been entirely unused since the four of us took reign here.

And yet, something took me down these forgotten halls during my search for Ezryn.

Sure enough, he kneels beneath the Shrine of the Queen, a stone statue of a faceless woman, one hand extended to the sky, the other to the earth.

It used to be common practice to spend quiet moments of meditation in the Sanctum, to offer gratitude for the joys in one's life or to shed one's worries into the void. Though the Queen created the Vale, she also abandoned it five hundred years ago. My thanks and concerns are no better heard by the Queen than they are by that slab of stone carved in her memory.

It's a simple room, the Sanctum, small and almost cramped compared to the other sprawling chambers of Castletree. The walls and floor are made of wood, the ceiling lush with branches filled with green leaves and hanging ivy. It would be considered beautiful if it weren't for the briars and bits of rubble.

Four giant stained-glass windows let in a stream of multicolor light. The rain has finally passed.

I kneel beside Ezryn, bowing my head before the statue.

Ezryn quirks his helm toward me. "You don't have to join me. I know how you feel about the Queen."

"I haven't seen you in here in decades. Maybe you've remembered something I've forgotten."

"Unfortunately, no." Ezryn sits on his heels. The light from the stained glass paints his armor in red, blue, yellow, green, and purple. I find myself drawn to the swirling colors. It's not often I get to see Ezryn bathed in light. "The Queen is as silent as ever," he continues.

"And why is it now that you've come for her wisdom after all these years?" I raise a brow.

Ezryn stands and turns away from me. "I am leaving for Spring tomorrow."

I knew this decision was coming. Ezryn hasn't had word from his father, Prince Thalionor, the steward, in months. Neither Thalionor nor Ezryn's brother attended Princess Niamh's funeral.

Yet, still, I see how it weighs on him. I understand.

For men like us, looking into the past is a far harder thing than running blindly into the future.

I stand and place my hand on his shoulder. Blue light plays across my knuckles. "I understand. Wish your father well for me. I would travel with you if I did not need to return to Winter."

Ezryn looks over his shoulder, catching me in the dark gaze of his visor. "How long will you be gone?"

"We funneled a great amount of magic into Castletree. It should remain strong for several weeks, at least. That should be enough time—"

"Keldarion," Ezryn growls, "how long will you be gone?"

I drop my hand. Damn this fae. My inner thoughts could very well be an unraveled scroll for him. I can't meet his gaze, so I stare at the Queen's stone face instead. "I've given Eirik Vargsaxa temporary leadership in the interim while I secure a permanent solution. After

Perth's betrayal, I know I must leave Frostfang's rule in the hands of someone completely trustworthy."

"Perhaps a steward is no longer needed," Ezryn offers quietly. "If you were to break your curse—"

"That is not an option." The mere thought of it sends the blood rushing through my veins.

Since the moment that fated woman entered Castletree, the Enchantress's magic has been more than a curse. It has been a torment, an endless suffering where my every breath is a battle between agony and the few weak moments where I give in to her.

Rosalina.

The fae disguised within a human's body. My vision of the stone statue blurs. *I understand why our fates are so. But hers?*

I had thought her mating with Farron would ease some of the guilt in my chest. But instead, it's only worsened my suffering. How easy, how simple, it is for him to take her in his arms, to breathe in her scent, to promise her he will stay by her side.

And how hard it is for me to fight back every instinct.

To complicate the matter, the princeling is now the mate of my mate. I've always held a deep affection for Farron, but now he is another heart I must protect at all costs.

The tangled web my bargain put me in will ensnare them, too.

Unless I do something.

"So, you are returning to Frostfang, then?" Ezryn asks.

"No. I will be traveling across the Anelkrol Badlands—"

"Kel—"

"Until I arrive at the Great Chasm. I have business at Voidseal Bridge."

Ezryn spins me around, forcing me to stare into his helm. "What business could you possibly have there? That place is a pit of despair."

"And the Deep Guard are the only ones holding that despair back from the rest of Winter," I growl. "It's home to my last living blood relative."

Ez snorts. "You haven't seen Irahn in years. Quellos was more of an uncle to you than Irahn ever has been."

"Quellos was a traitor. He put his own ambitions above the law, above the good of the people. Irahn may be … eccentric, but he loved my mother, and he's dedicated his life to the defense of the realm."

"So, that's your plan. To make Irahn the new steward?" Ezryn tilts his helm.

"For now, at least."

I can tell Ezryn's evaluating my decision by the length of time it takes him to react. Not that it's unusual. Ezryn hasn't agreed with one of my decisions since we've met.

It's a wonder he's followed me for most of them.

Finally, he speaks, his voice low and reverberating. "It's not a decision to take lightly, Kel. Your uncle's kept the Great Chasm protected for the last two decades. That's why you named Quellos steward in the first place. Besides, Irahn hasn't been part of civilized society in years."

I wave an idle hand. "Winter has been sick with Quellos's politics for too long. Irahn could be the ruler Winter needs."

"*You* are the ruler Winter needs."

I walk toward the door, stepping into a beam of red light. It drips over my hair, my skin, drenching me in glowing blood. "I am Winter's bane."

Ezryn exhales heavily. "If you name Irahn steward, then what of the Voidseal? You would leave the Deep Guard without a warden."

"No, I wouldn't," I say lowly. My hands squeeze into fists. "If all goes as intended integrating Irahn as the new steward, I shall remain at the Voidseal as Warden."

A heavy silence fills the room. I want him to yell. Want him to attack me.

But I knew this was the most likely outcome: the quiet.

"You can't be saying what I think you're saying, Kel," he whispers.

I take a breath, then, "I am. Irahn is my blood. If he accepts the role of steward and proves himself a worthy leader, I will pass the Blessing of Winter on to him and give up my rule as High Prince."

A crack of lightning sounds outside, and the clouds roll in again.

"I can't believe this," he says, his whisper turning to a snarl. "The

Sword of the Protector belongs to *you*. Your father chose *you*, not Irahn, to inherit his Blessing. You are meant to bring peace to Winter!"

"I am not meant for anything," I say. "At least in Irahn's possession, the Blessing would not be hindered by this curse."

"A curse you need not bear!" Ezryn storms toward me and shoves my chest. Ah, yes, here it is. That anger. This I can manage.

But Ezryn doesn't push me again. Instead, he grabs my face, his gloved hands rough against my jaw. "Let me help you, Kel. Let me bring Caspian to justice. I will see him to a quick end, and this bargain would be broken forever. I will go to the Below for you, and he would not feel pain. I can free you and Winter and Rosalina—"

I clasp Ezryn's wrists and remove them from my face. "I can't let you do that."

"Bah!" He shoves past me, then slams a fist against the doorframe. "You know once you pass the Blessing on, it will be gone from you forever. It cannot be returned without great danger to your life."

"I understand."

"So, that's it then. You'll leave Castletree. Leave Rosalina. Leave *us*." Ezryn's body collapses against the frame. "All to protect the traitor."

I close my eyes, fighting back the emotion that threatens to consume me. It's not anger. And for once, not even guilt.

There's just a sadness that there is no other way to protect those I love.

So, I go to him. I clutch Ezryn around the shoulders and he falls back against me, his breath heavy and uneven. "This is what we do, Ez. For each other. For her. Let it be known, no matter how many times we stumble upon this treacherous path, our resolve shall forever remain unbroken. Each time we fall, we rise again. Do you hear me, brother?"

"Yes," he whispers. "We will rise."

I hold him tighter against me. "Now, go to Spring. Reestablish the true rule. Find your mate and break your curse. And claim the glorious destiny that awaits you."

4

ROSALINA

My hand is steady over the grip of the bow, but I can't seem to stop the pounding of my heart. Breathing deep through my nose, I draw back the string, feeling the tension build. My focus narrows to the target, a stuffed straw goblin with a bullseye painted on its chest.

As I release the arrow, time slows, and for a moment, I think it might finally strike. Then the arrow veers off course, hitting Castletree's wooden wall.

"Dammit," I say, lowering the bow and wiping my forehead of sweat. Does everywhere in the Summer Wing need to be so hot? I look around to see if anyone witnessed my failure.

The training hall is large.. One side hugs tight to Castletree, showing the lovely wooden bark—and snaking thorns—and the other is open air, looking through the branches to the Briar and hills beyond. Beams of sunlight drift over the sandy floor.

Ezryn and Farron are sitting cross-legged in a corner, facing each other. Farron's palms are skyward as Ezryn hovers his above them. He's been teaching Farron the art of healing. While the Autumn Realm's innate magic is fire, Spring's is rejuvenation. Farron taught Ezryn fire in Autumn, and now Ezryn is passing along his knowledge.

As I stare at them, I understand for a moment why the Queen built this Castle with a piece of each of the realms. Four rulers together with access to each of their homes. United, we are stronger.

There's a clatter over by the weapons rack, and I whirl to Dayton, stumbling over them. The weapons lean against wooden planks, a collection of swords, lances, bows, and quivers brimming with feathered arrows.

Dayton has made sure I try them all, though I like the bow the best.

"Why did no one tell me there's a party in the Summer Wing?"

"You're late," I say dryly. "Astrid said she told you to be here half an hour ago." His words are slurred, movements uneven. How much did he need to drink to be this inebriated since arriving back at Castletree?

Dayton narrows his gaze and grins. "Hmm, the training grounds look good with a few more feathery decorations."

I grimace, looking at the collection of arrows dotting the far wall. My first request upon returning to Castletree was to be taught how to defend myself. I'd expected Keldarion to put up a fuss, but he'd agreed it was a good idea. Though I left out my inspiration for this plan. Caspian's words from the battlefield come roaring back to me: *Those princes are ever foolish; they should have taught you to defend yourself.*

But it's not all because of the Prince of Thorns. I hated watching the princes go off to battle and feeling left behind and useless. So, I'll practice my magic, my thorns, and I'll use the tools of this world. I have no intention of leaving the Enchanted Vale. But this world isn't like the human one. I must learn to survive, and that means being able to protect myself.

Dayton's been at Castletree the most of all the princes. He'd been teaching me the fundamentals of each weapon before he would leave for a quick visit to check on his sister in the Summer Realm. Training is the only time we've spent together.

Farron told me not to worry about Dayton's avoidance. He's been living with the mood swings of the Summer Prince for years. I don't understand how Dayton could make love to us like that, with such passion, and then be so distant.

Farron said Dayton will be falling into bed with us before we know it. But what if he's wrong? What if Dayton was looking for his mate in the Summer Realm? It's better that I don't know.

I'm not sure I could bear it. I was so certain that night we spent in the Autumn Realm, the night we had almost made love … I thought the same magical light that had bloomed between Kel and me was happening between us.

Three mates, Rosalina? I chide myself. I can't keep them all.

"Okay, show me up close." Dayton waves an idle hand, drawing me from my thoughts. "Hit the target."

With renewed determination, I retrieve another arrow and notch it in my bow. Pulling my arm back, I line up the bullseye in my sight, then let loose the arrow. It strikes the wooden wall behind the target.

"Arg!" I say, frustrated. "I don't understand. I'm doing everything you do! Finger in the proper position, elbow raised, and—"

"That's the problem, Rosalina," Dayton says, stepping closer. "You're very smart. We all know that. But you're thinking of all these things separately."

"What—"

Then he's behind me, and because he's Dayton, he's not wearing a shirt. I feel his muscular skin against the training garb Flavia fitted me in: a white dress with shorts underneath and a leather chest piece for protection.

Though when Dayton had first seen me in the outfit, I wasn't sure if he wanted to teach me or …

"Are you paying attention?" He's grabbed an arrow. With his hands over mine, he starts guiding my movements. "You know what to do. Trust your body. When you shoot a bow, it's not all separate things, it's an extension of you. It's a *feeling.*"

"I don't think a feeling is going to help me hit a goblin," I sneer.

His face is close enough I can smell the sweet wine on his lips. "Feel for the heartbeat of the bow, the pulse of the string. Visualize where it will land."

I try not to scoff at him, but let myself become fluid, his arms over mine as we pull the string back together.

"Find your anchor, a calm in the storming waves around you."

I inhale deeply, tasting salt on my tongue, feeling the sand beneath my feet and the heat of his touch like a blazing sun.

"That's my girl," Dayton breathes, releasing his hold and stepping back.

Warmth blooms through me, and I narrow that focus to the goblin target and release.

The arrow whizzes, striking the target and exploding in a spray of water.

A spray of water?

"W-what?" Dayton calls.

I can't even celebrate finally hitting the target because all I can do is stare at the wet sand beneath the utterly destroyed goblin target. There's a hole through its belly, straw sticking out at strange angles.

Both Ezryn and Farron jump up. "Did you use water magic?" Ezryn asks.

"I don't know."

"Not just any water," Farron says, leaning in front of the target. "Seawater."

Shells and seaweed cover the sand. But there's no arrow to be seen.

"That wasn't me," Dayton says.

"Water magic is fairly common for fae in the Summer and Winter realms but ..." Farron looks up. "You completely changed the arrow into water. Rosie, not even Kel and Day can do that."

"I ... changed it?" A knot of unease settles in my stomach. I shouldn't be capable of doing that. Many fae can control the elements, but to *change* things completely ...

As far as I know, there's only one fae who's ever been able to do that.

"Add that to your research notes," Ezryn says. "Thorns, flames, and now this."

I stare down at my palms, unsure how I accomplished it.

"At this point, we should realize nothing about our Rose is expect-ed." My heart sings at the deep, gravelly voice, and I look up to see Keldarion leaning in the doorway.

"Keldarion," Ezryn says, inclining his head.

"I'll be departing for Winter now. My wolf will make good time overnight." His eyes only briefly pass over mine before he turns. "The staff will have dinner prepared for you."

Before I would have run after him. I would have followed that ache in my heart.

But I stay put.

If Keldarion can ignore our mate bond, then so can I.

No matter how much it hurts.

Besides, I have other important things to worry about. I look back down at my hands, Fire, water, thorns … What else is locked inside of me?

5

EZRYN

One step.

The Spring Realm is one step away. That's all I have to take in order to be back in the place of my birth.

My birthplace, but not my home, I think curiously. When did my mind shift so that the crumbling walls of Castletree and the dark, twisting vines of the Briar were more home than my own realm?

I stand in the entrance hall before the enchanted mirror, its surface glistening like nectar. All I need to do is step through it and think of Florendel, the capital of Spring, and there I shall arrive.

I've thought about going through this mirror every day since I arrived home from the Autumn Realm, thought about it every time no tidings came from Spring. But I told myself I was needed here. When the other princes took leave to visit their realms, I had offered to stay behind to watch over the castle. To watch over Rosalina. Spring has waited a long time for my return; a few weeks would be nothing in the span of my absence until now.

But I have been as poor a protector of Castletree as I have been a High Ruler.

Though Farron and Keldarion have been gone much of the six weeks—with Farron returning for short stints to visit Rosalina—

Dayton has only been gone for the last two. Something has shifted in our dynamic, a sort of solidarity between Dayton and me. Though Keldarion may still remain cursed, at least he knows his path to freedom. But Dayton and I ...

How does one hold on to hope when it has waned to but a sliver of moonlight?

I exhale roughly, the sound echoing in my ears. The stone beneath my feet should be worn into trenches by how long I've paced before this mirror. One step. Why can't I take it?

Perhaps it's for the same reason I couldn't stay in Castletree with Rosalina when the other princes left. Castles and keeps cannot contain what I've become.

Rosalina deserves a man of honor.

Not the Black Beast of the Briar.

That's what they scream, the goblins. The last name on their lips as my wolf's jaws tear out their throats, as their skulls crush beneath my paws. I tell everyone I patrol the Briar for their safety. But that's not the only reason.

The rage inside of me needs to come out. Better the goblins than someone I love.

I square my shoulders and face the mirror. One step. One step—

"Another silent getaway, I see."

Her voice drifts into the entrance hall, and I turn, my armor clattering with the movement.

She's leaning against a pillar, arms crossed, one eyebrow raised.

"Rosalina," I breathe.

"Not running off to the Briar this time. Home to the Spring Realm, then?"

There's a sharpness to her tone. She's ... angry with me.

In the heat of the moment in the library, it was easy to pretend everything was fine, that I hadn't left her alone, or that I wasn't leaving again. But with me on the edge of another realm, there's no hiding from the truth.

"Yes. That's the plan anyway," I say lowly.

She raises her chin in the air, eyes averted. "Well, you've been staring at that mirror for half an hour. You're usually so eager to leave."

No wonder she's Keldarion's mate. In this moment, she could rival him in iciness. Who am I to blame her?

I owe her an apology for leaving her with Castletree in this state. For leaving her at all.

What do I say? That I never feel fear around the goblins or during the long, lonely nights, but she frightens me beyond measure? That each smile or touch she offers me is like a lightning strike, rending me to my core? And more than all of these things, I know it is only a matter of time before my determination breaks, and I will be hopelessly lost to her?

"Rosalina," I manage, "I'm sorry."

She sighs and walks over to me. Her every movement, from the sway of her hips to the exasperated pout, sends my heart pounding. "It's okay. I know the goblins are wonderful company. Next time, I'm going to paint myself green and sharpen my teeth, so you'll want to hang out with me." She makes a ridiculous attempt at a scary face and holds her hands up like claws.

A low laugh escapes me and I reach forward, tucking a strand of hair behind her pointed ear. "They certainly don't have your sense of humor."

She sighs and rolls her eyes, pushing herself closer to me. "I just missed you."

Despite my better judgment, I place my hands on either side of her face, lightly stroking her cheeks with my thumbs. "It's easier this way."

"Tell my heart that."

The honesty of her words tears through me. What would she say if I offered every piece of myself to her? Would she have me? Would she break me?

One step to the Spring Realm. One question asked of Rosalina. I have the strength to do neither.

Bright pink floods Rosalina's cheeks, and she gives an awkward laugh. "I shouldn't keep you."

Reluctantly, I drop my hands from her face and turn back to the mirror. "You're not. I'm the one delaying. It seems I cannot get my feet to work."

"You're nervous?" she asks.

"Terrified," I admit softly.

She reaches out and laces her fingers through mine. "Are you afraid to see your people?"

"No. I'm sure I will be welcomed warmly, despite my extended absence. There's even a member of Keep Hammergarden's staff I'm looking forward to reuniting with. It's—"

"Your father."

"How did you know?"

She blinks up at me. "You mentioned he was sick. It's hard to see our loved ones like that."

Especially when I know it was my actions that made him so. A numbness tingles through my chest as I fight away the memory. "My father, Thalionor, is serving as steward over Spring. I call him sick, but it's not exactly that. Physically, he's still sound. After my mother died, he fell into a daze. It was as if he was the same person on the outside, but on the inside, he was ... empty."

Rosalina squeezes my hand. "Your mother's passing was hard on everyone in your family."

A small crack emerges among the numbness in my chest, words trapped within waiting to get out. "My father, my brother Kairyn, and I... We were all so hard all the time. That's the way it is in Spring, in the royal family. You must be the foundation for your people to grow upon. But our mother was this filament of softness that held us together. Like the moss that grows over the rock. She was beloved as a High Princess, the fated mate of my father. She taught me everything I know of honor, of duty to our realm. For Kairyn, she was the only person he ever truly felt at home with."

"I'm so sorry, Ezryn," Rosalina whispers, leaning her head against my shoulder.

The pearlescent colors of the mirror swim before my eyes. "My father was a brilliant man before her passing. Though my mother was

High Princess, Father often went abroad, directly serving the villages away from our capital. The people adored him. Still do, despite his condition. He was a great warrior, valiant and bold. Honor to the realm is everything to him."

"How was—is—he as a father?" Rosalina asks tentatively.

I sigh. "Strict. He demanded a lot of Kairyn and me. He wanted us to be great." I shake my head. "It was easier for me to follow in his example. But Kairyn was never good at following instructions or trusting in the process of something. It created tension between him and Father."

"Is that why you're afraid to see your father?" she asks. "Because he was so stern?"

"No," I say slowly. "I was never afraid of him." My mind reels trying to find the truth, trying to put this pain into words. "When I visit my father now, I see everything I'm missing. Not only who he used to be. But he's the last remaining tie to my mother. I wish more than anything I could be the ruler she was." I close my eyes, voice hoarse. "My father was her mate. Watching who he was vanish before my eyes … It feels like watching her die all over again."

Rosalina wraps her arms around my waist and hugs me so tightly, my armor jingles. "Tell me something about her," she whispers.

I sigh and hold her tight. "She wore a starlight silver helm. I never saw her face, but in my mind, she was beautiful."

"Of course she was," Rose says. She blinks up at me. "And no matter what, she's always with you, Ez. There's a piece of her inside of you that will never leave."

"I suppose that's why I must go to Spring and make sure the realm she left me is in good order," I say.

"Wait. Before you go—"

My heart lurches. *Ask me to stay.*

But instead, she scrunches up her face and says: "Anon caria mirel baelorin. Yavanthy caeotin. Darisfeli em onore. Ezryn."

The words are choppy, labored. But I'd know them anywhere.

"That is a language of Spring," I tell her.

She places her palm flat on my chest plate and stares at her spread fingers. "I know. You said that to me down in Cryptgarden."

"You remembered?"

She reaches up to caress my helm. Her brown eyes shine as she holds my gaze. "The mountains told me your name. The forest sang your song. My heart has been searching for you since the first dawn."

Of course, the first thing Rosalina would do upon hearing a new language is find a way to translate it. I can picture her in the library, poring over a dictionary. My chest tenses. Those were words I meant to keep secret ...

"My heart searches for you, too, Ez," she whispers. "Let me find you."

As much as I wish I could sweep her into my arms and tell her again and again and again that I'm right here, the mirror beckons me forward. "I'll be back soon."

"I'll be waiting for you," Rose says and lets me go. "I promise."

With her promise giving me the strength I need, I take one step forward and enter Spring.

6

CASPIAN

M y palm smacks against the back of the wooden armoire, and an annoyed growl sounds in my throat. *Not here either.* I've covered the floor with Rosalina's dresses, emptied every desk drawer. And the fae woman is still sleeping peacefully in her bed. She must be a deep sleeper.

Or my presence soothes her. The thought disturbs me.

I limp to her bedside table, ignoring the biting pain shooting up my leg. You don't lose the Autumn Realm without a little retribution. The drawer is brimming with paper, pens, and a half-eaten cookie. *But not my book.*

"Where exactly did you hide it, Flower?" Her dark hair is loose, pieces curling around her face, with full lips slightly parted. She's kicked her blankets low, and it's so easy to make out the delectable curves of her body through the thin fabric.

Clutching my hands into fists to resist touching her, I proceed to the other side of the room. Of course, she could have hidden it anywhere in Castletree, but there's this peculiar feeling that it's here somewhere.

I sense the exact moment she wakes up, like a shock through my chest. But I don't turn, busying myself in a drawer I've already checked. I pretend not to hear her stupidly loud breath or feel her taking control of *my* thorns and snaking them around my ankles. The floor creaks. Stars be damned, does she actually think she's being sneaky?

The thorns yank me off my feet, and I slam to the ground. Rosalina straddles me, pinning me and pressing an elongated thorn to my neck.

"What are you doing here, Caspian?" she snarls, her face poised in an adorable grimace.

"I could ask you the same question." I smirk. "If I'd thought this was what you were after, I'd have bargained for a lot more than a kiss." My eyes snap to the thin thorn bracelet around my wrist, and the two matching ones around hers.

Her expression changes into a silent O, and she eases up from the position her little assault has put us in. Her thighs are spread on either side of my waist, one palm flat on my chest, and of course, the thorns around my ankles. Those I take control of now, untangling myself and coaxing them to slide up her legs.

She gives a sharp hiss of pain, and I can feel her pushing to take command of them again, but I don't allow it.

"You let me surprise you," she says.

"How else was I to get what I want?" I glide a hand up her milky white thigh. "And I always get what I want."

She hisses and presses the thorn a little harder against my neck, but she doesn't realize nothing she can do at this point can hurt me. Not after what's already been done. My fingers graze beneath her nightdress, and her scent fully consumes me. "Do you have an aversion to panties, Flower?"

Her cheeks flush and she jerks back, but the thorns around her legs prevent her from getting far. I pierce her with my gaze, and it takes everything in me not to lift her up and bring her down on my face. I can't survive for long in the world up here, but I bet I could survive on her.

"*You're* the one who came into *my* room in the middle of the night."

I tilt my head, changing my thorns so the brambles fall away and they're nothing but delicate vines that snake higher and higher up her thighs. "And your mate is away in the Autumn Realm, the other in the cold and ice. So, who exactly were you dreaming of creeping into your bed and feeling this exposed pussy? The Summer Prince with a dawn awakening? Hmm, what is his name again?"

"Shut up," she hisses.

"Or," I release my hold on the vines, let her consciousness ease in, as we both coax them higher and higher, "was it me you were thinking of?"

I expect her to spit at me, or curse, or call me disgusting. I don't expect the flush on her cheeks. Her long sigh as the vines slide to brush the edges of her center. Through them, I can feel how slick she is. Her desire is a palpable weight in the room, and for a moment, I feel I may lose all control and plunge these vines deep inside her just to fill her aching need.

I manage a raspy breath and my senses return. Retracting the vines, I snag one in my palm, licking the tip. "Just as delicious as I remember."

She seems to have regained her composure and growls, "You're a pig."

"No." I spin us, so she falls to her back. "I'm the one in control. And if you're tired of this little dance, tell me where my book is and I'll be on my way."

"What book?"

"My princess is learning, but you have no idea what you've got."

She wiggles beneath me but can't quite break free. The long ears suit her, matching her large eyes and perfect lips. "I know some things. Parts of it were written by the Queen. But I don't understand what interest you'd have in her."

"The Queen was the most powerful fae who ever lived. You can't blame me for being curious."

"It's more a diary than a spell book," she says.

So, she has been studying it. That wasn't part of my plan, but I wonder ... It might not be such a bad thing. "You'd be surprised what you can derive from someone's raw thoughts."

"I'm not giving it back. It's hidden somewhere you'll never find it. I don't trust you. You *betrayed* us, Caspian."

"They've been calling me a betrayer for years," I say. "It was your mate who made a bargain with me. It wasn't my fault the little pup wasn't careful about his wording."

"You don't get to insult Farron," she snarls. A tangle of thorns strikes me in the chest, and I fly back across the room, landing in a heap with my hair falling over my brow.

Rosalina stands, looking down at her wrist where two thorn bracelets writhe like living snakes.

I stand and dust off my tunic. "Speaking of bargains, there's one you haven't paid for. A kiss for those convenient thorns, remember?"

"Just playing by the same set of rules you are, Cas," she says. "Besides, why would I want to fulfill it and let you take away my thorns?"

"You're a fae, but you still don't understand me." We begin to circle each other. "Why don't you give me a kiss and see if I let you keep your little trinkets?"

"I'm not kissing you," she says, then narrows her gaze. "You knew I was fae, didn't you?"

"From the moment I first laid eyes on you." Though the Fates had shown her with pointed ears in their prophecy, so I can't exactly take credit for that one.

"You do love your secrets." She keeps stepping in a circle over the objects I've scattered around her room.

"And just because you're fae doesn't mean you're safe. Being fae isn't all sunshine and roses, Flower. Even the Queen knew that."

"What do you mean?"

"Keep reading my book and maybe you'll find out."

"Stop talking in riddles and actually give me some answers. Then perhaps I'll give your stupid book back." She spreads her arms wide in frustration, the moonlight through the window casting her curves in a dangerous silhouette.

Her breasts are free and heavy beneath the nearly sheer nightgown, and it's so easy to see the sharp points of her nipples. She gives a little gasp when she notices my gaze, and her own flicks to her robe on the ground.

But she moves past it.

I prowl after her. *You really are intent on torturing me, aren't you?*

If she's still shocked about hearing me in her mind, her expression doesn't show it. Only a flicker of concentration, then I hear: *Being desired by you isn't as flattering as you think it is.*

I cut off her path, and she nearly bumps into me. "Now, what could that mean?"

"You want what belongs to Kel. You delight in tormenting him."

"I do." My control falters, and I grip her around the waist, slamming her against the dresser. "But I could learn to delight in tormenting you too, Princess."

She gives a sharp gasp as I dip my head, lips hovering right over her neck, then down to her breasts. Her pulse quickens. My words are lies. I don't think I could ever torment her in the way she does to me; being in her presence is agony.

Satisfying my lust and watching my lovers appear before Keldarion, seeing the brief flash of emotion in his eyes, has been great amusement these last twenty-five years. But it doesn't bring the same joy with her. I can still hear her voice in my mind from the party when I was fucking the fae on the dais: *Stop or I'll die.* I'm not even sure if she realized the gravity of her words. And now even the brief relief I'd found in the Below is lost to me. I shake my head, angry. *She doesn't control me. I am at no one's mercy,* I remind myself. But the longer I spend around her, the harder and harder it is to believe.

"What do you want to know, Rosalina?" I whisper.

She blinks up at me then gently guides my hand behind her to touch the brambles snaking up the wall.

"Your thorns," she says softly. "They're not sapping Castletree's magic, are they? They're keeping it standing."

7

ROSALINA

Caspian's violet-flecked eyes widen. "Now, why would you say something like that?"

"Because I can *feel* them." I started to piece it together when the princes were away, when it was just Castletree and me. These briars aren't the source of its sickness; they're like a second layer of foundation keeping everything standing.

The Prince of Thorns only lowers his hand from the briars, swallows, stays silent.

"I'm right, I know I am. From my first day in this place, I always knew these briars weren't evil. So why are you letting everyone believe you're taking the magic? If anything, it's taking *your* magic."

I study him. He's still stupidly gorgeous, of course. But there are dark circles beneath his eyes, and he's got a limp he's been trying to hide. Not to mention the way he'd disappeared on the Autumn Realm's battlefield, hacking up blackness; I haven't puzzled that out. "Caspian, why are you letting everyone believe you're the villain?"

"Who says I'm not?" he snarls.

"Because!" I spread my arms wide. "These thorns—*you*—are the only thing stopping Castletree from falling."

The flash in his eyes confirms my suspicions. The briars aren't evil, yet he attacked the Autumn Realm. But then he was fighting in disguise to help it. Or at least help me.

"Maybe there are things within these walls even a monster from the Below can't stand to lose."

I touch his arm. "I'm not sure what happened between you and the other princes, between you and Kel, but if you were to just tell them then—"

He pulls his arm away and snarls, "If you want me to keep my thorns here, you will not breathe a word of this to *anyone*. Do you understand?" And it's not anger flashing in his eyes …

"Caspian," I say, cupping his cheek, and this time, he lets me touch him, "what are you afraid of?"

Something sharp cuts across my vision, and a ringing reverberates in my ears. I'm no longer seeing the world through my own eyes. Flashes of moments tear through my mind. There's a torturous sting along my back, my arms, the crack of a whip and a scream. A scream that sounds like Caspian. Then a haunting woman's voice: *My darling boy.* Tall pillars of green gems, her kneeling before them, long dark hair blowing as emerald flames erupt around her.

I gasp, pulling away from Caspian. And for a second, it isn't flecks of purple dancing in his eyes, but flames of green. *Did he see the same vision I did?*

My heart beats wildly, and I realize this is the first time I've felt fear since Caspian has come into my room. Even when I awoke to him prowling around, the only emotion I'd felt was mild annoyance. And … other things I wish I hadn't.

"I've seen her, those flames, before," I stammer. "When I tried to break Lucas's crown. But we shattered it, and Perth's too. Is he back—"

"Perth was nothing but a pawn." Caspian coughs, then wipes his mouth to reveal a line of black. He gives a little sigh, then stares at me. His eyes have returned to the deep purple.

Thorns twine around his hands and form … a bow. Twisting briars curve to create a delicate bow with a taut string.

He holds it out. "Yes, I'm afraid of the green flames. And you should be, too."

Gingerly, I accept the bow, never once shifting my gaze from his.

And with that, the briars rise around the Prince of Thorns and take him back to the Below.

8

ROSALINA

The sinewy string of the bow Caspian created pulls back with ease, and the thorn arrow sails through the air, striking the cherry blossom tree in my room. This thing is certainly easier to shoot. *Or am I able to control the arrow because it's made of thorns?*

I stare down at the bow. The thorns entwine and overlap with each other in an almost delicate beauty.

My traitorous body still heats from his visit. I wish I could hate him, but a part of me knows there's so much more to the Prince of Thorns. The most unpleasant aspect of him is the secrets he's making me keep from the people I love. First our bargain, the book I stole, and now the truth of the briars weaving through Castletree.

Guilt simmers in my stomach. I have to tell my princes. At least about my bargain and the book. The last one doesn't exactly feel like my secret to tell. But now they've all gone back to their own realms. Except for Dayton.

"Waffles and fresh strawberry syrup this morning," Marigold says, pushing a cart into my room. "Prince Dayton brought home a basket from Summer."

I give a long sigh, then raise my bow and craft a thorn arrow from my bracelet on to my waiting fingers. It had been tricky to figure out how to create the shape at first, but I'd laid a normal arrow beside it and practiced sculpting a thorn, a little like molding clay in your mind. The arrow flies, this time going wide and shattering a vial of oil on my dresser.

"Girl!" Marigold starts, hands on her hips. "Are you even listening? What did I say about using weapons in here?"

"Sorry," I say sheepishly, lowering the bow. "I just don't want to suck at this anymore."

"You can't get better if you're not bad at something first," Astrid says from my armoire, wrinkling her nose at the haphazard mess inside. Last night, I'd scrambled to put back everything Caspian had strewn about.

My eyes flick to the side of my room. There's a tangle of thorns, my own grown from the bracelet. Hidden within is Caspian's book. I'm eager to read it again. *Why is he so interested in the Queen?*

"Come now," Marigold says. "Breakfast is getting cold."

I slink over to sit on the edge of my bed and pull the tray closer. The waffles are still steaming, and juicy red syrup slides down the sides. I stab the fluffy cakes with my fork and sigh as they melt on my tongue.

"And don't forget about the tea," Marigold says. "Especially after yesterday in the library."

"How do you know about that?" I ask, flushing.

"Nothing stays secret in this castle." Astrid laughs.

"Ugh." I grab the tea and take a sip. It smells like a field of wildflowers, with an almost nutty aftertaste. Marigold said a cup of this a week prevents me from being able to conceive. I know Farron's been drinking it, too.

One day, we'd both like to have a family. He mentioned as much the other night as we sat before the library's fireplace, adding to the memory book in honor of his mother. His childhood stories filled my heart with such warmth. But our future is a discussion for after curses are broken and Castletree is healthy.

"Knock, knock," Dayton says, peering into my room.

My heart skips, and I quickly wipe my mouth of strawberry syrup. "Hey."

"I'm heading to the training grounds if you want to meet me after breakfast."

"Sure."

He nods then pauses. "You still have that?"

I follow his gaze to where a stuffed lion with wings sits on my pillow. I giggle and grab it. "Of course, I do."

Dayton waltzes into my room, and from the corner of my eye, I catch Astrid leading Marigold out, who has a devious expression on her face.

"I haven't decided on a name for him, though," I say, holding the soft toy in my lap. It might be silly to have this as an adult woman, but it's special to me.

Dayton takes the little lion in his hands. "What about Aeneas? He was the first High Prince of Summer. Myth says he wielded a legendary trident blessed by the Queen herself."

"Like Kel's sword?"

"You mean that decoration? That's all it is, for the amount he uses it." Dayton chuckles. "If I had a weapon like that, I would not let it rot beneath my bed."

I laugh. "Aeneas. Ani for short. It's cute."

"You did not just give the hero Aeneas a cute nickname."

"But he's so adorable." I snatch the lion and fly it up into his tangled golden hair.

"All right, all right. I'm glad you kept it."

"Of course, you bought it for me on our first date—" I stammer and quickly correct. "Not that it was a date."

"Pretty sure I had your thighs wrapped around my face that night."

"Right, but we didn't even spend the night together. I ended up …" I trail off. Probably not the best time to bring up Kel figuring one of the last times Dayton and I were about to get intimate, Kel's name came out of my mouth. It was all a misunderstanding, but I don't think Dayton will ever forget it.

But the mention wipes the smile off the Summer Prince's face, regardless.

"You ended the night in the arms of your *mate,*" Dayton says, standing. "How's a guy supposed to compete with that?"

"Day—"

He heads to the door. "Get ready, and for star's sake, have a dip in the hot springs and wash off the Prince of Thorns' scent."

My fork clatters to my plate. "I—"

"And," Dayton growls, "you better damn well tell me what he was doing in your room last night."

9

ROSALINA

I take my lunch to the library, puzzling over my father's latest letter. I've entrusted Astrid and Marigold to hunt for texts that might help. He sent a rubbing of an ancient ruin depicting a woman with her hands extended to a flock of birds. In his letter, he wrote that the image felt important. But I wonder if perhaps my father is just biased. The birds looked like Pacific Wrens, my mother's favorite animal.

A part of me smiles at that, him looking for any connection back to her. But then again, Papa has always had great instincts. Maybe it is a clue.

I give a deep sigh and tuck the paper into my book bag, my thorn bow leaning against it. Dayton put me through quite the workout this morning. Plus, he only let me use the thorn bow a few times before we decided, yes, it was easier to shoot with.

"You have to learn the old-fashioned way, Blossom," he'd said. "You might not always have that with you. Learn to shoot with a wooden one and you can wield anything. And then be extra deadly with that thorn monstrosity."

Which had led to hours of hitting the back wall, but I had managed to nail the target four times. Three more than yesterday.

But no more water arrows appeared. I'm not sure I could recreate one even if I wanted to. The same with my own golden thorns: whatever magic I tapped into is still sealed inside.

When we finally finished training and started stretching, Dayton confronted me about Caspian. The truth came pouring out of me ... At least, most of it.

Caspian saving me on the battlefield, him being dressed in Autumn armor, me stealing his book and that's what Caspian had been looking for last night. It was just the part about the bargain that I left out. What would Dayton think of me? Especially after Farron's bargain with the Prince of Thorns went so horribly wrong?

But Dayton had been surprisingly understanding. He told me to show the book to Farron, which I know is a good idea. I need to tell Farron the whole truth. I need to tell all of them.

Something shimmers at the edge of my vision. I stand, narrowing my gaze, and absently grab my bow. Fae sight is far superior to humans, and I've found myself caught off-guard by the detail in the world these last weeks.

Rounding the corner, all I see is Astrid on a ladder, dropping books down to Marigold. Nothing out of the ordinary. But there, amid the orange and red trees, is green.

A phantasmal green.

"Look out!" I draw the bow and create a thorn arrow from my bracelet. I shoot.

A blur of green flame advances on Astrid and Marigold. My shot isn't straight, but I feel for my arrow. The thorn catches in my mind and careens toward the flame.

A horrible keening sound fills the air, followed by a thud.

The breath is heavy in my throat, and my vision clears. Astrid has leapt from the ladder and become a trembling white hare in Marigold's arms.

"What in the Above?" Marigold gasps.

A quick scan of the library shows no more flickers of flame, and I approach to see what exactly I shot.

It's a goblin, but not like one I've ever seen before. It's got the same rotten appearance as the ones that frequent the briars around Castletree, but veins of fluorescent green snake around its body. Dying flames curl over its hands and feet.

"What are you?" I gasp in horror.

The creature blinks its unnaturally green eyes. Black blood spews from its mouth, and it seems to notice my arrow piercing through its stomach for the first time. It doesn't look afraid.

"So much more than before," it says, words descending into a maddening laugh.

"How did you get into Castletree?" I snarl.

Its head flops to the ground. "Easy to infect something that's already dying. Sick, so sick, from Brother Caspian's magic."

Brother? Even these goblins think Caspian is poisoning Castletree. I remember being so afraid of these things when they first ambushed me in the Briar. But now, all I feel is anger. I yank the arrow out of its stomach. "Leave and tell your kind anyone else who comes here will not be shown such mercy."

But the creature does not try to move. It only smiles wider, showing rows and rows of razor-sharp teeth. "Death is the greatest gift one such as us can be given." Then it takes its gnarled hands on either side of the belly wound and rips.

A terrible squelching sounds, as blood and guts gush out.

I clutch my own stomach in horror, but the creature only laughs. "My kin has already retrieved the gift for Sister."

"There are more of them?" Astrid peeps, her little pink nose peering out from Marigold's golden tresses.

Pushing back bile, I turn from the horrific sight before me. "Hurry, warn the rest of the staff. Tell them to barricade in the closest room. I'll find Dayton."

"No goblin is going to wreck *my* castle!" Marigold says, a ferocious glint in her eyes. With a horrible squelch, she drives her boot down upon the creature's throat, putting it out of its misery.

"Be careful. These things are dangerous."

Marigold only gives me a sly grin, then pulls up her skirt to reveal a dagger strapped to her thigh. "There isn't a citizen of Spring that doesn't know their way around a blade, girlie."

I nod at her, and we rush toward the exit. The floor creaks behind me. I urge Astrid and Marigold on. Then I turn.

The goblin's body has completely been consumed by green flame. And it's catching the brittle leaves.

"No!" I scream. I will not let my favorite place in the entire world be taken from me. Salt tingles in my nose, and I throw my hands forward. A torrent of water erupts from my fingers.

It washes over the flames, dousing the fire and revealing a skeleton clawing out of the goblin's body.

Just like the soldiers from the Autumn battlefield. A familiar wave of fear rises, but I don't let it take over. If I do, I'll never get to Dayton. The flames will return and the whole library will fall.

I can't let that happen.

The goblin skeleton hobbles toward me just as I draw my bow. I shoot, guiding the arrow to strike its ribs. The sharp thorn pierces the bone, cracking it.

But the creature doesn't stop moving.

"Oh shit, oh shit, oh shit." How do you kill a creature who's already dead? Farron needed a whole ancient ass death spell to do it.

A terrible howl sounds from the monster as it reaches its bony fingers toward me, green flames already beginning to flicker along the bone.

"No, no, no," I stammer, trying to get out of its way. But its sharp claws rake across my chest.

I scream, scrambling back. It's only nicked my leather covering. Thank goodness I was too eager to get to the library to change out of my training gear.

What do I do? I slide my bow on my back, and then, on instinct, grab the biggest tome I can see off a nearby shelf.

The goblin lunges, and I swing the book as hard as I can against its head. Its skull dislodges and breaks into a pile of ash as it hits the floor. The body follows suit.

I let out a gasping breath. All right, so my zombie reading phase wasn't all for naught: a solid headshot will do the trick. It looks like these things aren't as hard to kill as Perth's undead soldiers.

I need to find Dayton.

I sprint out of the library. Where had Dayton said he was going after training? The hot springs? I rush into the muggy corridor but pause. *He's not here.* Something tugs painfully in my chest, and I turn on my heels without even checking the springs. *He's in his room.*

My boots kick up sand as I run fast down the hall. But there are small footprints in the dust, dozens of them—all leading to the Summer Prince's room.

10

DAYTON

I've woken up in some unusual places with unique company. Like in that rowboat with a mermaid tail wrapped around my legs—I swear she didn't have fins when we fell asleep. Or on shore, completely naked, head filled with memories of a silky-haired woman, but only seals on the horizon.

But today has to be the absolute fucking worst.

Passed out for an afternoon nap, I'd heard my door open, then felt a shift on my bed. My delirious mind had pictured Rosalina crawling in beside me. Instead, I turned to face a damned goblin.

Now, standing on my bed, surrounded by a pack of five goblins blazing with green flame, my hand burned from trying to punch one, I'd be lying if I said my prospects weren't a little precarious.

A goblin lunges at me and I rip down the gauzy canopy. It smothers the creature, but then the whole thing goes up like a green bonfire. *Fuck.*

Summoning Summer's Blessing, I bring forth a tide of water, knocking the creature back. I just wish my magic didn't feel so far away. Here at Castletree, my magic should be at its strongest.

One of the goblins breaks off and goes to inspect my swords on the side table.

"You stay away from those, you moss-ridden asshole," I yell.

It turns to me, hissing, then knocks them off the table like a disgruntled cat before brandishing its own weapon, a glistening silver dagger. There's something familiar about that steel—

One of them lunges, grazing my calf. Fuck, I've got to get out of here. Got to find Rosie.

I strike two of them with a gust of wind and leap through the opening, heading for my blades.

One of them blocks my path. "Not so scary without your swords, are you, Prince of the Arena?"

I manage to escape the swipe of its blade, my fingers grasping my swords, when a sharp pain cuts against my back. The familiar wetness of my own blood drips down my spine. I groan, doubling over.

"Dayton!"

Rosalina stands in my doorway, and I don't even have time to be frightened for her, because the instant I see her face, I know it's the goblins who should be afraid.

Her delicate features shift into a snarl, and her hair is a wild tangle. "Don't touch him!"

The flame goblins all turn to her, chittering, but it dies when the heavy energy of magic crackles in the room. Dies when Rosalina's eyes transform from brown to pure fucking gold. And for a single moment in that flash of light, dressed in the Summer training garb, she looks like an ancient hero in the Sun Colosseum. My heart all but stops.

Golden briars erupt from the ground, tear through the ceiling, and strike the goblins. They don't even have a chance to run before they're pierced by the sharp thorns and ensnared completely.

Rosalina lets out a gasp and drops to her knees. "Remove their heads," she says. "They're under similar magic as Perth's soldiers. They'll come back to life if we don't do that."

She doesn't have to tell me twice. Quickly, I grab my blades and relieve the goblins of their heads. They turn to ash as I do. When the last one fades away, Rosalina drops to all fours, the briars crashing to the ground with her.

I kneel before her. "You saved me, Blossom."

The briars remain, and golden roses bloom among the leaves. Just like the ones that destroyed Lucas on the Autumn battlefield. She hasn't been able to summon that magic since, but here it is today. Here to protect me.

"One of the goblins mentioned they were looking for something," she pants. "Do you have any idea what it might be?"

"Could they know about the High Tower? Our roses? Maybe they're trying to destroy them."

"No, High Tower hasn't been breached. And they didn't want anything in the library." Rosie's fingers curl into the sand on my floor. Then her eyes widen. "They're in the Winter Wing. Earlier, you mentioned Kel's sword was blessed by the Queen herself. Could they be after that?"

"Only one way to find out." I help her up, and we take off to the main corridor. There, running from the Spring Wing, are Marigold and several other staff.

"The castle is secure," Marigold says. "The last pack of goblins ran from the Winter Wing and out the front door."

I exchange a glance with Rosie. "Can you run?"

She nods, seeming to have caught her breath.

"Then let's go."

Swords firm in my hand, we sprint out of the castle, immediately hit with a sharp torrent of rain. I blink through the water, finding a cluster of goblins streaking green flames just about to cross the bridge.

"If they make it to the Briar, we'll lose them for good!" I yell. Our feet splash in the puddles. Shit, we'll never catch them.

"Keep running!" Rosalina yells. But she stops and draws her strange thorned bow.

Her gift from the Prince of Thorns.

But I obey, hitting the edge of the bridge as the goblins reach the other side. And there, glinting in one of their hands, is something wrapped in old cloth. If I fucking lose Kel's sword while he's gone, he's going to kill me. I pick up my pace.

A thorn arrow sails through the air, but lands wide of the goblins. I glance over my shoulder. "You missed."

"No, I didn't," Rosalina says. Then she swipes her hand overhead. The thorn arrow expands, exploding into a patchwork of briars, blocking off the exit of the bridge.

The goblins careen to a stop, chittering in agitation, trapped.

Trapped with me.

Perfect.

I draw my blades and take the moment of surprise to dispatch two of them. The others panic, slipping on the slick stone. They may be covered in green flame, but they're not so fucking scary when I'm armed. Going for the head, the last four are goners before Rosalina even catches up with me.

She slows to a stop, wind and rain tousling her hair and soaking her clothes, so they cling to her full curves. Her eyes widen, shifting back to dark brown. She stares at the piles of ash and black goblin blood at my feet.

"We make a pretty good team," I say.

"That we do." She smiles, then retrieves the hastily wrapped package from a pile of ash. Carefully, she unfolds the old cloth, revealing the sheath with an icy hilt sticking out.

"Careful," I say. "Don't touch that without the sheath."

"Wouldn't want to get fingerprints on this prized possession," she says sarcastically. "Kel might stick me in the dungeon again."

A lot worse would happen to her than that if she tried to wield the Sword of the Protector. But my mind is still stuck on why the goblins would attempt to steal it. "They really were after Kel's sword. I wonder what use they could have for it."

"One of them mentioned a gift for Sister, whatever that means." She carefully sets the sword down, then walks over to me, running a delicate hand over my bare chest until she reaches my back. "They hurt you."

"Just a scratch."

Her expression turns steely. "Do you remember when you told me if anyone touched me, you'd kill them and fuck me in their blood?"

I run my hand through her rain-soaked hair. "What are you imply-ing, Blossom?"

She lets her hand rest on my chest. "They hurt you. Now they're dead. So—"

I step away from her. "We should get the sword out of the rain."

Her eyes flash. "Dayton, when I saw you in danger—when I *felt* you were in danger—every part of me exploded. I don't think that type of magic just happens. The only other time was when I needed to protect you all. Protect Farron and Kel, my—"

"Don't go there, Rosie."

"Why not?" She grips my arm. "Can't you feel this?"

A growl sounds in my chest, and I yank my arm away. "Do you want to know what I feel, Rosalina O'Connell? What I really feel?"

"And what is that, Prince of the Summer Realm?" Her mouth has shifted into a snarl. I've made her mad.

Good. I'd rather her mad than whatever the hell she was trying before. "Relief."

"Relief?"

"Yes. When I found out you and Farron were mates, all I felt was relief. Relief neither of you belonged to *me*."

Her face crumbles. "Day, that night we all spent together ..."

"Of course, I *want* you and Fare, but I also know how fucking awful that would be for both of you."

She shakes her head. "That's not true."

"Everyone I've ever loved has met a terrible fate, Rosie. Every single person." My voice breaks. "I thought for sure I'd take Fare down with me because I can't give him up. But you saved him from *me*."

"Stop it." Rosalina grips my arm over the bargain cuff Farron and I share. "There's nothing terrible about the love you and Farron have for each other. And there's nothing terrible about what's between us. I haven't been brave enough to say it yet, but Dayton, I ..."

My entire chest feels like it's caving in, and I haven't cried in fucking years. It might be salty tears running down my cheeks, or maybe it's just rain. "Rosie, stop. I can't bear it, please."

But she doesn't stop. Of course she doesn't.

"Daytonales, you are my mate." She snatches my jaw. "Let me fuck you in the blood of the enemies we slayed and prove it."

I can't keep her. I can't own her. But I could give myself this moment. One time with the most perfect woman to ever live. My resolve is weakening, every part of me aching for her. One night with me won't kill her. She'll have Fare. She'll even have Kel.

My death has always been hovering just beyond the horizon. And here it fucking is. Maybe not the death of my body. That'll carry on. But my soul, my heart—they're not going to survive losing her.

But I've never been one to make the best decisions.

Rosalina stares up at me, eyes flashing like the raging storm.

"Fuck it," I growl and take her in my arms.

II

ROSALINA

Dayton pulls me against him with such force, I'm completely thrown off my feet and into his arms. What was it he had said to me once? That he wanted to crash beneath my waves. Well, now every part of us is colliding.

Rain slides down our faces as we kiss. His tongue parts my lips. I wrap my legs around his waist, and he holds me tight, one hand gliding up my back, the other firmly cupping my ass.

"Fuck, Blossom." He peppers my jaw with sweet kisses. "You have absolutely no right to be this beautiful, this fierce, and this damn good a kisser."

A feeling of absolute freedom washes over me, and I burst out laughing. I told Dayton I think he's my mate.

He sits me on the edge of the bridge's railing, his hips pressed between my legs. My body thrills at the feeling of his hardness. Blinking through the sheets of rain, I make out his signature cocky grin, golden hair a wet tangle.

"I once tried to escape over this bridge," I say.

"You're not going anywhere now," Dayton growls. He grips my leather breastplate and tears it off in one swift movement.

"I liked that—"

"I'll get you another one." Darkness passes over his eyes as he takes in my body, clearly visible beneath the soaking wet fabric. A purely male groan sounds in his throat as he lowers his mouth to my neck and drags his teeth to my collarbone. "I intend to rip this thing to bits."

"Do it."

Tearing sounds through the air as my dress becomes little more than tatters, and the Prince of Summer desperately claws for my skin. Drops of water fall off his eyelashes as he blinks back the rain to take me in.

"You are more beautiful than all the goddesses in the Vale," he breathes and kisses me, pressing our bodies together. My breasts push against the rock-hard planes of his chest. Then he leans me back, hands easily gliding down my slick body.

My breath catches as I realize he's leaning me over the side of the bridge, nothing between me and the open air but his hand on my back. But I'm not afraid. He won't let me fall.

He drags me back up, and I gently touch his jaw, the beautiful square shape. He's so masculine, but at the same time, there's a sculptured beauty to his features.

"What did you think the first time you saw me in the hot springs?" I ask.

"That you were the most beautiful person I'd ever seen."

"Be serious."

Dayton's hand slips between my legs, and I cry out. He rubs tenderly, and my core clenches. *So good.* His touch feels so fucking good. "I am being serious."

"I was just some human."

"Come on now." His fingers lightly dance over my molten core. "You were never *just* some human."

"Day," I moan, my hair catching in the wind.

He tucks a curl behind my ear and flashes a crooked smile. "Meanwhile, you thought I was *just* some staff member easy enough to manipulate."

"That's not—" My words are stolen when Dayton dips his head, kissing my breasts. He takes a nipple between his teeth and bites.

The smirk still plays on his lips when he lifts his head. "I get it. You were desperate to save Fare. Your bond must have been calling out to him even then."

Frustration pushes through my pleasure. This isn't about Farron right now, and I wish there was a way I could make the stupid Summer Prince see that.

"Dayton." I drag a hand down his chest, feeling the muscles ripple beneath my fingertips. "You were the first of the princes to kiss me, you know."

He bends to bite the point of my ear. "I was the first to taste you, too, if I recall," he says, rubbing my pussy harder as if for emphasis.

I bite my lip, savoring the exquisite waves of ecstasy. "I'd never felt anything like that in my entire life. Do you understand what I'm saying?"

"That I'm good at making you come?"

I let out an annoyed breath and take his face between my hands, forcing the stubborn prince to listen to me. "You were the first person to show me what love is supposed to feel like."

He stills his hands, his breath. The only movement is a slight quiver in his lips.

Can you feel it now?

"Are you asking me if I love you?" he says. Says as if he heard my every thought.

I don't answer because it is what I'm asking, and he knows it. He grips the back of my neck and pulls me into a deep kiss. He tastes like salt and sun. I feel like I'm drowning, but I don't need air. All I need is him.

His wet mouth slides to my ear, where he whispers, "Come in my arms, Baby."

Wordless whimpers escape me. I shake, then he slips a finger inside, and I'm lost. "Dayton," I moan. "Please."

He slips a second finger inside of me. I'm so wet. Pleasure spirals out of me in waves.

"Not yet," he says, and places his thumb over my clit. "Not until I know you're completely mine."

"I am," is all I can gasp.

He rubs me and I feel that delicious pressure building. I'm so close, so damn close.

"Look at you, outside on the bridge." He strokes faster. "Naked and mine."

Tears well in my eyes and I claw at his shoulders, as wave after wave of pleasure begins to wash over me, dragging me under. I can't breathe, can't think, can only feel. He keeps rubbing, keeps pushing me higher and higher until I'm shuddering and moaning and crying out his name.

"That's it, Rosie," Dayton says. "Come for me."

He slides a third finger in, and I climax hard against his hand. The orgasm rocks through me, body trembling. Dayton doesn't stop, doesn't let me come down. He just keeps working me, his fingers thrusting in and out until I'm nothing but a quivering mess.

"Don't stop," I gasp.

"Never." He kisses me. His mouth is relentless as he licks a path down the curve of my neck. His fingers continue to pump in and out of my aching pussy as my orgasm finally slows.

"Day," I murmur against his lips. "Day, Day."

"I can't wait. I need to be inside you." He pulls out and begins to work furiously at his pants, dropping them to reveal his massive cock. Dayton looks magnificent on a good day, but having him standing before me, wet and wanting …

Wanting *me*.

"I'm yours," I gasp. "I'm yours, Dayton."

He raises a dark brow and chuckles. "Well, that's splendid, love, because I think it's obvious how much I want you."

I grasp his cock, not able to fit my fingers all the way around it, and stroke. "Thank the gods," I say, adding a lilt of his accent and deep voice to my own, "because this is positively the most glorious cock that ever did hail from the Summer Realm."

Dayton grabs a knot of my hair, tugs. "Are you making fun of my cock, Blossom?"

"Wouldn't dream of it."

"Good." He draws me closer until his lips are by my ear. "Because this cock is going to fucking claim you, going to make you scream *my* name, going to fill you with so much cum it'll be leaking down your legs, and there won't be a soul in the Enchanted Vale that won't recognize my scent on you."

I whimper, completely and utterly melting for him. "Yes, yes, I'm yours, I'm yours."

"Spread your legs."

I do, and he stares at me for a moment, sizing up how to best claim what belongs to him. It bursts in my chest, this part of my heart that has always been his.

"I need you now, *please.*"

"Rosalina." Roughly, he grips the back of my neck and pulls me into a kiss at the same time he enters me. But he does so gradually, and I moan against his lips as his length pushes slowly, so slowly. I let out a groan as I feel my body expand to accommodate his size. "More, please."

He takes my lips between his teeth. "Patience, Blossom. I don't want to hurt you."

I give a little whimper of protest but allow myself to enjoy the utter bliss of this sensation, of finally being this close to him. He stares where our bodies meet.

A deep growl rumbles in his throat as he pushes in the last few inches, sheathing to the hilt. And I scream, scream at the sensation of being filled so completely, my body already clenching around him, never wanting to let him leave.

"Fuck," he growls, holding us tight, not letting either of us move. His lips dip to my neck. "You feel so fucking good, Baby, do you know that? You're so soft."

"Do I feel as good as I taste?" I smirk.

"The gods themselves will have to pry me out of you." He gives a little pump, not fully leaving, but enough to jolt my whole body with white-hot heat.

I moan, and he moves his hand to rub my clit. My core tightens, nearly coming with the sensation. I wiggle on his cock, needy for friction. As if he can sense my desperation, he begins to move, holding me tight by the waist at the edge of the railing as he pumps in and out.

"Dayton!" I cry, clinging to his neck, pulling at his hair. He pulls out, almost to the tip before sliding back in slowly. "You're torturing me."

He does it again, grinning like the Cheshire Cat as inch by agonizing inch, he slides deeper inside. Then he lifts me off the bridge railing and into his arms, pumping faster and faster. I have no idea how he has the strength to do that and hold me, but I am completely and utterly at his mercy.

He brings a wet tongue to my ear, then says lowly, "I do recall you promising to fuck me in a goblin's blood. The blood has washed away, but ..."

He lowers himself to the slick cobblestone, me still on top of him, legs falling to either side of his waist, cock still deep inside me. His teal eyes blaze. "You're in control now, Rosie. So, fuck me like the wild, uninhibited goddess I know lives inside you."

I slam my hands on his rain-slicked chest, and a smile rises on my face. I move, lifting myself to the tip of his cock before slamming down hard. The sensation rattles us both. He tilts his head back, neck muscles straining, and groans. So I do it again. And again. Faster and faster, until my fingers are leaving red scratches along his chest, my breasts are bouncing, and he's lifting his hips to match me thrust by thrust.

My voice is hoarse from calling his name. Something feral flashes in his eyes as he rises, holding me in his lap as we continue this pace, our bodies working in tandem.

My inner muscles tighten, and he slams me down hard, and I know I can't hold on much longer. "Day, I'm—"

"Come, Baby. Take it, take this cock." His teeth graze my neck, hands tangled in my soaking hair. I'm his. My body wracks with euphoric bliss as I come undone around him.

He roars and I feel his own release explode, cock spasming as he spills deep inside me. I press down on his lap, wanting to take it all. Somehow in the daze, his lips meet mine, and we tumble to the cobblestone.

I'm not sure how long we lie there, him still inside me, the rain cooling our heated bodies, but eventually he pulls out and rolls to the side.

Pure euphoric bliss fills me as I fall to my back, blinking as the rain pours down, the taste sweet on my tongue. A laugh bubbles up within me, but when I don't hear Dayton answer it, I turn to him.

He's staring straight up, one hand clenched to his chest, an almost pained expression on his face. Pain? Why, when what happened was just so wonderful?

It hits me with shocking clarity.

He didn't feel it. Did *I* feel it? I let out an animalistic cry, my own hand flying to my chest. Desperately, I try to recall how it felt with Kel, with Farron. It had been the same, hadn't it? This feeling had been answered by them, but with Dayton …

No, no, no. It's not possible. He's my mate, too. I *know* it.

Dayton sits up, sighing. The rain clouds begin to part, and it feels more ominous than it should. Like an ending.

"Let's go inside." He grabs his pants and laces them up.

Tears fall down my cheeks, now no longer hidden by the rain. "I was so sure …"

Dayton picks up Kel's sheathed sword and only gives me a quick, sympathetic shrug. Like that's all this loss is to him—a shrug. But what this really means is … There is someone else out there for him.

I shake my head, drawing my knees up to cover my naked body. "No, something is wrong. It hasn't awoken yet. It wasn't the right time. We can go find some will-o'-wisps and see if your bond is still all tangled and—"

"I died in front of you." Dayton turns, anger lacing his words. "You watched me get pierced by three arrows and collapse, and the bond didn't awaken." He kneels and cups my face. "We made love, fucking glorious love. And the bond didn't awaken. Because there is *no* bond between us. We're not mates, Rosalina."

"But Day—"

He stands swiftly. "Stop."

It's the second time he's told me to stop today. And this time I do.

My training dress is tattered on the ground, and I stand naked, chest heaving. The storm has blown away the ash, the rain has washed the blood, and now only the rags of the goblins' clothes and their weapons remain.

"Oddly nice weapons for goblins," I say absently. As if my heart isn't ashes itself.

"I was thinking the same thing." Dayton leans down to inspect a piece, then another, and another.

"What is it?"

"These weapons are practically new," Dayton says, brow furrowed. "And they're made of Spring steel."

"What does that mean?"

"It means we have to warn Ezryn."

My heart clenches at his name. "So, we're going to the Spring Realm?"

"Yes, Rosalina, we're going to Spring."

12

EZRYN

Each step I take into the Hall of Vernalion—the throne room of my home, my ancestors—is slower and heavier than the last.

It's been months since I've returned to the Spring Realm —a long time for the High Prince to be away, but also merely a blink in the eyes of the fae.

And yet everything has changed.

It looks the same, the lush greenery draping the stone walls. Delicate tendrils of vines and leaves trail down like emerald tears. Gleaming veins of Spring steel trace intricate patterns across stout pillars, entwining with golden filigree. The earthy scent of moss mixes with the wet stone. Keep Hammergarden is built into the base of the mountains, an eternal mixture of Spring's bounty and the rich ores in the rock.

Servants bow their heads as I pass. They weren't expecting me, but they never are. Usually, my presence is cause for bustle and gossip. Now, they shrink back, eyeing me warily as if I am a stranger.

The ornate, domed ceiling makes the throne room appear even more spacious than it is, though it does nothing to stop the oppressing weight that hangs throughout the hall. Though I have stood here many times as a boy and a young man, never have I felt such a heaviness in this space.

Someone has planted massive red flowers in every corner of the throne room. A few have bloomed but most are still buds. They appear too vivid for this sacred area.

But the biggest difference of all is my father. He's not sitting on the throne as he rightfully should as steward.

Instead, sitting there, leaning back, hands grasping the armrests with curved gloved knuckles, is my brother.

The brother I banished decades ago.

"Well, well, well, the silver son has returned," Kairyn calls from the throne, his voice a dark timbre.

"That seat does not belong to you," I say. "Where is Father?"

Kairyn tilts his black helm. Two long protrusions jut out above the dark visor, reminiscent of a Great Horned Owl. Like all Spring royalty, he covers his face for all but his immediate family or fated mate. Though by creed, we could take off our helmets in the presence of the other, our parents raised us with the strictest of principles. I remember the last time I looked into his eyes as a boy before he put on his helm. There was innocence there. Fear.

Now, his visor reveals only darkness.

"Father," Kairyn says slowly, "has fallen ill. He is under our watchful care."

"I did not grant you leave from the monastery."

"In these dire situations, I thought it necessary to take command in Father's place."

"You should have sent word," I growl. "However exceptional the circumstances, you are still banished."

"Spring *needs* me."

My brother has always been rash, reckless, but for him to break a royal order … Have things truly become so grave that Kairyn would risk such a thing?

"There is more to being steward than sitting on a throne. If you have so valiantly been serving in Father's stead, then why did you not respond when I sent a letter of the Autumn Realm's plight or the invitation to attend the funeral of Princess Niamh?"

Kairyn's helm rolls in a circle, a bored and agitated expression he's done since boyhood. "Apologies, big brother. But with Father ill, I could not step away. Spring needs a strong and attentive ruler, after all."

His voice ... The haunting intensity, the brooding rasp. I want to claw at my skull to get it out. He's been in my head for so long, and now to hear him in person ...

He's your little brother, I think.

But I notice he's still made no move to get off my throne, as law demands of the steward when the High Ruler returns.

On the contrary, Kairyn leans forward, resting his helm on his fist. He's dressed entirely in black, his suit of armor shining and pristine. His cape drapes over the seat like spilled oil. The only color is a pure white stardrop flower tucked into the top of his breastplate.

You do not belong there. The throne is ancient and sacred, crafted of the helms of all the previous High Rulers. Each one has been melded into the seat, imbuing the throne with the indomitable spirit of its previous wearer. The collective wisdom and resilience of each High Prince and Princess of Spring forms a single, formidable seat of authority.

I purposely avoid looking in the top right corner of the back of the chair, where I know I will see a starlight silver helm with a slanted visor reminiscent of cat eyes.

"So, you've broken your banishment and decided to claim the stewardship in Father's place without seeking the approval of the High Prince," I respond to my brother. Idly, I wonder what the staff think of all this. Many I recognize: footmen and butlers, ladies-in-waiting and advisors. But I do not see the one I'm looking for, the keep's majordomo, Eldy. He has always been my father's closest advisor. And come to think of it, neither do I see any of my father's princeguard.

And there are many faces I have never seen before. Clustered by the throne are a group of acolytes from the monastery, their white and gold gowns clearly defining them as members of the clergy. I scan their faces, landing on one. A fae woman, her blue eyes piercing. She seems familiar—

"What would you have me do?" Kairyn growls. "I will not stand by while Spring falls into the clawing hands of the power-hungry."

"A curious turn of words for a banished prince who is now suddenly sitting atop a throne." My voice is steady, calm, but it's a fight to get out. My head swims with the heavy despair that hangs like clouds over the room. "You were sentenced to a lifetime of servitude at Queen's Reach Monastery."

"And I have given it a lifetime's worth of service." Kairyn stands, and his shadow falls over me. Despite being younger, he has always been taller, broader of shoulder. Now, he looks like a giant shadow, only the feathered brow of his helm distinguishable from the black void of his other armor. "I freed the monastery from the tyranny of the High Clerics, who were exerting their power over all the mountain villages after you left Spring in the hands of our poor, ailing father. Now, it is Florendel that needs me."

I suck in a deep breath. *You ran,* I imagine Kairyn saying in my head. *You forced my hand.*

Who am I to stand before my brother and cast blame?

Kairyn stomps down the steps toward me. That oppressive weight nearly makes my body dip, but I hold steady. "The High Clerics don't rule the monastery anymore," he rasps. "I do."

Heavy footsteps sound, and from the back door of the hall come two figures, clad in huge armor and helms.

Kairyn gestures to them. "I have replaced Father's princeguard with my own loyal conclave. Rest easy that I have ensured all of Spring's citizens are in good hands. You need not worry, brother. Return to Castletree with the knowledge that I, your blood, will continue the stewardship here with the same wisdom and integrity in which you would rule."

A moment of silence passes, then he whispers in my mind: *I wouldn't have killed her.*

My brother's shadow is too heavy, his words ringing both outside and in my head. I stumble back, wanting to rip the invisible clouds from the room. What's going on here? My father bedridden, Kairyn on the throne, the High Clerics deposed, a new princeguard—

A set of bright eyes in the doorway catches my attention, and I see Eldy staring in. One recognizable face in a place that suddenly feels so unknown. His frown is framed by a familiar gray goatee, and he opens his eyes wide, gesturing for me to follow him.

I grit my hands into fists, then stare up at my brother. "You speak highly of your accomplishments, Prince Kairyn. But you have disobeyed the High Prince. Let me observe the state of Florendel before you make such claims as to absolve your banishment and take command of *my* realm."

With that, I turn my back to my brother and storm out.

13

ROSALINA

My heart leaps in my throat as my body shimmers back into corporeality, arms still wrapped tight around Dayton. He had summoned the magic mirror to take us to Florendel, the capital city of the Spring Realm.

My feet land on dark pink cobblestone, the edges filled with fluffy green moss. Dayton still has a grip on my shoulders, but quickly lets go. I look around, making sure Astrid and Marigold made it safely through.

As soon as we realized the goblins were wielding Spring steel, Dayton and I rushed back to Castletree and sent word to Farron and Kel. I got dressed quickly and packed a single bag. Then I grabbed Kel's sheathed Sword of the Protector and met Dayton at the mirror.

"You aren't thinking of heading to Florendel without a guide, are you, toots?" Marigold had chastised Dayton, digging a finger between his pecs before giving them an affectionate pat.

"I've been to Spring plenty of times," Dayton had groaned, but Marigold had made up her mind.

"Things are different in Florendel. You'll get eaten alive."

"If Marigold's going, I'm coming too!" Astrid had cried, snatching my hand.

Now, the four of us stand in a tight cluster, staring around at the capital city of Spring.

I take a deep breath; the air is humid, a lush, fresh dampness to it. But there's something else—the tang of metal and wet stone.

"Ezryn will be staying at Keep Hammergarden," Dayton says. "This way."

"You mean *this* way," Marigold says, brow raised. She waves her hand. "Follow me."

Dayton rolls his eyes but obeys, while Astrid and I toddle behind. But I can barely walk in a straight line: there is so much to see, to hear, to take in.

A majestic cityscape sprawls around us, all overlooked by a towering mountain range that seems to scrape the very sky itself. The metropolis is infused with ornate buildings, wrought-iron balconies, and colorful pastel-hued facades. The streets, made of cobblestone, are adorned with lush gardens, where bubbling fountains and decorative tilework make them appear as serene oases. The buildings are all made of brilliant pink stone.

"This place is amazing," I whisper as I stare upward, trying to glimpse the tallest peak.

"That's Mount Lumidor," Astrid says. "It's one of the highest mountains in all the Enchanted Vale."

Its sheer grandeur dominates the skyline. Cascading waterfalls and emerald patches of vegetation dot the slopes. It feels as if the city itself is cradled in the mountain's embrace.

"Florendel is renowned as one of the most magnificent cities in all the Vale," Astrid says, her red eyes darting around almost as much as mine. "Both a natural wonder and a place of industrial craftsmanship."

I understand what she means. I turn in a circle, taking in the vibrant city. It's the busiest place I've ever seen in the Vale, with fae bustling past us, pulling carts or running in and out of storefronts. No one even gives us a second glance, many with blank expressions focused on their intended task.

"Don't be intimidated by the hustle and bustle, girlie," Marigold calls from up ahead. "We Spring folk can be single-minded in our work. But that makes the place even more exciting, doesn't it?" She nudges Dayton playfully in his side.

But Dayton gives no reaction back. A severity has taken over his expression, one that doesn't seem to belong to him.

My heart aches. *I truly thought, in the deepest depths of my soul, you belonged to me. How can there be someone else?*

I take in a shaky breath to stop my thoughts from spiraling further. That's it. It's done. Dayton is not my mate—there's someone else for him.

As foreboding as goblins wielding Spring steel is, perhaps it's just what we need to refocus our attention.

Both delicate and massive flowers adorn every storefront, every walkway. We pass under a moss-covered archway that drips petals in a variety of colors. But it's not the pastel meadow I'd once imagined when I thought of a faerie city of Spring: there are glimpses of mining and metalwork underneath the vibrant blooms. In the distance, I hear the clash of metal on metal and the hum of a machine.

"The stone is so beautiful," I say to Marigold, looking around at all the rose-colored buildings.

"It's made from volcanic rock mined in the Starweaver Mountains," she says. "Is my city not magnificent?"

"Stay vigilant and mind your tempers," Dayton says, his voice low and serious. "Ezryn's father, Thalionor, is as straight-edged as a blade."

"And not exactly your biggest fan, if I remember correctly," Marigold says.

Astrid heaves up her skirt to hurry beside Dayton. "Didn't you accidentally set his Royal Botanical Garden on fire one Spring Solstice?"

"It was a long time ago," Dayton snaps. "That damned thorny prick thought it would be fun to make our own fireworks—"

"You mean Caspian," I say lowly.

Dayton picks up his pace. "Like I said. It was a long time ago."

"The Prince is right though, Rosalina," Marigold says. "The royal family has always been very strict. Best to keep your wits about you until we find Prince Ezryn."

I nod and walk closer to Marigold. It's like being back in her home realm has imbued her with extra confidence. She struts with chin held high, hips sashaying back and forth.

The buildings are low-pitched with clay tile roofs. Each door is elaborately carved with a façade depicting everything from nature to epic battles. I find myself lingering to take everything in, and Astrid yanks hard on my elbow so I don't fall behind.

As we turn a corner, my eye catches on something up in the mountains, and I gasp. A massive cherry blossom tree juts out of the side of the cliff, seeming to defy the laws of nature. Its branches stretch and intertwine, forming an intricate network of paths and chambers. A castle.

Not just any castle. Castletree. Spring's version of the illusion that appears in every realm.

And at its base lies a formidable keep carved into the very mountain itself. Huge rose-colored stone walls covered in ivy block our path, hemming in giant wooden doors engraved with spiraling leaves. It reminds me of Ezryn's necklace. Castletree's pale pink blossoms drift down like confetti, creating a pink walkway up to the gates.

Two guards stand sentinel on either side. They're clad in steel armor with heavy helmets, yet their faces are not covered. Come to think of it, none of the citizens wore helms like Ezryn. *It's only the royal family who must cover their faces,* I remind myself.

"Let me do the talking," Dayton whispers as we approach the guards. "Hail, good servants of Spring. I, High Prince Daytonales, seek entry to the Hall of Vernalion for an audience with High Prince Ezryn."

The guards look at each other, then back at Dayton. "Do you have an appointment?"

I catch the tic in Dayton's jaw. "No, I don't have an appointment. But if you tell Ezryn—"

"The *High Prince,*" the other guard interjects, "is in a meeting with the steward. They are not to be interrupted."

Dayton flashes a grin that could coax a smile out of stone. "I appreciate your diligence, but Prince Thalionor will be more than delighted to hear I've come—"

"Prince Thalionor is no longer the steward," the guard says dully. "Prince Kairyn rules Florendel now."

A strangled beat of silence passes between us. Dayton blinks. "Kairyn? That's impossible. You must let me through—"

"No appointment, no audience." The guard shrugs.

A cloud falls over Dayton's face, brow furrowing with anger.

"We have to do something," I whisper to Marigold, "otherwise I think Dayton's going to be the first one to break his own minding-temper rule."

Marigold clears her throat and pushes past me and Astrid to stand beside Dayton. "Why, if it isn't little Antonio and little Filipe. I see you've finally made guard duty! Quite the improvement from when I was last here. Weren't you both on latrine duty?"

"L-Lady Marigold!" the one on the left—Antonio—cries. "We weren't expecting you!"

"You look as beautiful as ever, my lady," Filipe mumbles. "Radiant as the sun…"

"Save it," she barks. "A High Prince would never have been treated this way when I ran the household. And I can only imagine if the majordomo hears about such insolence—"

"It's orders, milady!" Antonio cries. "Only those approved by Prince Kairyn may enter."

"A High Prince requires no such approval. Bring me Majordomo Eldor and we shall get to the bottom of this idiocy."

Filipe snaps to attention. "T-that's not necessary. Prince Daytonales, we shall show you to the throne room. But … the others have to stay here." His eyes flash to me and Astrid.

"They stay with me," Dayton growls.

"With all due respect, High Prince, unvetted visitors are not allowed in the Hall of Vernalion. There have been dark deeds conspiring of late," Antonio says.

I place a hand on Dayton's arm. "It's okay. You and Marigold go ahead. Astrid and I will wait right here. Once you find Ezryn, this will all be sorted."

A pained expression flashes across Dayton's face, but Marigold nudges his arm. "I'll stay too and watch over her. Don't get that pretty face in a knot."

"Fine." He heaves in a breath. "I'll find Ezryn and be back as soon as possible. Don't wander off."

"My feet are planted." I stomp my feet for emphasis.

Dayton sighs again then leans toward me, face tilted … A kiss?

But as quickly as the action overcomes him, he jerks back, cheeks flushing. "Uh, okay. Be back soon."

The guards wave for another set of sentries to take their place, then march on either side of the Prince of Summer as he disappears within the walls.

14

EZRYN

My head feels lighter outside of the Hall of Vernalion. I take a deep breath, reveling in the rich, familiar smell of my home. My gloved hands clutch the stone barrier on the ramparts of Keep Hammergarden as I gaze over the city, the Starweaver Mountains, and finally to the top of Mount Lumidor. Eldor, the keep's majordomo, hovers nervously at my elbow.

"What is going on here, Eldy?" I turn to him. After leaving my brother in the hall, our head of house was quick to get my attention. I'd almost pulled him into a hug, I'd been so happy to see a familiar face that wasn't standing vigil at my brother's side. But I'd restrained myself.

The fae man taps his fingers together, one of his many nervous habits. His gray hair falls straight to his jaw, and he stops tapping only to pluck at his mustache.

"I wanted to send word, sire, but all messages in or out of Florendel are being surveyed. Prince Kairyn does not take kindly to anyone who questions his leadership. He brings to court a great … paranoia about the outside realms."

I keep walking again, gaze out at my city, if only because I need to do something with my body. "Tell me, what has happened to my father?"

"It's hard to say, sire." Eldy shakes his head. "You know he's never been the same since … since the loss of your mother."

"Let us not mince words. I know it is you who has been the true steward in my absence. My father's state did not allow for such work."

"A duty I gladly served. But even so, in the last months, it's as if a fog has settled over his mind. He looks without seeing. He eats without tasting. He speaks without meaning."

My jaw tightens. "And Kairyn has taken this opportunity to revoke his own banishment."

Eldy stops in front of me, holding my gaze with his huge, watery eyes. "Kairyn has taken the opportunity to do much more than that. He's enacted a coup against the High Clerics, declared himself the new leader of Queen's Reach Monastery. He's brought many of the Golden Acolytes down to the keep. I don't know what for. They just amble around. All except for the woman he put in charge of your father's wellness. And his princeguard, of course. He's calling them his Penta Conclave."

"What of my father's princeguard?"

"They were assigned to various posts around the realm." Eldy's nose twitches. "It was all quite sudden."

"He's always wanted my attention. I just never thought he'd go to such lengths to get it." Collapsing over the barrier, my helm suddenly too heavy. "I was too hard on him, El. It was a mistake to send him away from Florendel. Now, he's seeking to prove himself here, but he's still only a wild boy."

Eldy puts a hand on my shoulder. "By law, you were justified to enact far worse than a banishment, sire. To tell the truth, Kairyn's actions may be radical, but he's protected the people. His conclave has destroyed several goblin raids, and he's housed and fed refugees from villages that have fallen."

"At least some good has come from his disobedience." I shake my head. "But I cannot allow him to bend the rules of his banishment however he likes. Regardless of how justified he believes his actions, there must be a consequence for his defiance." I only wish I didn't have to be the one to decide it.

Eldy leans beside me, wrinkling his nose. He has a large white flower pinned to the lapel of his green vest.

"A stardrop?" I ask. "Haven't seen one of those in ages."

"Oh, this?" Eldy looks down. "Yes, quite the pretty flower, isn't it? Usually only used for medicinal purposes due to its antitoxic properties, but I saw a couple of the newcomers from the monastery wearing them. They are alpine flowers after all, only growing at high altitudes. But I figured it was all the rage with the young fae, so I procured one for myself. Quite the trek, mind you!"

I huff a laugh and clap him on the back. "I've missed you."

He smiles at me, and I hold on to that. I never admitted my sin to him or Marigold, but after my mother's death, they looked at me as if they knew the truth and forgave me anyway.

A forgiveness I do not deserve.

"—never seen her before."

Voices filter up from below the rampart, and I look down. We've wandered nearly all the way along the keep and have arrived above the gates. The two guards standing watch are jabbering at each other—a lack of duty my father would never have stood for.

I, however, cannot be bothered when my mind is so full—

"Pretty thing, ain't she?"

"Looks like a village maiden. You know the type. Not much going on between the ears, eh?"

I roll my eyes. The two guards are nattering on about a woman. Not only a lack of duty, but a lack of chivalry as well.

One of the guards lets out a howling laugh. "That's how I like them! It's not what's between the ears, but what you can stick between their legs."

"Come on, Eldy," I say. "Let's head down to the gate. It appears our soldiers need reminding about the meaning of vigilance."

But Eldy's not listening to me. His eyes are cast over the ramparts, chest heaving. "I-It's her. She's returned!"

I follow his gaze to see two fae women examining a cluster of bright red buds, the same as in the throne room.

It can't be. For it appears to be Astrid and Marigold.

"Marigold has come back," Eldy whispers.

Before my mind catches up to what Astrid and Marigold being here means—or what is sure to be another dramatic tirade in the ongoing chronicles of Eldy and Marigold's love affair—one of the guard's voices echoes up to me: "All right then. If you're so confident, off you go then. Go show that village hayseed just what you've got."

"Why not?" One of the guards drops his lance and steps out from his post. He starts walking along the wall.

Not toward Astrid or Marigold.

But if they're here...

Who are the guards looking at?

I practically throw my upper body over the ramparts, staring down so I can see the edge of the wall.

And there she is, standing still and straight, hands clasped before her pretty pink dress, expression completely lost in a daydream.

My Petal.

Damn the stairs. Damn gravity itself.

I leap over the side of the barrier and land in a harsh clatter right in front of Rosalina. The guard jerks to a halt, and Rosalina gives a peep. I bring one arm up and slam my fist on the wall over Rosalina's head. Slowly, I turn toward the scum, holding him in the darkest glare I can muster through my visor.

I don't say a word. I don't have to.

"H-High Prince!" the guard yelps, staggering backward. "I was..."

"Leaving," I growl. "And take him with you." I gesture to the guard who's holding his lance so tight it looks like he'd fall to the ground without it.

"Of course, sire! Right away!" The guard turns on his heel and disappears through the gate.

I let loose a huge exhale, relax my body, and look down.

Rosalina's staring up at me, doe-eyed and breathless.

My cheeks suddenly heat, and I drop my arm from over her head, instead clutching the back of my neck. "Sorry about that."

Rosalina's still staring at me with those shimmering eyes, her lips parted in an O. Then she shakes her head, and a beautiful smile crosses her face. "Ezryn! You found me."

My words feel caught in my throat. When I don't say anything, she cups the side of my helm and tilts it to look at her. I place my hand over hers. "I always will."

There's something in the heave of her chest, the curiosity in her expression as she stares at me.

"What is it, Petal?" I whisper.

"I suppose," she pauses, "I'm just happy to see you."

A smile crests my lips.

A smile she'll never see, Kairyn sneers in my mind. I grit my teeth until his laughter stops.

"What are you doing here?" I ask.

"Oh!" She grabs my hand. "Ezryn, it's Castletree. Goblins attacked it. And they were wielding Spring steel."

15

CASPIAN

There's a list in my head of all the things that frighten me, with losing to Ezryn at a board game and finally inheriting my birthright being near the top. Being summoned to the Abyssal Sanctum fits snugly between them.

I pause briefly outside the iron doors and stretch my calf. My leg is almost healed, but I can't let a single tremor show. Any sign of weakness would be especially problematic, as this is the first time I've been called upon since enduring my punishment for losing Autumn.

Throwing open the doors, I step inside. Towering columns line the walkway to a massive throne. Tall stairs lead to an elegant chair.

Crystals surround the throne, flickering green flames caged within them. Their jagged edges jut out at odd angles, casting a luminescent glow across the shadowy figure draped there.

Each stone seems to hum with its own arcane heartbeat, making the air heavy with magic. I resist hunching my shoulders. It always feels like I have two sets of judging eyes on me here.

I wasn't the only one summoned today. Another figure already kneels before the green monstrosity. The Nightingale has her head bowed. The perfect servant. *Not that she really has a choice.* She's dressed in her full armor, besides her mask. Sira loves to watch her expressions of fear.

I mimic my adopted sister's movement and whisper quietly, "So, did you mess up or did I?"

Her blue eyes flick to me, and she hisses, "Shut up. I've done nothing wrong."

A haunting voice cuts through the din, and we both fall silent. "My children. Rise."

We both follow the command instinctively. My mother inclines her head. The green light slashes across her sharp jawline and that serpentine smile that often mirrors on my own lips.

A smile the Nightingale can never quite master, no matter how much hatred our mother fills her with.

"I've heard some disturbing rumors sifting down from the Autumn Realm," Sira, Queen of the Below, says. "It appears I may have been too hasty when I discounted Quellos's report of the girl who destroyed his army. I hear whispers of a woman who can wield briars."

Inside, my blood goes cold, but I keep my expression neutral and avoid flicking my gaze to my sister.

"Some say she's a human. Others, a fae." Sira taps a pointed nail on one of the crystals lining the arm rest. "Now, Autumn is sending out decrees that the High Prince of Autumn has found a mate. Yet, I also hear she's mated to the High Prince of Winter. So many stories. My son, have you gazed upon this woman?"

"Yes," I say carefully, so carefully. "I've seen her."

"Tell me, Caspian, was she familiar to you?"

That echoing serpentine smile spreads up my face. "Like a vision."

My mother laughs, the dark sound resounding through the rocks. "The Fates never lie, do they?"

No, but they certainly withhold much of the truth, I think bitterly. "I've been keeping an eye on the girl. They keep her at Castletree. As expected, the Winter Prince's magic remains bound as he refuses to break the curse."

"Because of your bargain?"

"Because of my bargain." Absently, I touch the frosted thorn bracelet around my wrist. The Nightingale's calculating gaze falls over me. Even she doesn't know the full extent of what happened between Keldarion and me.

"Clever boy," Sira praises.

"That she is also Farron's mate is news to me," I continue. "Or that she can wield briars. I've noticed no such thing."

One dark brow rises on Sira's face. *I shouldn't have said his first name.* The Nightingale is still staring at me. We need to be dismissed before she mentions a certain party guest who summoned a patch of thorns in the Below.

"The people of Autumn call her the Golden Rose." Sira keeps her voice steady, but the words have a sharp edge. There's a reason she's only speaking of this to us, and not her entire court. *Has something frightened the Queen of the Below?*

"I'll look into it personally."

"As will I." The Nightingale steps forward.

"No need, sister. I'm sure you have your hands full controlling your wild dog of Spring. Didn't you also recently accept command of the mission to take the Summer Realm?"

"Don't fret, brother," the Nightingale says with a steel-laced voice. "Our Queen requires someone with follow-through. You've been draining Castletree since before I was born, and where has that gotten us?"

"I want information on her magic and her bonds with the High Princes, but tread carefully," Sira says. "If she has mated with the High Prince of Autumn, he will have regained much of his magic. Interferences from Castletree would be most detrimental to our plans. The Below cannot yet take on the entire Enchanted Vale and hold it under our control." Sira turns to gaze deep into the green flame swirling within the stones. "Not yet."

RISKY. It had been too risky bringing Rosalina down Below for my birthday party. Now, the Nightingale knows of her magic, more rumors are surfacing, and it's only a matter of time before Sira hears of the golden briars she summoned in Autumn.

It was a necessity. Rosalina had to awaken her fae self. I'd thought the only way was to bring her closer to the source of her magic, but my Rose was able to unlock it all on her own.

"Caspian." The Nightingale grabs my arm as we exit the Abyssal Sanctum. "We need to talk."

That we do. "Come on, then, Birdy," I say, using the nickname I gave her. "Let's get a drink."

The Below is vast, stretching beneath all the Enchanted Vale. Just like the world above, some parts are more populated than others. Cities and small villages dot the deep chasms and interlacing tunnels.

Using thorns, Birdy and I traverse our way back to Cryptgarden, but I don't lead her to the palace, where we both live. Instead, we descend the hundreds of steps to the city in the valley beneath. There, I take her to the seediest pub in the most twisted alley.

The entrance isn't even labeled; there's only a rundown sign with a sigil of a unicorn slashed with blood. *The Bloody Unicorn.* Not the most original or welcoming name, I'll grant, but it's among the few places in the Below where I'm sure my mother's spies won't overhear us. Besides, Dex, the barkeep, makes a damn good drink.

Birdy wrinkles her nose as she always does when we come here. The air is thick with the scent of fried food and the earthy undertone of strong spirits.

And blood, of course. There's a whole splatter of it stained into the entranceway. The ne'er-do-well patrons know better than to stare at us as I procure a corner booth tucked into the natural rock wall.

Birdy puts a hand on her hip and glares down at me. "What do you want?"

I offer her a sweet smile. "Surprise me."

She rolls her eyes and stomps off to the bar. I run my fingers over the sticky wood table. Just how much does Sira know of Rosalina? More than she let on? Less? And what exactly will she do when she figures out the truth?

The Nightingale plops two bubbling pink drinks on the table and slides into the booth. I grab one and down half of it before my thoughts can consume me. "This is delicious. What did Dex make today?"

"Who knows? I just told him to make it strong."

I lean back in my seat. "You wanted to talk, so let's talk."

"You know more about Rosalina O' Connell than you revealed to Mother."

"Not so loud," I hiss. But no one's paying attention to us. Everyone here is deep in their own problems and drink, and the eerily upbeat music drowns out our speech.

"You're the one who proclaimed her name during the party," the Nightingale says. "What was it again? Whoever touches her dies a painful death?"

I clutch my drink to still my shaking hands. A stupid, rage-filled mistake. When that man had *touched* her—I inhale through my nose. Luckily, that name means less than nothing to anyone in the Below, and it doesn't seem to mean anything to Sira. "Your point?"

"How can she summon thorns? You told me that magic was from the Below. She's not *from* here."

"Actually, I told you the magic of thorns was *in* the Below." I take another sip of my drink.

"Is that why the Autumn Realm is so taken with her? Because she can control thorns? Why are they calling her the Golden Rose?"

"Not just thorns," I say. "Golden briars and golden roses, too. Alive, magical, and as beautiful as she is."

I look down at my cup, then back up to my sister. "You poisoned my drink. Truth serum, is it? Always playing with your potions."

Her only answer is a knowing smile.

I'm not even surprised. Because this is how it is with Birdy and me. How it has to be between siblings who have been raised for a single purpose. *Take the Vale by any means necessary.*

I shake my head. I want to summon my thorns and escape somewhere until the effect wears off, but then she'd know I'm hiding something big. And maybe there's a part of me that's tired of keeping all these secrets to myself. At least, some of them.

"You're intrigued by her, aren't you, Cas?" Birdy asks. "Why?"

I tilt my head. Her potion just demands my words be truth, but it doesn't dictate what truth. "She's Keldarion's mate. Of course, I'm intrigued."

Birdy downs the rest of her untainted drink. "I've never understood your obsession with those princes. They're selfish rulers who hide away in their castle, abuse their magic, and forsake their realms. They look down at all of us Below. The princes wouldn't reach out a hand to help us if the whole underworld was burning."

"Come on now, Birdy," I say. "Tell me how you really feel."

"No." She slams her hands on the table. "It's your turn to share information, Cas. You are *never* honest with me. You always leave me out. I'm not a child anymore. Can't you see what I've already accomplished in Spring?"

"Oh, I've seen."

"Enough stalling. There's something else about that girl at Castletree. Tell me."

Two secrets war inside of me. The serum coursing through my system brings them both to the surface. I need to choose which one will escape my lips. Maybe this is fate, because one of them is a secret I've wanted to share with her for so long.

My gaze drops to the Nightingale's calloused fingers. I can't help but remember how small her hands were when Sira first commanded that I show her how to wield a blade. Better me than the weapon masters who would whip her for one wrong move.

Not that I could spare her from much of the terrors growing up. It's hard to protect someone else in the Below when you can barely protect yourself.

For a moment, I think of taking her hand but quickly disregard the idea. "Well then, listen carefully."

As the story leading up to the secret spills out of me, I watch her every movement. This truth will either heal her or break her. Her expression remains unreadable as I talk. Until I say the last word.

That's when I see Birdy's face fracture into madness.

Summoning my best impression of a certain icy fae bastard, I growl, "Oh fuck."

The Nightingale stands, eyes alight with a sort of unhinged insanity. "How could you have kept this from Mother? I have to tell her."

I stand and grip Birdy's arm. "Go ahead, sing like the pretty canary you are. But tell me, *sister*, what do you think will happen when Sira learns the truth? Do you believe she'll have any use for you when she could have someone that can summon gold itself? You would be discarded again, just like you were by your real mother."

Pain flashes in her eyes, rare tears brimming. She can't deny my words—she'd know they're true even if this damn serum wasn't coursing through my veins. Guilt rises within me, but I push it down. This is the only way to keep them both safe.

"Leave Rosalina to me. Forget about her," I growl. "Return to Spring."

The Nightingale shakes out of my grip, something feral flashing in her gaze. "I'll never forget this."

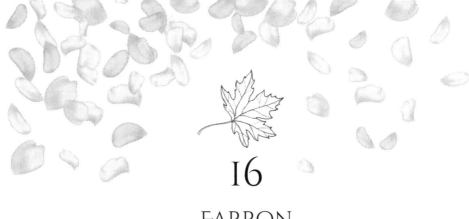

16

FARRON

Papers fly out of my fingers as I throw the useless scraps over my shoulder. I've read and reread these texts and accounts a thousand times now. And yet, I'm still no closer to understanding.

I heave in a breath and clutch one of the wooden shelves in the alder tree. This sacred, secret space is the resting place of Autumn's Great Scriptorium of Alder, and it has been a sanctuary to me before. Today, it feels like a prison, a tomb of worthless information.

Guilt creeps through my mind. *I lied to Rosalina, to all of them.* I'd told everyone I was spending so much time in the Autumn Realm so I could help situate my father as the new steward. Truthfully, my father doesn't need my help; he'd been assisting my mother run Autumn for decades. With the winter wraiths gone, our crops are once again thriving, the once displaced villagers back in their homes.

No, I've been in Autumn for a different reason. One I will not voice to Rosalina. She's been through so much already. I can't add another burden.

But I have to know the reason why Caspian is able to speak in her mind.

And if it's for the reason I fear, then I must figure out how to break it.

I collapse to the ground, fingers digging into my hair. There's nothing left. I've scoured everything in here; so much was lost to my beast and Caspian's most recent betrayal last month.

I ripped his notebook, and he returned the act by forcing me to destroy centuries of sacred literature and bringing an army of goblins to slaughter innocent soldiers. If there ever had been good in Caspian, it has been torn out of him root by root until only his selfish heart remains.

Forcing in a shaky breath, I remind myself to be grateful for what is left within the alder tree. Before George O'Connell left on his expedition with my little brothers, he painstakingly reconstructed what he could from the wreckage. There's no doubting where Rosalina gets her tenacious spirit.

"I must accept what is," I whisper to myself, a phrase I've repeated over and over these last few weeks. There is nothing here that will explain why the Prince of Thorns can speak in my mate's mind. Or at least, no information that contradicts my worst fear.

But I won't stop. Rosalina's just discovered an entirely new life: her faedom, her dormant magic. Her mate. Caspian destroys everything he touches. I won't let him destroy her.

Though Kel won't speak to me of his bargain, I've finally begun to understand him. Maybe it's through the connecting bonds of our shared mate, but I feel it deep within my chest. Kel would die for Rosalina.

But more than that, he'd let everyone else die for her, too.

I put back the papers I discarded and tidy up the strewn-about texts. Perhaps I need to learn from Keldarion. The best way I can protect Rosie is to be with her.

I should return to Castletree.

As I make to leave the alder tree, I cast a glance to a pedestal pushed to the dark shadows. A faint green glow illuminates the space. *I'll come back for you.* I think.

Perth's crown was capable of reanimating the dead. If one could harness the Green Flame energy differently, could it halt death forever?

My chest tightens as I think of my mother, of her own lance cracking through her ribs. *And the monster who did that to her escaped.* Rage barrels past the grief, and I can almost feel the ghost of the wild beast thrashing to break out. But the beast is gone. Only I remain.

I step out into the chilly air. My elk Thrand and Rosalina's horse Amalthea graze nearby on the new grass that has grown over what used to be ruins. I walk over and run a hand along Thrand's flank. "One day, I'll bring you home to Castletree. The briars will be gone, and grass will grow again. Streams of crystal-clear water will flow, and meadows of flowers will stretch over the hills."

What did we even call the Briar before it became such? *The Queen's Realm,* I remember. A place where all the wonder and magic of the Vale merged together.

But for now, the Briar is my home, and I must return to Castletree, to my mate.

A flutter sounds, and I look up to see a white bird flying toward me. A sea bird, a sandpiper. *You don't belong here.*

But the bird is not a bird at all, with wings of paper and markings of ink. A message.

I pluck it from the sky and unravel the note.

Goblins. Spring steel.

Dayton and Rosalina are in trouble.

17

ROSALINA

I keep right on Ezryn's heel as he storms through the gates into Keep Hammergarden, nattering as fast as I can at him, catching him up on what conspired at Castletree. "—and that's when we saw what they were wielding. Spring steel, Dayton called it. He immediately sent letters to Farron and Kel letting them know what happened, and then we came right here."

"The goblins have long used crude imitations of our weapons," Ezryn says. "For them to have stolen our own resources is unprecedented."

I stare up at him, silent. I don't think I even understand the gravity of what Dayton and I discovered. But a sense of comfort rushes through me, being here, being with Ezryn. He always bears his burdens alone.

Not anymore.

A fae man scrambles down the steps of the wall and stops in our path. He leans over, hands on his knees, panting. "Sire, must you always be leaping off buildings? You could twist an ankle, or more likely, dent our lovely cobblestone. Oh!" He notices me. "Why, hello there. Have we met before?"

I smile at the newcomer. He's got a nervous jitter to him, but his eyes are kind. "I don't think so. I'm Rosalina O'Connell."

"This is Eldy, Keep Hammergarden's majordomo," Ezryn says. "And a good friend."

"Rosalina O'Connell." Eldy says my name like each syllable is special in its own way. "A pleasure to meet you. I wasn't aware," he looks between me and Ezryn, "the High Prince was currently courting anyone."

"I'm not," Ezryn says bluntly, and I flinch. The feel of him between my legs when we were in the Below floods through me: the dark shroud of his backward helm obscuring my vision until there was only his mouth and tongue. Call me old-fashioned, but bringing a lady to a private arboretum and eating her out like your own personal buffet kind of feels like courting.

"She's High Prince Farron's mate," Ezryn continues.

And there it is. I know Ez and Day are thrilled for me and Farron; they're the only ones I think who might love Farron as much as I do. But it's just another reminder that their curses worsen, that they're missing out on someone who could love and cherish them with every fiber of their being, who would see them for more than the beasts and the sins, but the wonderful, strong men that they are—

And that person isn't me.

"Oh!" Eldy gives a little hop, covering his mouth. "Prince Farron has found a mate? What joyous news! Dear Farron! I am positively chuffed!"

Ezryn crosses his arms. "How have you not heard? Letters were sent to all the realms."

"Like I said before, sire, Spring has been a bit … closed-off from the other realms." Eldy looks past me, and something shifts in his expression. His mouth falls open in a gasp. "It truly is you."

Astrid and Marigold approach us. Astrid's biting her lip, eyes shifting rapidly between the majordomo and Marigold. But Marigold crosses her arms, pops a hip, and levels Eldy with a glare that would frighten even the princes' beasts.

"You are as beauteous as ever, Lady Marigold," Eldy whispers, eyes suddenly at his feet.

"Save it," she snaps. "I'm not here to listen to you grovel. I'm here to do my job." She gives him another withering stare. "Something you struggle to do."

"I … I never!" Eldy says, but Marigold's already sashayed past him toward the keep. Ezryn claps him on the shoulder as he follows her.

"You're going to need to catch me up," I whisper to Astrid as we walk behind.

"Have you got three years?"

But there's no time for details as we approach the door leading into the cavernous Keep Hammergarden. I've never felt so small in my entire life: the colossal mountains loom above, and the keep is built directly into the rocky surface. It blends almost seamlessly with the natural contours of the mountain range, appearing as if grown from the earth itself.

It's strange: the imposing stonework of Keep Hammergarden, and the delicate gardens that dot either side, bursting with blooms of every color. There is both strength and fragility, power and peace.

Guards lower their heads as we pass into the building, showing the utmost reverence to Ezryn. He walks with confidence, and the man who was competitively playing board games with Caspian, stealing chocolate muffins, or tenderly healing my arm, feels far away.

"For some reason, this place has always given me the heebie-jeebies," Astrid whispers as we walk through the huge hall. "It's like I can't tell if I'm inside or outside."

I kind of understand what she means. The walls are the rough stone of a cave, with moss and trickles of water running over it. And yet, it's decorated with finery. A dark green carpet lines our way, and the guards are dressed in shimmering armor.

A familiar, loud voice echoes through the space. "I *told* you, I don't need an appointment. If you don't let me in to see Ez right now—"

"You mean His Highness, High Prince Ezryn?"

We round a corner to see a red-faced Dayton squabbling with a guard outside of two large wooden doors.

"You know who I mean," Dayton sneers. "Now, I'm going to kick your ass if I can't see Ez in the next—"

"High Prince Ezryn!" the guard calls, suddenly straightening.

"That's who I *said*," Dayton sighs.

Ezryn comes up beside him and crosses his arms. Why do I get the feeling he's raising a brow and smirking under that helmet of his?

"Thank you for your vigilance. But this is High Prince Daytonales of Summer. He is to be treated with the same respect as I."

"Oh, Ez!" Dayton wraps an arm around his shoulder. "Tight ship you run around here. Would have thought I was Kel by the way the folk are treating me."

Another realm that has issue with Kel?

"Apologies, High Prince," the guard says, lowering his head. "I was merely following protocol established by the steward—"

"The steward," Ezryn growls, "is bedridden. The person sitting on the throne is a usurper."

And with that, Ezryn throws open the doors and strides into his throne room.

18

DAYTON

O f course.

The usurper Ezryn mentioned is none other than that little shit, Kairyn. Rosie, the majordomo Eldy, Marigold, Astrid, and I, thunder into the Hall of Vernalion after Ezryn like his own personal army. Damn, this place has never been the cheeriest, but it feels like a funeral hall. A sense of despair washes over me the moment I step through the doors.

It's really not surprising, though. Kairyn's always made me uneasy, even when he was just Ezryn's little brother following us around. Now, he's sitting on the throne like a damned tyrant, legs spread, and hands clenched. And there's a bunch of creepy people standing nearby, dressed in long robes of white and gold.

Golden Acolytes, I realize. *What are they doing here?* Though the Queen's Reach Monastery operates close to Florendel, it has never been involved in the rule of Spring.

One of the acolytes catches my eye, a fae woman with short dark hair and startlingly blue eyes. She's staring straight at me. A soft smile graces her lips. I look away. Something about the disciples has always freaked me out.

Two knights standing on either side of the throne give me pause.

The position establishes them as princeguard, but they're helmeted like the royal family of Spring. And their armor is warlike instead of the usual ceremonial style that is tradition, one a shining amber, the other a deep turquoise.

Ezryn plants his feet before the throne. His voice is steady but loud: "Everyone except my brother. Out. *Now.*"

Immediately, the staff shuffle out the front and back doors, but the acolytes stay where they are. Kairyn says nothing, only tipping his head in a way that is both mockery and a challenge. There have been so many times throughout the years I wanted to punch him straight in that ugly owl helm, and I have a feeling I might get the chance.

But I hang back, letting Ezryn handle this his way.

When the acolytes still refuse to move, Ezryn's voice deepens. "I said everyone."

"Come on." Rosalina tugs on my sleeve. "Everyone includes us."

I look around at my crew. "Rosie, trust me on this. Ez might need us."

"We must obey His Highness's wishes," Eldy says, as uptight as I remember him. "Chop, chop, we can wait for him outside."

"Abandoning the Prince again, Eldor?" Marigold snaps. "Follow me." She waves us toward the back exit of the throne room. As soon as we step outside, she yanks my arm and directs me to the wall.

A worried expression crosses Eldy's face. "Marigold! This is highly uncalled for!"

"And so is letting that banished prince call himself steward. I've been watching over Ezryn and Kairyn since they were boys. I will not stop now." Her eyes blaze as she taps a particular pattern on the wall. Suddenly, a lump of stone spits out a door knob.

She opens it and ushers us inside. The five of us are now crammed in a small room no bigger than a closet. But...

The far wall shimmers with translucent light. An enchantment lets us see and hear into the throne room. On the floor, there is a wooden hatch.

"Where does that go?" I ask.

"It's an escape route out of the castle. This space is only to be used by the royal family for security reasons," Eldy hisses.

"This *is* for security reasons," Marigold snarls back. "Who knows what that mad boy will do to Ezryn? We might have to send the muscle after him." She claps my bicep, lingering for a moment. I give it a pulse for her, and she thanks me with a wink.

Rosalina barely seems to be listening to us. She's drifted right to the translucent wall, long fingers running along the shimmering line. "Is Kairyn dangerous?"

Eldy, Marigold, and I exchange a look.

"Not dangerous exactly," I murmur. "Just unpredictable."

"I will tell you only once more." Ezryn's voice filters through the enchanted wall. We're positioned to the side of the throne, and Ezryn's body is as still as ever. "Everyone but my brother, *out.*"

A female voice resonates: "With all due respect, High Prince, we are the Golden Acolytes. We answer only to the Queen herself, and in her absence, the High Clerics. Of which Prince Kairyn is one. And you are not."

It's the fae woman with the blue eyes who spoke.

Ezryn's only tell is the slight tilt of his helm. "So be it. Let your followers listen then, brother. High Cleric you may have named yourself, but you have no dominion over my realm. You are not steward. Remove yourself from my throne and return to the monastery. Your banishment is not absolved."

Kairyn tears up from the throne. Seven realms, he's gotten big since the last time I saw him. His shadow covers Ezryn in darkness. "You can't do this. I have saved Spring! I deserve to be named steward!"

For a second, I think Ezryn's going to scream back at him. But he stays still. "Thalionor is steward. While he recovers and I appoint a new steward, I will retake command of Spring. See yourself back to Queen's Reach or I will have you escorted there." His voice lowers to a gruff whisper. "Do not test me, brother."

Kairyn doesn't move. His heavy breathing reverberates from beneath the helm. "I have quelled the goblin raids. I have rid the

Queen's Reach Monastery of corruption. I have brought peace to Spring!"

Ezryn takes a step. "I will be the judge of that."

"How dare you doubt me?" Kairyn roars. "I bring order to Spring! You have brought only death!"

I intake a sharp breath, my own heart pounding. Images flash in my mind: standing alongside my brother Damocles in the Hall of Vernalion. Beside him was High Princess Niamh, and beside her, High Prince Erivor of Winter.

Ezryn, newly coronated, sitting upon the throne. And Kairyn, seething beside him.

"Careful, Ez," I mutter under my breath.

Rosalina presses herself harder against the translucent wall, her brown eyes huge. "Why is he saying that to him? 'You only bring death?'"

Kairyn thunders down the steps of the throne and circles Ezryn, his black cape snapping like a raven's wings. "You come back to Spring, thinking you belong here. Thinking all should bow down and kiss the favored son's boots as they always have. But things have changed, big brother. I have changed."

"Don't do this, Kairyn," Ezryn says lowly.

Eldy plucks at the hairs on his chin. "No, no, no. The last time they were like this..."

Marigold squeezes her eyes shut. "Kairyn evoked the Rite."

The words flood the memory back into me.

Spring has always been secretive about their ceremonies, but the High Rulers were invited to attend Ezryn's coronation. My brother was High Prince at the time.

Damocles, as he always did, chose me to be his honor guard.

I knew Ezryn pretty well at that point, but the fae sitting on the throne was barely recognizable. He was clad in brilliant silver armor, anointed in both a crown and cape of wildflowers.

And though I couldn't see his face, I sensed it from him.

A darkness. It was like shadows I couldn't see, a wind I couldn't hear. An invisible calamity fighting within his steel.

I told myself it was grief—something I knew blessed little of at that point.

Because right before Ezryn's coronation, there had been a different ceremony.

A funeral for his mother, the former High Princess Isidora.

"What is the Rite?" Rosalina whispers, looking back at us.

I take a heavy breath. "An ancient practice in Spring where anyone can challenge the High Ruler to the throne. It is a battle of physical and magical combat where the winner takes both Spring's Blessing and the crown ... and commonly the life and honor of the loser."

Rosalina gasps, and Astrid grabs her hand.

Eldy shakes his head sadly. "This would not be the first time Kairyn has attempted it."

The throne room echoes with Ezryn's voice: "Stand down."

"You sent me to the monastery to rot," Kairyn says, "because I know the truth. I know what you did to her!"

"*Stand down.*" Ezryn still does not move.

Dammit, how is he so still? If I was in his position, I would have pummeled that jerk ages ago. But Ezryn's like an impenetrable fortress, just standing there as Kairyn circles him, helm twitching.

"What happened last time?" Rosalina breathes.

I close my eyes as the images play across my mind. Did Ezryn even realize I was there? I was nothing then, not a High Prince, just Damocles' escort. "It was Ez's coronation, decades ago. Rosie, his mother ... She died passing her Blessing on to Ez."

"It's a dangerous thing, for the living to move the Blessing to another," Eldy says. "The realms celebrated when Niamh's passing to High Prince Farron went so smoothly."

Rosalina's gaze is intent on Ezryn. "He never speaks of his mother. I wonder if he feels responsible."

"He shouldn't. Isidora knew what she was doing. She was the brightest and bravest lady one could ever know." Tears streak down Marigold's face and she quickly wipes them away.

I wrap an arm around Marigold and pull her tight against me in a half-hug. I know she served Princess Isidora directly. "You know how Ez is, Rose. Even if he doesn't blame himself—"

Her eyes drift over to Kairyn. "His brother does."

"Look at you, High Prince," Kairyn says, a haunting rasp. "High Prince of what? Of a realm you abandoned? A father you left a widower? You should be on your knees, begging me to take the realm off your hands!"

Ezryn lifts his chin. "It's time for you to leave, Kairyn."

Kairyn's voice sounds like a snake's hiss. "You stand there so certain, so still. You think you can fool them like you've fooled the rest of the staff." He gestures to his acolytes. "But you can't fool me. I see it in you. The *rage*. You want to kill me, don't you, brother?"

"If I wanted to kill you," Ezryn says so low I can barely make it out, "you'd be dead."

Kairyn throws his helm back and laughs. "And there it is! My brother, at heart, a beast."

At that, Ezryn steps into Kairyn's path, stopping his incessant pacing. "What did you call me?"

"I am not afraid of beasts. Name me steward. Let me show you the true potential of Spring."

"A deserving steward would not allow Spring steel to come into the hands of our enemy," Ezryn growls.

Kairyn stills, then flashes a quick glance behind him at the acolytes. "I-I don't know what you're talking about. But I will continue to eliminate all threats to our resources. Name me steward and see Spring to glory!"

Rosie turns around and catches my gaze, her eyes frightened. "What happened at his coronation, Day?"

I suck in a breath. "Kairyn accused Ezryn of the murder of Isidora, and then invoked the Rite, challenging him for the throne."

I'd thought in that moment Ezryn might hand it over. There had been such a sadness to him, a despair unlike anything I'd ever seen. "Ezryn seemed to consider just abdicating the throne to his brother, but Kel's father, High Prince Erivor, told him Kairyn was unfit to wield the Blessing of Spring. So, Ezryn chose to fight."

"Ezryn defeated him easily," Marigold continues my story. "As is custom within the royal family, Ezryn had the right to unhelm Kairyn for his insolence."

"Unhelm..." Rosie whispers.

"The most shameful and dishonorable punishment imaginable for a member of Spring's royal family." Eldy's voice trembles as he speaks. "A fate worse than even death."

"But Kairyn still wears his helmet," Rosie says.

"Ezryn couldn't do it, not even to the man who accused him of killing his own mother," I say back. "So, he banished him to servitude at the monastery instead."

Eldy nods. "A most merciful act."

Rosie turns back to the translucent wall, lip quivering. "But if Kairyn challenges Ez to the Rite and wins—"

Before us, Ezryn turns his back to Kairyn and begins walking up the stairs to the throne. "You will *never* be my steward."

Kairyn lets out a howl of rage. One of his acolytes leaps forward—the blue-eyed woman who spoke earlier. "Sire, don't!"

He shoves her out of the way and screams: "I challenge you to the—"

Before he can finish the words, Ezryn turns and surges at his brother. In a feat of raw strength, he lifts Kairyn up and slams him on to his back. In the same fluid movement, he draws his sword, Wind-scythe, and holds it to Kairyn's neck.

"*Do not* challenge me," he growls, a voice more wolf than man. "*Never* challenge me again."

Utter silence fills the throne room. In our small space, not one of us takes a breath.

Then Ezryn stands and sheathes his blade. Kairyn stays down. With staggering steps, Ezryn walks up the stairs to sit on the throne.

"You will return to the monastery and await my judgment for breaking your banishment. Until my father recovers, I shall remain in Spring." He turns to the acolytes, then gestures to the fallen Kairyn. "If anyone has an issue with that, you can take it up with your High Cleric."

PART TWO
ENSHRINED
MEMORIES

19

CASPIAN

S o. Much. Wind.

Does there truly need to be so much wind? I know we're up on a mountain, and yes, it's one of the highest peaks in all the Vale, and there's nothing but the sky and stars and the Above, but I'll never be able to get my hair untangled from the points of my ears.

Maybe I wouldn't be as bothered if this damned monastery wasn't so distastefully eerie. The art carved into the walls makes the Queen look dead-eyed and ghastly, and the presence of open-air windows everywhere—to be closer to the Above—means any torch is instantly snuffed out. Only the moon and stars light the chamber.

She would find this whole place garish, I think.

I sit on a narrow stone windowsill, one leg draping over the edge. The view below is at once awe-inspiring and vertigo-inducing. The rush of the river down the mountainside sparkles in the moonlight. Far in the distance, Florendel shimmers with twinkling lights of fires and glowspells.

Rosalina is there. She has no idea the danger they've put themselves in…

For better or worse, there's no time to be alone with my thoughts. The mass of black fabric and shining armor before me gives another roar, slamming a hand against the stone wall. Kairyn's breathing rages like a slumbering beast.

"Behaving like a child won't help either of us," my sister scolds him. She crosses her arms, her slender, jewel-encrusted armor the only color up here in the dark. "We knew Ezryn would return to Spring sooner or later."

"All I've done for my realm," Kairyn rasps, "and he dismisses me from the throne like I'm some common thief. Now, he is deliberating on my punishment? I've saved Spring, and he will not see it!"

I pretend to examine my nails, as if entirely disinterested in their conversation. Truthfully, I am. It was no surprise Ezryn wouldn't allow Kairyn to keep a stewardship that the High Prince didn't instigate himself. It's also no surprise Kairyn's storming about, puffing out his chest like a fool. He's been both worshipping the ground Ezryn's walked on and cursing his every breath since long before I met them.

But the Nightingale's hovering presence behind him ... That's interesting. Her hand on his arm. The way she's staring into the dark void of his helm until he turns and stares back. How she's not wearing her usual mask either, the one that shrouds everything but her sapphire eyes. Now, her hair blows freely in the harsh wind, her mouth in a scowl.

She's a pretty little thing. A deadly, pretty thing.

Kairyn truly has no idea what he's gotten himself into.

"He does not see me as an equal," Kairyn says lowly, though the Nightingale's hand has steadied him somewhat.

"He sees you as a threat," she responds. "An act we must mitigate quickly. Your brother needs to trust you. You were a fool to challenge him while he still wields the Blessing of Spring."

Kairyn pulls away from her. "I can face him!"

"And if you won?" she snarls. "Would you be able to thrust the blade into his heart? Rip the helm from his head? Or are you still happy to walk in his shadow?"

Kairyn says nothing.

I slip from my perch on the windowsill and drift over to these two young fletchlings. "Sira wanted a report. What am I to tell her? Temper tantrums and bickering?"

A growl surges up Kairyn's throat, and he makes a move to come at me, but the Nightingale grabs his arm. "Now, now, Kairyn. My sweet brother has never been a man of patience. What I have crafted here in Spring is something of beauty. Not like that sloppy goblin raid you organized on Autumn. Apparently, Autumn is thriving now, brother. Mother wasn't very happy about that, was she?"

My back and legs throb as I think of the punishments I received for not delivering Autumn, but I keep a smirk plastered on my face.

Kairyn staggers to the door and rips it open. "You need something to report? Tell Sira soon the five divine weapons will be in my control."

The Nightingale and I exchange a glance. She puts her mask back on, and we follow the Spring Prince out into the hallway.

Kairyn's voice bounces off the walls as we trail behind him. "I know what they call you, Caspian. Traitor. Betrayer. So, this may be a confusing subject for you, but what we have cultivated here is called loyalty."

A muscle feathers in my jaw. I can't believe I'm being insulted by this walking hunk of scrap metal. But I let him continue—why interrupt someone when they're likely to reveal their own weaknesses?

"Cast your eyes upon the Vale's reckoning." Kairyn stops before a huge, open-air archway. I step beside him and look down into a stone courtyard.

Hundreds of soldiers spar, their steel spears clanging together in near-perfect unison. They all wear identical armor, that same moon-light-gold emblazoned with celestial sigils: suns and stars and crescent moons.

I raise a brow. "I'm not sure if you've forgotten, Kairyn dear, but I haven't spent my whole life in the Below. In fact, I traveled from Florendel to the monastery escorted by your very brother only several decades ago. I've seen the Queen's Army train before."

And they are as mesmerizing now as the first time I saw them. The monastery is not only home to strange acolytes who still revere the long-lost Queen and worship the sky as if it still housed the Above, but to an ancient guild of highly trained warriors from across the realms. The Queen's Army was formed centuries ago, serviced by elite and disciplined soldiers who would come to the Queen's call only. Their dedication is unmatched.

Hilariously so, if you ask me.

They've given their lives to training and wait for the day the Queen will call upon them, regardless of the fact she's been gone from the Vale's eye for over five hundred years. Like dogs waiting on a doorstep for a dead owner who will never return.

Kairyn snorts, a puff of air coming from beneath his helm. It shouldn't bother me, but I find myself straightening and pushing myself up on my toes to get closer to his height. By gods, he's like a giant.

"Why are you snorting at me?" I snap. "Do you intend to fool me —to fool Sira—into thinking you have an army? They serve no realm, only the Queen—"

Kairyn raises his fist into the air. The clang of spears stops; every soldier turns in a single, uniform movement to look up at him.

My pounding heart is the only sound.

"Hail, great warriors!" Kairyn roars.

"Hail!" the army cries back, hundreds of voices now one.

The Nightingale drifts beside me. Though I can't see her mouth, I can see it in her eyes: the reverence, the hungry awe.

Kairyn's voice is a raspy echo. "Who do you serve?"

"High Cleric Kairyn," they answer.

"It's not possible ..." I stumble away from the edge. "This army has spent centuries awaiting the return of Queen Aurelia."

"Like the rest of the Vale, they can wait no more. We may have lost a legion or two in the upheaval, those who could not see the true cause. Let them flee across the realms, seeking a Queen who will never answer." Kairyn turns with a flick of his black cape and stomps down the hallway. "When my brother banished me to the monastery, I knew I could rot, or I could grow. Like the ivy that strangles the dying tree, it was my duty to Spring to turn the minds of those clouded by corruption."

The Nightingale grabs my arm and whispers in my ear, "You doubt him, brother, but wait and see. He is a great leader. He has gained the soldiers' and acolytes' trust not because of his blood, but despite it. They serve him because they know he leads the way to glory."

I yank my arm free. "I didn't realize throwing old men off a building was the path to glory."

She clicks her tongue. "Do not pretend to weep for the High Clerics. They ignored the plight of the villages and treated the people here like property. You'd have done no different than Kairyn."

Perhaps that's what's bothering me. She's right.

He *did* stop the goblin raids against the mountain villages. I think our own goblins Below are nasty business, but the ones that wander the Vale preying on the fae, the ones that don't follow Sira's commands ... Why, they're nothing more than barbarians.

I pull her back, so we fall behind the young Spring Prince. "What did you promise him, Birdy? He's already got a position of power in the monastery. If he minds his temper, likely that tin idiot Ezryn *will* name him steward. So, why's he giving you an army?"

"This army is not for me," she says. "I have my Dreadknights, and they will follow me to the ends of the realms. No, the Queen's Army is for something much greater."

"What's Kairyn's game? Why is he throwing everything away for ... for Sira?"

The Nightingale blinks. "Throwing it away? Listen to yourself. Maybe if you spent more time with Mother and less spying on those beloved princes of yours—"

"Birdy," I warn.

She shakes her head. "Kairyn understands something you don't. This world wasn't built for people like us. We must fight for every scrap. No matter what he does, Ezryn will never respect him. Spring will never see him as anything but the banished brother."

"Ah." I stroke my chin. "If he can't make his brother love him, he'll make him hate him instead."

The Nightingale's eyes drift away from me. "Anything is better than nothing."

A clang sounds before us. Kairyn heaves open a huge metal door leading to a staircase.

My chest burns as I climb up, not thinking we could get any higher. I quickly wipe a drip of black gunk from my nose. This report better wrap up soon.

We enter through a door at the top of the staircase. "Who are these charming folk?" I raise a brow.

Standing in the room are two armor-clad figures, one finished with a bronze sheen, the other in a turquoise blue. Tucked in their breast-plates is the same white flower that both Birdy and Kairyn don.

"This is the start of my Penta Conclave, a new order of High Cler-ics," Kairyn says.

"I don't recall the old High Clerics wearing helms of Spring steel."

Kairyn stomps over to one and almost tenderly caresses the shining metal. "I have forged these helms with my own hands. They are not only High Clerics, but my own princeguard."

The Nightingale looks at me with gleaming eyes, almost as if she's just showed off that her new puppy knows how to roll over.

Five pedestals loom behind the conclave. On all except one is a grand weapon: a lance, a trident, a hammer, and a brilliant golden bow.

I examine the two warriors, both still except for their heavy breath-ing. "So, you've chosen these poor souls to wield divine weapons."

Kairyn nods toward the bronze-clad one. "Shenzo wields Autumn's Lance of Valor." Then he gestures to the one in turquoise blue. "Pike bears Summer's Trident of Honor."

I stroll over to the massive hammer, intricately crafted, both a thing of beauty and power. "You, of course, have chosen Spring's Hammer of Hope?"

"No one shall wield Spring's divine relic but I," he growls in response.

Now, my voice deepens. "Then you do realize you have sentenced yourself and your men to death?"

Before Kairyn can respond, I'm upon him, yanking his wrist and pulling off his huge leather gloves. Dark black veins mar his skin, running from the tips of his fingers up the wrist, beyond to what is hidden by his armor. A sneer escapes me. "As I thought. The corruption has already set in."

Kairyn pulls his hand away.

"Idiots," I bellow. I turn to my adopted sister, stalking toward her like an animal. "And you! How could you be so stupid as to allow him to do this?"

The Nightingale steps back. "I thought—"

I grab Kairyn's arm again, pointing to the lines of rot running through his hand. "These weapons are enchanted by the Queen. They cannot be wielded by any who do not possess her token."

When the Nightingale gives me a confused stare, I smack my chest. "The High Princes' necklaces, you fool! The more you use these weapons without one, the deeper the rot will sink."

Kairyn hunches over, his gaze somehow burrowing through the closed helm. "I am no fool. We shall get the necklaces. The High Prince of Summer is already here. It's only a matter of time before the rest arrive and they're under our control."

The Nightingale smacks her palm against the empty pedestal. "And you, Caspian, were the one instructed to retrieve the fifth weapon! Where is the Sword of the Protector?"

Now it's my turn to roll my eyes. "Do you think Keldarion just leaves it lying under his bed, discarded and unprotected? It's not so easy. I heard even Perth's new pets couldn't recover it."

"Well, figure it out. You know we need all five." Her gaze shifts to the golden bow. Her movements are so lithe, she appears to float toward it. "And we need to find someone strong enough to use the very weapon the Queen once wielded herself. Her token was lost when she left five hundred years ago." Her hand drifts up, fingers nearly touching the brilliant string.

"Stop!" Kairyn lunges forward, wrapping his arms around the Nightingale and pulling her back.

"I can do it, Kai," she snaps. "Let me try!"

Crossing my arms, I raise a brow at the two of them, his arms still laced tight around her. "Do tell what this is all about."

She sighs. "We know about the corruption. But there's something different about the Bow of Radiance. Whereas the rot sinks in slowly with the other weapons…"

"The bow has instantly killed anyone who touches it," Kairyn finishes.

"A shame," I say.

Kairyn releases the Nightingale and thunders over to me. "Perhaps the almighty Prince of Thorns should like to give it a try."

"Oh, no thank you. I work hard for this perfect complexion."

"Enough." My adopted sister steps between us. "You have more than enough to report to Mother. Kairyn, you must return to the keep. There is work to do with your brother."

Kairyn glowers down at me, the long owl brow furrowed in a permanent scowl. Then he storms from the room, the two members of his conclave dutifully following.

The Nightingale lingers for a moment. "I have everything under control, Cas."

"Of course you do, Birdy." I flick my eyes to the door where Kairyn last stood. "You're very good, aren't you?"

"What are you talking about?"

"The little charade you've got going with the young prince. I saw how he moved to protect you against the bow. You have him eating out of your hand."

She snorts and crosses her arms. "He's not so bad." Then her gaze softens. "There's something … endearing about him."

"Oh, what's that? The murderous tendencies? The rageful outbursts? The *stomping*?"

Birdy pushes past me and makes for the door. When she arrives, she shoots back one withering glare. "He understands how it feels to be the unloved child."

20

EZRYN

It's amazing how even among all the vibrant life, my father's room still smells like death. The draping curtain of vines around the bed, the moss-covered stone walls, and vases of fresh green flowers do nothing to mask the heaviness in the air.

An acolyte from the monastery sits beside the bed, dipping a cloth into a basin of water and placing it on Father's wrists, the only exposed skin she can see.

"His plate and cup were empty when I arrived for my duty this morning," the acolyte says, without turning. "Though, he is now in a deep slumber."

"When did he last leave these chambers?" I step into the room.

"A week now, sire. When he does awaken, his words have lost all rhyme and reason. Many healers have come. Physically, there is nothing ailing him. I fear his spirit is lost."

I still, my chest tightening. It has been this way for some time, but I've never seen him in such a state before. True, he has wilted, but he has always been able to hold court.

The acolyte stands, wiping her hands on her apron. Her dark, wavy hair is pulled back by a stardrop, the same white flower Eldy was wearing. I recognize her from the throne room.

But that's not the only place I've seen her before. "What is your name, acolyte?"

"Wrenley, sire."

"Wrenley." I snatch her arm, pulling her easily toward me. "I saw you in the Below. Why were you there?"

Her blue eyes flash, and she struggles out of my grip. "I—"

"At the Prince of Thorns' party," I growl. I'd accidentally grabbed her, mistaking her for Rosalina. "What business did you have there?"

She straightens, regaining her composure, and stares me straight down in a way that reminds me of Rosalina when she sets her mind to something.

"High Prince, I was indeed in the Below." Her blue eyes water. "Unfortunately, there is sometimes a need for even a servant of the light to descend to such depths. Do you command me to bear my shame to you so publicly?"

Guilt roils through me as a single tear trails down her cheek. Many fae travel to the Below for what cannot be procured above, some reasons more sinister than others. But if she is to be directly tending to my father, I need answers. "Your loyalty is to your monastery?"

"Yes," Wrenley says. "And to Spring. Indeed, Prince Kairyn lets his heart guide him instead of his head, if I may be so bold. But he has saved so many on the mountain. And now that you have returned, I believe … I believe it may be enough for Prince Thalionor to regain his strength."

"I shall sit with him. You are dismissed."

She nods, gathers the basin, and pads to the exit. "I'm sure the steward will be glad of your presence in Spring again. Prince Thalionor was never the same after what happened to Princess Isidora. Such a tragedy she didn't survive the passing of the Blessing, for one so strong."

"Get out," I growl.

She inclines her head and darts from the room.

Falling into the chair beside the bed, I let out a deep sigh. My head aches, and fatigue consumes my body. My father lies on his back, helm polished, the only sound a raspy echo. His bare wrists look dry and wrinkled. Even this small bit of skin feels too much for me to glimpse.

For I have never seen his face. If my parents had interpreted the royal creed differently, I could gaze upon his face now. Tend to him and feed him warm broth.

My mother, his mate, was the only one he allowed to witness him. My parents were not mates in the way I witness Rosalina and Farron, love blossoming like a wild meadow. But they were bound as tight as chain mail. A blade and a shield, an arrow and a bow, an anvil and chisel. There was no one without the other.

I've never seen their smiles or frowns or ever known the color of their eyes. I'd lamented once as a child on it, long before I donned my own helm, and begged my mother to remove hers.

We wear our helms as a sign of devotion to Spring, my mother had told me. *Our greatest love must be given to the people first. It is the duty and honor of the royal family.*

My parents showed me their love through their devotion to our people, by teaching me our ways, instilling discipline.

It was a different sort of love than what I witnessed when visiting Keldarion's family in the Winter Realm. Of long nights curled by a fire with hugs and old stories and warm, shared food. But I treasured the love I received from both my parents.

And I felt that same honor the day I was old enough to bear my own helmet. Not since, has another soul gazed upon my face.

But my love for my realm? My duty? Did the Enchantress steal that from me as well?

I've tried to help in what ways I could, protecting the Briar and patrolling Spring's borders.

It hasn't been enough. Spring is suffering.

And it's my fault.

At least my brother had the courage to do something about it.

I bow my helm until it rests against my father's. "Tell me what to do." There's a shake to my voice. "I must deliver punishment to Kairyn. Do I imprison him? Execute him? Take his *helm*?"

The only answer is my father's rattling breath.
I squeeze my eyes shut. "How did our family become so broken?"
But I know the answer.
I'm the one who broke it.

21

ROSALINA

I awaken to a soft knock on my door. Sitting up, I stretch and call, "Coming!"

That was an insanely good sleep. Maybe it's because the room I've been given in Keep Hammergarden is so similar to my room back home. The pastel décor, the blooming flowers in vases, and the canopied bed, could be straight out of the Spring Wing. The only thing that's different is the walls are made of the mountain's stone and not the bark of Castletree.

I snag a cream-colored robe off the armchair to cover my thin nightgown. Despite our strange welcome, Ezryn ensured Dayton, Astrid, and I were set up with food and lavish quarters. I know he took care to place us in private spaces where no one would find us during the night.

The warm face of Eldy, the keep's majordomo, greets me as I open the door. The older looking fae man has gray hair that curls only under his ears and a goatee streaked with white. He carries a tray brimming with pastries, fruit, and a floral-painted teapot.

"Good morning, Lady Rosalina. I do hope I didn't wake you. I wanted to bring you some breakfast while it was freshly made from the kitchen."

"You're so kind! Come in." I open the door wider when I hear a strangled, gasping sound.

Down the hallway, Marigold pushes a trolley, a betrayed look across her face. "Excuse *me*, Eldor, but Lady Rosalina is *my* charge. I won't have her drinking that watered down leaf juice you call *tea*."

She uses her trolley as a battering ram to shove Eldy out of the way so she can get into my room. "Come in," I say meekly.

"This *leaf juice* is the realm's finest lavender tea, steeped at a precise temperature so as to bring out the floral notes." Eldy sniffs and raises his nose in the air. "I highly doubt Lady Rosalina would prefer the boiled mud water you always serve."

Oh boy. It's too early for this.

Marigold's face turns a concerning shade of red. "At least my tea has taste."

"Unlike its maker," Eldy shoots back.

Thankfully, I notice Astrid poking her head around the corner, white hair a mess and dressed in only a simple white shift. I gesture her in, and we sit down on the edge of the bed. She places her head on my shoulder.

"I figured you'd be well taken care of, so I didn't even bother to check on breakfast," Astrid says.

I smile. "You should use this time as a vacation. I think we're going to need it with these two."

Eldy and Marigold seem to have forgotten Astrid and I are even here. They stand inches apart, her finger jammed into his chest, his eyes glowering down.

"Take your stale muffins and begone! Rosalina is more than cared for!" Marigold snaps.

"Prince Ezryn specifically requested that I make sure Rosalina's every need is tended to! I could never go against his wishes," Eldy retorts.

"Oh, yes, you could never disappoint His Highness, but you have no worries about disappointing others."

"You're the disappointment—"

Quickly, I stand and step between them. "Thank you both so much for bringing me breakfast. It looks delectable. And I can drink two pots of tea, no problem! But I'm more than capable of feeding myself and I'm sure you both have more important things to do than watch me eat."

Marigold narrows her eyes at Eldy. "This place has fallen apart since I was last here. Your staff are wandering in circles, useless without directions! Time for someone to whip them into shape."

Eldy's words come out through gritted teeth, "I have been doing the best I can."

Astrid flops on the bed. "I saw Prince Ezryn wandering the halls on my way here, saying something about needing a cup of coffee."

Marigold and Eldy both stare at each other, then practically sprint out of the room, trying to muscle each other out of the way to get through the door faster.

Their words echo after them: "Your coffee is like swill, woman!"

"At least my coffee doesn't give people the *runs* for three days after."

When their arguing is far enough away, I shut the door and raise a brow at Astrid. "I don't think I've ever seen Ez drink coffee."

"Yeah, well, they needed something to keep them busy." Her red eyes shine with mirth.

I chuck her a muffin then pour us each two cups of tea: one from each teapot. "So, what's the story?"

"I've only witnessed the end of it myself, but from what I can gather, Marigold and Eldy had a sweeping love story back when they both served here in Spring."

I widen my eyes. "A torrid love affair?"

"That's what Marigold told me." Astrid takes a long slurp from one cup. "Both Marigold and Eldy were offered service under High Prince Ezryn when he went to live at Castletree. Eldy felt like he couldn't leave Prince Thalionor after Princess Isidora's death, while Marigold wanted to stay close to Ezryn."

"So, the distance tore them apart?"

Warm sunlight drifts from a window carved in the rock, making Astrid's hair shimmer. "On the contrary, at that point, the way was open between Spring and Castletree, and their love only grew. In fact, Marigold thought perhaps a wedding would be on the horizon."

"No!" I gasp, crumbs flying from my stuffed mouth.

"Oh, yes. At this point, I'd come to Castletree under service to Keldarion, so I can tell you with certainty, Marigold was absolutely smitten. She left one evening to go on an extended leave in Spring, as they were to travel together through the realms. The plan was to meet Eldy here at Hammergarden."

"Well, what happened?"

Astrid shakes her head sadly. "He never showed. She waited and waited and waited, but he was nowhere to be found."

"Cold feet," I murmur.

"I guess. But here's the thing. Marigold returned to Castletree that night." Astrid squeezes her eyes shut. "The same night the Enchantress came and cursed us all."

My chest tightens, and my teacup clatters to the saucer. "If Eldy had showed, she wouldn't have been at Castletree."

"She never would have been cursed," Astrid confirms.

I drift to the window, looking out at the courtyard of the keep, covered in cherry blossom petals. "All these years as a raccoon, she's probably blamed him."

"And perhaps he wonders why he never saw her again." Astrid shrugs. "Whatever the case, their hearts are closed to one another."

I lean my head against the cold stone. This curse hasn't just destroyed the lives of the princes, but the staff, too. If Ezryn were to find his mate, he could free Marigold. Perhaps she could regain her happiness. The happiness she deserves.

My thoughts drift to Ezryn and his brother. Thinking of the way Kairyn spoke to him in the throne room sends a chill up my spine. Ezryn has returned to his home to find his father deathly ill, his resources stolen by goblins, and his brother making a play for the stewardship. All of this on top of needing to find his mate ...

The tangled light I saw in his chest while we were in Autumn flashes in my mind. If only I could whisper into his heart and unravel those threads one by one.

I could do it, I think. *I know I could.*

But these thoughts are dangerous. My heart already feels like it shattered yesterday. *Oh Rosalina, you're so selfish.*

"Are you okay, Rosie?" Astrid asks.

I run a hand along the soft skin of my left wrist. "Yeah, I'm okay. But I need to find Ezryn."

22

ROSALINA

I follow the winding path through the cavernous halls of Keep Hammergarden, counting doorways and turns until I'm standing before a set of beautifully carved oak doors. Last night, Ez gave Dayton and me instructions on where his chamber was located, but this place is a maze. It's as if a castle, a forest, and a cave were combined.

Oh well. If this is the wrong room, what's the worst that could happen?

That terrifying masked man could answer, I think. Kairyn, Ezryn's brother. Everything about him sets me on edge. Before I lose my nerve, I rap my knuckles on the door.

"Who is it?"

A breath of relief floods out of me at the sound of Ezryn's muffled voice. "Rosalina."

There's a beat of silence, then: "Come in."

Slowly, I crack open the door and slip inside. The chamber is stunning, flooded with light from massive windows looking out to the city. Like most of the keep, the walls are made of the mountain's natural stone, creating a sense of raw beauty.

My eyes are drawn to the huge bed, draped in gauzy fabrics. The pillows look heavenly soft, and it seems far too big for one person. For some reason, the perfectly made-up bed looks like an unkept promise, an invitation to muss the sheets and send the pillows flying.

I take a breath and search for Ezryn. The rush of water sounds adjacent to the bed, and mist sprays out from beyond a pane of frosted glass. My throat clenches. Behind the glass is a man's silhouette, light and shadows teasing his shape.

Water streams from a hole in the wall, cascading down the rocky surface. It's like an indoor waterfall, a shower that seems carved from nature itself. And Ezryn's in there right now.

My mouth suddenly feels bone-dry. Though he's only a blurry silhouette, I can make out the lean lines of his body, usually hidden behind his armor. His arms raise up, fingers running through his hair. I remember when I was able to tangle my own hands in his thick waves, both wanting to cherish the feel of him and being terrified of how temporary I knew it was.

I drift closer. He turns, his face nothing but obscured shadow. But I swear I can make out the line of his nose and the curve of his lips. My fingers remember everything, a phantom touch.

Unconsciously, I take another step. This single pane is the only thing between me and that mysterious smile I've seen in my mind's eye. The only thing between me and his skin...

My eyes drift down. His back is to me now, and I chide myself as I wonder if he only turned—

"Just finishing up washing," he says. "I'll be out in a moment."

"Oh! Uh, yeah. No hurry." Heat rushes from my chest up to the tips of my pointed ears, and I stiffly walk back to the bed and sit on the edge.

A shuffle and the *ting* of metal sounds from beyond the glass, and then Ezryn steps out.

He's wearing a helm I've never seen before; the same style, but a brilliant starlight silver.

And he has a towel wrapped around his waist.

And that's it.

Every nerve in my body lights up. There's a voice in my head screaming at me not to be a lecherous perv, but the lecherous perv part is too strong, and I fully drink him in from the bottom of his long legs to the crest of his helm.

He stands with one arm leaning against the pane of glass, well-defined chest, covered in dark hair on full display. Water drips down his tawny skin, begging to be licked. Muscles ripple over his arms and abdomen.

He tilts his helmet, and the glint of light on the visor almost makes it look like he's narrowing his eyes. "So..."

"Huh?" I answer. Then I realize my mouth is half-hanging open, and my eyes are practically out of their sockets. And I was the one who showed up in his room. Words would be nice right about now.

It's just that I've only ever caught glimpses of his skin: the line of wrist between his armor and his gloves, the beautiful curve of neck under his helmet. And each of these were like treasures to be squirreled away. But now...

Now he's on display like a piece of art, and merely looking doesn't feel like it could ever satisfy.

"You needed me?" he adds. I always thought it was his armor that made him seem so still, but even like this, he barely moves. The subtle nods of his helm are all I have to go on.

I look down, folding my hands in my lap. "I wanted to make sure you were okay. Everything happened so quickly yesterday."

He sighs. "Everything may have happened quickly for us, but I think things have been brewing in the Spring Realm for a long time. In my heart, I knew I was needed here. I only hope I'm not too late."

"We'll get to the bottom of this. Dayton and I can start investigating the stolen Spring steel. And Kel and Farron should be here any day." I stand up and close the distance between us. It feels like the easiest thing in the world. "You're not alone, Ezryn."

His hand drifts up and pushes a curl of hair off my face. "Trust me, Petal, I have never doubted your intrepid heart."

I place my hand over his, holding the warmth of his palm to my cheek. "Then what are your doubts? Ever since we've returned from

Autumn, you've been distant. If you're not in the Briar, you're training or alone in your chamber."

His other hand cups the opposite side of my cheek. "You find the good in all things. But trust me when I tell you, every decision I have ever made has been the wrong one. Even coming back to Spring and sitting upon the throne ... Who am I to claim myself a better leader than Kairyn? Now, I must decide his fate once again."

"I don't buy it." My fingernails dig into his skin. "Every decision has been the wrong one? What about choosing to stand with Farron in battle? What about saving Dayton's life? What about—" My voice breaks with laughter and emotion. "What about not killing me on the bridge all those months ago? What about this?" I grab his hand and place it on my left wrist, on the skin he healed for me back in Autumn.

His helm shakes side to side. "Those weren't choices to be made. They were just the right things to do."

"Everything is a choice." My hand drifts to his chest. I flick a smoldering gaze up at him.

He's quiet for a long moment, breath reverberating through the helm. "Rosalina, I've warned you about the decisions I make."

"Tell me," I whisper, "does this feel right?"

Because for me it does. Like all the anxiety I've felt since I arrived in Spring and saw him facing his brother alone in the throne room, all but ebbs from my body. Like despite everything on the horizon, this moment could protect us from the world.

Another aching beat passes in stillness, my pounding heart and the rushing water the only sound. Then Ezryn grabs me around the waist, spinning us until my back is against the mist-sprayed wall. His hand tightly grips my jaw, the visor's gaze penetrating. "Isn't that just it, Petal? Why does this feel so right? You are mated twice over—"

"My mates love you. They love you, Ezryn. For once, stop thinking about everyone else. And choose me."

My words seem to electrify him. A growl resounds from beneath his helm, and he drifts his hands over the curve of my waist to my hips. We're so close to the spray of the shower, and I push away from him, walking backward and holding him with my gaze.

The water rushes over me, plastering my hair to my face and soaking through the thin pink dress I'm wearing. Ezryn's palms press on the wall and the glass pane, trapping me.

I run my hands along the dress as it clings to my curves. The outline of my breasts is visible, and the helm's gaze is laser focused on them.

"Come into the water with me, Ezryn."

He does.

His hands tear the soaking dress up over my body. Water *tings* off his metal helm. I stroke along his collarbone, his muscular shoulders, clutch his biceps. I'm as starving for his touch as he is for mine.

He cups my breast and moans. The cool metal drops to the crook of my neck as he rocks his hips against mine. Through the towel, his hard length juts forward, pressing against me. Now it's my turn to moan.

"Get rid of this. Now. Right now." I tug on the towel.

He laughs, then hooks his fingers under the fabric. I push back so I can get a better view.

"What are you doing?" he asks.

I cross my arms. "Come on, don't make it weird. I've been waiting for this moment for a long time."

Now I've done it. He takes his hands away from the towel and instead leans over me. "A long time?"

A flush spreads across my face. How can I tell him the first time I saw him sitting at the dining table in Castletree, I pictured him throwing me over it? "I mean, a respectable amount of time that is not at all creepy or weird."

"Don't worry." He takes my hand and guides it over his bulging length hidden by the towel. "I've been thinking of you for a long time."

I gasp, caressing the hardness. "You saw me when we were in the Below."

"I could pass a thousand seasons staring at you and never have my fill of your beauty. I want you when the cherry blossoms fall in spring, and during the balmy nights of summer. I want you on a forest floor filled with autumn leaves and shivering in winter's snow."

My hands tighten around his length. "Then take off your damn towel."

He drops it with a wet thunk, and I intake a deep breath. Ezryn stands before me, completely bare except for his helm. The massive cock between his leg bobs, and a stream of water runs down its length.

Our hands are over each other in a moment: my lips on his shoulder, the steady stream of water beating over us, his steel hardness in my hand.

He groans and dips his head to my breasts. I shiver at the cold metal pressing against my nipples. Then he makes an agitated growl. "I crave the taste of you."

His huge hand cups the apex of my thighs before I have a chance to respond. I cry out and grind against him.

"You're so beautifully wet for me, Baby Girl," he murmurs. "I want you to come around my fingers."

"Yes, yes!" My lips give way to teeth as I bite his shoulder. Two large fingers press against my entrance before sinking deep. My grip tightens on his cock, and I stifle my cry against his skin.

Bursts of pleasure erupt through my core as he curls his fingers inside me. My pace increases along the length of his cock. I clutch it for dear life, barely hanging on through the rush of ecstasy.

"Ezryn," I gasp, "if you keep—"

"If I keep what?" The fingers buried in me whorl and pulse, and his other hand snatches my dripping hair and pulls.

The sensation sends my climax roiling over me like the pulsing waterfall; I collapse against him, my heart near feeling like it will take flight from my chest.

"So good, Baby Girl," he murmurs. "You're so good for me."

He holds me up by my waist, and I lean against his chest, blinking tears and water out of my eyes. His cock is pressed against my lower belly, and I pull myself tighter against him. It's so hard and thick ... I find myself drifting down to my knees.

"What are you doing?"

The misty water highlights his body as I glance up. "Worshipping the High Prince of Spring."

And he does look like a High Prince now more than ever, his body like a statue, the starlight silver helm gleaming.

"Rosalina," he begins, but I don't give him a moment to protest.

"You're not good at letting people take care of you. But I'm going to take care of you, Ezryn."

With that, I take the head of his cock in my mouth and twirl my tongue. He groans, sinking against the stone. With one hand, I grip his shaft and with the other, I cup his balls.

His body goes rigid as I run my tongue up the seam, taking time to taste the pearly sheen on his tip.

"Fuck," he breathes. "You're such a good girl."

Encouraged, I open my mouth and take him deeper. My hand clutches the base of his cock. He grabs a fistful of my hair, legs shaking. I suck in a breath through my nose, reveling in being able to take so much of him.

I blink up, a half-smile on my stuffed lips, and he rolls his head back, groaning. "Seven realms, you're beautiful."

His praise makes my chest heave, and I work him with my mouth and fingers until he starts thrusting against me. His tight grip on my hair keeps my head steady as he fucks my mouth, gently at first, and then harder and harder.

"You're so good," he groans. "Too good."

I drop my hand from his balls and press against his hips to stop his movement. Then I pop off his cock, a line of spit dripping out of my mouth. "Are you going to give me your cum?"

His cock twitches in front of my face. "What?"

My voice becomes a whine. "Will you come in my mouth?"

He runs a hand over his visor, slicking away the water. "You want me to…"

"*Please.*"

"Fuck." In answer, he grabs the back of my neck and shoves his cock into my mouth. I suck him greedily, dragging my tongue around his swollen head, desperate for him.

"Rose, I-I'm—"

I open my throat as much as I can and squeeze his balls tight in my hand. With a roar, his cock throbs, then erupts in my mouth. I take him deeper and suck harder, eager not to miss a single drop. His hands are like vice grips in my hair, and then all at once, he relaxes. His hands lower, his knees buckle, and I swallow one more time.

"Come here," he murmurs, and pulls me up by my elbows until we're chest to chest, the hot water streaming over us.

He runs a hand over my lips, cleaning me. "Perfect."

I smile, his praise addictive.

Ezryn leans his helmet against my forehead. "I choose you, Rosalina," he whispers. "Whatever you're willing to give me."

The words nearly escape my lips: everything, everything, everything.

But maybe it's the rush of the water waking me up or I'm not the same idiot girl I was yesterday, but I know I can't say yes.

Because I'd given everything to Dayton, only for the world to remind us that it doesn't work like that. It's not enough to want something with your whole heart. It's not enough for every part of you to be screaming that *this* is right.

I can't break my heart again.

"Will you let me have you, Petal?" Ezryn continues when I don't say anything. "Let me lay you on the High Prince's bed. I will take you in a way that only a fae of Spring can."

My heart feels like it may rip from my chest in order to get to him, but I push out of the shower, grabbing a second towel from the floor and wrapping it around myself.

"What's wrong?" he asks, following me.

Tears cloud my vision. "I want to be with you, Ezryn. I want it more than there are words. But I can't give myself to you in that way."

He looks down. "I understand."

"No, you don't." I intake a shaky breath. "This is going to sound crazy and greedy and selfish, but in *here,*" I tap my chest, "I feel like you should belong to me. And I feel that way about Dayton, too."

"So belong to me," he growls. "I will take you and keep you safe and—"

"And *what,* Ezryn?" I cry. "Leave me when your mate finally comes along? Or refuse to find your mate altogether and abandon Spring to the curse? I thought I could break Dayton's curse. No, I *knew* it. But you know what happened? Nothing. Nothing, Ez. We made love and everything stayed the same."

Ezryn shakes his head back and forth. "No, nothing stayed the same. Because Dayton is different because of you, whether you're mates or not. He is a better man, Rosalina, and fuck the curse, fuck the Enchantress, and fuck these damned bonds that get to dictate our lives. It doesn't matter—"

"It matters to me!" I scream. "I'm not going to just sit here and watch as your roses wither, and you and Dayton lose more and more of yourselves to the curse. When Dayton and I made love, it didn't help him. It only hurt."

Ezryn rushes to me, guiding my face to look up at him. "Listen to me, Rose. One day, Dayton and I may meet our mates. It doesn't change what's happening between us right now. I would never ask you to do anything you're not comfortable with. But don't think for one second you are a burden."

I pull away from him and stumble to lean against the bedpost. Looking over my shoulder, I whisper, "I can't do it again, Ez. Can't keep hurting people. Everything felt so alive in my heart when Dayton and I made love. But it didn't matter. The curse didn't break. We're not mates."

A choked cry escapes his lips. "What does it matter if you're not mates? Why can't I love you?"

Heavy silence thunders through the room. Did he say...

Ezryn looks to the side, fists clenching. "Why can't he love you ... I meant why can't Dayton love you."

I close my eyes, fighting back tears. "Because my love will only hold him back."

Only hold you back.

Ezryn staggers to the wall, and it seems like he's barely holding himself up. "So, what now? We pretend like none of it matters?"

I wrap my arms around his waist, burying my face into his back. I inhale his scent: that sweet and earthy blend that smells like home. "You will always matter to me."

He sighs and turns around, pulling me into a hug. I take a deep breath, fighting the sob that wants to wrack through my chest. Because I don't know where to go from here. I know for my own sake I can't give myself to Ezryn. But I can't remove myself from him either.

"Do you trust me?" I ask.

"Always."

I close my eyes. Then I reach up and put my hands on either side of his helmet. He doesn't stop me. Slowly, I inch it off, then hold the heavy metal in one hand. And with it, I hold his trust in a single blink.

Softly, carefully, I stand on my tiptoes and brush my lips against his. His warm breath caresses me. My free hand traces his jaw, rough with stubble, as our kiss grows from soft to needy. *One second more*, I tell myself second after second until finally I pull away.

I place the helm back on his head and tug down, feeling to make sure it's in place. Then I blink my eyes open. "You have a realm to rule and a curse to break, High Prince. And I'll be at your side looking after you for as long as I can."

23

KELDARION

The letter shakes in my gloved hands. Dayton's messy writing is nearly obscured by the constant snowfall, but the words mean less than that incessant tugging in my chest. Castletree has been attacked. Everyone is safe. They're going to Spring to seek answers and to give aid to Ezryn.

My entire being screams to use my necklace to open a portal to Castletree right now, then jump through the mirror to Florendel and find Rosalina. But out here on the edge of the Vale, the magic is too weak for my necklace to work. And besides, my heart says otherwise: *She's safe. She's unafraid.*

Of all the terrible places I have placed my trust, I know it is safe with them, my brothers. Dayton, Ez, and Farron will never let harm come to her.

And I must see this through.

Icy wind whips my hair across my brow. I blink rapidly, trying to unfreeze my eyelashes. Living in Castletree for so long, I truly have gone soft. Winter's bite has never felt so sharp.

Though to be fair, the Anelkrol Badlands make the capital of Frostfang feel like a summer day.

I pull my heavy jacket tighter and walk down the length of Voidseal

Bridge. My weary eyes scan the desolate expanse: Voidseal Bridge is a frozen behemoth, a colossal structure that spans the Great Chasm below. The freezing air burns my nose as I take in a breath, staring straight ahead instead of looking down into the void. Flecks of torch-light flicker around the edge before the whole thing descends into darkness.

It's been years since I've been out here. Not only is it a treacherous journey from Frostfang, but there's never been anything for the High Prince to do.

All the dealings of the Deep Guard are managed by *him*.

I reach the watchtower, walking up the steps until I stand beside a flickering torch and a fae man clad in robes of ice blue. The howling wind whips through the jagged rocks of the chasm, a mournful symphony. It carries with it the shouts and orders of Deep Guards as they operate the lifts that lead them down into the chasm or back upon the bridge.

The fae man doesn't say anything at my approach. Finally, I can take it no longer. "Have you considered my offer, Uncle?"

Irahn says nothing, his visible breath ripped away by the wind. The acrid tang of burning tar stings my nose from all the torches lit. "Speak, Uncle."

"Aye, I've considered it, boy." My mother's brother turns to me, his face heavily weathered and wrinkled. He's the oldest looking fae I've ever seen, though not truly the oldest. Years upon years serving on the outskirts of Winter have aged his body.

But not his mind. He's as sharp as ever.

"And?" I growl.

He turns, gray hair and white cape flapping as he descends the watchtower. "I refuse."

"Uncle!" I storm after him. "You are my only blood left. Who else am I to pass the Blessing to?"

Irahn throws his hand in the air. "I don't care! Just keep your politics and magic away from me."

I take a steadying breath, but every inhale feels like the cold seeps into my bones. I knew Uncle Irahn wouldn't be easy to convince.

That's why he was the only choice to replace me as High Prince. I'd already put too much faith into power-hungry men like Quellos.

And I see it in the eyes of the Deep Guard, the Winter citizens who have dedicated their lives to the protection of the realms. Voidseal Bridge is a marvel of recent craftsmanship, less than three decades old. It's a mix of stone and crystalline ice that spreads fifty miles across the chasm. It is home to only the strongest of heart and spirit. Most have lived here since its creation, those who would give up comfort and personal pride in order to make sure the chasm is guarded at all times. Those who serve here look to my uncle as more than a warden. To them, he is a father, a guardian.

That is what Winter deserves in a High Prince.

Something I can never be as long as my selfish heart has rule.

Uncle Irahn storms toward the largest structure on Voidseal, the bridge house. It appears like a small fortress, crafted of ice-covered ironwork and massive stone blocks. A shiver passes through me as we walk through the doors; great fireplaces chase away the badlands' chill, at least for the moment.

"My office," Irahn growls. "Now."

My own steps are as angry as his. "You're a stubborn old man. I'm offering you more than a throne. I'm offering you glory, the chance to be a hero to the Vale, to be remembered in history for eons—"

We thunder into his office, and he slams the door. "You're offering me your chains."

"What?"

Irahn's eyes darken. "Do you truly think so little of me, nephew? Aye, glory, legacy. These things you offer me like they have any meaning. You know what has meaning? Actually saving lives. Protecting the vulnerable. Being the one shield between us and the Below."

"I did not intend to insult you."

My uncle laughs. "I cannot be insulted, boy. All you showed me is you truly have no idea how close we are to seeing everything we love swallowed by the void."

"I understand you guard the Great Chasm—"

Irahn walks to the window and slams a hand against it. From this vantage, sweeping views of the chasm unfold before my eyes. Icy rock gives way to limitless darkness. On the bridge, watchmen keep vigilant posts, constantly scanning the void. "You know where this leads, don't you, Kel?"

Through gritted teeth, I say, "I am familiar with the Below and the monsters there."

Now, Irahn laughs. "You've got goblins in the Briar. We've got goblins everywhere. Winter, Spring, Summer, Autumn. You remember what crawled out of here all those years ago? How they made their way to Frostfang? Aye, the things that slither down here … They're different. And they're not senseless beasts like the gobs. They hunger. They plan. They think."

I stay silent, stretching my fingers to get some warmth back into them. *Of course I remember. I remember everything about him. The good and the terrible.*

Uncle Irahn turns away from the window and holds my gaze. "I don't know why you're giving up the throne your father wanted for you. That's your duty, your fate. My duty and fate are here. The Deep Guard needs a warden. I won't leave them without one."

My voice is steady as I say, "The Deep Guard wouldn't be alone. I will stay as warden."

Irahn doesn't laugh in my face as I thought he might. Instead, one wiry eyebrow raises. "What is going on, Kel? Why would you give up the Blessing to serve here?"

"I am not fit to be High Prince," I say lowly. "And you're right. The Below is getting stronger every day. More threats will come. It will take a monster to fight a monster."

And I know deep within me, I am finally doing what is right.

Keldarion, son of Erivor, was never fit to be High Prince. For it was my actions that led to the awakening of the Great Chasm in the first place.

I know I will never be able to break my curse. But if I pass the Blessing on to Irahn, he at least has a chance to save Winter, to save Castletree.

And no harm will come to Rosalina.

No harm will come to *him*.

I shed my clothing and let my body shift, let the beast rip his way out of my flesh, to show my uncle exactly why I cannot keep Winter.

When the white wolf stands before Irahn, he does not flee. His eyes widen and he takes in a sharp breath. "So, the rumors out of Autumn were true. There are beasts in the Briar."

"What say you now, Uncle?" I growl.

"It's a fancy trick." He crosses his arms. "But I don't trust that you're capable of being warden yet. Come on then, boy. Let us descend into the bellows of the earth and truly see what you are made of."

24

FARRON

There's a chill in Rosalina's room, but then again, there's a chill in every room of Hammergarden. That's what building your castle into the literal side of a mountain will do. At night, it's not so unlike the weather of Autumn.

I drop my satchel on the stone desk and unbutton my vest. It was late when I arrived, having come through Castletree's mirror. Thankfully, Ezryn had alerted the guards to watch for me, and they escorted me to my mate's room. As much as I'm eager to check in with Dayton and Ezryn, I know they'll have secured themselves in their chambers so no one will see them as their wolves.

Kel hasn't returned. Through the shared mate bond with Rosalina, I can sense he's still very far away. He must have received the same letter I did. Is he on his way here?

Rosalina makes a soft sound in her sleep. I stride over to the bed, dropping my vest and pulling my tunic over my head.

Despite the cold, my mate has kicked off half the blankets, and her perfect form is on display. She's wearing a short lacy nightdress, the sharp points of her nipples poking the fabric. Quickly, I drop my trousers and begin to palm my cock. Stars, I could come just looking at her.

But that's not nearly as fun as what I have in mind. I know she loves these little wake-ups as much as I do. It was something we established when we first arrived back at Castletree, when we were absolutely feral with need. Our schedules didn't always line up, especially with me being in Autumn so often. But we agreed our bodies belong to the other, no matter when, no matter where. Of course, that came with the trust and love that we can rescind the agreement at any time.

Climbing on to the bed, I spread her legs apart, running a hand along her soft thighs. How sweet it will be for her to wake up, filled by my cock. Will it be as I'm riding her? Or as my pleasure erupts and I'm spilling deep?

I raise the edges of her nightdress so I can gaze at her supple curves, breasts full and prickling with goose flesh.

I lightly palm her breast, and she barely stirs. Must be deep asleep. Damn, I can't remember anything hotter than the time I awoke in the library to her mouth around my cock. I sputtered awake to see her licking my cum from her lips.

So fucking hot. How did I get so lucky to have a mate like her? Even after all these weeks, I don't take being a man at night for granted. Especially if it means being able to have her every night.

I pull off her panties and run a finger along her center, feeling her slickness. "So ready for me, Sweetheart."

I can't wait another moment. I plunge my cock deep inside her and let out a wild groan as I sink deep into her warmth. She feels so good. Her body twitches slightly, an instinctual movement, but her breath remains heavy.

Bracing my hands on her hips, I try to keep my movements soft and even, but it's hard not to lose control. My entire body pulses with pleasure at being so near my mate. She moans, eyes moving rapidly beneath her lids.

I bend to kiss her neck and whisper, "You don't need to wake up, Sweetheart, but I couldn't wait. I need your body. I need you."

She takes a deep breath, and a soft, sleepy smile forms on her lips. "Farron."

I lick along her jawline until I reach her plush lips, all the while continuing my rhythmic movements on her pussy. Her inner walls clench tightly around me.

"I missed you," she says, running a hand through my hair.

"You have no idea how much I crave you," I groan, my movements growing faster now that she's waking up. The sound of our bodies slapping together fills the silence of the night.

She moans deeply, her legs coming up to wrap around my waist, drawing me deeper. "Not the way I've been thinking about you, Fare."

"Hmm?"

"Thinking of the way you feel inside me, the way you touch me."

I cup her face, increasing my pace, getting more and more turned on as she writhes beneath me. Suddenly, a scent hints at me, one of earth and metal. I clutch her jaw and make her look up at me. "Tell me, Rosalina, have you been a good girl for the Prince of Spring?"

Her whole body trembles and something devious flashes in her eyes. "Maybe."

"Don't stop now," I growl, slowing my pace, holding her at the edge of release.

Her eyes squeeze shut, and she bites her lip. "A shower, his cock in my mouth and—"

I bury myself all the way.

"Then he spilled down my throat."

"Stars," I moan, and almost explode inside her at the thought. On her knees before Ezryn ... I only wish I had been here, figuring how hard I came when he watched us in the library. I can only imagine what it would be like to have our girl at his mercy.

"Farron, I—" Her nails rake down my back.

"Almost there, sweetie." I suck on the sensitive skin beneath her ear. "I'm not done with you yet."

"You better not be." She presses her palms flat on my chest and uses that new fae strength of hers to flip us. Her brown eyes lock with mine as she strips off her nightdress and begins to ride me hard, breasts bouncing.

"Stars, you feel so good," I moan, rising to sink my teeth into her neck. Her muscles contract, sending me into a frenzy. I thrust up, pressing into her slick heat, and drive us both closer and closer to the edge. Rosalina slams her hips down, circles them, and I'm completely at her mercy.

"I can't take it anymore," she cries, her voice a tempest. "I want to feel you come inside me."

"Not yet, Rosie." I pin her on her back, knees over my shoulders. "Scream my name first."

Her gaze darkens, and her inner muscles clench around my cock. "Farron!" she cries. Her pants turn into screams, and her fingernails rip at the sheets.

Her shudder of pleasure is all I need. I throw my head back, sweaty hair sticking to my brow, and groan out my hot release.

The breath is heavy in our throats. I collapse on top of her, and we slowly untangle from each other. Still needing to touch her, I stroke the point of her ear. "I was worried about you with the goblin attack on Castletree. But Day kept you safe, didn't he?"

A wash of sadness flows through our bond at his name, but then her face turns determined.

"I saved him."

How could I ever doubt her? "Of course, you did."

"I used my thorns. When I saw Day in danger ...." She trails off, blinking. "Something in me fractured, and I created gold thorns that sprouted roses. Like on the Autumn battlefield."

My heart constricts, both with fear for her safety and relief that she was able to protect Dayton, to protect herself. "It's a most unusual magic. Even Ezryn can't create plants, just control them. No other fae has been able to summon plant matter from nothing—"

"Caspian can."

Fire bursts in my heart. I can't stand his presence at the best of times, but to hear his name on her lips right after we made love—

In a whirl, I pull her on top of me, wrapping her in my arms. "I don't want to talk about the Prince of Thorns right now."

"Okay." She leans down to kiss my nose, then crosses her arms over my chest, just staring down at me.

She looks so beautiful now. Ethereal, even. She could be the subject of a portrait or crafted of stained-glass. A strange thought strikes me. "You know, there was another fae who made roses."

"Who?"

"Tomorrow, I'll show you." My eyes close, comforted by the beat of my mate's heart.

She kisses the side of my face. "I love you, Farron."

"In the starlight way," I whisper back.

25

ROSALINA

Everything in the Spring Realm seems at odds with itself. Delicate plants bloom between hard slabs of rock. Bushels of flowers drape over shop awnings carved into the mountainside. And the people are no different, wearing soft pastel hues beneath gleaming armor.

As I walk down the market street between Dayton and Farron, I wish Ezryn was here with us now. However, he's traveled up to the monastery to pass his judgment on Kairyn. My stomach twists in a knot. I don't know what his final decision is, but it's been tearing him up inside.

The Spring Realm is not unlike Ezryn. On the outside, he's as hard as the helm he dons. But I've been able to glimpse within, from the gentle way he healed my scars, to the devotion in which he protects the other princes. And there's humor there, too, small glimmers of it —usually a joking laugh with the staff or a sardonic insult to Kel that has the other princes chuckling under their breath.

And there's the passionate lover. My cheeks heat as I recall our encounter yesterday, as well as the welcomed wake-up call from my mate. He's gotten ahead of me now, bumping Dayton's shoulder with a smirk.

Explaining to Farron what happened between Dayton and me—or more so, what didn't happen—had been hard. I think we both had hoped that Dayton belonged to us in some way. But Farron took my hand and tried to reassure me. *It's all right, Rosie. Day doesn't have a mate yet. No use fretting about what hasn't happened.*

Except we shouldn't be fretting about Dayton finding his mate—we should help him find them.

"Want to buy a fish?" a loud voice draws me from my thoughts, and I blink as a fish is presented in front of me. Except it's not a real fish, but a metal one, iridescent scales glistening in the light. A white flower spouts from its mouth like a spray of water. "Stands on its tail fins, it does. Great for over the mantel. Comes with its own stardrop flower! They're said to ward off the Malice Spirit."

"She's all right." Dayton grabs my arm and tugs me away from the vendor. "This one has plenty of gadgets and gizmos already."

"Hey, it was kind of cute," I say.

"Don't come to me when the spirit sucks your wits!" the vendor calls after us.

Dayton gives a dramatic sigh and stomps back, digging in his pockets for a coin. I give a beaming smile as he presents me with the trinket. A new friend for Ani.

"What's a Malice Spirit?" I ask as we fall into step beside Farron.

Farron wrinkles his nose. "Not a legend I'm familiar with. I know the Spring folk have lots of tales of monsters crawling up from the caves, but those are usually just creatures of the Below."

A gentle breeze brushes my hair back, thick with a floral fragrance. "Have either of you been to this smithy before?"

"Draconhold Forge," Dayton corrects. "Don't let them hear you call it anything less. And yes, a few times. Spring exports more than half the metal for the realms, and about eighty percent of all weapons."

Our mission today is to investigate the forge and see if they know anything about the stolen weapons. This could have been one of the places the goblins got the Spring steel.

"This city is truly fascinating," I say as we continue down the streets. Florendel is like an extension of the mountain itself, the stone and earth expertly shaped by the hands of ancient fae. Intricate floral motifs decorate the surfaces of the buildings, bridges, and walkways that are seamlessly carved into the mountainside. Delicate vines cascade down the stucco walls, tendrils swaying with the gentle rhythm of the mountain's heartbeat. The whole city is carved from volcanic rock, the buildings crafted of pink brick. It feels like walking through a daydream.

As we enter the main market area, the path widens, and the crowd grows dense. Dayton pulls me protectively against his side. A huge flower fountain spouts crystal-clear water.

Stalls are adorned with a stunning array of wares, showcasing the talents and artisanship. There are weapons, clothes, and quite a bit of jewelry, along with potent herbs and colorful spices. The bottles of fragrant potions and elixirs are embellished with gemstones and jewels, their facets reflecting the sunlight and casting dazzling rainbows upon the cobblestones.

The vibrant chatter of the fae fills my ears. But I notice more than a few glances in our direction. "They must recognize you as High Princes," I whisper.

Dayton's eyes darken. "Some, but use that fae hearing you've got now, Rosie. Listen."

Most changes have come naturally, like the new vibrancy of the colors I see or clearer vision. But Farron said my body may repress some changes that could be too overstimulating.

Stilling my breath, I try to reach out my senses, focusing on a conversation between two women, both in pale green dresses with armored spiked shoulder plates.

"It's the High Prince of Autumn all right," one of them says. "Every time I've ever seen him here, he's with the Summer Prince."

"And the girl? Do you think it's her?"

"Gorgeous, isn't she? Whispers have come from Autumn. The Golden Ro—"

A fae child sprints across the path, trailing a kite in the shape of a bird, laughing loudly. The sound splits into my sharpened hearing and a ringing fills my ears. I grit my teeth, hissing in pain.

"It's all right. Takes practice," Dayton says softly. He leans down, as if to kiss my ear, before he straightens.

"Interesting." Farron narrows his eyes at the crowd. "That name has traveled here as well. Come along. There's something I want to show you."

We retreat from the bustle of the market, passing a troupe of musicians playing an upbeat tune. Outcroppings of gardens pop up along these streets. Most are filled with unique flowers or plants, but some are vegetable and fruit patches, all snuggled in the rock.

"We're almost there." Farron smiles. "Spring is a wonderful realm, isn't it? They've mastered the harmony between stone, nature, and themselves."

"It's amazing," I say.

"The Queen herself blessed this place," Farron continues. "As she did all the realms. And she left a gift for the people of Spring. I told you last night, you're the only one who can create roses. But then I remembered she built an archway leading to the Draconhold Forge. An archway that would forever be in bloom."

My hands gently touch the pendant around my neck. Two gems dangle from it: a golden leaf gifted to me by Farron's father, and a moonstone rose. Keldarion had said it was the symbol of the Queen. Papa told me this was a trinket my mother had found at an archeological dig site …

Something pricks at the edge of my mind.

My mother was fae. Perhaps she had some connection to the Queen.

"Hey, Fare," Dayton says. "How sure are you about that 'always in bloom' part?"

Ahead of us sprawls an archway, a tangle of magnificent briars covered in red roses. But an earthy and too-sweet smell fills my nose. The roses on the briars … They're wilting. A dusting of dark petals lines the walkway like a trail of blood.

Farron bends down to scoop up a handful of petals. "It's like at Castletree," he says softly. "The Queen's magic ... It's fading from the Enchanted Vale."

26

ROSALINA

"It's like another world," I whisper, gazing at the Draconhold Forge.

A narrow passage has led us deep within the heart of the mountain. Smoldering embers dance on thick smoky air. The forge is a mesmerizing sight to behold. The cavernous chamber is bathed in the warm glow of molten metal, casting flickering shadows upon the stone walls. The rhythmic pounding of hammers on anvils reverberates through the space, a symphony of creation in progress.

"Come on," Dayton growls, ears twitching. "Let's find the person in charge."

Hundreds of fae artisans move with fluid grace, despite their bulky protective coverings. Tools of various sizes and shapes are meticulously arranged near glowing anvils, which seem to pulse with their own sort of magic. Glimmering ores and precious gemstones lie in stone containers, waiting to be transformed.

"Hail Above! The light must not be with me today to find two princelings disturbing my forge?"

Farron gulps. "I know that voice..."

We whirl to see a female blacksmith standing before us. She's clad in leather armor, covered by a sturdy black apron. A protective shield covers her face, the light making it hard to see her features. She's much shorter than all of us, but the way she has her hammer thrown over her shoulder and the tight corded muscles in her arm, she's not someone to mess with.

"Oh hey, Tilla." Dayton steps in front of me, voice dripping with charisma. "Didn't know you worked here now."

Tilla ... I know that name from somewhere.

The blacksmith pulls off her shield with a long sigh. She's beautiful, with tawny skin, dark eyes, and long black hair swept back in a tight tail. "What are you doing here?"

"Ezryn sent us," Farron says.

Tilla's gaze sweeps over all of us before landing on me.

"Kel didn't travel with us," Dayton says. "He's in the Winter Realm."

"Did I ask, Sunshine?" She rolls her eyes. "Follow me. I command the east sector. If High Prince Ezryn sent you, it must be important."

Dayton and Farron explain our situation to Tilla, but I fall behind, mind working. Tilla ... Caspian had brought her up at a dinner we had months ago. She was with Kel romantically, at least for a time. Does she know who I am? That Keldarion is my mate?

Sickening jealousy courses through me as I realize he's probably done more with her than he's ever considered with me.

Tilla leads us around a corner to an outcropping that overlooks the entire cavern. From this high, the workers all look like little ants scurrying about. There are deep chasms as well with swinging bridges leading across. If someone were to fall...

My stomach drops.

Tilla stops beside a grand anvil, throwing her hammer down. This must be her own personal workspace. "Ezryn sent you. Why?"

"Goblin forces have been spotted wielding Spring steel," Farron explains. "We're trying to figure out how they came by it. Have there been any attacks against the forge or any missing stock?"

Tilla narrows her eyes. "We often hear the goblins chittering from the deep, but they don't dare come up here. They burrow out of the tunnels across the Starweaver Mountains, sure, but we've had no attack or loss of our weapons. Everything is accounted for."

Once again, the immensity of the Below staggers me. I've been to Cryptgarden but have since learned the Below is so much bigger. Tunnels, caverns, and cities stretch beneath all of the Enchanted Vale. It's like a whole other world.

"But the goblins had the steel. Steel that only comes from *this* forge," Dayton insists.

Tilla's face hardens. "I'm not doubting you, Daytonales. But they didn't get it from Draconhold."

I bite my lip and breathe in the warm, smoky air. "Have there been any reports on attacked shipments? If you export the steel, perhaps one of the wagons was overtaken on the road."

Tilla crosses her arms. "Not that I've heard."

Reaching into the bag slung around Dayton's chest, I pull out one of the swords we retrieved from the goblins. "We found this in the possession of a goblin. The others were armed similarly."

Tilla takes the sword and places it on a stone slab. She runs a hand over it, her palm glowing with flame. Red markings begin to spark across the sword. "This is recently made, from our latest batches. One we sent to..." She pulls her hand away, the red marks fading.

Dayton opens his mouth, but I gently place a hand on his arm. This isn't the type of woman who can be pressured into revealing anything.

She eyes me carefully, then hands Dayton back the blade. "There has been an unusually high shipment of weapons up to Queen's Reach Monastery since the boy prince took over."

"Kairyn." Saying his name makes me feel like I have shadows on my tongue.

"What do a bunch of holy folk need weapons for?" Dayton asks.

Farron smacks him on the chest. "Probably for the Queen's Army. Though they haven't seen combat in centuries." He must notice my blank expression and continues, "They're an elite force of fae soldiers, training day and night until our Queen has need of them."

"Prince Kairyn sent word that the weapons they had were naught but rusted toys. It might have nothing to do with it, but there have been troubling reports of goblin raids in the high mountains by Queen's Reach Monastery," Tilla says.

"Perhaps Kairyn thought reporting a goblin raid on his weapon shipment would make him appear weak, so he hid it," I suggest, though even as I say the words, something darker simmers in my stomach. "Either way, it's obvious where we should go next."

"No," Dayton whines. "I don't want to go to the creepy monastery."

A deep laugh fills Tilla. "I helped you, now you help me. There's a bucket of raw gold at the bottom of this slope. Be good strong fae princes and carry it up. More than a quarter of our workers are away today."

Dayton and Farron both sigh before going to retrieve it. I move to follow when Tilla says, "Stay. They can handle it."

I swallow, my throat dry and wonder if she plans to throw me off into the depths of the Below.

The thought is not as troubling as it should be.

"A quarter of your workers away," I whisper. "That seems high. Is there a holiday I don't know about?"

Tilla shakes her head. "If only it were so. A strange illness seems to be passing through the city. Fever and hallucinations. Saw one bugger drop his hammer and start swatting at the air. Nearly threw himself off the bridge before we caught him."

"Was he all right?" I ask.

"Physically, but the gal who walked him home said he just stared straight ahead as if—"

"As if all his wits had been snatched?"

"Yes." She narrows her eyes. "How did you know?"

"A man at the market said Malice Spirits would come steal my wits if I didn't put this fish on my mantel."

"Hmm." Tilla crosses her arms. "Hopefully the healers get to it. We're busier than ever here. Seems like the Below is belching out more and more monsters lately, and there's no finer weapon or armor to defend yourself than what comes from Spring."

"I don't doubt it," I say.

"And you've been practicing with a bow, I assume?" She nods at the red marks along my arm. This morning, Dayton had insisted I practice without my thorn bow. And that, of course, had led to the string hitting my arm numerous times.

"Still learning. Ezryn ensures that I know which weapons in Castletree's armory were forged in Spring. They're always the best. He told me all about this place."

Tilla gazes at me. "I've heard about you. The Lady of Castletree. I thought you were human, but it appears that rumor was wrong. And is it true, you are mate to two High Princes?"

I flush, but don't feel defensive. Instead, Tilla's curiosity strikes me as genuine. "I'm sorry. I should have introduced myself sooner. I'm Rosalina O'Connell. And yes, Farron and ... and Keldarion are my mates."

"That look on your face when you say his name tells me he hasn't changed at all. I'm sure you've heard about me and him?"

"Only a little," I admit. "Something about frogs in a bed?"

She snorts and bends before a large chest by her anvil. "Honestly, I should thank the thorny bastard for his interference. Kel leaving me on our wedding day was the best thing that ever happened to me. Our marriage would have been my family's dream. Once it was over, I realized I could find my own."

My stomach clenches. They almost got married?

Tilla stands and crosses her arms. "No reason to get your brow in a knot. He never loved me."

Kel had a great love, Dayton said once. And it wasn't Tilla. But then who?

I shake my head. "Well, he told me being my mate is *utter torment.*"

Tilla meets my gaze and then we both burst out laughing. "He truly has not changed."

A great deal of huffing sounds behind us as Dayton and Farron drag the gold up the hill, red dust billowing behind them. "Now, what's so funny?" Farron wheezes.

"Talking about how terrible Keldarion is," I answer.

"Oh, can I join in?" Dayton smirks, dropping his end of the bucket, leaving Farron to scramble to hold it up. "Did I ever tell you about the time he turned my hot springs into a frozen pond? Just because he was in a pissy mood—"

"You two haven't changed either." Tilla sighs, then narrows her gaze at Farron, who has dragged the bucket the last bit by himself. "Maybe you look … older."

He gives a sheepish grin. "We should get going." He and Dayton start to walk toward the exit.

I turn to Tilla. "Thank you for your help today. I'm happy to have made your acquaintance."

She grabs my arm. "In Spring, you are often gifted your first piece of armor for an act of selflessness. I heard what you did in Autumn. Now, having met you myself, I can see you are deserving of the steel of Spring."

In her hand, she reveals a metal bracer overtop a woven leather piece, meant to tie around the wrist. The metal itself is silver and smooth, with the edges gilded in a floral pattern.

"It's nothing fancy," Tilla says, expertly tying it around my wrist. "But it'll last you a lifetime and stop those pesky welts on your arm."

"Thank you." I hold it up, the metal catching the red fire of the forge. My own armor from the Spring Realm. "How can I ever thank you?"

"You don't need to—"

I pluck the white flower from the fish trinket Dayton bought me and put it on her anvil. "It's no Spring steel, but it's all I have right now."

Tilla picks up the flower and gives it a sniff. "I have a feeling there are great things ahead of you, Rosalina O'Connell. And besides, you're mated to one of the iciest bastards in the realm. You're going to need all the help you can get."

27

KELDARION

T he mechanical lift stutters down into the darkness. I stand in my fae form beside my uncle, neither of us speaking. My heart pounds with a mix of anticipation and trepidation. I'm dressed in the heavy fabrics made specifically for the Deep Guard, which blocks out most of the cold.

I'm familiar with Cryptgarden, but the rest of the Below, I've only heard about in stories. Irahn's stories ... and Caspian's.

Memories threaten to take over my mind: the feeling of nimble fingers pushing hair away from my brow, the teasing whisper. *The dark hides things even a Winter prince should fear.*

Gears grind and chains clink in a discordant symphony. Thankfully, Irahn begins to speak, tearing me from my thoughts. "This is a lost world, boy. In the Badlands, the elements conspire to torment both our body and soul. But it is nothing compared to the chasm. Only in our unity can we survive. Each step we take, each blow we strike, is a testament to our resolve to the realm."

"It would be my honor to serve among the brave men and women of the Deep Guard," I respond.

Irahn laughs, a sound as hard and grating as the gears. "Things like honor and glory have no place in the chasm. Chasing after honor will only bring you death."

Torches flicker by as we descend. Deep Guard fae walk along wooden parapets, carrying swords, spears, bows, and knives. They're armed to the teeth.

A strange sensation lifts through the pit of my stomach as we plunge deeper. I instinctively grasp the cold railing, seeking an anchor. Every level that goes by is marked by a jolt, a brief pause, before the descent resumes. The temperature seems to drop with each passing moment.

We shudder past a cave opening, and a roar sounds from within. I turn to my uncle, eyebrows raised. He shrugs. "One of the guards assigned to this level will handle it."

"And what level are we going to?"

Irahn grimaces. "We're going beyond where there are levels."

I roll my shoulders and feel for the Blessing of Winter. A deadly sharp ice blade grows in my hand. Just in case.

One by one, the torches along the wall give out. Irahn strikes a match and lights a lantern attached to the lift. Now, there is only a dim bubble of light.

The seconds stretch into eternity. The jolts signifying various stops come further and further apart. Finally, Irahn pulls a lever; a metallic screech erupts through the air as the lift clangs to a stop on the edge of a rocky cave opening.

I blink. There's light here, but not from torches. Ghastly green lines scar their way through the cave, leading deep into a tunnel. A green I will never forget: the same glow that came from the traitor Quellos's crown. *Was he truly harnessing the same magic that created this place?*

Irahn is terrified of the monsters in this place. But I'm terrified of the magic that created it. Memories fly through my mind's eye: green flames flashing in a purple gaze as Caspian weaves me a legend of a terrible god from beyond even our own stars. One that doesn't just conquer cities, but entire worlds. *Is this magic the same?*

Irahn stretches his neck from side to side. "Won't be long now.

They don't like the sound of the lift," he says just as it clatters to a stop. Then he draws a broadsword from its sheath and steps into the cave.

"This should be fun." I shed my clothing, the cold biting at every piece of exposed skin. Before I even have a chance to shift, a deafening roar echoes through the chamber.

Irahn flicks his gaze to me. "I've already buried my sister and my brother-in-arms. Do not make me bury my nephew, too." Then the old fae raises his broadsword and roars back into the dark.

A colossal shape emerges from the shadows. A hulking figure of at least twelve feet, the monster's thick muscles bulge beneath mottled gray-green skin. Its gnarled face is a twisted mask of rage, yellow eyes flickering with an inward fire.

In some ways, it's similar to the goblins that plague our lands: the body like rotten earth, the jagged teeth, the malevolent anger in its gaze. But this creature is bigger than anything I've seen before. A cave troll.

A surge of adrenaline pumps through me. Tapping into my power, my form shimmers and transforms. Fur sprouts from my skin, my limbs elongate: the white wolf stands beside my uncle, hackles raised.

The troll stalls for a moment, taken aback. In its hand, it clutches a rusted claymore glowing with green light. Then it charges.

My body is the epitome of agility and grace as I run forward, drawing the troll away from my uncle. It drives down with the claymore, but I dodge, and the blade digs into the icy ground. Chunks of ice shatter against the cave wall. I strike back, jaws snapping at its forearm, tearing through sinew and muscle. Rotten blood spurts into my mouth.

The troll swipes at me with its free hand. I move, but the claws catch my haunches, cutting deep. But Irahn is there with his broadsword, slicing the back of the troll's ankles. It bellows and wrenches the claymore loose.

Irahn and I flank the beast, and a strange elation rushes through me. I remember doing tours with him out in the wilds, fighting under his service as a young fae. The years have not dulled our coordination.

The troll swings its claymore at me again, but I anticipate its move, leaping over the blade. My uncle's sword beams with ice magic. Like my mother, he was always adept in both blade and the arcane. He clashes his sword against the troll's, but his magic sends a freezing burst of icicles right at the monster's face.

Seizing the opportunity, I sink my teeth into its vulnerable leg, eliciting a roar of agony. The cave troll staggers.

My paws pound against the icy ground as I propel forward, leaping on to its back.

"Kill it!" Irahn cries. He unleashes another barrage of dagger-sharp icicles.

My fangs sink deep into the troll's neck, severing the rotted life coursing through its monstrous veins. It gives a mammoth bellow of pain that weakens, becoming less of a roar and more of a lament. Then it topples forward.

I leap off its back, landing beside my uncle. The cave falls silent.

Irahn exhales loudly, then shakes his sword, scattering droplets of troll blood across the icy wall. "That beast of yours is quite something."

"The beast and I are the same," I rumble back, the wolf's voice low.

"Come on." Irahn gestures deeper into the tunnel. "More where that came from."

I follow on silent paws as he leads me past the dead troll and into the cave mouth. As soon as we enter, the green lines illuminate a familiar sight.

Thorns. Thorns everywhere, overtaking the walls, the ground. Except these are all frosted over. A rough-cut path has been made through the brambles.

This chasm truly is my doing.

"That monster is only the beginning of the threats you'll find down here," Irahn says. "Without the Deep Guard, they'd pour up out of the chasm and make their way across the realms."

"You see now I am capable, Uncle. Let me serve here in your stead. I will keep the monsters at bay. I owe the realms that."

"I don't doubt your skills in battle or even as a warden." Irahn stops and turns to me. "But I will not take the stewardship."

My heart hammers in my chest. "Why not?"

"You came to Voidseal to prove to me why you cannot rule. Instead, you have only shown me it must be you."

I close my eyes. "My people would never follow a beast like me."

Irahn places a hand beside my ear. I startle, realizing this is the first person to ever touch me in this form besides Rosalina … and *him*. One of the only people to ever look upon my wolf without fear. "Keldarion, nephew," he says, "have you tried?"

28

DAYTON

I grip the reins tightly, feeling the rough texture of the leather against my hands as the ibexes carry us up the treacherous rocky mountain path. Farron has taken to his, though he's always had a way with animals, from ponies to horses to his great elk. He can look into a beast's eyes and know its soul.

Maybe that's why he likes me, I think.

"Little bumpier than riding Thea," Rosie says, bent so low, her stomach is pressed to her ibex's back. Its black horns curl around her.

"You're doing fine," I call over.

"Trust your mount." Farron spurs his ibex closer and gently pats her beast's nose. "These animals know the route well. They'll get us there safely."

Rosalina nods, and we continue up the long path to the monastery, riding the local ibexes. We rented a couple from a farmer outside the city, though he insisted we keep a wary eye out for goblins. Thank the stars we chose the mounts. My feet ache just thinking of trekking all the way up here.

The ibexes' sure-footed steps harmonize with the rush of the nearby river and the distant roar of cascading waterfalls. The path steepens ahead, and the scent of pine and earth mingles with the fresh afternoon air, filling my lungs with each breath.

As we ascend higher, the monastery comes into view, perched majestically atop the mountain. "Who the hell would give up everything to live on the top of a bloody mountain with not a tavern in sight?"

"It was built on one of the highest peaks in the Vale so as to be close to the Above." Farron gives a light chuckle. "It's a sign of devotion, Day. The monastery is situated in the Spring Realm, but Spring does not abide over it. The Golden Acolytes and the Queen's Army answer only to the Queen. But with the High Clerics gone and Kairyn governing it now, I'm sure much has changed."

"Including the need for a mass number of weapons," Rosalina says, running a hand along the new metal bracer Tilla gifted her.

Damn, that woman is incredible. Receiving a gift from her mate's former lover? It would have been so easy for Rosie to put up her guard upon meeting Tilla, to hate her for the simple reason she was with her mate before. But of course, Rosie offered her the same respect and kindness she offers everyone.

She's perfect. Far too perfect for me. Something the world has no shame in reminding me of. It laughs in my face when I dare to try. Dare to have a single perfect moment with her.

The ibexes quicken their pace, their powerful muscles propelling us forward. I lean into their movements. My heart pounds in rhythm with their hoofbeats.

The path winds perilously close to the edge of a steep cliff. On our other side, roaring sounds as a waterfall drops to a small pond before narrowing back into the river.

"This river runs all the way from the top of Mount Lumidor to just outside of Florendel," Farron says. "Parts of it are waterfalls like this with a few shallow pools, but there are rocky rapids, too."

"Do you hear that?" Rosalina asks.

We still, and I lay a gentle hand on my ibex's back. A bleating sounds in the air, followed by a woman's scream. We exchange a worried glance, then urge our mounts forward. Figures take shape at the top of the slope before us.

A fae woman dressed in long white and gold robes: an acolyte of the monastery. She holds a stick and waves it back and forth in front of her at—

"Goblins," I growl.

Four of the creatures edge closer to her, though at least these look like old-fashioned nasties, no green flames surrounding them.

"She's protecting the babies!" Rosalina yells.

A small cluster of baby ibexes cower behind the acolyte. The fluffy, cream-colored creatures huddle close, eyes wide, with horns no more than stubs.

"Get back!" the acolyte snarls venomously and cracks one of the goblins over the head with her stick. Another one charges her, and she stumbles, feet at the edge of the river.

"We have to help!" Rosalina shouts, sitting straighter as she urges her ibex up the hill.

Farron nods and I follow their lead. "Guess they warned us about goblins."

"Tasty, tasty for our lunches," one of the goblins chitters.

"Tenderest meat, the babies have," another one says, licking its lips.

"I told you to get back!" the woman yells again. She's young, with dark hair and a vicious scowl. She brings her stick down hard on one of the goblin's feet and it howls.

Heat washes over me as Farron gathers his power. As a High Prince with his curse broken, there's nothing holding his magic back, except the overall health of Castletree.

A goblin lunges for the baby ibexes, and the woman careens her stick toward it. The goblin catches it and pushes her. She doesn't even have a chance to scream. One moment she's there, the next she's in the river. She pops up, sputtering, before the river ensnares her, and she plunges down the waterfall.

Her form stills on the small pool below, but it's not long before the river turns into vicious rapids.

"I'll get her," I say, leaping off my ibex. "You two handle the goblins."

Running a few paces to the cliff, I jump. The cold hits me with a jolt, and I break through, gasping. The acolyte has floated further away, the water before her turbulent.

"Fuck," I swear. Arm over arm, I surge toward her. She's not moving, and a thin line of red trails in the water.

Over my shoulder, I glance up to see Rosalina and Farron fighting the goblins, a torrent of red and white flames. *They're okay.*

The woman slips under. Gasping for air, I follow. It's deeper than I thought. I only catch a glimmer of gold, sinking, sinking, sinking. But I grew up among the waves and surf of the Summer Realm, and water is as much a home to me as the land. Kicking hard, I easily reach her and grip her around the waist.

Damn, she's heavy in these clothes. How much fabric does a holy person need? *Wouldn't be the first time I got a priestess out of her robes,* I think. I shove off the bulky cloth until she's just in a silk slip. Clutching her tightly, I kick to the surface and break through, gasping.

"Dayton!" Rosalina screams.

I blink the water from my eyes. Both she and Farron are on the shoreline, a tiny herd of babies clustered around our ibexes' legs.

"I'm all right," I call, holding the woman against my chest and swimming to shore. I lay her upon the grass. Farron and Rosalina circle me.

Farron places a hand over her mouth. "She's not breathing."

I touch my seashell necklace, searching for the particular token that houses the mirror, the one blessed by the Queen. In that, I feel my fading magic. But Summer's Blessing was made from water, of the deep oceans and tides. I position my hand over her body, feeling for the water that shouldn't be there. The water in her lungs. I drag it up out of her throat, a gentle stream coming from between her lips before misting away.

A moment passes, then she coughs, sputtering for air. The four of us breathe a collective sigh of relief.

"Easy now," I say, putting a hand behind the woman's back. The movement shifts her slip, and I catch the glimpse of a necklace, a string of seashells. Strangely similar to mine. "Are you all right?"

Her brown hair is a tangle around her face, and she brushes it away before she looks at me with the bluest eyes I've ever seen. Blue like the sea, like the endless horizon. She clutches my arm and rasps, "Y-you saved me."

29

ROSALINA

I don't know if it's because of the altitude or the immensity of the structure before us, but I'm struggling to breathe.

Queen's Reach Monastery towers above us, an unbelievable skyscraper of gothic architecture and fae elegance. It stretches so far up that the top is completely covered by clouds. And we're already so high in the mountains, it's no wonder it's said to be the closest point to the fabled Above.

It is a single building composed of thin and jutting towers, the walls made of golden stone, the spires gilded. Flying buttresses support the main structure, while ornate domes crown the other turrets.

Farron holds out his hand to help me down from my ibex. I let him but can't tear my eyes from the building. It makes me uneasy; maybe because I realize just how small I truly am.

"Quite the sight, isn't it?" Farron asks as he ties our steeds beside a patch of stardrop flowers.

"I always dreamt of seeing the Eiffel Tower or the Empire State Building," I whisper, not even able to blink, "but this would put them both to shame."

"The Queen made quite an impact on the people of the Vale. This is their testament to her."

"I'm sorry Dayton isn't here to see it."

After he rescued the drowning fae woman, Dayton had offered to escort her down the mountainside.

"He's seen it before. Come on." Farron places a hand on my back and guides me toward the doors.

They open as we arrive. Ezryn stands there, arms crossed. Farron had sent him one of his enchanted flying letters informing him of our impending arrival.

"I'm glad you've arrived safely. How was your journey up the mountain?" he asks.

"Eventful," Farron responds. "As you can see, we've lost Dayton. But I'll tell you about that later. Have you spoken with Kairyn yet?"

"No, I was just about to find him when I received your letter. Come. Tell me what is so urgent. Mind your words, though. There are ears everywhere."

We step inside the entrance hall of the monastery. I gasp, chills surging up my body. I don't know if I've ever seen anything so beautiful. The entire hall is lit with colored light drifting through the many stained-glass windows. It reminds me of High Tower in Castletree, but grander, more spectacular. Even the long rug we walk upon is opulent, the swirling designs telling a story I don't understand.

It's a hive of activity: a staircase disappears upward on one side, and an elevator shaft hums with movement on the other. Acolytes dressed in white and gold robes busy about, barely paying us any attention.

Ezryn and Farron's conversation drifts in and out of my ears as I try to focus, but the surrounding sights are so distracting.

"I have to admit, my brother is right," Ezryn says. "There seems to be a great improvement here since he replaced the High Clerics. The acolytes are well-fed, morale seems high, and the surrounding villages are protected from goblin raids."

"Who's been protecting them?" Farron asks.

"The new High Clerics. Kairyn calls them his Penta Conclave."

Farron's voice lowers: "Isn't there only three of them? Kairyn and those other two helmet-wearing soldiers he's always with?"

Ezryn hesitates. "My brother is a great warrior."

"And he could be stashing Spring steel up here," Farron urges. "Listen—"

He begins to reiterate what we learned from Tilla, how a great number of weapons have been moved up to the monastery.

My focus breaks as a little girl dressed in white walks by holding a bouquet of stardrops. She smiles up at me and waves. I wave back.

Then her cheeks turn bright red. "Sorry. I thought you were someone else."

Before I can respond, she scuttles away.

I continue trailing after Ez and Farron, their voices now too low for me to hear. We pass an arched doorway, and I cast a look inside.

My heart stutters. It appears like a chapel, stone pews set before a dais. Behind the dais is a mosaic.

I stop, eyes completely caught by the artwork. It depicts a woman, her eyes closed, her body silhouetted by an ethereal glow. And all around her are the seasons I've loved so much throughout my life: in the upper-right quadrant, the cold comfort of winter depicted in pieces of blue and white ceramic. Below it, the gorgeous pinks and green of spring. On her other side, turquoise and coral make out the heat of summer. Above are the fiery reds and oranges of fall.

And hanging over the woman's head is a briar blooming with red and gold roses.

Before I know it, I've slipped into the room, drifting over to the image as if drawn by an invisible string.

This must be a depiction of Queen Aurelia. I feel a sense of kinship with her, a part of all the seasons that make up the Vale.

Something scratches at the tip of my mind, a feeling and a thought all at once. I squint my eyes at the mosaic. That feeling ... It ripples down from my head to linger by my heart.

I touch my necklace. The Queen is gone. But what if some of her magic stayed behind? "Beautiful, isn't it?" a voice says from behind me.

I whirl. Blocking the doorway like a living shadow is Ezryn's brother, the banished prince of Spring. Kairyn.

30

DAYTON

The late afternoon breeze tousles my wet hair, and I wrap my poncho tighter around my shoulders. My gaze drifts up to Mount Lumidor, where the monastery gleams like the point of a sword. *When will Farron and Rosie be back?*

"Hello?" A quiet voice draws me from my thoughts. The acolyte stands at the doorway of my balcony.

After our encounter on the mountainside, Rosie and Fare had continued up to the monastery, and I'd escorted the acolyte down to Florendel. She'd been on her way to deliver a special medicine they brewed at the monastery for the ailing Prince Thalionor. We'd been soaking, and despite being given Farron and Rosie's dry cloaks, it had been a long, cold journey. Pressed against me on the back of a single ibex, I'd felt her shiver all the way down the trail until she finally drifted off to sleep.

Of course, I had no idea where to bring a damned acolyte, so I placed her on the couch in my room until she finally woke up.

She seems better now, some color returned to her cheeks. One of my tunics is notched around her waist with a rope belt, and oversized socks are pulled up to her knees. "It's a little big on me."

I can't help but give a soft chuckle. She looks ridiculous. "I'd be more worried about your gods smiting you for changing out of your holy garb."

That earns me an eye roll as she pads closer. "It doesn't work like that. We worship the Queen. We give our energy, light, and prayers to the Vale in hope of calling her home. Some even believe that she'll open the way to the Above."

I peer through the clouds, but there is nothing to be seen except a blue sky. "Do you really believe that's where we came from?"

The acolyte follows my gaze skyward. "The High Clerics gave many sermons on it, of the great wars between Above and Below. How the Below destroyed the Gardens of Ithilias—"

"But the soon-to-be-Queen stole four clippings from the rosebush, and from them, created the entire Enchanted Vale, a haven for all fae. We have myths in Summer, too." I flash her a grin.

"I'd counsel you not to call it a myth next time you enter Queen's Reach." She sits next to me on the balcony edge. "And these clothes are fine. I'll only be wearing them until I return to the monastery. Quite comfortable, actually. They smell ... salty."

"Sorry," I say. "Can't seem to shake that. I swear in the Summer Realm, your tongue is coated in a never-ending layer of sea salt."

"I like it," she says so softly I'm not sure I'm meant to hear.

My gaze returns to the monastery, and I give a sigh before turning to the woman. She plays with the ends of the rope tassel. Her short hair is drying into thick curls, and one piece falls across her brow. I think about reaching out and tucking it behind her ear.

A year ago, I certainly would have. Damn, even a few months ago I would have. But ever since Kel sent Rosie away, it all changed for me. Everything. Objectively, I'm sure this fae woman is pretty, even if it feels wrong admiring a holy person. Large eyes, chestnut hair, plump lips. She reminds me a little of Rosie. Or maybe my every thought leads me back to her.

"I've been incredibly rude," I finally say. "I never asked your name, or do you have to give that up in service of the Queen?"

She shakes her head, letting out a musical laugh. "You certainly have a unique view of our order. I get to keep my name. It's Wrenley."

"Wrenley, huh? That's kind of cute." I flash her a grin, and deep crimson stains her cheeks. "And my name—"

"You're the High Prince of Summer," she says. "Daytonales. Everyone knows who you are."

"Call me Dayton. I hope my reputation hasn't scared you off too much."

"The feats of your bravery are certainly true. If you hadn't been there—"

I shake my head. "You were the brave one. Most people would have left those animals to the goblins."

"You wouldn't have." She lightly touches my arm, and I notice her fingers are calloused. "As for the rest of your reputation, I guess I'll have to find out for myself."

Shaking out of her grip, I pace away. "Rumors are always more fascinating than the real thing."

This isn't like me at all. A year ago, I would have already had this woman flat on her back in my room, just for the challenge of getting her to scream my name instead of the Queen's. And why not? She's pretty and she likes me, clear enough in her touches and glances.

But I can't stop looking at the monastery on the hill. Why? To catch a glimpse of the two mates returning, mates destined to be in love with each other *forever*?

"It's fate."

"What?"

I look back to Wrenley as she reaches under the collar of her tunic. "With such a cynical view of the world, Summer Prince, I don't expect you to believe in such things, but ... There was a reason you were climbing the mountain at that time. The first thing I saw when I opened my eyes was a necklace like mine."

She pulls the string around her neck and holds out a seashell necklace. I walk back to her as if in a trance because damn if I hadn't noticed that, too.

"My father was from Summer, you see," she says. "But my mother and I lived in a village on Mount Lumidor. He'd go back to Summer for the fishing season, and every year he'd return with a shell for me."

Gently, I run my hand over the shells, and immediately I know they're from the white sand beaches of my home.

"What about yours?"

"Me?" I touch my fingers to my own necklace. "Well, this one is the token of the High Prince of Summer, but I added it to a string of shells I already had. Someone really special made it for me."

I can still see him: one of our first Summers together, his nose burnt, and cheeks spotted with freckles, sand in his auburn hair. He lay beside me, stringing a necklace of shells. *Fare.*

Wrenley gives a soft smile then delicately unstrings her necklace and pulls off a shell, a nautilus, the edges so bright it almost appears gold. "I want you to have this as a thank you for saving my life."

"I couldn't—"

"Please," she whispers, then stands on her tiptoes and gently brushes away my hair. She unties my necklace and adds the golden shell to the string.

I grab the new shell and slide it until it's under my nose, holding it up so it catches in the sun. "It's beautiful. Thank you."

As she smiles, I can't help but think of someone else, and I try to push the thought down. Wrenley puts her necklace back on and heads to the door. "If you really want to thank me, Summer Prince, then promise me this isn't the last time I'll see you."

31

FARRON

E zryn and I walk through the cloistered halls of Queen Reach Monastery. An elderly acolyte named Silvio leads us toward the armory, his back bent. There are even wrinkles on his pointed ears. *He must have been serving here since the Queen left.*

I look behind me. We lost Rosie a while back. I'm not surprised— it's such a Rosalina thing to do, to get caught up in a painting or the glimmer of a sunbeam. A sense of curiosity whispers through our bond. I'm sure she'll tell me all about whatever wonder was so fascinating when I find her.

Admittedly, I catch myself wishing I could wander the monastery for no other purpose than to take in its history. But I have to help Ezryn get to the bottom of this. Tilla said shipments of Spring steel have been moved up to the monastery. What reason would a sanctuary need for weapons?

Thankfully, we found Silvio, the master armorer. His age and constitution seem another indication of how little weapons are used up here.

Silvio's hand trembles as he unlocks a wooden door and gestures us in. I follow behind Ezryn. The room is dark, lit only by torchlight, but clean and well-organized. Racks line every wall, holding all manner of weapons, from spears and lances to swords and axes. They all glint with the familiar sheen of Spring steel.

"As requested, High Prince Ezryn," Silvio says, holding out his hand. "Here is our armory."

Ezryn strides over to one of the racks and examines a blade. "Freshly forged. Tell me, armorer, when did these weapons arrive?"

Silvio taps his chin. "We've had various shipments over the last few months. With the goblins growing bolder in the mountains, High Cleric Kairyn decided that the Queen's Army should be equipped with more than rusty kitchen utensils. His words, not mine."

"The Queen's Army only answers to the Queen herself," Ezryn says.

Silvio shrugs. "The High Cleric says peace comes from preparation. He wants the acolytes trained as well. Why, the other day, I held a blade for the first time in three hundred years." Silvio shivers and gives a breathy laugh. "Invigorating!"

I cross my arms. "So, does everyone in the monastery have access to these weapons?"

"Only the High Clerics and I have a key, and the steel is regulated. One must pass certain training before they may wield it in the practice grounds. Each weapon is signed out until its return. Kairyn keeps quite a watch on things. He's even taken it upon himself to teach some of the younglings a lesson or two!" Silvio's wiry eyebrows raise. "Lessons I'm sure you passed on to him, High Prince Ezryn."

Ezryn turns away and looks back at the steel.

"So, you haven't noticed any of your weapons missing?" I ask.

Silvio shakes his head. "No, High Prince."

"Thank you, armorer. You are dismissed," Ezryn says.

Silvio bows and takes his leave.

When the door shuts behind him, I lean against a rack, the steel clattering. "I thought we might have finally found a lead, but everything seems accounted for up here. With how bad the goblin attacks have become, I understand why the acolytes want to learn to defend themselves."

"I'm ... relieved." Ezryn's voice is slow, considering.

I raise a brow. "That our sole clue has turned out to be a dead-end?"

"I wasn't sure who I would find when I came up here."

"You mean *what* you would find?" I clarify.

Ezryn shakes his head. "No. Who. I couldn't be sure of my brother's true intentions for breaking his banishment. But coming up here ... He's beloved by these people. They've taken in so many displaced by the attacks." He sighs. "Kairyn's done more for Spring as an exile than I have as its High Prince."

I walk over to him. "You had reason for your suspicions. Kairyn defied your order of banishment and deposed your father's prince-guard in place of his own. Have you decided on his punishment yet?"

Ezryn turns from me, and his reflection wavers in the many blades hanging upon the wall. "No. I thought I'd figure it out on my way up. What is the proper sentence for breaking a banishment? By all rights, I could exile him from Spring entirely. Cast him out forever."

"Why don't you?" I breathe.

His voice is a broken rasp. "Because I don't *want* to."

He faces the wall, shoulders slumped with defeat. I wonder how hard that was for him to admit to me. In this way, he's so different from the rest of us. He's not like Rosie, who wears her heart on her sleeve and often lets her thoughts rush out, no matter how strange. Or Dayton, whose emotions are so easily read in the crashing waves of his eyes. Damn, even Kel, as secretive as he is, won't hide away his feelings.

For Ez, he's always let his actions speak for him. He fought for me when I needed it most. Now, I'll do what I'm good at.

I'll give him the words.

"I understand." Walking quietly, I come up behind Ezryn and place a hand on his shoulder. "Kairyn's all you have left."

Princess Isidora and Prince Thalionor were fated mates. When she died, Ezryn's father nearly closed off completely. I've never known him well, but my mother used to whisper that he'd become a shell of himself, a ghost in fae flesh. Then she'd always hug my father so tightly.

My chest becomes heavy at the thought. Anytime I think of my mother, I'm right back on the battlefield. It's as if the soldiers' cries and the clang of metal are happening in this room. *I miss you so much.*

I've had my father and siblings to lean on, to grieve with. Not to mention, Dayton and Rosie don't let a day go by where they're not checking in on me.

But after Isidora's death, who checked on Ez?

Ezryn lifts his hand to cover mine and holds it tight.

"It's okay to be conflicted about this," I say quietly. "Take your time."

"We were always so hard on him, Fare. My father and me. You remember Kai as a boy, don't you? He was always so distracted. A dreamer. There are so many moments in our childhood where I was so focused on fulfilling my own duty, I never stopped to look behind me and wait for him to catch up."

I'd spent a little bit of time with Kairyn before his banishment. He mostly struck me as … odd. Come to think of it, I can't think of a time when I saw him and Ezryn really get along. Even when they were younger, it was always Ezryn and Kel working together, fighting together, doing everything together. "You were the heir. You had to worry about yourself."

A deep rasp comes from beneath Ezryn's helm. "He needed someone. Mother was the only person he was close to. She understood his strangeness. I took her away from him."

My throat tightens. How many times have I felt like that since the death of my own mother? That if I had done something different that day, I could have saved her life, and not left Dom, Billy, and Nori motherless?

I squeeze my eyes shut. In my heart of hearts, I know I deserve forgiveness. And Ezryn does, too. "It wasn't your fault, Ez. Passing the Blessing is dangerous. Isidora knew the risks."

His body stills, and he peels his hand away from mine. A moment of silence passes before he says, "How did it feel when your mother passed it to you?"

I can never forget it. The memory is treasured within me. "It was like a dormant flame caught to light in my chest. As if my core self ignited and radiated out, and suddenly I was a part of every living thing in the realm. The leaves were brighter, the sun warmer. I could hear words on the wind I'd never understood before—"

"To me," Ezryn says, voice a husky growl, "it felt like I was being ripped from the inside out. Like in order to settle within me, it had to carve its way into my bones. I thought I was strong. No. The Blessing showed me just how weak I was. How weak I *am*. I couldn't control it. It all happened so fast. I—" He cuts off and turns away, body drenched in shadows.

A shiver runs up my spine. "You what, Ez?"

Another weighty pause courses between us before Ezryn stalks to the door and opens it. "My father is dying, Farron. What if this decision about Kai's punishment is the last chance to do right by my family?"

He was about to tell me something. I could push him …

No. He'll find his words in time. When he's ready, he'll tell me.

I stand beside the High Prince of Spring and peer into the dark shadows of his helm. "We're your family, too. You've done right by us. If you don't believe Kairyn has anything to do with the missing Spring steel, I trust you." Again, I search my mind for what I think he needs, arming him with words instead of weapons. "Kairyn is still here, Ez. If there's something you need to tell him, it's not too late."

32

ROSALINA

"Prince Kairyn," I breathe, fully turning to face him. The hairs on my arms rise, and for some reason, the idea of having my back to him feels wrong.

I shouldn't be surprised to see him here. He's the leader of the High Clerics. And I know I'm not in the wrong for entering this space; Ezryn told me the monastery is open to everyone. But between his height, the broadness of his shoulders, and the sweeping black armor, the exit to the hall appears shrunken behind him.

"Apologies. I was walking with Prince Ezryn and Prince Farron and became distracted." I look down. "They're just up ahead. I'm sure they're wondering where I am."

"It's understandable. The artwork throughout the monastery can not only be distracting, but enchanting." His voice is a reverberated timbre through the black helm. "I would know. I've lived here for decades."

Been banished here for decades, he means.

Kairyn stands beside me and looks up at the mosaic. A white stardrop on his breastplate, reflects the low light. "The Queen, in all her glory. The Golden Acolytes honor her memory and pray that she will return to the Vale."

My breath is heavy in my throat. I blink up at him. "Is that what you pray for?"

He stays silent for a moment, reminding me of Ezryn. Then he says: "Waiting for someone else to save you is a hopeless endeavor. The Queen is renowned as loving and just. She would not want us to sit in denial. A truly selfless ruler would want a new power to rise and shepherd the Vale as she had done before."

It's strange to see him speaking like this, quietly and with such thought. So different from my first impression of him when he confronted Ezryn. And yet...

I see it in his clenched fists, the heave of his heavily armored chest. A storm brews beneath the surface.

"My name is Rosalina O'Connell," I say, straightening. "I'm ... friends with your brother."

"Oh, I know who you are, Lady O'Connell." Kairyn turns and walks toward the door. "Everyone knows who you are."

"Everyone?" I say more to myself.

Kairyn stands in the doorway. "My brother is a great many things, but a connoisseur of the arts he is not. It would be my honor to show you the monastery's other masterpieces."

Slowly, I step toward him. Looking down the hall, there's no sign of Ez or Farron. But they know I'm here.

Kairyn is Ezryn's family—maybe I can help soothe whatever resentment lies between them. We need allies more than ever.

"I'd be delighted," I say.

Kairyn sweeps a huge hand behind my back and shivers run down my spine.

He leads me up a staircase and into a grand hall filled with tables, desks, and resplendently carved pillars. "This is the study chamber, a place for contemplation, meditation, and scholarly pursuits. It is also home to one of my favorite pieces of art."

He directs me past a row of bow-necked acolytes and into a hallway capped by a beautiful arched window. Golden light from outside filters in onto a tapestry.

I drift over to it, eyes searching the threads. It goes from ceiling to floor, depicting an epic scene.

Stretching across the top are colorful, nebulous clouds. In the very middle, blooms a glowing rosebush.

I point up. "What is that?"

Kairyn's voice echoes in the hallway. "The Above, of course. The first realm. A place that now only exists in memory … or so they say."

My eyes drift lower to the very bottom. In a perfect parallel, it depicts caverns and dark mist. "That is the Below, I suppose."

Kairyn quirks his head at me. "You do not recognize such sacred art. It must be true then."

"Hmm?"

He takes a heavy step, his shape blocking out the light of the window. My heart pounds; he's the only thing I can see, towering over me, his body silhouetted by the light. He reaches out a massive, gloved hand, and I shrink back—

But he only gently touches the point of my ear. "It's true. You were not fae-born. Or you were and…"

I give a nervous laugh. "Yeah, I wish I could tell you the whole story, but I don't even know it."

"The Princes of Castletree have truly kept their little treasure to themselves."

My voice finds strength: "The princes and I make the best decisions we can for Castletree."

"Our dying hope," he murmurs. "Twenty-five years they've been searching to heal the source of all magic, and still nothing. Some people may think they hoard the magic for themselves."

"Some people would be wrong," I growl.

"Rumor has it more problems plague our dear princes. Their home rots, goblins run wild, and some say they've even caught sight of a horrible monster running through the brambles. A beast in the Briar."

Now, it's my turn to steady myself, to be like Ezryn and think before I speak. "I find the scariest beasts aren't the ones with teeth and claws, but the ones that hide behind a smile."

We hold each other's gazes—his that terrible dark void beneath the protruding metal brow—before he chuckles, deep and haunting.

"I happen to love things that scare me, Lady O'Connell." He turns to the tapestry. "As you are a new-born fae and my brother has not seen fit to educate you, let me. I have often taught the youngest acolytes of our history."

I shift back to the art, keeping Kairyn visible in my peripheral.

"At the dawning of time, there was only the Realm Above, a place of ethereal beauty. And it owed its radiance to the Gardens of Ithilias, a celestial rosebush that bathed the realm in its divine light."

He sweeps his hand up toward the top image. A celestial rosebush … My heart thuds with anticipation.

"The fae lived here in peace and serenity. And yet, not all were happy to be bathed in the light. A fae woman coveted a land of her own. So, she stole a precious flower from the rosebush and, with its magic, forged the Realm Below."

My eyes catch on the scene underneath the nebulous clouds: a fae woman is sewn into the threads, her eyes glinting even in the fabric. Her black hair flows behind her as she pulls a rose from its stem.

"In her new realm, the woman used the stolen rose to breed creations of her own, monsters crafted of the darkened soil of her realm."

"The goblins," I whisper.

"And the like." It almost sounds like there's a smile behind Kairyn's lips, and I realize I must appear captivated.

Because I am.

"The fae woman who stole the rose," I breathe. "What was her name?"

Kairyn's fists clench. "Sira, Queen of the Below."

I've heard the name. Farron's words drift back to me from months ago: *Someone even Caspian is afraid of.*

Kairyn continues: "For her treachery in stealing the rose, Sira was banished from the Realm Above. In retaliation, she waged war upon those who had wronged her, unleashing her creations onto the celestial city. Despite their courage, the fae of the Realm Above knew not the ways of war. Sira destroyed the rosebush, and the Realm Above was lost."

I can't help it; my fingers drift over the images Kairyn depicts: the rosebush throttled by darkness, the clouds caving in on themselves. "That can't be the end."

"It wasn't." Kairyn reaches out and takes my hand in his, directing me to a new image. One of an ethereal fae drenched in light. Four roses float around her head. "A brave fae named Aurelia sensed the impending doom and severed four flowers from the rosebush before its demise."

"Aurelia," I whisper. "The Queen."

"From the ashes of devastation, she crafted a new world and grew a grand castle, a tree imbued with the fallen magic of the Realm Above." His voice lowers. "A twisted throne of power."

I trace the edges of the brilliant tree, my heart blooming like its branches. "Castletree." *Home.*

Kairyn's movements are slow, languishing, as he leads me across the tapestry to the next image: a fabric version of the mosaic I saw earlier. "From the plucked roses, she created four realms, and bequeathed them to her four most loyal servants. She named them princes and princesses, forever binding the magic of these realms to hers. The self-proclaimed Queen of the Enchanted Vale sat upon her throne with vengeance in her heart."

I turn to Kairyn. "What do you mean, vengeance?"

"The war was far from over, Lady O'Connell. Aurelia had lost her first home and suddenly had dominion over not one realm, but five. And she intended to make Sira pay for what she had taken."

Before I can ask another question, Kairyn places his hand on the small of my back again. "Come. I will show you more than art."

Kairyn leads me into an elevator shaft: a strange combination of mechanical engineering and the spark of magic. The back is completely open, revealing the twisting river down the mountain and Florendel far in the distance. He places his finger on the door and traces a rune. My stomach leaps into my throat as we shoot up.

Seconds turn into minutes as we continue flying up, up, up. Kairyn says nothing. I twiddle my fingers around and around. The silence sits between us, heavy and awkward.

Finally, I can't take it anymore. "So, you live here?"

"Yes."

"Do … Do you like it?"

"No."

Okay, this has transitioned from awkward to super awkward. At least in front of the tapestry, we could talk about the artwork.

I glance over my shoulder. "At least your view was nice?"

A heavy exhale sounds from beneath his helm. "I suppose there are certain benefits to residing in this place."

"Oh yeah? Good food? Comfy bed?"

The elevator shudders to a stop, and Kairyn grabs my elbow, steadying me before I pitch forward. The doors creak open. "My brother doesn't live here." Then he stomps out on to the floor.

Let it go, Rosalina, I chide myself. But I guess becoming fae didn't make me smarter. "You don't like being around Ez?"

Kairyn stops walking. "Ez…" he mumbles, shaking his head. "*Ez.* You sound like that fool Keldarion."

We're now in a narrow stone hallway. I look out of a small arched window to my right, and my legs nearly give way. The horizon is long-gone; only clouds are visible. I have never been this high up in my life.

Kairyn swings around, black cape swishing behind him. "Even you. They call you the Golden Rose after what you pulled in Autumn. Fated mate to High Prince Farron. And even you…"

I cross my arms. "*Even I* what?"

His words are slow, as if speaking to a child. "Even you don't see it. No one ever has." He turns and storms down the hallway. "Until I make them see."

"Wait!" I pull up the hem of my skirt and run after him. The narrow hallway opens up on one side, overlooking a courtyard. I gasp; hundreds of soldiers are training in perfect unison, their movements fluid as a dance.

Kairyn stands above them, watching.

"What can't I see?" I pant to catch my breath.

He sighs. "It doesn't matter."

"Then tell me the rest of the story." I touch his forearm. The act seems to startle him, and he looks down on my fingers upon his armor.

There's something almost innocent in his apprehension. I try to hold his gaze through the visor. Ezryn was like this when I first met him: stern yet skittish. Maybe I can show Kairyn that things have changed at Castletree, that he and Ezryn could rebuild the bonds that were broken.

Kairyn's helmet tilts, and he seems to look lower, below my eyes. "There was still more blood to be shed. And the Queen was quick to spill it."

He pulls away from me and continues down the hall. I scurry to keep up. "Not only acolytes and clerics live here, but also the Queen's Army, an elite army that the Queen would call on in times of war. And she would call on the High Rulers, too. The first High Prince of Spring forged five divine weapons, one for each of the rulers of the realms: Winter, Spring, Summer, Autumn, and the Queen's Realm."

The Queen's Realm. The home of Castletree, what we now call the Briar. It must have looked so different back then.

"When wielded together," Kairyn continues, "the five weapons were said to be able to summon an impossible magic. Some legends even say they could open a way to the remnants of the Above."

Kairyn leads me up a winding staircase. My heart beats at a frantic pace, the story like electricity. I can barely breathe, let alone speak.

"Though war raged for many years, Sira and her creations were eventually defeated. They slunk back into the Below ... at least for a time. Queen Aurelia decreed that in periods of peace, there was no need to wield weapons of such immense strength. The monastery had just been created, and so they were kept here, at the very top, for safe-keeping."

"Isn't that dangerous? Anyone could come up and take one."

"It is not so simple. Aurelia was clever. She enchanted each of the weapons so that they could only be wielded by one who wore her token."

"No one else could pick them up?" I breathe.

Kairyn gives another dark laugh. "Oh, anyone could pick them up. It would just drain their life and corrupt their blood until they were nothing but shallow husks."

"Heck of a system," I mumble.

We reach a door at the end of the stairwell, and Kairyn stops walking. He's looking at me again. Not at my eyes. Further down.

At my moonstone necklace.

I quickly slip it beneath my dress.

Kairyn turns away and throws open the door. We come to a small, circular room. Wind whips through the open arched windows. Five pedestals arc around the space, all except one gilded with a beautiful weapon. There's a massive hammer carved with steel vines, a glowing teal trident, a copper lance sparkling in the sun, and...

I step forward.

A bow.

A bow unlike anything I've ever seen. Its delicate frame, crafted from shimmering moonstone and steel, is adorned with golden constellations. Its string pulses with radiant energy.

I extend my hand toward it—

"I wouldn't do that if I were you." Kairyn grabs my shoulder. "The Bow of Radiance was Aurelia's own weapon. The corruption seems to work ... quicker on those who touch it. Unless," his voice lowers, "you somehow wielded the Queen's token."

"Why would the Queen create a token for her own weapon? Wouldn't she be able to wield it?"

"Of course. The Queen could brandish any with no consequences. Some believe she made a token for her bow in the happenstance she ever came upon her fated mate and wished for them to take up arms."

I nearly clutch my necklace but stop. I suddenly have a great desire to get Kairyn's eyes off of me. "Do the others have names?"

"Of course. There's Summer's Trident of Honor, Autumn's Lance of Valor, and Spring's own Hammer of Hope."

Gesturing to the bare pedestal, I say, "What belongs there?"

"The Sword of the Protector. Before the Queen disappeared, she granted Winter protection over the realms in her absence. It has been passed from High Ruler to High Ruler and is now in the care of the current High Prince."

"Keldarion."

Kairyn walks to a window and looks out. "He must have it with him in Castletree. Perhaps you've seen it?"

An embarrassing memory flashes through my mind of being blackout drunk and swinging this sacred sword around like a toy. I guess it's a good thing I didn't hold it for longer or it probably would have started to taint my blood. I hadn't felt any corruption at all when I'd held the icy hilt in my hand. "Can't say I have."

"A shame," Kairyn mutters. "Perhaps if we had all five weapons, we could rid Castletree of its corruption."

A chill runs down my back. "I should probably head back to the entrance hall. I'm sure Ezryn and Farron are looking for me."

Kairyn nods and walks back over to the door, holding it open. "Thank you for indulging my stories, Lady O'Connell," Kairyn rumbles as I walk past him. "It has been a great pleasure to finally meet you."

I stop and stare up at him. "They are simply stories, aren't they? Legends?"

"Oh, I'm not so sure, Lady O'Connell. Legends have a way of becoming all too real when the time is right."

The weight of his answer hangs over me as I descend the stairs. I place a hand on my necklace. What if these are more than stories?

What if I'm part of them?

33

EZRYN

The shadow of the monastery stretches long before me. Rosalina gives a wave from atop her ibex, and Farron offers me a smile as he mounts his own.

"You're not going down with them?" Kairyn stands beside me.

"No. I came up here to speak with you."

Farron and I found Rosalina and Kairyn in the entrance hall after we were done inspecting the Spring steel. She explained she'd run into him while investigating some art, and he'd shown her a couple of the other relics in the monastery. I'd felt a twinge of unease seeing them together. My brother has never been what I would call a gracious host. Rosalina didn't appear bothered by his presence. If anything, she seemed distracted, lost in her thoughts. Though that is not unlike her. Perhaps she's someone who could find common ground with Kairyn—they're both dreamers, in that sense.

Kairyn doesn't turn to face me. "You have come to deliver my punishment."

"It is my right. You deliberately disobeyed your banishment." My words are steady, even if my mind reels. *I need to make a decision.*

Kairyn's breathing quickens. "I did not disobey you out of arrogance or spite, I swear it, brother. Spring was in danger; someone needed to act. How long was I to wait? For Father to recover? For the Queen to return? For the High Prince to—" He cuts himself off before muttering, "I couldn't stay up here, rotting away while I watched my people suffer."

I pause before answering. Instead, I search his dark helm as if I could find answers there.

Arrogance and spite—that was exactly what I sensed when I saw him atop my throne. But maybe those were the easy things for me to see. A resentful boy disobeying his brother.

When I look at him now, I observe the tremble in his fingers, listen to the hitch in his breath.

He is frightened of me. Of the judgment I may pass.

The realization makes my chest tighten.

Farron told me I'd done right by my family. It isn't true. If I had done right, I wouldn't hear Kairyn's voice as the narrator of my every painful thought.

In our youth, how many times had I been invited to councils while Kai was stuck waiting outside the door? How many times had I chosen to spend months in Winter or entertain Keldarion here, instead of paying attention to my own blood? Whenever my father needed a second in a tournament, he chose me. Whenever I needed one, I chose Kel.

I always had my reasons. Kairyn was too blunt for councils, too rash for tournaments. Despite being brothers, we never saw the world in the same light as Kel and I did.

Is it too late?

Wind rips at our capes, blowing them in near synchronicity. I square my shoulders to Kairyn. "Tell me the truth about the Spring steel."

He speaks quickly. "Villages all across the Starweaver Mountains were falling to raids. Our people were dying. *Our* people. The acolytes must be able to defend themselves—"

"I'm not asking why you brought the steel here. I understand your reasoning, and I agree with it."

Kairyn quirks his helm. "You … agree with me?"

"I need to know how the Below got their hands on it. Speak honestly. Did you lose one of your shipments?"

Kairyn pauses, the hesitancy itself a confirmation. The prideful boy won't admit ...

I stop myself. Not pride, but shame. Something we brothers of Spring know too much about.

That painful tightening in my chest triggers again, realizing how much of that shame I instilled in him. I took every opportunity I could to correct his errors. To prove to Mother and Father I was worthy of being the next High Ruler of Spring.

"I have made many mistakes," Kairyn finally says, voice a low tremble. "But each one has been made in service of a greater vision. This, I swear."

The sun has slowly shifted across the horizon, taking the monastery's shadow with it. Kairyn's own silhouette now stands apart.

"You're not the only one who's made mistakes, Kai," I murmur. "If we're to rectify them, then now, more than ever, we must trust each other."

I stare down at his shadow, the void engulfing the grass. Would Spring have been better off if I had trusted Kairyn back when he first challenged me to the Rite? If I had let him take my rule?

He may be disobedient and arrogant. But he's never caused the harm that I have.

"Trust each other?" Kairyn repeats. "You are asking for my trust?" There's anger in his voice. Hatred.

All this time, I've thought he should be grateful when I chose to banish him to the monastery. I could have had him killed, or worse: unhelmed. But why would he be grateful? He saw the life vanish from our mother. Watched me leave Spring in the hands of our father, whose grief had claimed every piece of his spirit.

No wonder he hates me.

And it would be so easy to hate him. I close my eyes, and my thoughts drift down the mountain toward Rosalina. She offers her kindness for free and shows forgiveness to those many would deem unworthy. I've seen how her compassion has chased the darkness from my brothers—my *other* brothers, the ones who live at Castletree.

If I learn from her, then maybe I can chase away the darkness between Kairyn and me. We can find a new path forward.

"I do not want to be your enemy, Kai," I say.

Kairyn paces toward the cliffside, then spins back to the monastery. Finally, he stops with a deep sigh. "I never wanted to be yours."

This is my opportunity. I need to speak with Kairyn about the one thing we've never spoken about before. The reason he evoked the Rite against me. The reason I can't stop his voice from repeating over and over in my head.

The reason I will always doubt if I made the right choice keeping the Blessing instead of passing it to him.

I part my lips to speak, but instead, the haunting echo of her scream reverberates in my mind. My blood rushes as it did the day the Blessing first passed through me. Kairyn remains as motionless as when he bore witness to my actions.

I can't speak about it with him, not yet. So, I choose other words instead. "Come back to Florendel with me."

He goes still. "What?"

"Due to your courageous actions in protecting the Starweaver Mountains, I hereby lift your banishment."

"You're not going to punish me?" he asks hesitantly.

I try something I've never done with Kai. Lightheartedness. "I could send you to the Anelkrol Badlands, but I have a feeling even that wouldn't keep you from our people."

His gaze drifts over the cliffside, toward Keep Hammergarden in the distance. "I don't understand."

"I want us to return home. Together."

"I … am absolved." A strange sound emits from under his mask. I think it may be a laugh. "And you accept me as your steward?"

That makes me pause. Of course, I cannot allow Kairyn to keep his own imposed stewardship. I told him as much in the throne room. *You will never be my steward.* "No. Father will maintain the title of steward, and I shall remain in Florendel to rule. It's what I should have been doing all these years." I place my hand on Kairyn's shoulder. He looks down at it, and his body goes rigid. I realize this is the first time I've touched him since his banishment. "Kairyn, you have shown your loyalty to Spring. Now, you must show your loyalty to me."

34

ROSALINA

S nowflakes melt on my heated skin, and a chill weaves through the loose fabric of my nightdress. I'm dreaming—I feel it in the way the edges of this place become like clouds of mist and I can't quite make out the horizon through the window, only a wavering line of snow-capped mountains.

The white wolf is very clear. He's curled in a ball next to a drab bed. *Where are you, Kel?* Slowly, I kneel to gently pet his ears. His fur is soft beneath my fingers as if he were right in front of me.

"Rosalina?" he asks, sharp blue eyes cracking open. His head tilts, the great snout pressing into me, sniffing. Something about my scent must have awakened him because he stands in a flurry. He gives a low, playful growl and knocks me to my back—and suddenly the floor feels very real beneath me.

A rough tongue drags from my collarbone to cheek, and I giggle at the sensation. The wolf stills at my laughter, and I realize he likely thought he was in this dream alone. Those blue eyes narrow.

"I'm really here. At least a part of me is." I wrap my arms around his massive neck. There's a strange rippling beneath my fingertips. Then a large and completely naked fae male hovers above me.

"It seems even in dreams you have power over me," he growls. Then he scoops me up. "Though I'll not have my mate suffer a cold floor."

He takes us to the bed, which is comfier than it looks, with thick quilts and a soft mattress. Kel lies down with me atop of him, head on his chest.

"I know I shouldn't be touching you," I whisper, my fingers running along his soft chest hair. "Though if I move away, you'll become a wolf again."

"Perhaps I need not stay away from you in my dreams."

My body thrills at this notion, this moment where he's not pushing me away. I snuggle deeper. "I thought you'd return when you received our letter. Kel, the goblins wanted your sword."

His arms tighten around me. "I wanted to return. But I knew you were safe."

"How long until you come back?" He doesn't reply, and a wave of anxiety washes over me. "How long?"

Keldarion is silent for a moment before he says, "I keep trying to do the right thing. But my choices always lead someone to suffering."

I lay my palm flat on his chest. "Your heart will tell you the right thing to do."

He rolls slightly, white, messy locks falling across his face. "I fear I lost ownership of that when a certain human wandered into my castle."

How can I have your heart but not your love? I wonder. His gaze saddens. *Did he hear me through the bond?* "Half-human," I say, smiling.

"Ahh, yes." He caresses the sharp point of my ear.

The way he's gazing at me, that look he gets … It's almost reverent. I trail my fingers along his jaw to the dip in the middle of his chin.

"I want to help you with your choices, but I can't with all the secrets you keep. Don't you trust me?"

"I do, Rose." He shakes his head. "But if you knew the things I have done in my past, you would not look at me the same."

"You've seen my scars and never judged me. You said your heart is mine, so *trust me* with it." Gently, I touch the bracelet of frozen thorns on his wrist. "Tell me about your bargain with Caspian."

He stiffens, then sighs. "When I return, I will try to tell you, but—"

"All I ask is you try," I whisper. And I see my own wrists as well. My own thorn bracelets with Caspian, two thin circlets. I'll tell him of my bargain with the Prince of Thorns then, and afterward, explain it to the other princes.

The promise seems to relax us both, and he pulls me into his embrace until I'm wrapped up in the scent of pine.

"I wonder if you shall stay with me all night," Kel says almost wistfully. I haven't been able to lie with him like this since our time in the Autumn Realm, when we would all make a little nest outside Farron's room.

"I hope so," I whisper. "I feel better now."

He stiffens. "Were you ill?"

"A slight fever before bed, and my stomach cramped a little." A different kind of heat rises in me. Could these symptoms also be...

Kel's large hand slides down my side before settling on my belly as he begins to rub soft circles over the silky fabric of my nightdress. I inhale and squeeze my legs together as an intense wave of heat envelopes me.

I feel the ripple of change in Kel's body as he senses my immediate and all-consuming arousal.

"I think I know why our mating bond took me here, tonight of all nights." The ache in my stomach tightens, and I resist the urge to grab his hand and shove it lower.

"Isn't Farron there to help you with your needs?" Kel asks, a rough edge to his words.

"We made love earlier, but he went to Hammergarden's library before bed. Most likely fell asleep there," I say, voice heady. "This is different. The bond with him is satisfied. But—"

"I cannot satisfy you in the way a mate should."

Is this what Farron and I read about, the *wilde courtship*? A jolt of satisfaction ripples through me at all the places my body touches Kel's. "It's the mating frenzy," I try to explain, "due to the fact we haven't completed our bond."

He inhales sharply. "I will not chance anything with you, Rose. Even in this dream."

I nod. "I need to wake up." Pressing on his chest to rise, a throbbing courses through my body. My skin grows feverish and hot, the silky fabric of my nightdress rubbing teasingly against my aching breasts.

"Yes—" Kel cuts off. His eyes darken like dye swirling in water. Is this the *wilde courtship* taking him over as well?

Before I have time to question further, he pulls me down. His lips crash over mine, and I sigh at the contact. All the discomfort evaporates into delicious pleasure.

My legs spread on either side of his hips, and his hard length grinds against my already soaking panties.

"Kel, wait," I gasp when I break away for air. "There's nothing I want more than this. But you don't.."

He ignores me, his mouth trailing along my neck. "You are mine," he growls before he bites down. I cry out at the euphoric thrill of pain and pleasure.

"I'm yours," is all I gasp back.

He licks the tender spot before he reaches down and all I hear is a tearing sound before I realize he's ripped my underwear completely off. There's a quick flutter of cold air, then the hard length of his cock rubs against my entrance. Our moans mingle at the sensation.

"No, stop," I whimper as I glide against the steel-hard length, wanting more than anything for him to move inside of me. "I could never regret being with you, but I don't want you to regret being with me."

It's all I can manage through this haze, this mating frenzy. Every part of me craves him. Pure male sounds erupt from the back of his throat. I'm under his complete control. His arms wrap around me like a vise. He's so strong. He tears my nightgown easily, parts of it sliding away to expose one of my breasts. His large, rough hand runs over the softness and squeezes. His other reaches under my dress to cup my ass.

Lapping a tongue over a nipple, he continues a wet trail up my chest, along my neck to my lips. "Mine," he growls, deep and possessive.

"Yours," I breathe, completely at his mercy.

He flips us until he's hovering above me. Power ripples through him, veins bulging in his neck and arms. Light flashes in from the moon and for a moment, his eyes almost appear to glow. Right now, he reminds me more of his wolf than any fae man. Raw, animalistic with strength and desire. And every instinct in him right now is to mate with ... me.

Claim me.

I am nothing but willing and eager. My knees fall open, revealing my slick entrance, and his gaze goes feral with hunger.

He's going to have me. Something I have dreamed of, longed for. Will it break his curse to make love to me like this here? Will it free Winter and restore his magic?

Trying to fight through this haze of fog and *need*, I shut my eyes. I will not have him like this, not until I know he really wants me. If I don't leave now, I don't know how much longer my self-control will hold. I try to ground myself in my bed, thinking of the smell of flowers and stone, the soft sheets. Try to think of something far, far away from the cold, away from my mate.

I open my eyes just as he's about to descend on me. "I'm sorry, Kel." And then I'm falling. Sheets and pillows tumble around me. With a jolt, I sit up.

I'm in a dark room, my chambers in the Spring Realm. My skin is still feverish and, without Kel's touch, the ache in my body returns. And strangely enough, my dress is still ripped, panties gone. My core throbs, the scent of pine still lingering over me. But I wasn't really there, was I?

Something blooms in my chest, light and sparkly. A shadow moves in the corner of my room. For a moment, I wonder if somehow Kel came here with me.

"Farron?" I ask breathily.

"No." The darkness wavers, then the Prince of Thorns staggers out of the shadows.

35

ROSALINA

"What are you doing here?" I gasp, pulling my ripped dress over my exposed breast.

Caspian doesn't reply. He only staggers and grips on to the bed's banister as if it's the only thing keeping him upright. The loose strands of dark hair shadowing his face make him look utterly disheveled. He wears an oversized tunic, laces undone to show most of his chest, and tight breeches. And curiously, no shoes.

"What are you doing here?" I ask again, still fighting for control of my voice. The incessant heat refuses to leave even without Kel's presence.

"I—" His voice is a broken rasp, and in the shadows, I can't see the flecks of purple in his eyes. They're only black.

"I'm not giving back your book," I spit.

A low, dangerous laugh echoes from him. "I'm not here for the book."

What is he here for then? I think of Kel's sword, tucked protectively under my bed. Does he know it's here? Blood pounds so fast in my ears I can't hear my own thoughts. Caspian pushes himself off the bed post and the mattress sinks as he crawls on top of it.

As he crawls on to *my* bed.

I scramble back, hitting the headboard, drawing my knees up to my chest. "If you're here for the payment of your bargain, remember I get to choose when and where."

He laughs darkly. Then a thorn wraps around my ankle and drags me down until I'm flat on my back, legs spread, ripped dress awry. He places a hand on either side of my head. "So, choose now."

Choose me, he purrs inside my mind.

I blink up at him, the soft full lips, thickly lashed eyes, all fixed in an utterly desperate expression.

"Caspian," I whisper.

The effect of his name on my lips, travels through him like a current. His hands tighten into fists in the blanket.

He dips his head, lips traveling to my neck. A sharp jolt of pain courses through me as he presses his tongue into the mark Kel made. "Fulfill your bargain, Rosalina."

"Not yet," I say, but the words are only a breath. A half-formed thought.

I could use the thorns to push him away. I could reach out through my bond for Farron. I could call for help.

But I don't.

Instead, I stay still. I let him crawl over me. Let him put his hand on my face and smooth the hair back.

Because it soothes this ache inside me. Because despite everything, I realize with sickening horror, I *want* the Prince of Thorns to touch me. Maybe a dark part of me has wanted this since I first saw him in the garden of Castletree.

His teeth nip the space right above Kel's mark, and I squirm with the sensation. His breath is warm as he brings his face right in front of mine.

If he kisses me right now, I'm not sure I'll stop him. I'm not sure I want to.

The thought ignites me with anger, and I growl, "I have a mate."

His eyelids flutter, and a devastatingly handsome smile spreads on his face. "I know you do."

36

CASPIAN

Her lips are parted, brown eyes wide, cheeks red as roses. If I kissed her right now, she wouldn't stop me.

Thorns wrap around my ankles, curling up the rest of my body. Her chest heaves in deep breaths of air, and maybe it's my cruel imagination, but when the thorns and shadows drag me back to the Below, I almost see a flicker of disappointment on her gorgeous features.

My magic isn't as precise as it used to be, and I arrive in a Cryptgarden corridor close to my room. A heat courses through my body, every muscle as achy as when I woke up an hour ago in sweat-soaked sheets.

Coarse laughter sounds from down the hall, and a fae sentry flanked by two goblins rounds the corner. Aldridge Menzies, one of my mother's favorites. Though she doesn't *actually* have favorites … Moreso, he's one of her more tolerated sentries.

"Quite an unbecoming sight, milord." Aldridge laughs. "Perhaps retire to your room before the liquor takes over."

The goblins beside him chitter with laughter. Normally they wouldn't dare, but they're emboldened by his insolence.

Drunk, is that how I look? Stars, I'd rather be drunk than feel *this*.

"I do not recall giving you permission to speak," I snarl. Using the wall as leverage to stand, I push past them.

Behind me, thorns break through the stone, and I hear Aldridge's gasp of shock. Most days I can stand his impertinent comments.

Today isn't most days.

By the time I round the corner, his cry of pain as the thorns rip off his hand is muted. Mother won't be pleased, but depending on her mood she may overlook it, figuring I let him live.

I pass an open veranda to where another party rages in the courtyard. The smell of sex mingles with liquor.

There are always any number of willing participants lurking around Cryptgarden ready to lie with the Prince of the Below. And though Kel may have cast me as his villain, even I won't send any of these hapless souls to the icy wasteland that bastard has sequestered himself in.

And besides…

Stop or I'll die.

The agony in her voice, the pain that coursed through her body, though she didn't realize why. No, I can't do that to her.

But I have to do *something*. Do something now before I go back and—

A growl rises within me, and I strike the stone wall with my fist. It leaves a solid crack, along with blood on my knuckles. *I shouldn't have gone there.*

He would kill me if I lost control. He would rip me apart and tear me limb from limb. The death of his parents, the downfall of his realm, the betrayal … Keldarion let me live through all of it. But I do not suspect he would let me live through that.

Though how sweet it would be. Perhaps even worth my life.

I won't make it to my room. I push open the next stone door I can find. Nothing but an abandoned corridor full of dusty artifacts from the Vale. A single window lets in a strip of murky gray light.

My clothes feel itchy, too heavy on my heated skin. I pull off my tunic and unbutton my breeches, stepping out of them until I'm completely naked. Running my hands down my body, a pained sound leaves my throat as my fingers grasp my aching cock.

But it's not the touch I want.

Falling hard to my knees, my hand begins to move furiously as I curse. "Fuck, fuck, fuck." I try not to think of her at all. I especially try not to think of her in moments like this.

But tonight, Rosalina has invaded every aspect of my being.

She'd been there—and yet not there—when I'd arrived in her room. Body still in sleep, but eyes moving rapidly beneath the lids. Things were happening even I couldn't explain. A bruise forming on her neck, a ripped dress. The smell of her arousal filling the space like a toxic perfume.

She'd been with him. The desperation of her want for Keldarion sang through my blood like a familiar tune.

Until she'd returned.

"I should have kissed you," I gasp out, slowing my strokes, watching the pre-cum drip out of my tip. "Should have kissed you and filled you."

The words are a desperate promise that can never be. My cock aches for release, but I don't give it to myself yet. Inside, I follow my mind's wondering of how it would be. Pushing Rosalina's hair back and filling that long neck with more marks until she was properly claimed.

Peeling her dress off and taking in her body. Then I'd run my mouth over every dip and curve until I got lower. My lips quirk. *Kel had already taken care of her panties.* Not that my princess is overly fond of those.

Her sweet nectar would be readily available. I lick my lips, groaning, cock twitching. How easy it is to imagine taking her, the sounds she'd make, her face...

What sort of expressions would she make?

The way she looks at me with a hatred that doesn't reach her eyes. *And why is that?* There's no goodness in me to see, that's for sure. Maybe there's a small part of her that recognizes that I would *never* hurt her. That I would never let anyone else hurt her.

I know one thing. I'd fill her, claim her, make her watch only me as we exploded in pleasure together.

Then I'd watch her disappear. To him.

The vision changes...

Her lying before Kel, naked and completely wrecked by me. What would he do? Take her right away, trying to establish his claim like a big, brooding alpha? He'd do it fast, with strength, powerful strokes that would wrack her whole body. And oh, she'd melt into him, every soft curve of her against his hard edges. His giant cock sliding in and out of her pussy, already filled with my seed.

The thought is enough to send me over the edge. My cry echoes off the walls as I spill into my palm, collapsing to the ground as the pleasure of it courses through me. My lashes flutter closed, and I allow myself one moment to revel in this bliss.

Well, did you feel that, lovers?

37

EZRYN

My brother's footsteps thud in the cool stairway as we descend into the bowels of Keep Hammergarden. The sporadic torches along the walls are the only light in this place.

I want to show you something. He'd found me in the throne room this afternoon and said those words to me. For a second, I almost heard them in his small, boyish voice, the one he had when we were but children running about the mountains on our own until returning to the keep covered in dirt. Back then, he'd wanted to show me colorful frogs or crickets. How many times had I dismissed him? Now, I follow behind.

"During my servitude at the monastery, there was much time for contemplation. I dreamt of Florendel, of how we could restore peace and stability to our realm," Kairyn says, his voice echoing off the cloistered walls.

My brother, the visionary. He has not changed in that regard. "What did these dreams entail?"

We're taking the underground path only accessible from the keep by the hatch in the secret room behind the throne. Only the royal family and our most trusted staff know about it.

Kairyn stops before the metal doors that lead into the caves within the mountains. "Follow me."

He yanks open the door and gestures me into the massive cave beyond. It's lit by a large opening in the mountainside, where dusky light streams in. My breath catches as I stumble, looking up. "Kai, you made this?"

"Designed it. With help from a team. Engineers, artists, forgers. Do you want to see inside?"

A laugh erupts from my throat. "Of course I do."

Stationed inside the cave is a vessel unlike anything I've ever seen before.

It is a ship cast in dark wood, the sharp, pointed features giving it an ominous elegance. Atop its prow stands a mythical drake figure-head, its jagged teeth jutting forth in an eternal battle cry.

The smoky black sails unfurl from the towering masts, resembling the outstretched wings of a gargantuan bat, as if the vessel itself were a creature of the night.

Kairyn nearly runs forward, and I follow him, eyes fixed on the creation before me. "An airship. Kai, how did you manage it?"

"That's just it. I fixed the monastery, and then it was time to turn my attention to Spring. We used to be inventors, great forgers and steelworkers. What creations have come from Spring in the last century? Nothing. But this ... This will change everything. Travel to other realms, moving resources, transporting armies—"

"Well, hopefully we won't need any of those soon." I clap my brother on his back. "It's magnificent."

Maybe I'm imagining it, but Kairyn seems to grow an inch taller, pride shimmering off him like heat from the sun. "I'll take you aboard."

"Perfect—" My gaze shifts to the opening in the cave, to the orange sun dripping down over the horizon. "Actually, can we do it tomorrow? I have somewhere I need to be."

Kairyn follows my gaze to the fading light. "Of course. Tomorrow then."

He escorts me back up the stairs, and we part ways with a handshake.

I never knew Kairyn had the ability to design such an invention, let alone see it through to fruition. My mind reels with all the possibilities. Perhaps we could load it with supplies and take it to Autumn to assist any villages that were damaged during the frost, or even use it to visit Kel in the—

"Where have you been?" A voice cuts through my thoughts as I turn the corner toward my chambers.

Dayton leans on the wall outside my door, arms crossed and a scowl on his face.

I walk past him, opening the door and going inside. He follows me. "I was attending to matters with my brother."

"That's who I came to talk to you about." Anger laces Dayton's voice. He runs to get ahead of me, blue eyes shining. "You absolved his banishment? Are you mad?"

"It is my right to decide when Kairyn has atoned for his crime. I would have him here at the keep with me."

"It sounds more like you let *him* decide when he was done. You know as well as I do that Kairyn's stability hangs by a thread on a good day."

I shove Dayton out of my way and walk to the window, staring out at my keep. "He's not the same person he was."

Dayton doesn't understand. His oldest brother, Damocles, cherished and mentored him. The two of them were inseparable. But I never gave Kairyn so much as a kind word. The Summer Prince rushes after me, grabbing my shoulder. "What about the missing Spring steel?"

"A shipment was raided. I will work with Kairyn to ensure it does not happen again."

"So, that's it? He would have willingly killed you during the Rite. You know that, don't you? Now, you're just going to let him go free?"

How do I explain to Dayton that if Damocles were still alive, he would do everything he could to give Dayton a second-chance? "Kairyn had his reasons for challenging me. I respect that."

Dayton scoffs. "Your honor will be the death of you."

"Enough!" I push Dayton back. "What is this? Keldarion is gone and now you have to step up and fill his role? Are you trying to be like him?"

"Are *you*?" Dayton growls. "Willfully ignorant, trusting someone against everyone else's judgment, turning away from the facts when they're right in front of you—now *that's* like Kel."

"He's my brother!" I roar.

Dayton steps back, a look of hurt on his face. He turns and walks to the door. "Just remember, 'brother' is what you once called Cas. Didn't stop him from betraying all of us."

38

DAYTON

My world narrows to the points of my swords and the sound of metal hitting the wooden dummy. Step, slash, step, slash. I put myself through every routine and exercise my old trainer beat into my thick skull. Step, slash. My arms twirl, my feet falling into a practiced rhythm as my breath evens to a familiar cadence.

I push past the ache in my muscles and the frantic beating of my heart. Sweat coats my brow, my palms, and I tighten my grip. Roaring, I spin and bring my swords down.

Wood splinters and the dummy cracks in half. My chest heaves, and I blink sweat out of my eyes. The dummy is reduced to rubble, nothing but a carved-up husk. Around me, the training yard is completely still, and everyone that had been practicing is watching me. *Didn't realize I'd garnered an audience.*

One of the squires rushes up to me. "It's not often we get to witness someone from Summer train, especially of your skill, my Prince. It is a most exceptional feat. Please allow me to replace this for you."

Nodding, I step away from the gravel square. Florendel's training ground is located on an upper level of Keep Hammergarden, partially covered. Half of it looks over the city to the landscape beyond.

Certainly is beautiful for such a hard people. Below us are the royal gardens. I can see they dragged out old Thalionor for some air. Sun glints off his armored helm, but the rest of him is covered in a thick quilt. A few acolytes mull around him, picking flowers. One of them turns to look up, then lowers her hood.

Wrenley. She smiles and gives me a wave before turning back to the prince. I grasp the string of seashells around my neck, tilting my chin to look at the beautiful golden shell she'd gifted me. *It's fate.* I can't help but drift my gaze to the rolling hills beyond Florendel where two people are walking through a rainbow of wildflowers.

Rosalina and Farron. I take a drag of cold water from my flask. Their movements are delicate, almost as if in a ballet. They're two small figures on the horizon, no bigger than dolls, but it's like I can feel the love between them. A dusky pink line blankets the horizon. I hadn't realized how long I'd been in here. Fare doesn't care if the sun sets.

Not anymore.

On the other side of the rolling wildflower hill is a bobbing cluster of blue lights. "Those lights over there … Are they—?"

"Ahh, yes. The Lights of Fate." The squire comes up beside me. "We often see them on the hills. They like the flowers."

"Lights of Fate," I repeat, absently rubbing my chest, trying not to think of the last time one of those buggers landed on me. Showed me the tangled mess that is my mate bond. The Spring Realm may have another name for the will-o'-wisps, but I still don't want to get anywhere near them again.

"I've replaced the training equipment, sire." The squire nods, then retreats.

"How about training against something that fights back?" a voice calls from the entrance. "I think that block of wood is a bit below your skill level."

A smirk crawls up the corner of my mouth. "I suppose the High

Prince of Spring ranks a little higher than wood, but we'll see by how much."

Ezryn steps closer. We haven't spoken since our fight yesterday evening. He's in his usual helm, though his armor is lighter, looser, good for movement. He swings a large broadsword in one hand. The crowd moves to the edges of the training ground and murmurs with anticipation.

Ezryn turns to them and says, "You are dismissed."

A laugh booms out of my chest. "Don't want an audience for your defeat?"

"Only trying to protect the Summer Prince's reputation."

I step on to the gravel. Dressed for training, my chest is bare besides a leather wrapping around my waist. Sturdy sandals don my feet. But none of it really matters beside my twin swords. They're an extension of my arms, as much a part of me as my own hands. I twirl them, wondering how they'll hold up against that Spring armor.

The Spring Prince is as stoic as ever as he steps forward. "Ready?"

"Always." I grin.

He rushes me, positioning his sword over his head before bringing it down in a wide arc. Tucking my swords into my chest, I somersault out of the way and come up behind him. Ez may be stronger, but I'm faster. I honed my training in the arena, where I learned to fight with unmatched agility and speed. I'd like to see him duck in that heavy metal.

We've sparred countless times before, but something feels different about today. Our disagreement from yesterday still sits in the forefront of my mind.

Eh, better for men like us to fight it out than talk, anyway. Letting out a fierce roar, I smash both my blades against his back. He pitches forward before whirling and catching me across the stomach, leaving a thin red line.

Hissing, I retreat a few steps. We haven't used practice weapons against each other in years, counting on our quick ability to heal and trusting each other's skill to never land a truly damaging blow. But damn if it doesn't sting sometimes.

With a resounding clash, our swords meet again. The impact reverberates through my arms, but I hold my ground. Ezryn's brute force pushes me back across the loose gravel.

"Just admit it," I growl.

"Admit what?"

I dance out of the lock. "That your brother is up to something. I'm not going to apologize for saying it." I strike with precision, aiming for the gaps in his armor.

Ezryn dodges. "I'm not here to talk about Kairyn."

Frustration grows heavy in my chest. The swords flurry through the air. Sparks erupt each time our blades collide, the sound echoing through the training ground like a battle cry. "Then why are you here?"

Ezryn ignores my question and swings his broadsword in a wide arc, attempting to knock me off balance. I sidestep the attack, my feet moving with the agility of a summer breeze. I strike low, aiming for his exposed leg, but Ez's reflexes are swift, and he parries.

Sweat drips from my brow, and my muscles ache from my already-long training session. But the Spring Prince doesn't relent. The sparring match continues, a dance of steel and skill.

Ez's strength pushes against me, but I evade his strikes with practiced ease. Neither of us can gain an advantage.

"Why are you here?" I scream again.

His silence is worse than any answer he could give, and my frustration only grows.

"Why are you here?" I strike at him with each word.

He blocks me every time.

I hate that I can't see his expression and the way I can't even hear his breath. He won't listen to me about his brother. But why would he? I'm just the drunken Prince of Summer who let his own brothers die. Who doesn't deserve his Blessing, only this curse—

My anger grows hotter, and my wolf rears inside me. He knows night is close. And maybe my eyes are glowing because there's a strange reflection in Ezryn's armor.

But it doesn't unnerve the armored asshole. He counters every attack, and it feels like the black T of his visor stares into my soul.

"They're mates!" The words come out of me unbidden in a half-feral snarl. And I'm so shocked by them I lose my grip and fall to my knees in the gravel. Pebbles fly up around me.

My body begins to shake. Shake like I walked into the damned Winter Realm. My sweat feels cold over my skin. "They're mates," I say again, as if it's the first time I realized it.

First time I really let it sink beneath my bones.

Ezryn carefully lowers his sword and puts a gloved hand on my shoulder, but the gesture causes me to lose the last of my strength. I fall against his chest.

Not unlike the time he healed my broken body in the Autumn Realm.

"They're perfect," I say, voice laden with exhaustion. "The two of them are perfect. Beautiful and kind and brave. Why shouldn't they be together? It makes so much sense. Kel, too. Someone to protect them when their hearts make them vulnerable."

"Dayton," Ezryn says. "Rosalina and Farron may be mates, but they love you."

Salty tears run into my mouth, and it reminds me of home. "There's no need for me. There's no place for me."

"That's not true." Ezryn touches my bicep, over the golden cuff that marks my bargain with Farron. I gave him access to my magic at any time as long as he never forgets the moment we made the bargain.

"A weak imitation. I don't suspect it's anything like a mate bond." I give a long sigh.

"My mother used to tell me not to mourn the flower in bloom because you know one day it will wilt, for then you are forsaking its beauty." Ezryn tilts his gaze to the horizon. "Their love for you blooms now, and you do not yet have a mate."

I inhale a shaky breath, grasping at my seashell necklace, and manage to sit up. "Is this why you're here? You knew I was about to break. How?"

"There are signs when a person has strong emotions caged," he says.

And just how long have you been caging your emotions, Ez?

39

ROSALINA

Carefully, I unroll the paper, taking caution not to smear the chalk rubbing. "Well, what do you make of it?"

Farron leans over my shoulder, golden glasses sliding down his nose. "It's old, certainly. This art style is ancient. Remember the stained glass in the monastery? You can see how they took inspiration from it."

I stare down at the paper, a rubbing my father sent in one of his latest letters. His travel companions, Farron's little brothers, use their magic to make his letters fly through the air, finding me wherever I am. Each letter contains updates on his quest to find my long-lost mother. A mother we now know is fae.

There are so many questions. How did she disguise herself as a human? Why didn't she tell him? Why did she leave a year after she had me?

This rubbing depicts a woman with hands spread high above her head as birds fly away. Papa's note reads: *It's a Pacific Wren. I know it. Your mother loved those birds. She always pointed them out. It means something, Rosie. I know it does.*

Farron hovers a hand over the picture. "The letter said he took this rubbing from ruins in northern Autumn. Do me a favor and grab that map we were looking at the other day."

Nodding, I make my way across the Spring archives. Though they don't hold quite the cozy charm of our library in the Autumn Wing of Castletree, they house many treasures. Books, records, and texts are all organized on metal shelves. High stone pillars lead up into the cavernous mountain side, and arched windows let in bright streams of light.

When we first entered, Farron had sniffed something along the lines of, "Books in a cave? The humidity!" But really, everything has been quite dry. Maybe it's an enchantment.

Standing on tiptoes, I grab an old scroll we'd taken down a few days ago following another lead from my father. He'd sent: *Can't get the word 'Aerantheis' out of my head. Mean anything to you?*

Turns out Aerantheis was an ancient city of Summer. Farron explained there's a legend that it sunk to the bottom of the sea, but the Queen blessed the fae who lived there with tails so they could live in the ocean. Quite the origin for mermaids. Though the mystery still stands on how my father knew that name. Maybe Billy or Dom mentioned it to him.

Did you grab the ancient map? Not the new one, Farron says in my mind.

I have it, I send back. We've been getting good at chatting in each other's minds. It's easy to do this close, but we've also managed from opposite sides of Keep Hammergarden. Unfortunately, we haven't quite figured out how to communicate when we're in separate realms, but I'm sure that will come. When Farron and I work together, I feel like we can do anything.

I make it back to our long stone table, and his gaze slides down my body like a touch. I can't help that the Spring dresses are so beautiful. Today, I'm dressed in an off-the-shoulder blouse with a billowing skirt, the hem embroidered with tiny flowers. My cheeks heat. Researching in a library reminds me of when we first met. He's so gorgeous like this: vest, glasses, and floppy hair.

Farron straightens and clears his throat. "Ah yes, that's the one."

"I know it is," I say, smirking.

We unroll the map, and he tracks his finger to the northern Autumn realmlands. "This must be where your father was. The ruin used to be a city called Calandorin." Farron gets that determined look, then he taps the side of his nose. "You know, there was a legend about that place. I wonder if these stony archives will have it."

He straightens and darts off into the stacks. While I wait, I take a seat next to another set of books. These texts are on mate bonds. One of the more fascinating is a collection of accounts trying to describe what it feels like to have a bond.

Mind speaking, a connection of the spirit, a sweeping fire that consumes body and soul. *Like the other night.* My mating frenzy. I'd explained to Farron in great detail how I felt like I was there with Kel, the mark on my neck … But I'd left out the other part. The visitor in my room.

Caspian had not been himself in that moment, and neither had I.

"Unfortunately, no luck. Not that I'm surprised. This is more of a tomb than a lib—" Farron rounds the corner. "Is everything all right?"

I breathe out a long sigh and tuck my hair behind my neck. "I'm fine. That's too bad there's nothing here about— What did you say the place was called?"

"Calandorin."

Calandorin. The name sparks something at the back of my mind. Quickly, I scramble in my pack. My fingers clutch a smooth leather spine. "I've been meaning to show you this. I think I saw mention of that city in here."

Farron hovers over me. "What is it?"

I thump the book on the table. Farron's eyes widen. He runs a long finger over the letters. "This book is ancient. There's a strange aura to it. Wherever did you find it?"

"I kind of stole it," I admit. "From Caspian. He took it from your Scriptorium. Technically, it belongs to you."

"I don't think this kind of book belongs to anyone," Farron murmurs.

I prepare myself for a deluge of questions, but my mate stares entranced, his touch tentative and curious over the leather binding.

"Let me show you," I say and slowly open the book, flipping through the delicate pages until I find the image I was thinking of, a mountain etched in inky lines, spewing black smoke.

"Calandorin's original location lay at the base of a volcano," Farron says, reading the text. "One day it erupted without warning, and only the Queen was able to make it there in time. But she couldn't find a way to get all the fae off the mountain before the lava reached them."

My eyes drift back to the rubbing. "So, she changed them…"

"The Queen used her magic to transform them all to birds so they could safely fly down the mountain."

"And that's how birds were created. Like the mermaids?"

Farron flips the pages. "No, she changed them back. They built a new city and must have paid homage to her with the plaque your father found."

"The magic of change," I whisper. "Man to animal. Is there any other fae with that power?"

Farron shakes his head, auburn hair falling across his brow. "There are some fae who transform themselves, such as from fae to unicorn. Or mermaids can have legs for a time. But there's no magic of transformation on others, such as Queen Aurelia had."

"No," I say, an idea hitting me like a stroke of lightning. "The Enchantress who cursed you … changed you from fae to beast." My chest heaves with breath. "Could she be the Queen returned?"

Farron gets a faraway look. "The thought has crossed my mind before. And she would have just cause, for we four failed her realms. Sometimes people do horrible things to protect something they love."

"But if the Enchantress was the Queen, why would she leave after?" I continue. "Castletree is sick. Why wouldn't she help it or any of the realms? In all the stories about her, she's always doing good."

"Indeed. And how does this legend aid your father's search?"

"I don't know," I say, turning back to Papa's letter. "It's a good story, but what does it have to do with my mother? Why does Papa think the type of bird is important?"

"Perhaps she was one of the citizens who was transformed into a bird?" Farron suggests.

"Maybe." I stare at the rubbing of the Queen. There's a tiny spiral around her throat. Is it a rose?

My hand unconsciously drifts to my necklace. Is it possible my mother had some connection to the ancient Queen? Maybe she didn't find this necklace.

Maybe it was a gift.

"I'll start a reply to your father, detailing what information we've learned." Farron sits down at the table and pulls out a quill and ink. "Keep that book safe, Rosalina. I'm sure there's more to be gleaned from it. But we should get back to our other research. Figure out more about this mating frenzy of yours."

I tuck the book back into my bag. The thought of the *wilde courtship* turns my thoughts back to purple eyes and a leering smile. I smooth out invisible wrinkles in my skirt. "Farron, I need to tell you something. Something I've kept hidden because I'm ashamed and scared."

Farron jumps up so fast, his quill falls and drops blotches of ink on the paper. He wraps his arms around me, and I realize I'm shaking. "It's okay, Rosie. You can tell me anything, you know that." He sits back in his chair, pulling me on to his lap.

"It's about Caspian."

Farron stiffens beneath me. "Go on."

I touch the two bands of thorns around my wrists. "I didn't only see Kel the night my mating frenzy took over. When I woke up, Caspian was in my room."

Farron inhales sharply but says nothing more.

"He looked possessed, Fare, like his body wasn't his own. He wasn't there long, but … but it was like he was drawn to me."

"The Prince of Thorns likes his games," Farron says, but his voice holds little conviction.

My fingers dig into his vest. "Farron, are you able to feel him like you do Kel?"

Farron touches his neck. "If I feel anything for the Prince of Thorns, it's only remnants of our bargain. It's deep magic, Rosie. It clouds the soul."

Maybe so, but there's something more going on. Something I've been trying to ignore for months. The yearning for Caspian, the jealousy. And when I was searching for Farron, it was him I found instead. I jump off Farron's lap, voice growing frantic. "He can *speak* in my mind. I feel a pull to him. Farron, what if the Prince of Thorns is also my mate?"

Farron's golden eyes widen, then he slumps forward in his chair, hands in his hair. The Prince of Thorns attacked his home, and before that, Caspian betrayed Keldarion and the entire Enchanted Vale.

I clutch at my heart. "What else could it be?"

Farron stands, then walks on shaky legs towards me. "There is so much magic in this world we don't yet know about. It could be any one of his tricks. And if it is true, we'll figure it out together."

He cups my face and I lean into his touch. "You don't hate me?"

"Of course not, Rosalina. There's nothing you could ever do to make me hate you. Besides, if the stars have matched your light with that vile darkness, you don't have to accept the bond."

"That's true," I whisper.

"We need more information. And in the meantime, be wary of what you feel. Ask yourself if it's truly the same as with Kel and I."

"Why don't you hold on to Caspian's book for a while?" I ask. "It does technically belong to you, after all. Maybe you'll find some clue in it I missed."

"Okay, I'll give it a read." Gently, he brushes the hair from my brow. My heart melts at his tenderness. This softness, this forgiveness ... I've never felt as open with anyone as I do with him. With Farron, my secrets will always be safe. I look down at the thorns winding around my wrist. My bargain. "Farron, there's something else."

"Well, I never!" A voice smooth as honey caresses down the hall, followed by the wheel of carts.

I pull away from Farron, wiping my eyes. "That would be Marigold."

"Never too late for afternoon coffee," he says, tucking a strand of hair behind my ear. "Please do not fret about Caspian. Don't think you can't tell me what's going on in that glorious mind of yours. If you need to follow your feelings, I will stand by you. But I promise, Rosie. I will find the answers to your questions."

Relief floods through me from his response. From his warmth and understanding, though I know inside, the idea must be truly haunting. Nodding, I turn as Marigold enters the room, rolling a tray cluttered with ceramic carafe, elegant cups, and a tower of cookies. Behind her, in a flurry, is Eldy.

"Lady Marigold, I've never been bombarded with such attitude." The majordomo flaps his arms at his side.

"What's the problem?" I ask.

Marigold slams the carafe down with such vigor, little droplets fly out. Quickly, I grab the rubbing as Farron rolls up the map.

"The problem is Eldor has dared ask to escort me to Prince Ezryn's welcome home jubilee tonight!"

Farron raises a brow and tries to reach for a cookie before Marigold swats his hand with a rolled napkin. "A plate first, Autumn Prince!"

"I thought you'd like to attend the jubilee, Marigold," Farron says and gives Marigold a knowing look. "It's a full moon tonight, after all."

"Aye, I do, but not with someone that has more butter than biscuits for brains."

"The nerve!" Eldy says. "In my day, an invitation of such caliber would be met with at least appreciation if not acceptance."

"Appreciation," Marigold scoffs, loading Farron's plate with a teetering pile of cookies. "He expects appreciation from *me*? Me, who's been serving in naught but Castletree for twenty-five years?"

"A place of highest esteem." Eldy scrunches up his face. His features do look rather birdlike: the large nose, pointed chin, and gray hair pulled back like slicked tail feathers.

But he doesn't know about the curse, doesn't know that if he hadn't stood Marigold up, she wouldn't turn into a raccoon each night.

"A lady like Marigold cannot simply be asked to events such as this," I begin. "You have to entice her to go with you."

Marigold gives a huff of approval and finally hands over the plate of cookies.

"How would I do that?" Eldy asks.

I place a hand on his shoulder and laugh. "I'm sure you'll figure it out."

Eldy bobs his head. It's like I can feel his magic through the connection of my hand on his shoulder. Really, deep down … He could be very birdlike.

Feeling a little strange, I remove my hand and pluck a cookie off Farron's plate. The powdered sugar smells divine. Before I take a bite, I notice it's divided into three different sections: one pink, one brown, and one yellow.

Marigold notices me examining it. "The pink represents the stone which shelters us, the brown represents the earth from which we grow, and the yellow represents the sun that gives us life."

"All things that make the Spring Realm what we are," Eldy finishes. Carefully, he picks one up and looks at it. "It's been a long-time since I've had one of your famous polvorones, Marigold."

She crosses her arms, but her voice is soft. "Been a long time since I've made them. They never tasted right when I made them in Castletree."

Eldy takes a bite, crumbs dotting his beard. "I would have eaten them gladly."

Farron and I exchange a look, and I sense an opportunity. I lean into Eldy, pretending to whisper, "Did you even tell Marigold about the present you got her for the occasion?"

The majordomo gives a raised brow, which I return with a wink. Ezryn had already shown me some of the beautiful jewels they craft here. I'm sure I could procure a trinket or two that Eldy could offer Marigold.

Eldy clears his throat and chuffs, "Well, I didn't want to ruin the surprise."

Marigold purses her lips, and I can see her resolve weakening. "Fine, I'll go. But I'm not saving all my dances for you."

"Very well. I'm glad you see reason." Eldy gives a loopy smile, before his face creases. "Wait, who else would you dance with?"

The two of them continue the argument as they leave the archives.

I turn back to Farron, wipe crumbs off his cheek, and give him a quick kiss. "Come on, Autumn Prince. We've got a party to go to."

But his hands tighten on my waist, and the kiss deepens until my whole body melts beneath his touch. "First, Princess of Autumn, it would be a shame to waste this perfectly cleared table," Farron whispers against my neck, before throwing me on it.

40

CASPIAN

B irdy is cackling. When I was a child, I thought cackling was
something only described in fairytales, like witches brewing a
cauldron they threatened to put naughty children into. That
was until I met my sister. Though I suppose she's like a witch now,
hunched over in her lair, brewing …

"Always playing with your potions," I say, leaning against the
entrance to her chamber. "Planning on poisoning your dear brother
again?"

Those of the Vale always say the citizens of the Below have a fasci-
nation with the realms above, but my little sister takes that to an
extreme. And why wouldn't she? A little girl growing up down here.
When she was younger, I felt guilty and brought her back the odd
thing from time to time. She's like a crow. It matters not to her if the
item is from the human or the fae world, if it's shiny, Birdy covets it.

Now, she lives in one of Cryptgarden's highest towers and has
filled it with trinkets. In every nook and cranny, there are brightly
colored bottles and chalices teetering precariously on ledges, and the
floor is a million shades of spilled and splattered colors.

Currently, she's curled over a stone table staring intently at the
blue bubbling concoction.

"You should have seen it, Cas," she says without looking up. "The potion I made the other day ... It was incredible."

"Hmm." I stroll in. Her messy desk is a disaster waiting to happen. Containers filled with all sorts of—I wrinkle my nose—*ingredients,* I suppose she'd call them. Herbs, insects, crystals, water with messy labels depicting different stages of the moon, as well as a variety of flowers, shells, and an assortment of blue blobs bouncing against a glass jar. Now, those were tedious to catch for her.

"Took me ages to get it right, but I finally got it! Worked like a charm." She rubs her nose, smearing soot across her face.

She's not wearing her Nightingale armor. Instead, her hair is pulled back, and she's dressed in an oversized tunic and leggings.

"Let me guess." I smile. "A love potion for that armored owl of yours? I told you before, he's enamored. You don't need it."

She blows a tuft of hair out of her eyes. "No. And besides, love potions don't exist. But what I made was the next best thing."

There's a snapping of heels, the brush of long robes. I straighten, breath catching in my throat, and recognize the same stiffening in Birdy.

Sira storms into the room without knocking. "Would you like to explain why the High Prince of Spring is back on the throne and those other miserable princes are with him?"

Birdy's lip trembles, the smile from a moment ago completely gone.

My mother seems to notice me for the first time. "What are you doing here? They've neglected to defend Castletree. Take it now!"

I give a long sigh. "Do you really think they would have all left Castletree without several wards in place?" They'd left a few, but like their magic, their wards are weak. Maybe enough to stop a few wayward goblins. Not enough to stop me.

Birdy bows her head. "Presently, I'm in talks with Prince Kai—"

Sira grabs a potion from my sister's desk and smashes it against Birdy's face.

To her credit, the Nightingale barely flinches. She stands perfectly still as the blood and sticky blue liquid trickles down her cheek.

Sira snatches Birdy's chin with one hand. Shadows flicker around the tips of her fingers. "I thought I could mold you into something worthy, but it seems I was wrong. I do not tolerate failure."

Birdy's lip trembles. She blinks rapidly. Dammit, she knows better than to cry in front of our mother.

Leaning on the table, I examine my nails. "I suppose I could help her, Mother. Not much to do while I wait for my magic to siphon their wards."

Sira pushes my sister away and turns to the door. "Do not disappoint me again, my children."

As her footsteps fade down the hall, I pluck a pair of tweezers from the countertop. "Sit down, Birdy. You've got glass in your cheek."

41

KELDARION

The water is a milky blue, steam rising from the surface and curling at the rocky roof. This cave is one of the few comforts allowed to the Deep Guard of Voidseal Bridge. Located a few hours' march from our base, it's a popular destination for mandatory rest days. I hadn't wanted to accompany the host of soldiers heading this way, but my uncle had insisted, eventually convincing me by stating, "If your sword doesn't kill the creatures of the Below, by the seven realms, Kel, your smell will."

These secluded caverns contain large pools of natural hot springs, though they lack the salty air of the one in Castletree. But up here, any warmth is luxurious. All modesty is stripped away, and fae men and women bathe alongside each other. I've found my own space, secluded in a stony alcove. From here, I can still see the mouth of the cavern, where snow falls from a gray sky.

Large white bubbles float past me, carrying a sweet scent. The smell of roses. A deep warmth blooms in my chest.

Whirling, I tread through the water, following the floating bubbles. Then I see a figure, her back to me, hands massaging bubbles through her hair. *How is she here?*

She's out of the view from the rest of the company. I tread faster, then grasp her arm. "Rosalina?"

Magic sparkles between us, a humming in my ears, and I have the strange sensation of pulling something over a vast distance. Of pulling *her*.

Rosalina spins, blinking wildly, and wraps her arms over her chest. Her gaze settles on me, and she lowers her arms. The water comes up to her collarbone, anyway. "Kel?"

"How are you here?" I growl.

She tilts her head, looking adorable with her hair piled in bubbles. A grin spreads across her face as she looks around. "Whoa, where are you? A snowy hot spring? This is so cool."

"Did our bond bring you here?" I wonder. It's nothing I've heard of before, but like in the dream, she feels very much here and present with me.

"I think so," Rosalina says. "I was in the bath, getting ready for a Spring jubilee tonight, but then I felt … Well, I felt you."

Memories of the last time we were together flood back to me, how desperately I'd craved her, how in that moment I'd have done anything to claim her. I can't let that happen again.

"You should go," I growl.

"This place is magical," she sighs, wading about. Her long neck tilts up to stare at the large, cavernous ceiling.

She glides around the rocky corner. "Oh, sorry. I didn't see you there."

I swivel to see she's face to face with one of the Deep Guard. Lars, I think his name is. A good soldier, broad shoulders, with long blond hair, currently dripping with water.

"Don't apologize," Lars answers. "I haven't seen you around before. Are you new?"

Lars doesn't see me from behind the rock, but I don't think it would matter if I was right there. His eyes are entirely on Rosalina.

"Uh, kind of," she replies, taking a step back.

He has the gaze of a starving man as he takes her in. She's a rare bloom in this barren place—perfect skin, sweet full lips, and just how much of her body can he see beneath the water? His own naked form is only inches away.

"Hair wash. Good idea." He smirks and reaches for her head.

I'm in front of him in an instant, grasping his wrist almost hard enough to snap. "She's with me."

Lars' face shifts instantly from lust to terror. I release him and he slinks back. "High Prince Keldarion."

I say nothing more. He retreats, rejoining the rest of the group far away from us. I stay still, breath heaving in and out of my chest. My fists are clenched at my side to stop myself from following him and doing something I'll regret.

"Kel?"

Her voice drives me into a different sort of trance. I cannot let anyone else see her. Not here when she's naked. Not when she hasn't been properly claimed by me.

I grab her around the waist and drag her deeper into the cave, secluding us behind another cluster of rocks. No one else can have what's mine.

She squirms against me, and I feel her soft naked body against my hard planes. I can't let her go, not yet. I press her against the rock wall. Warm water curls around us as I shelter her in.

"Kel," Rosalina says softly, her fingers threading through the white strands of my hair. "This is a side of the *wilde courtship* I haven't seen before."

"Is that what this is?" We're far away from the crowd now, their voices a muffled murmur.

"Your pupils are huge," she whispers. She's no longer squirming against me, but writhing. Her body moves in a rhythm, and her legs wrap around my waist. Seven realms, is that her slick pussy rubbing against my stomach?

"He shouldn't have touched you. Shouldn't have even looked at you."

"It was an accident." She smiles, then still holding on to me, dips her head back, rinsing the suds from her hair. "You're not this jealous and possessive around the princes of Castletree."

"They may see you. These men can not."

"What does that make you want to do?" she whispers. She gently touches the snowflake necklace, then curls her fingers in my chest hair.

"Rose," I warn. My cock is hard with her body pressed so close to mine. "You know I can't. I can't let this *thing* take over again."

"Fine, but there's something I want you to know." She takes my hand and presses it against her chest. "Can you feel my heart?"

"Yes."

"Right now, it's beating just for you."

The rapid rhythm seems matched by my own heart. I close my eyes, relishing the sound. "I feel something else."

"That is?"

I lower my hand, unable to stop myself from grasping the full weight of her breast. Gently, I knead the soft flesh with my fingertips before palming the entire mound *hard*.

Rosalina pushes against me, mouth opening against mine, and we both desperately gasp in the humid air. I cup her ass, allowing myself one single moment of bliss, her center sliding against my aching hard cock. "Oh, the things I want to do to you. The sounds I want you to make for everyone to hear. There'd be no doubt that you are mine."

Her brown eyes widen before she kisses me, tongue slipping across my own. For a moment, I imagine it: sliding deep within her, and fucking her hard against the rock wall.

But too quickly, she pulls away, gaze sultry as she purrs, "Are you sure that's not just the *wilde courtship* talking?"

"I want the entire world to know you belong to me," I say.

"So, you wouldn't like it if anyone else saw me like this?" She rises out of the water and onto a low rock shelf. The drastic chill in the air instantly pebbles her nipples and gooseflesh spreads across her legs.

"Rosalina." She isn't alone in her nudity; others walk around on the bank, gathering their things.

But she alone is a work of art. She doesn't understand just how gorgeous she is with her perfect breasts, the curve of her stomach, her soft thighs.

"You can't touch me, but if you could," she says, "what would you do?"

I step closer, eyes half watching her, half keeping an eye on any Deep Guard getting too close. "First, I'd tell you to spread those long legs and let me gaze on what's mine."

"You think this pussy belongs to you?" she asks playfully, but does as she's told, her fingers playing in the soft line of hair before spreading apart her pretty pink center.

I groan loudly, and my hand instantly dips beneath the water, grasping my cock. It's steel hard, so ready to stretch and fill her.

She circles her fingers along her entrance. Water from the hot springs slides down her thighs, adding to her slickness. "It is yours, Kel."

A possessive growl escapes me, and I drop down between her legs, barely able to contain myself from devouring her right now. "Fuck yourself with your fingers."

She sighs, and I hear the wet sounds as she enters herself. Her scent fills me, rich with desire and lust. Her free hand grips my hair, and she cries out.

"That's it, Rose," I say. Then I push myself back. "I have very little control around you."

Her mouth loops into a smile. "Are you touching yourself?"

I am, gripping the base of my cock hard.

"What would your soldiers think if they knew you were making your mate come just behind these rocks?"

"You're making yourself," I say.

She looks at me through a hooded gaze. "You have no idea how much it turns me on to have you watch. To even be near you. Gods, you're so hot, I could come just looking at you. And the fact you're watching, that you may want me—"

I grip myself tighter as her fingers slip in and out of her pussy. She bites her lip, and I can see the desire in her eyes. The need.

"I can't want you, Rose. I can't have you."

"Just watch me then. I'm so close."

Her words send a shiver down my spine, and I can feel the lust, the need, coursing through me. "Fuck."

She pulls her fingers out, and the wet sound nearly sends my cock into a spasm. Stroking faster, I ache to feel her tight heat enveloping me.

"I wish I could suck on your cock."

I groan. Can the others hear us? I don't even care. "I want to lay you out in front of everyone and fuck you, Rose, so they know you're mine."

Her eyelashes flutter, and she bites her lip, head falling back, hand moving faster. My rhythm increases to match hers. "Would you like that, Rose? To be covered in my scent, my seed?"

"Oh, Kel, I'd prefer for your seed to be inside of me."

Unhinged desire surges through me, from this *wilde courtship*, from my own need for her. Something in me snaps. I drag her off the rock wall and into my arms, kissing her deeply. I take her bottom lip between my teeth, then drag my mouth up to her ear, nipping at the soft point.

"How would you like to be bred? Filled with load after load of my cum until your belly swells with our child?"

"Oh," she gasps. Her hand still works furiously on her pussy.

"Could you take it, Rose? Take that much of me?"

"Let go of me," she breathes. "I'm going to come."

She floats out of my arms, and I see her hand move desperately beneath the water, my own grip frenzied on my cock. "Don't stop looking at me."

Her chest heaves, breast bouncing as she begins to come. It storms through our bond. I'm inundated with pleasure, her orgasm shooting up my body, too. There's no point resisting as it consumes me.

I keep my gaze locked on hers as I come, spilling my release into the water. "Rosalina."

"Kel," she whimpers.

That was close, too close. But I can't say it wasn't worth it.

She tilts her head to look outside. "It's beautiful, Kel."

Figuring enough time has passed to be safe, I gather her against me, and she molds perfectly into my arms.

"Promise me something," she whispers. "One day, you will show me your realm. Not just the ballroom or through these dreams. I want to see it all for real."

Sweeping the wet hair from her brow, I smile down at her. "I would love nothing more, my Rose. But I cannot promise you that. I do not even know when I will return."

Her smile falls, sadness flickering across her features. "I have to finish getting ready."

"Promise me something."

"Of course."

"Tonight, when you dance, look at the stars. Know that I'll be looking at them, too, thinking of you."

She grazes my jaw with her fingertips. "Goodbye, Kel."

I blink and she's gone, only rose-scented bubbles swirling around me.

PART THREE
SPRING'S AWAKENING

42

EZRYN

At moments like these, I wonder how I dared stay away from my realm for so long.

The Meadowmere Forest outside of Florendel has been drenched in all the splendor of Spring, decorated with magic and the beauty of our craftsmanship. If this weren't a jubilee in my honor, perhaps I could enjoy it.

The air is filled with the sweet scent of wildflowers, carried by a gentle breeze that rustles through the ancient trees. In this magical hour of twilight, the sunlight shimmers purple through the dense canopy, creating dappled patterns on the forest floor. More than ever, I am thankful for the full moon tonight so I can savor this moment without transforming into my beast.

Savor it, because she's on my arm. She who glows more beautifully than anything from the cosmos.

"Wow," Rosalina gasps, eyes darting around to take in the celebration. I find myself smiling at how unabashedly she feels everything; there's no thought to hide her joy or mask her pain. I wonder what it would be like to feel everything so freely.

Behind me, Dayton is speaking in a low voice to Farron. I offer the youngest of us princes a smile, then realize he can't see it. Yet, Farron gives me a smile back. It is his right to enter the party with his mate on his arm, but he held no objection when Rosalina grabbed my elbow. I know she'll go back to him—back to where she belongs—soon enough. But for this moment, I revel in the feel of her beside me.

The sound of laughter and mirth grows louder as we draw into the heart of the gathering. The jubilee is in full swing, and the woods have been transformed into a playground of wonder.

"What are those?" Rosalina points upward. Giant leaf pods move gently through the trees and down to the forest floor. One lands near us, and laughing partygoers step out. In a similar fashion, massive flowers, the size of a small room, keep their petals closed as they drift from one end of the party to another, before blooming and letting guests in or out. Each one is a tiny sanctuary of its own, providing quiet solace from the event or transporting guests around the clearing.

One flower pod, petals unfurled, carries the harmonious melodies of the orchestra. Their music fills the air, and Rosalina perks up, swaying to the rhythm.

Seven realms, has she ever looked so beautiful as when she is donning a dress of Spring? I knew Marigold would never miss the opportunity to show Rosalina the wondrous fashions of our home, but she has truly outdone herself.

Rosalina shines in vibrant colors and floral motifs. The sleeves, made of brilliant white lace, drape gracefully over her shoulders. Scarlet red, turquoise blue, and emerald green flowers are intricately embroidered over the bodice, seeming to come to life every time she sways. The pleated skirt hugs her hips. Each tier is adorned with embroidered blossoms in every color from the indigos of twilight to the golden hues of dawn.

She spins in a circle; her hair flows around her in soft waves, hundreds of tiny petals woven throughout. When she catches me looking at her, her eyes sparkle with a mischievous glimmer.

I want to kiss that smirk off her face.

She skips over to me and takes my hand. "Your home is magnificent, Ez."

"I can take no credit for this. Kairyn is the one who organized the jubilee." I wave away a cluster of fireflies that dance near my face.

Fae nod to me as we walk through the party, though some have already partaken in too much drink, for their eyes are glazed, movements slumbrous.

Rosalina waves to everyone.

When a leaf pod dips near us and opens to uncover a table laden with food, she squeals and insists we try one of everything. When across the party, a flower blossoms to reveal a harpist, she grabs my hand and yanks me through the whole event to stand before them. Tears prick her eyes at the music. And when we catch sight of Dayton and Farron swaying together under the rising moon, she stares at them wistfully.

"You should go dance," I tell her. "I've taken you away from Farron for far too long."

The glitter dusting her cheekbones and eyelids sparkles. "Why don't you come dance with us?"

"I should probably find my brother."

She chews on her lip, then grabs hold of my elbow. "One more lap through the party, then I'll let you go. Promise."

I couldn't say no to her if my life depended on it.

We drift under the darting lights—both enchanted and cast by fireflies—and walk along the edge of the clearing. I feel her eyes on me. "Something on my helmet?"

"I like this color on you." She strokes a hand down the side of my helm. I'm wearing a suit of armor that has long sat dormant here in Spring, an elegant set of starlight silver that is more ceremonial than battleworthy. "You look like Sir Lancelot."

"Another friend of yours?"

She barks a laugh. "No, no. He's a character in a great legend. There have been thousands of stories written about him and Queen Guinevere."

Rosalina and her books. Since her time at Castletree, I've heard about all her favorite characters. "Tell me of this Sir Lancelot and his Queen."

Rosalina leans against the trunk of a tree. "Lancelot was renowned as one of the bravest and most gallant knights who ever served great King Arthur. Yet, he had a passionate streak, a fiery temper that he had to repress on behalf of his honor."

"Hmm, sounds like an interesting fellow." I brace a hand beside her head. "And who was this Queen Guinevere?"

"She was a beautiful maiden. So beautiful that Lancelot fell madly in love with her upon first sight. And she loved him back." Rose blinks her huge brown eyes at me. "Their love was such that they forsook all honor, all commitments, to be with one another."

"Why could they just not love each other?" I breathe.

"Because," Rosalina whispers, "she belonged to his best friend. And he had a duty to his people, to the throne."

"Oh." Something shifts in my chest, like coals smoldering, fighting for life against the ash. "What happened to them?"

Rosalina's eyes drift down, staring into nothing. "Lancelot is consumed by guilt and remorse and disappears from Guinevere's life in a self-imposed exile."

"What of the Queen?"

"She is nearly burned at the stake," Rosalina whispers, "for choosing to love a man who could never belong to her."

The music and chatter of the party fill the air, but it feels like there's nothing but emptiness around me. "Such is the fate for foolish dreamers."

"It's just a story," Rosalina says, and I hear the pitch in her voice, an attempt at merriness.

I force myself to emulate her tone. "Look, there's Dayton. You should give him a dance."

"Right." She nods and starts to head out before turning back to me. "There are thousands of versions of that story, Ez. Maybe one day I'll write my own. One where Lancelot and Guinevere end up together."

"I will be the first to read it."

She smiles, then drifts away from me, petals in a breeze.

I sigh and collapse my weight against the trunk. I need a moment to collect my thoughts—

"You've hardly left her side all night and here I was, thinking my big brother would seek me out." Kairyn disengages from the shadows as if he is merely an extension of them.

"I hate parties," I growl.

"I know."

We look at each other in silence; the whole thing is so ridiculous, I nearly laugh.

"A sword at a party?" Kairyn muses, looking at Windscythe on my back.

"Trust me. I've been to enough parties now to know it's always best to be prepared."

Kairyn's gaze leaves mine and searches the clearing before landing on Rosalina. "You care for that fae."

"She is mate to the High Prince of Autumn," I say quickly. "I swore to Farron I would protect her with my life."

"No." Kairyn seems wrong in this place, his armor absorbing the light instead of reflecting it. "It's more than that. She is … precious to you."

"It matters not."

"Tell me," Kairyn says, "do you think she will still smile so sweetly at you when she learns the truth?"

Ice floods my veins. "I don't know what you're talking about."

"But how could you tell her, when you've never admitted it to me?"

A growl rumbles in my throat, and I grab his arm firmly. "We will not speak of this here. And I will not speak of this with *you*."

Kairyn shakes his head. "Typical. You are more than willing to look into the future of Spring with me, but will never look to the past. Tell me, have you even deigned to pay your respects to Mother yet?"

When I don't answer, my brother melds back into the dark edges of the party. I am left dancing with the fireflies.

43

ROSALINA

T hough this is the fourth fae party I've attended, each one feels like the first time. The realms are all so unique and wondrous.

"Hey, silly." Dayton smirks at me. "You've got petals on your face."

His rough hand rubs at my cheek, and I can't help but wrap my fingers around his wrist. In the gentle glow of the stars, his hair looks like burnished gold, topped by a crown of flowers.

"It was a cake with edible flowers! How cool is that?"

"Very cool, Rosie." He doesn't take his hand away. "Are you done eating your cake so we can dance?"

The prickling sensation of being watched travels over me, and I scan the party. Hovering beside a lily pond is the acolyte from the temple. She's not dressed in her robes, instead wearing a blue gown that falls above her ankles. Pink daisies cover the gauzy fabric of her dress, and a matching crown adorns her short, brown hair.

Wrenley. Dayton had told me her name. "You should ask her to dance."

"I don't feel like dancing."

"You literally just asked if I was finished with my cake so we could dance."

Dayton puts a hand behind his head, raising the hem of the nearly transparent shirt high enough that I can glimpse the toned muscles of his stomach. "Changed my mind."

"Day…"

Farron has wandered off, but he wouldn't be any help in this matter. I think he's convinced himself Dayton will never find his mate and we'll be able to keep him forever.

If only.

"Rose."

I shake my head, and even though the words taste like ash in my mouth, I say, "Come on. You saved her from the river. She gave you a precious shell from her necklace that is similar to yours. You have to try."

Dayton grinds his teeth and reaches for his sweet lavender wine. "Is that really what you want?"

Of course not. But I grip his arm hard enough to spill his wine. "We can't be selfish. I can't keep you. Summer *needs* this."

His teal gaze locks on mine as he drains his drink and tosses the lily pad goblet into the water where it unfurls. He makes no move to leave.

"Fine. If you won't talk to her, I will."

Dayton shrugs as if he couldn't care less.

"Think of your people, Day," I whisper. "Of your little sister, Delphia. Wrenley might not be your mate, but you'll never know if you don't try."

Twisting through the party, I make my way to the acolyte. "Pink or blue?"

She turns to me slowly, raising a brow. "Excuse me?"

"Which color is your favorite? Your dress would say both."

"Oh," she says, and her full lips curve into a smile. "Black."

"Black?" I echo.

Wrenley's smile grows further. "Yes. It is during the darkest night we can most clearly see the light of the Above. The light of our blessed Queen."

I almost catch an air of sarcasm to her words, but she's an acolyte. Perhaps it's a practiced phrase.

"We haven't been properly introduced." I hold out my hand. "I'm Rosalina."

Wrenley looks down at my outstretched palm before delicately shaking it. "You helped with the goblins."

"As much as I could. I'm glad you're all right."

She picks at one of the flowers on her dress. "The Summer Prince's appearance was truly fate."

Fate? "Yes. Your necklace is beautiful. Dayton told me your father collected the shells for it."

Her blue eyes widen. Such a bright color, distinct and familiar at the same time. "My father," she murmurs. "Yes, he had a market stall selling trinkets in Hadria. It's where my mother met him. Convinced him to move to Spring, but he brought a handful of shells to always remember Summer. That's what my necklace is made of."

There's a hitch of pain in her voice, the same hitch of pain that catches in mine when someone asks me about my mother. "My father is an archeologist," I explain, "so he had trinkets from all over the world."

"What realm did you say you grew up in again, Lady Rosalina?"

Right. My childhood must be very different from hers. Wrenley looks about my age, but with fae, you can never really tell.

"Is Ez's lavender wine strong enough for me to see double?" Dayton waltzes up, holding two goblets. "Or are there truly two fae beauties standing before me?"

He's dripping in charisma and charm, the same way he was when I first met him. He hands us both a drink. A part of me is thankful for the interruption in my awkward conversation. Another part of me feels sick to my stomach.

"Are you enjoying the party, Wrenley?" he asks.

She turns her full attention to him, voice breathy and soft. "Oh yes, it's wonderful. Prince Kairyn was very kind in giving us the night off. Rosalina was telling me of her childhood."

"Right," I say. "You said you grew up in Spring?"

"Yes," Wrenley replies. "But we spent much time in Summer. I particularly enjoyed my trips to the Byzantar Isles."

Dayton smiles, a genuine one, remembering his home, and launches into a tale of the place. I take the opportunity to make an exit and let the conversation continue between them.

Every part of me aches to look back at Dayton, to see if he's watching me. But I don't turn around.

I need to let the Summer Prince go.

44

ROSALINA

L ooking around, I search the grounds for Farron. Last time he disappeared at a party, he ended up destroying an entire library of priceless literature. Though I'm not surprised he hasn't returned yet; he'd seemed fascinated with the plants around the clearing, and I don't doubt he's wandering around with an armful of samples.

I catch sight of someone else, though. Marigold twirls under Eldy's arm, her face completely lit up. Their love deserves a second chance.

I take a moment to glance up through the treetops to the starlit sky. *Are you looking at the same stars as me, Kel?* Our bond brought us together earlier. Surely, there will come a day when our separation—be it physical miles or emotional—will be a thing of the past.

The party continues before me like something out of a *Midsummer Night's Dream*. Unlike the wild celebration that occurred in the Below or the formal ball in Winter, this event seems more casual, like a gathering. Some fae are downright subdued. I wonder what Ezryn thinks of all this. I hadn't wanted to leave him earlier, but I also didn't want to stay on his arm all night; I'm only holding him back.

"Lady O'Connell, you look ravishing."

Kairyn stands beside me, nearly blending in with the dark shadow of the tree. My heart thumps against my chest, and I startle.

"Prince Kairyn! You scared me."

"Apologies. I merely wanted to compliment the Lady of Castletree on her beauty." He takes my hand and bows, lowering the cold edge of his helm to my knuckles. "Though I doubt she wants for praise. You seem to be followed by one prince or another wherever you go."

I give an awkward laugh. "Are you enjoying the party?"

"More so now that I've come across you." His voice is deep, yet I can't help but feel that he lacks the confidence of the High Princes. Like he'd rather be anywhere than socializing. "I was hoping you would indulge me in a dance."

My ears prick as a haunting melody seems to grow louder, drifting across the breeze. "Of course, I would be honored."

He nods stiffly, as if he didn't expect me to say yes. Then holds out a hand. I take it, seeing how small my own is against the black expanse of his leather glove.

In a whoosh, he pulls me into the soft grass being used as a dance-floor. My bare feet find purchase, and with my hand in his, the other on his shoulder, I realize just how short I am in comparison. I'm not used to feeling short—at least when I'm not around the four princes of Castletree—but Kairyn has me feeling positively miniature.

We move in rhythm to the music—or close enough to a rhythm. Kairyn's movements are more march than dance. Nothing like my waltz with Caspian last winter, when the very air had seemed to carry us.

"It's a beautiful necklace you wear," Kairyn says.

I look down at the moonstone rose. "Thank you. It belonged to my mother."

"Did it? And how did she come by it, if I may ask? I tend to be … a collector, of sorts."

The words are on my lips: *She found it on an archeological dig.* That's what Papa and I had always believed. But it's obvious my mother was hiding her true nature all along. Could it have been a gift from the Queen?

Could she have stolen it?

Regardless, something warns me away from the truth—or what I know of it. "She found it in the human realm."

Kairyn's owl helm twitches ever so slightly, and I know he doesn't believe me. He presses on. "It appears to be very old. I should like to examine it at the monastery. We have many precious artifacts. If I could only compare—"

"I'm sorry," I snap. "But it's very special to me. I never take it off. *Ever.*"

Kairyn's grip tightens on my waist. "Is that so." It's not a question.

The music picks up, and Kairyn spins me faster, nearly lifting me off the ground.

"Ezryn looks like he's having a marvelous time," I say, despite the fact I can't see Ez. I want Kairyn to remember he's around.

"My brother's always been good at appearing the perfect prince. He was trained and taught from birth to follow in our parents' footsteps. A silver son."

My dress swishes as I twirl under Kairyn's arm. "He's a powerful leader. Spring is lucky to have him."

A grinding sound reverberates beneath the helm. "He was *taught* that he is a powerful leader. But true power cannot be taught; it is something that one is born with. An innate ability to make the sacrifices required. And this is not always visible on the surface."

I stay silent, watching the dark visor for any clue of the fae beneath. I can't figure out if he loves Ezryn or hates him. There's both admiration and resentment in his every word.

Maybe that's the truth of it; love and hate merged so closely together, he can't see which is which.

I think of my father. When he was off on his adventures and I was stuck at home, I spent years resenting him. And as soon as he came home, I'd be desperate for any ounce of attention.

But we found our way back to each other. Maybe Ezryn and Kairyn can, too.

"I know Ezryn isn't really a man of many words, but he appreciates what you've done here," I tell Kairyn. "If you reach out to him, I'm sure—"

Kairyn snorts, an undignified sound for this armored giant. "I have reached out to my brother far too many times, and just when I think I'm breaking through, he leaves me dangling off a precipice."

I stare into the young prince's helm, wondering if I'm holding his gaze. I do know what he's talking about. "Sometimes the closer I get to Ezryn, the more it feels like he pulls away."

"Exactly," Kairyn says.

I can't believe this is what I'm bonding with Kairyn over, but I understand deeply what he means. Just when I feel like there's a crack in Ezryn's armor, when I think he might let me in, he pulls away and retreats within himself. I've only had to endure this for a few months, whereas Kairyn has lived with it for a lifetime.

"In his eyes, I'll only ever be a child," Kairyn murmurs, "unfit to stand at his side."

"I know it can feel like he's far away," I urge, "but he's changing. When I see him and Kel—"

"*Keldarion.*" The name is a hiss and a growl all at once. "Ah yes, I'm sure my brother is quick to reconcile with that one. He doesn't hold any ill-will against traitors. Only his blood."

I drop my hands and step back. "You're hurt, and it's not my place to pry. I'm barely more than a stranger to you. But for what it's worth: trust him. Trust Ezryn, and he will see through on any promise made."

"For what it's worth, Lady O'Connell, let me ask you something. Do you truly know my brother?"

"Yes," I say without hesitation. "Ezryn is brave and kind, and he'll do anything for his friends and his realm."

Kairyn closes the gap between us and runs a finger down my neck, under the thin chain of my necklace. Slowly, he lifts the moonstone rose on a single finger. The gifted golden leaf from Autumn dangles off to the side. I hold my breath, feeling as if he's wrapped his hands around my heart. "He's like his armor, shining on the outside, but have you ever seen within?"

"I know his heart, and it is *good.*"

Kairyn lowers the moonstone rose back to my skin, then turns, looking nothing more than a shadow. "If you are so certain, ask my brother what happened the night he accepted the Blessing. Ask him what happened to my mother."

45

FARRON

"Prince of Thorns, if you can hear me, answer this call." My fingers tighten around the briars. I watch the thorns slither through the library of Castletree. *Can you hear me?*

Silence is the only response. A low growl rumbles in my throat. Using my necklace, I managed to slip out of the Spring jubilee with ease and quickly return to Castletree. But it won't be long before my absence is noticed.

I fall to my knees in front of the thorns and place two hands on the vines, then with a sinking resignation, bow my head. "Please, Caspian. I need to speak to you. What do you want? I don't have any sacrifices around, though one of the staff turns into a goat at night. I could persuade them to—"

The vines ripple and shadows curl around my feet. I look up to see Caspian lounging on a thorn above me. A smirk curls up the side of his mouth. "Really, Farron, a goat sacrifice? How barbaric."

I shrug. "How am I to know what you dark princes like?"

"What I like is *you*, Autumn Prince. On your knees and begging for me." Caspian leaps off the vine and prowls closer. "Has anyone ever told you you're adorable? And so festive today. Don't say you dressed up just for me?"

I stand and cross my arms. My outfit is a combination of a lime-green robe with pink flowers and tight gray pants that flare at the bottom. I wrap the robe tighter to cover my bare torso. "You actually came."

"Why are you so surprised? It was you who called me. And I can't resist a man on his knees."

Heat burns in my core under the predatory nature of his gaze. Is this what Rosie felt when he came to her during the mating frenzy? The thought cuts through everything else and protective anger takes over. "I'm here to talk about Rosalina."

Caspian raises a dark brow and steps back. "Not as timid as you used to be, Pup."

We begin to circle each other. "You were in her room the other night."

"You should have joined us." He smirks.

"Tell me about your…" I pause. "About this *connection* with her."

His smile only widens, and he grasps my robe, pulling me closer. "What is it you're truly asking, Autumn Princeling?"

My teeth grind. I *hate* him. I knew I shouldn't trust him, and yet fear drove me to make a bargain with him. A bargain with twisted words that he used to attack my realm and set loose my beast.

"Say it, Farron."

A growl rises in my throat, and I push him away. "Are you Rosalina's mate?"

He laughs and closes the distance again, rubbing a hand along my neck. "What do you think? Don't you feel me there?" His thumb slides under my chin. "What else could connect us so?"

My eyes drift down to his wrist, to the twisting bracelet of frozen thorns. "Your bargain with Kel," I breathe. "The remnants of our own bargain. Are you using those to corrupt Rosalina's mind?"

Caspian steps back. A curtain of dark hair falls across his features, and he pouts his full lips. "They do call you the smart one."

A strange wave of relief pours through me. Fae bargain magic is potent. I don't know all the details of his deal with Kel, but I know it was one of the most powerful bargains one could make.

A giddy smile spreads over my lips, and I fall to a library chair. "You're not her mate."

"Sorry to disappoint you, Farron sweetness."

"I don't suppose you'll break your bargain with Kel."

"Never." Caspian turns away and shadows twist up his legs and feet. "But ... There is a way for *you* to break it."

The silence is loud between us, and I get the feeling this isn't something he planned on telling me. "What do you mean?"

Caspian's fists clench at his side. "There might be a way to break both my bargain with Kel and my connection with Rosalina."

My heart hammers in my chest. Caspian's voice is so low, it's like he doesn't even want the surrounding thorns to listen. "Is this another one of your tricks?"

"What tricks?" A strange smile crawls up his face. "You destroyed my book. I took one of yours. But your mate stole the book I wanted. And that's where you'll discover the answers I need."

The book he's looking for—the one Rosie trusted me with—is safely tucked in my bag back at Keep Hammergarden. It seemed innocent enough, mostly tales of the Queen, though I haven't had a chance to give it a thorough read yet. What is the Prince of Thorns hoping to find inside? "You were always going to betray me, weren't you? Take your goblins into my realm for that book?"

"Of course I was."

I gnaw on my bottom lip; I don't feel guilty about ripping the notebook Rosalina got him for his birthday. Not after he manipulated me, his games with Rosie ... And in the past, he'd betrayed Kel. He'd betrayed us, too. There was a time I believed the man before me had been a friend.

I don't feel guilty about it, but sometimes I remember the look on his face, the noise of anguish as he gathered the ruined papers. Like it had actually mattered to him.

"Admit something else," I say lowly. "You wavered that night. It was why you were arguing with the Nightingale. You wanted to call off the attack."

"I was only waiting for the opportune moment," he says too quickly.

"You still have it." I reach into the folds of his jacket and snag a tattered book, bound with a single ribbon.

Caspian gasps, and a strange expression flashes in his gaze, something akin to fear. But he relaxes as he realizes I'm not going to destroy it further. This present from my mate.

I nod for him to follow me through the stacks, weaving in and out of the patches of moonlight. I hadn't lit a fire, as I didn't want to alert the staff to my return. Finally, I stop at a workstation. It's where Rosalina and I bind our notes and repair damaged books. Carefully, I untie the ribbon and lay the remains of his birthday gift before me. It was a clean rip right down the middle.

"It seems we may have a mutual goal then," I say. "But I'll make no more bargains with you."

"This doesn't have to be a bargain," Caspian replies. "You could trust me."

With great care, I throw away the tattered pages, keeping only the first one Rosalina wrote on. "Why do you think I'm doing this gesture of good faith? As I hope you did, by telling me the truth about your connection with Rosalina."

"I didn't lie to you, Autumn Prince." His dark gaze tracks my every movement.

I grab a brush and dip it in sticky glue, carefully running a thin line along the torn leather, as well as the ripped pages, and gently smooth them down with my fingers. "Tell me how to break your bargain with Kel and why you can't do it on your own."

"It's not so simple," Caspian says, then, "And I'm not so scholarly as you. But I assume my bargain with Kel may break as a side effect of what I truly want."

Heat grows on my palm, and I use it to quickly dry the glue before carefully reassembling the book. Lastly, I grab a thick needle and twine to bind the edges. "And what is that?"

"Something you need to find. Maybe it's a spell, magic, a damned potion made of frog legs for all I care. As long as it does what I want."

I close the book. There's still a scar on the leather, but the notebook functions again. Rosalina's writing is so clear on the cover: Caspian's name and holly symbol beneath. Why had she made this for him? Was it simple kindness or something more? I hold the notebook out. "And what is it you truly want, Prince of Thorns?"

"To become a human."

The notebook falls from my grasp and Caspian quickly grabs it, tucking it into his cloak.

"What?" I stammer.

"You heard me. Find a way to change me. Really change me. Not some illusion. And I suspect all my bargains and bonds will fade with my fae self."

I can only gape in surprise at him. "You're one of—if not—the most powerful fae in the Enchanted Vale. You would give that all up to be human? Why?"

Shadows and thorns swirl around him as he descends back to the Below. "Because a human can't become what she wants."

46

DAYTON

"There he is!" I call, half-leaning out of the flower pod. "Farron!"

Farron stands on the edge of the glen, wandering like an idiot.

"I'll get him," Ezryn says. He spreads his palms, and the flower pod we're in shifts off its projected course. The petals unfurl to a staircase right before Farron. I hold out my hand.

Farron beams, and I pull him up. "Hey."

The flower petal coils again, trapping us in a haze of pinkish light. It's intimate inside this, like a secret enclosure. There's a small pool of nectar at the base of the pod. Stamen sprout forth, the anthers giving off a soft light. The interior of the flower curls up like a bulb, but parts of it push out to form a little seated area.

Currently, Ezryn and Rosie occupy that spot. After I finished my dance with Wrenley earlier, I'd seen their pod swing by and took the chance to escape. Rosie couldn't yell at me for not trying anymore. Something terrible nags in my chest. Maybe the reason I'd been so resistant to dancing with Wrenley was because Rosie is right. There is *something* there. Saving her in the river, the seashell necklace... And there's no way to deny how beautiful she is.

So, I did my duty. I danced, even though the whole time I felt every emotion inside me curling inward. The only place I wanted to be was in this pod with Rosie and the metal lug.

And with Fare here, I never want to leave.

"I missed you," he says, making his way to Rosalina. He pushes her on to her back and crawls on top, sliding her dress up to grip her soft thigh.

"I tried to reach you, but I couldn't," she says.

"I'm here now." Farron's golden gaze catches mine. Then he stands, grabbing my pants and tugging me closer. His tongue glides up my chest to my neck. "I missed you, too."

"Fuck," I growl, feeling my cock harden against the press of his hips. "What's gotten into you, huh?"

His eyes shine with an expression I can't place. "Let's just say I don't want to take anything for granted. Not you, or Rosie. Or you, Ez," he calls over his shoulder. Ez tilts his helm in acknowledgement.

I grab Farron's chin. "Everything okay?"

"It will be." He kisses me roughly.

Rosie watches us with a hungry gaze. The night Farron and I shared her comes to the forefront of my mind. "Ez, is there a way to stop these flower rooms from, uh, blooming?"

"Yes," Ezryn says. "Why?"

Farron reaches between my legs and grasps my cock. "I don't want this to open," I pant, "while anyone is in a compromising situation."

"Oh." Ezryn looks between the three of us. "I should go."

Rosie's eyes widen, and she crawls over to Ezryn, putting a palm on his shoulder plate. "You can leave if you like. But I want you to stay."

Farron turns, hair tangled, eyes glassy. "Stay, Ez."

"Come on, Ez, listen to the girl. Charm her." I smirk at him. "Tell her, 'Let me fill you with my pollen', or some such Spring poetry."

Of course, I can't see his expression, but I feel like he's rolling his eyes. He curses something in a dialect of Spring that I don't understand, then presses his palm against the outside petals. They ripple and the top closes in tighter around us.

Rosalina looks at me. The question wavers in the sweet-scented air. What about us? There hasn't been a single moment that's passed where I haven't thought of how it felt to be inside her. Mate out there or not, there's no fucking way I can have Rosalina only once.

"What about it, Blossom?" I ask. "I played your game. Socialized. Maybe there's someone out there I belong to. But in here, all I want is you. Stars above, in this damned flower, let me belong to you."

Her lip trembles as she looks up at me, then stands. Her gaze quickly passes over Ezryn and Farron, who are watching her just as spellbound as I am.

Rosie reaches behind her back and pulls on a single long ribbon, and in a whoosh of fabric, the dress falls around her ankles. But she's not naked. A lacy brassiere with a rim of flowers holds her breasts, and hugging her hips is a petticoat with layer upon layer of frills.

Her voice is a breathy rasp as she looks at me and says, "So, make me yours."

47

ROSALINA

It's selfish to want them all. But as the Summer Prince's ravenous gaze roams over me, I don't care. In here, for tonight, we can pretend.

Dayton smirks. "You look so cute, Blossom. I hope our sweet girl is prepared for all the naughty things we're going to do to her."

He grabs the frilly band around my waist and tugs me against his chest. "I discovered that even fae wear lingerie," I say. "Marigold said I might have need of it tonight."

"Marigold was right." Dayton shoves his large hand beneath my skirt to cup my wet and aching pussy.

I sigh into the touch, my whole body filling with bliss. "I wasn't sure I'd get to feel you again."

Sadness flashes in his eyes, and his lips part.

"As if any of us could refrain from touching you." Ezryn's deep voice ripples through me. His gloved hands move the hair off my shoulder, and I lean back against his hard metal body.

"That's true." Farron comes to my other side. He runs a hand up my stomach and tugs at the lacy frills of the brassiere. "This is cute, Sweetheart."

Three of the princes surround me. Somehow, it feels so right. If only there wasn't a hole in my heart that hasn't been filled. Something missing. *Someone* missing.

Dayton's mouth crashes over mine, and the desperate longing I've felt for weeks floods through me. "I need to be inside you," he murmurs.

I nod, and Ezryn guides us down to the seat. Dayton kneels before me, as Farron works on stripping the Summer Prince of his clothes.

"Are you ready for him, Baby Girl?" Ezryn pulls my knees apart, then slides a hand between my legs.

"Mmm," I moan. "You took off your gloves."

"I needed to feel you," he says. His fingers roughly slide me open, playing across my skin. "You're so wet. So willing to be filled."

I whimper and squirm against his teasing. Then the breath goes out of me as I gaze up at Dayton, looking like an ancient carved god. He's completely naked except for the flower crown on his head.

A longing mewl escapes me as I take him in, the rippling muscles on his chest, the thin trail of hair that dips between his sharp hip bones. And then his cock, throbbing, veins prominent and dripping with pre-cum.

"I did that to you already?" I smirk.

"You have no idea what you do to me," he whispers.

Something melts inside, and a burst of love at the vulnerability of the words travels through my mind. I know it's from Farron. He sits across from us, naked, legs spread and stroking his long cock.

"Why are you over there?" I ask.

"I get you every day. I'm going to enjoy the show. For now."

"She's ready for us." Ezryn flips my frilly skirt up to give a full view to the Summer Prince. The Spring Prince stands and begins undoing the laces of his greaves. I watch with eager anticipation as he slides off his armor, revealing only the tight black underclothes.

With strong arms, Ezryn maneuvers me so I'm lying lengthwise on the flower bench, facing up. "Rosalina, are you ready to be pleasured by three fae at once?" he says as he takes a seat behind me and cradles my head in his lap.

I nod, whimpering with anticipation.

Dayton snatches my jaw. "Use your words, Blossom."

"Yes, I'm yours. I'm all of yours."

"Good." Dayton kneels on the bench between my legs. Taking my ankles, he wraps them on either side of his waist, then enters me in a swift movement.

"Oh, fuck, fuck, fuck," I cry out as he drives in deep, my inner walls clenching around his massive cock. My head bounces in Ez's lap.

"Our cute girl certainly has a naughty mouth," Dayton says. The pink light of the flower petals casts his hair a rose-gold.

"I could take this outfit off and I wouldn't be so cute," I glower.

He slams to the hilt. "You'll always be cute. But don't you dare take this off." His hand slides between my legs to massage my clit.

The muscles in my core tighten and my heart pulses with anticipation.

"Don't tell me you're coming already, Rosalina." Ezryn slips a hand beneath the lace of the brassiere and pinches a taunt nipple.

I bite my lip hard enough to draw blood. "It feels so good."

"Yeah?" Dayton circles his hips, showcasing how full I am of him. His nimble fingers touch me just the right way.

"Tell us what you like, Baby Girl," Ezryn says, cupping my entire breast in his large hand.

"You, all of you," I gasp as the sensation of it sends my body writhing in waves of delicious heat.

"Oh, Blossom," Dayton groans, throwing his head back as my muscles clench around his cock. I'm so close to the edge.

"Beautiful," Farron gasps, watching us with wide eyes. "All of you."

Ezryn puts my head on the bench and reaches forward to grip Dayton around the back of the neck. "Don't let her come yet."

"Ez," I whine. "Please, I—"

Dayton's lips part, blond hair tangled around his face, then he smirks. "Aye, Daddy."

Ezryn groans. "Why do you call me that—"

But I only giggle. "He doesn't hate it as much as he pretends. I want to see how hard you are … Daddy."

"Rosalina," Ezryn says, a warning edge to his voice, and a strong hand grips my neck.

All I can do is moan in pleasure, completely and utterly theirs. Dayton stares down at us, then braces himself on the side of the petal and starts to move. Really move.

"Feel it, Rosalina," Dayton growls. "Because I'm not anywhere close to finished."

They continue to work me, my breath short gasps as the Spring Prince loosens and tightens his grip on my neck.

"Get on all fours," Dayton suddenly commands, and I hasten to obey him. It puts me face to face with Ezryn's lap, and the obvious bulge. "You see that?" Dayton says. "That looks to me like a sorely ignored cock for a waiting mouth."

I lick my lips and blink up at the Spring Prince. He swears again in the language I don't understand and works at his lacing before pulling out his cock, thick and steel-hard.

"Damn," Dayton says, gripping my ass and shoving into me from behind. "That's a nice cock. If you don't suck it, I will."

"Oh, Day," I moan, clawing at the bench for purchase as he drives deep inside me, hitting my G-spot in spurts of wondrous pleasure. "This cock is all mine."

I bring my lips down on Ezryn's length, sucking deeply. Not bothering with teasing, I wrap one hand around the base, sliding and twisting the parts my throat can't reach. I take on Dayton's urgency, barely pausing to breathe, my sounds only gurgles and moans.

Ezryn descends to a series of curses, deep breaths echoing from his helm.

"Oh Baby, you have no idea how hot you look sucking cock," Dayton groans. "Especially with your ass bouncing in this frilly little skirt."

Then he flips the petticoat up and smacks my ass. I release my mouth from Ezryn's cock long enough to let out a staggered cry.

"Did you like that, Baby?" Farron calls. "Do you want your ass nice and red?"

I chance a look at my mate, stroking his cock across from us. "That's a lot of talk for someone so far away."

"I could paint your ass, too, Fare," Dayton calls over.

Farron crosses over to us, and Dayton takes his hand off my waist and pulls him into a deep kiss. I feel a gentle tap. "You have the most perfect ass, Sweetheart."

Languidly, I run my tongue up Ezryn's cock before flicking my gaze to Farron. "Come closer."

He walks up to my face. Bracing myself on one arm, I reach out and wrap my other hand around his cock. Farron murmurs something unintelligible before grasping my hair and guiding my mouth back down on Ezryn's length. I take it greedily.

A low male groan rumbles through Ezryn, and his fingers slide along my spine. "Three cocks, Baby Girl. How does it feel to have us all at your mercy?"

It feels … euphoric. My head is spinning, lust and desire fogging my mind. I swirl the pad of my thumb over the tip of Farron's cock, and he tugs sharply on my hair. Ezryn tastes delectable, especially knowing how rock-hard I've made him, how he loves my lips around his cock …

Day's fucking me like it's his sole mission in life to fill me with his cum, fucking me like he'd die without my pussy. Or maybe I'd die without his cock. Either way, I never want him to stop.

Yet, at the same time, I want more. I feel so selfish thinking it, but my thoughts drift across the stars. Keldarion belongs here with us, too.

Gasping, I look up at Ezryn. "It would feel better if you let me come, Daddy."

His cock twitches. The dark visor of his helm seems to zero in on me, and I can only imagine how intently he's watching the saliva and pre-cum drip from my mouth.

"You will come when I say so," he says, voice all hard dominance.

"I'm not done with you," Dayton says, and he smacks my ass, hard. Then, he braces a foot on the ground to increase to an absolute brutal pace. I scream, tears streaming down my face. But the Spring Prince isn't done with me. He snatches my chin and tilts his helm. "I think this lovely throat can take it deeper."

I evaluate the massive size of the Spring Prince's cock before opening my lips. He knots a hand in my hair, guiding me deeper and deeper. And I take him. He feels so good between my lips, and the delicious, raspy sound he makes only spurs me on.

We find a rhythm, the three of us, as my mouth glides up and down Ezryn's cock, his fingers knotted in my hair. My Summer Prince pounds in and out of me, my breasts swinging with the momentum, as a light sheen of perspiration grows on my brow. My hand strokes Farron wildly, and he reaches between my legs to massage my clit.

Though Ezryn and Dayton aren't connected to us with a bond, I feel something building between the four of us. A wave cresting.

And we're all going to crash down together.

"Come for us, Baby Girl," Ezryn demands.

A muffled scream erupts from my lips as my orgasm overtakes me in a burst of light. Dayton roars, slamming in hard enough to rattle my whole body, his white-hot seed exploding deep inside me. Farron bursts his pleasure into my palm. At the same time, Ezryn's cock pulses, as a groan rumbles through him. His grip on my hair is near painful when he spills down my throat.

All of them cum on me, inside me. It feels so good, a deep well of satisfaction flowing within. I'm a sticky mess, but I am theirs. The pleasure doesn't stop rippling through me, so overwhelming I can barely breathe. My body spasms and clamps down on Dayton's cock. His male groans telling me he's feeling this just as intensely as I am.

Moaning, I swallow before looking up at Ezryn with a satisfied grin. He wipes the side of my lips with a tender touch, then, in a voice tinged with annoyance, says, "Someone kiss her for me."

"Gladly." Farron grips my face and kisses me deeply.

Dayton bends to layer kisses along my spine, his cock still inside me, as if he's reluctant to leave. My muscles pulse around him, and I wish I could keep him this close to me forever.

"Holy fuck, Rosie, you look so hot filled with all our cum," Dayton groans.

My arms start to shake. Dayton slides out of me, leaving his sticky release dripping down my legs. I miss the feeling of him inside me.

"Oh my god," I moan.

"You're not done yet," Dayton says, turning to Farron. "You're going to eat my cum out of your mate's pussy while I fuck you."

Farron and I exchange a look of pure and utter melting for this man. Then we both let out a collective whimper.

"You heard him. Spread those legs," Ezryn says, all dominance, as he positions me on my back.

Farron lightly kisses my inner thigh. "You smell so good, Sweetheart. Like Day."

His breath is hot between my legs before he licks me. Then one lick turns into an utter devouring. My overly sensitive pussy begins to throb.

Farron moans against me as Dayton enters him. The Summer Prince's expression is pure bliss as he drives in and out of my mate. Then he catches my gaze and winks.

Ezryn delicately pushes my brassiere down, freeing my breasts to the chilly air. "You're absolutely gorgeous, especially when your face is overtaken with pleasure."

Farron's tongue moves faster, deeper.

"Every drop," Dayton pants as he moves. "Get every drop, Pup."

Farron's answer is a sigh of ecstasy, his cock already hard again. I writhe on the flower petal, barely able to contain all the sensation.

"Come for us again, Baby Girl." Ezryn's nimble fingers work my breasts. "No one can hear you out there. Scream if you want."

And I do. His words send me over the edge in an explosion of euphoria. Farron moans, and through my blurry vision I see his cock spurt ropes of cum. Dayton pumps once more before roaring and emptying himself again. And Ezryn holds me tight through it all.

I lie in the bliss, wishing the flower could stay closed forever. That I could be theirs forever. And they could be mine.

There is more love within me to give. Deep within my selfish heart, empty spaces echo.

48

CASPIAN

"Well, well, well, Quellos, you've truly outdone yourself. Instead of playing around with old bones from the dirt, you've finally been able to keep your subjects alive."

I dangle a leg off a parapet and stare down into the open courtyard that is part of Perth Quellos's laboratory. Sira has truly surpassed herself in setting the old fool up with every toy and tool the Below has to offer. I must admit, it almost makes me think he made the right choice instead of languishing in Frostfang's prison.

Almost.

"Are you going to sit up there and judge, or are you going to be of assistance?" Quellos snaps.

"Sit and judge, thank you very much. I like to do what I'm good at."

Quellos mutters under his breath and turns his attention back to the goblin before him. The little creature stares around with wide eyes, eager to be the next pawn in Sira's game.

"Stay still," the old fae barks at the goblin, then, without a moment of warning, shoves it into a glowing green pit before him.

Mist that swirls like emerald fingers writhes around the screaming goblin. The creature crumbles in on itself, pitching forward, chitters turning to gurgles. Quellos sighs and wipes sweat from his bald brow.

"Such power in the Green Flame." Perth's eyes widen. "If only we could draw more of its magic into this world."

My insides to turn to ice. *Oh yes, let's invite a terrifying god-like being that could obliterate the entire Enchanted Vale and the human world with a snap of his giant fingers.* My jaws tighten, but I let nothing show on my face. All of Mother's prayers, all of Quellos's tricks with crystals … None of it compares to what lies within my own blood. It is a secret Quellos doesn't know, can never know.

I turn my attention back to Quellos's little experiment.

Green fire erupts through the creature and it straightens, crying out with renewed vigor. Its eyes flash with that same eerie flame. Its gnarled body climbs up the wall to stand before the former vizier of Winter.

"Very good," Quellos says, then points to the back wall. "With the others."

The goblin, now burning with an inward phantasmal fire, stumbles across the courtyard, where rows of other flame-riddled goblins stand in wait.

That must make … What? Two thousand of them now?

I keep a smirk plastered on my face. "Quite the little army you're brewing. They weren't any match for Castletree, though. Mother wasn't pleased with either of us."

The fingernail lines down his skull have just started to heal.

Quellos shakes his head. "I've only tried it on goblins. Just wait until I get it to work on fae." He looks up at me, blue lips stretched thin from his smile. "Care to be my first test subject?"

I leap down, landing the ten-foot jump with graceful ease. I waltz over to Kel's former vizier and bop him on the nose. "Not in the slightest." Then I turn and stroll through the archway into his lab. "Though I am fascinated by what other little creations you've been cooking up. What a wickedly twisted mind you have."

Quellos scuttles after me, breathing heavy. Vain fool can never resist showing off his work. And I do so like to be aware of everything all the time.

The lab is lit by the soft glow of luminescent jewels embedded in the walls and ceiling. Multiple workstations are set up throughout the large space. Glass apparatuses bubble with brightly colored elixirs, while shelves are stocked with vials.

To the side is a small greenhouse. I press my nose to the glass. "You've made significant strides in here. It's positively bursting." I'm not lying just to stroke his ego: the space is filled with huge red, yellow, and purple flowers.

"Yes, yes, we've had great success with our botany projects," Quellos says, too enraptured with his own work to remember he hates me. "You can go inside if you like, but you must wear one of these." He pulls down a vase and fishes out a white bloom.

I wave it away. "That's all right."

"Fine then." Quellos sniffs.

I continue my tour through the laboratory, randomly picking things up, examining them, ignoring Quellos's cries of displeasure, then continuing on. A horrid sound catches my ear, and I point to a cage on the desk. "What's going on there?"

Pale yellow foam oozes out of the mouth of a small brown rat, eyes rolled back to reveal the whites. It slams against the bars of the cage, squeaking and scratching.

Quellos strokes his chin. "Ah, this is a variation of bio botanical experiments. I was hoping this one would be trainable, but alas, it is still rabid." He darts his eyes around and says lowly, "Too bad I already authorized the use of it on my fae test subject."

I narrow my eyes. "Is this how you created that monstrosity you trialed last week? The one that escaped and took out the entire goblin unit?"

"I recaptured it," he says.

The eruption of a portal sounds outside the lab and bickering follows.

"Do not show weakness now." My sister's voice.

"I am not *weak*." The equally vicious retort of the young Spring prince, Kairyn.

The Nightingale and her rabid dog have returned.

Birdy's eyes are ablaze with anger as they walk in. Kairyn always looks the same to me, but I wouldn't be surprised if he were feeling the same.

"Cute look, Birdy. How was your party?" I ask. "I wasn't invited."

"I'm surprised you didn't crash it," Perth sneers as he uses tongs to try to feed the rabid rat. "You love doing that."

I flash a grin. "It's not as fun without Keldarion there."

Birdy storms over and smacks the tongs out of Quellos's hand, making him jump. "Enough of your rambling! We have an opportunity to take action tonight. Let us not waste it."

"We don't need to be so hasty," Kairyn rumbles. "My brother's trust in me grows daily. Besides, I have put measures in place to shake even his iron will. Soon, he will grant me the seat of steward officially—"

The Nightingale rounds on him. Though she is nearly a foot shorter, she surges up on her toes and gets straight in his face. "And what good is a steward if that damned brother of yours is always hovering about? We don't *need* a stewardship, idiot. We need the throne itself! We need Spring's Blessing!"

Kairyn bristles but says nothing.

"It is our purpose. I've only just begun, and I'm already so much further along than you at retrieving my own Blessing. These princes aren't our allies. They are the enemy, and they're only worth what we can take from them." A deep sigh escapes Birdy's lips, and she leans against the counter, head in her hands. "I've made my decision. Ezryn dies. Tonight."

Now it's my turn to bristle. "Well, well, well, the little bird has flown the coop. I don't think you've received the order for that yet."

"I'm taking initiative. Unlike you." She glowers up at me.

The black cape sweeps over the floor as Kairyn paces back and forth. "When I aligned with you years ago, it was for the good of my realm. For my people."

Birdy throws her head back and laughs, harsh and biting. "Is that what you're still telling yourself, love?" She swishes her short hair and drifts over to Kairyn, hips sashaying back and forth. Her fingers walk up his metal chest, and my eyes nearly roll to the back of my skull. "You aligned with me because you want that throne as much as I want to put you on it."

Kairyn's dark gaze burrows into hers, and I know she has him. She continues, "Ezryn left the realm to ruin. Remember what I showed you when we ventured into the Briar? He's a beast, Kai. A monster. But you knew that already, didn't you?" Her hand caresses his helmet. "Your brother is a murderer."

By gods, she is good. I mean, not that Kairyn is the most difficult of subjects—all fight, no facts, just like his brother—but she could talk him into laying down his helm, and he'd thank her for it.

"He is a murderer..." Kairyn repeats.

"It is your destiny to sit atop the Spring throne," Birdy says slowly. "We called upon the Fates, you and I, and asked them what they saw. They showed you your silver path. You will sit upon the throne of Spring and wield its Blessing. Only then can you usher in a new era of prosperity."

It's like a performance, and Quellos and I are mesmerized, watching as she completely wraps the prince around her finger like a piece of twine. It's equally fascinating and pathetic.

But the dog still has some bite. "The Fates never showed me my brother's death," Kairyn growls. "I can still gain the Blessing my way. I just need more time."

"You are afraid of your true potential," she says. "Of the life you deserve. Until you free yourself of this loyalty to the brother that banished you, you will always be his servant."

Kairyn stays silent, fists curling and uncurling. "I'm not his servant. He *will* see my worth."

The Nightingale grabs Kairyn's hand and places it over her heart. "Listen to me, Kai. I found you in the monastery when you were all but hopeless. I gave you purpose. I helped you retake the Golden

Acolytes and save the people of Spring. And what has Ezryn done? He betrayed you. He doesn't believe in you. Not like me."

I cross my arms. From the quiver in her voice, you'd almost think she actually cared for this fool of Spring. Except I know better. Birdy can't care for anyone; Sira beat that out of her.

Kairyn turns away. "I won't kill him."

Birdy fixes him with a scathing look. "Is loyalty such a foreign concept that you can't even recognize it when it's right in front of you? Tell me, Kairyn where does your loyalty truly lie?"

"You're wasting your breath, Birdy," I say and cast a smirk Kairyn's way. "It's hard to get approval from someone who's dead."

"I don't *need* his approval," Kairyn snarls.

I can't help taunting him—it's just too easy. "Is that what you tell yourself? I happen to remember you as a little bothersome boy, always chasing after Ezryn as he chose Keldarion again and again and *again*. One might think he views Kel as more of a brother than you."

Kairyn steps forward, fist winding back as if he intends to take my head off with a single swing. Birdy puts a hand on his chest then glowers at me. "You'll keep quiet if you know what's good for you," she warns.

Ah, but I love all the things that aren't good for me. "You know all about being desperate for approval, don't you, Birdy? I suppose that's why you two are such a good team."

Her glare is so cold, it could freeze the Summer Realm. "I won't kill Ezryn," Kairyn growls. "But I will break him. He will finally realize I am the worthy brother. I promise you I will have the Blessing of Spring."

"And how do you intend to break the High Prince?" she snarls.

Kairyn's voice grows so low and haunted, a shiver runs up my spine. "The Golden Rose. I saw the way he acts around her." He raises a fist. "Her death will destroy him."

The expression on my face remains the same: the smirk, the one raised brow. But inside, my blood rages and my mind whirrs.

Birdy begins to pace. "Yes … Yes. Lady *O'Connell* must die."

"I will send my Penta Conclave after her immediately."

Birdy makes an angry scoff. "Are you even more of a fool than I took you for? Spring must welcome you; you can't have yourself appearing as a renegade if your men get caught." She shakes her head. "I'll do it myself."

And that's when I see it in the glint of her eye. Something deeper than wanting to break Ezryn. A traitorous glint.

She asked for Kairyn's permission to slay Ezryn out of courtesy.

But she'll do what she wants when the time comes.

A yawn escapes me. "Quite the plan, you two. So imaginative."

"Something to say, Caspian?" Birdy shoots back.

I glide over to one of the shelves, start idly picking up the vials and shaking them for fun. The vein in Quellos's head looks ready to burst. "I'm just curious how my little bird and her little dog are planning to assassinate one of the most powerful fae in the Vale. The Golden Rose took down our own dear Quellos, after all."

"It will be quite difficult, mistress," Quellos says. "Besides, High Prince Ezryn is in constant companionship with her." The word comes out a slithering hiss. "She is more dangerous than she appears."

Birdy throws her head back and laughs. "You think I'm afraid of that wretch? I've been waiting for this moment. I will tear her apart thorn by thorn, and Mother will thank me for it."

My dear Birdy shows her colors, and aren't they a vicious sight?

Quellos shoves me away from the shelves and reaches up on his tiptoes for a vial. "The mistress would do well to heed my warning. I, too, underestimated the fae woman. And now I am a servant to the Below instead of ruling over the Winter Realm as I deserved."

Poor Perth has been in service to the Below for much longer than he realized. It was Mother after all who planted those little crowns for him to find. The crowns infused with magic of the Green Flame.

"Oh, shut it, old man." Birdy rolls her big, blue eyes. "You're lucky Mother saw any potential in you at all."

"It's that potential that might save your life." Quellos tips the vial over and pours out a large yellow crystal. "If things don't go as planned against the High Prince and the Golden Rose, you can use this as a contingency."

I throw myself in the path between Quellos and my sister. The crystal gleams like a living thing. "You can't be serious. That's not a contingency. That's *suicide*. This experiment devoured an entire unit of goblins before you contained it."

Birdy shoves me out of her way and snatches the crystal. She holds it up to the light, examining it. "I won't need it. Unlike you, big brother, I have follow-through. But I'll take it ... Just in case I want a little fun."

Kairyn places a heavy hand on her shoulder. "Just the woman. Ezryn is to remain unharmed."

"I will do my best," Birdy says, flicking her hair behind her softly pointed ear. "Though if he interferes, there are some things beyond my control."

My sister and the Spring Prince storm out of the laboratory, and Quellos returns to his rabid rat.

I stand quietly, thinking. Thinking. Thinking.

This is my little sister's opportunity to prove herself to Sira, to finally make something of herself.

Rosalina has no idea what's coming for her. If the Nightingale gets her way, both Rosalina and Ezryn will die tonight.

And it would be no fun at all if our little game ended so soon.

Sorry, sister.

I know what I have to do.

And I know I can't do it alone.

49

EZRYN

Rosalina skips beside me, long hair flowing behind her, laughter echoing through the night. I take her hand and help her leap over the small creek running through the other side of Meadowmere. Dappled moonlight shimmers in from the tree cover and paints her skin with an ethereal glow.

It's as if the forest were made for her, like it has been waiting all these eons for her arrival. *See? We've bloomed just for you.*

Although the foray with my brothers and our woman was not planned for tonight, it was a well-needed distraction. Watching Rosalina writhe beneath our combined pleasuring was a sight that will remain with me always. And it gave me the strength I needed to do what must come next.

Because Kairyn is right. I can't forever hide away the sins of my past, who the High Prince of Spring truly is. Not from her.

After cleaning up, Farron and Dayton took the opportunity to sneak up to the monastery and see if there were any more clues about the missing Spring steel while Kairyn is distracted by the party. But I asked Rosalina to come with me. To walk under the hallowed boughs of Meadowmere Forest and out the other side to Sylvanita Lake.

The death place of my mother.

Rosalina doesn't know that; she thinks I'm taking her to the lake. So, she spins as she walks, her dress trailing petals and her eyes full of stars. I revel in it.

Because though I don't even have her now, after this, I may lose everything.

A clearing opens in the trees ahead. I take in a deep breath. She must sense I'm anxious because she laces her fingers with mine and bumps my shoulder. Windscythe jangles in the hilt on my back.

"This," I say, "is Sylvanita Lake."

The full moon illuminates the clearing where a crystalline lake shines beneath its reflection. Water from the river above cascades over jagged rocks and into the lake. Trees drenched in pink cherry blossoms encircle the grove. At its crown is a massive willow tree. Its branches sway to the whims of the wind, its boughs adorned with tiny catkins as delicate as lace.

And piercing its trunk is a silver broadsword.

Rosalina steps forward, blinking. "This place feels like a dream."

"It's very sacred to our realm. Legend has it the Queen herself grew the willow tree."

Rosalina stares up at it and smiles. "I like it. It reminds me of the one back in Orca Cove."

I place my palm on the small of her back. "Come on."

Using my arm, I part the boughs of the willow like a curtain so Rosalina can enter. She runs a hand along the long branches. A few leaves drift over her hair.

I stand perfectly still watching her, but every part of me screams to grab her in my arms. My heart feels on fire, coals erupting into flame.

I have never felt anything like this before.

Seeing her here, in my realm beneath the cherry blossom trees, a deep and ancient knowing fights against my logical mind.

All the centuries of my life have passed with little meaning because I was waiting. Waiting to find her.

I rub at the silver plate over my chest, wishing I could grasp my heart. Months ago, I'd placed a will-o'-wisp there and seen nothing but tangled threads. Maybe I am broken.

And this ... This is what I must face to make it right.

"A sword?" Rosalina circles the trunk before she stops at the hilt. Only a small amount of the blade is visible, the rest absorbed by the tree.

I inhale deeply. I must tell her now. "It belonged to my mother."

"Princess Isidora," Rosalina says. "Why is it here?"

Every word is pain. "In memorial. This is where she lost her life."

"Oh, Ez," Rosalina breathes. "I'm so sorry."

There's so much more that needs to be said, but the words are stuck like arrows in my chest. I can't bear to look at Rose, so I turn my gaze to the ground.

Curiously, I notice a cluster of purple flower buds, unfamiliar to me. Much of the vegetation changed after my mother's death, but this is new since my last visit.

I kneel to examine them, just to give my hands something to do as I force the rest of the words out. "Do you know how my mother died, Rose?"

There's silence and then, "When she passed on Spring's Blessing to you. Eldy said that the act can be very dangerous. I'm so sorry that happened to her. To you."

I run a hand over the large bud and squeeze my eyes shut. "That's what everyone thinks. What all of Spring thinks. What even Farron and Dayton think. The only ones who know the truth are me, Kel, and Kairyn."

Her hand presses on my shoulder. "I will never judge your past, Ez. I know who you are now, and I see who you are becoming. You can tell me anything."

And I feel it ... The threads inside of me untangling, spreading out like petals on a breeze. I can trust her with my darkness, and she will shelter me.

I look up. "I ki—"

The flower bud in my hand blooms, spewing golden pollen into the air. A huge puff blows over my visor and under the edge of my helm.

And then the nightmare begins.

50

ROSALINA

"Ezryn? Ezryn!" I scream. He's staggered backward, clutching his helm, crying out with a voice I've never heard him make. Pollen smears across his visor and down his neck. His movements are jerky, frantic. I need to steady him.

I lunge forward to grab him, and a yellow blur shrouds my vision. My throat tightens, nose tingling.

My head spins. The trunk of the willow tree wavers in and out of focus, becoming two then three. My legs shake beneath me, and I look down to see the ground is moving under my feet, rolling over itself like waves.

Ezryn. I have to grab Ezryn. A horrible scream fills the air. Is it his voice or mine?

I need to get out of the willow tree. But the long dripping branches are gone. Spiderwebs surround me. I cry out, trying to push them away, but the sticky threads grab hold of me, pulling, pulling, pulling.

I fall to the ground. Hard. When I look up at the night sky, the moon is gone, replaced by the white face of the Winter wolf. The wolf howls, deep and mournful, but his maw is filled with blood. Has he just hunted or … The wolf coughs. Blood sputters across his jaw. It's his blood, his blood…

The wolf in the sky gags again, and the blood pours out, enough to make the waterfall run red. There are figures standing on the wet rocks beneath the tumbling water. I know them. Help. Help. I want to cry the words out loud but there are spiderwebs over my mouth. Help. Help.

The figures turn around, and Dayton and Farron stare at me with empty eye sockets. They wave at me, slowly and in unison.

Then I'm tumbling, and I can't remember where I was before, but it wasn't here because here is Orca Cove, and this place feels familiar and unfamiliar all at once.

A rainy street. Pieces of broken wood and a destroyed book. A pickup truck with headlights like an evil face. A man touching me with greedy fingers.

Somehow, my mind forms a coherent thought: this isn't a hallucination. This is a memory.

And that is so much worse.

The image shifts. My bedroom. Blood on a knife, on the ground. Tears and screaming and my own skin torn away from me.

No ... No more. I don't want these memories.

Then a strangled cry, one I wished I'd never have to hear again as my mate cradles his mother's body. And they're frozen, one by one, and there's nothing I can do.

Stop! Stop!

This isn't happening. I need to find Ezryn. The ground shifts again, and I'm back in the grove except the trees are closed in all around me and mud keeps swallowing my feet.

But I need to get to Ezryn.

"I didn't, I didn't, I didn't."

His voice. Each step fills my body with nausea, but I forge ahead.

"I'm coming for you," I think I say. I hope I say.

He's back under the willow tree. But the problem is it's so covered with spiderwebs, and I don't want to touch it.

Tears roll down my cheeks. When they fall to the ground, they're like acid, creating craters in the earth. I'm scared to know what they're doing to my face.

"I didn't!" Ezryn cries out, a mournful howl. "I didn't mean to."

I suck in a breath and throw myself through the spiderweb. Icky fingers cling to my hair and skin. But he's there, leaning against the trunk, hands digging at his helm.

"Ezryn, I'm here," I say, placing my palms over his.

My heart feels like it's imploding in on itself, a black hole bending all gravity. The rest of the world lurches away.

The grove again. Daytime. It looks different: more flowers, brighter. Ezryn's here, still right in front of me.

"No, no, no," he mumbles. "Get out. Get out!"

But it's too late. I can feel it now—my consciousness has been left behind, and I'm here with him.

In his nightmare.

Or rather, I realize as I stumble out from beneath the cover of the willow tree, his memory.

There's another Ezryn in pure white armor. I know it's him, because though I can't see his face, I can feel *it*, the way one feels the sun on their skin or the breeze through their hair.

There's a woman: tall and broad of shoulder and hip. A long jade skirt pleats out from under an armored breastplate. And she wears the most stunning helmet I've ever seen: starlight silver with a narrowed visor angled like cat eyes.

She's trying to grab his shoulders, but he's staggering away from her. "You must control it, son!"

This Ezryn ripples, flashes of magic sparking off his fingers like fireworks. "I-I can't!"

He pushes Princess Isidora, and my Ezryn does the same to me. The words are a haunting echo from them both: "Get out of here!"

But I can't move. I can only watch in horror.

This nightmare was once real. I feel it in the threads binding me to Ezryn in this moment. I feel it pulsing through the air: the Blessing of Spring passed from mother to son.

A Blessing too powerful for the son to control.

"I can't!" the past Ezryn cries and then he doubles over.

And erupts.

A guttural roar, a shockwave of power, and a pain in my heart so pure I fall to my knees. The grass in the grove shrivels, the trees wither, the leaves turn to ash in the breeze, and fish float to the surface of the pond.

And Princess Isidora cries out once, holding her throat, as she falls before Ezryn's feet.

"No," I whisper, my voice lost to the cry of the young fae man before me, clutching feverishly at the mother he killed.

And my Ezryn sinks to his knees beside me, silent.

"Murderer!" A new voice, a new figure among the dead trees. Kairyn. He turns and runs away.

Then more voices join the fray, coming from all around us: "Murderer! Murderer! Murderer!"

Some of them I recognize: Kairyn's, Eldy's, Kel's.

My own.

The world is shifting again, the voices turning to cackles, the trees growing eyes. The lake is now a bubbling pool of lava. No, no, we can't keep doing this. We have to get out. It needs to stop.

I need to stop it.

I struggle to my feet and look around, trying to see past what's real and what's not. The flowers ... They got their pollen on us. I need to get it off.

Lava boils and pops. I told Ezryn he could trust me. I need to trust me.

I sprint straight into the fire.

51

ROSALINA

Cold water rushes over me as I collapse into the lake. I plunge my head under again and again, scrubbing at my eyes, and gulping down the water to clear my throat.

With a gasp, I surge upward and look around. My brain is foggy, but my vision is clear. That fucking flower…

A growl rips from me as I stare at the purple flowers under the willow tree. Shooting my wrist out, thorns erupt, crashing under the roots of the plants, then smothering them. I won't chance getting blasted with that pollen again.

An anguished cry sounds, and I spot Ezryn pacing in circles, clawing at his breastplate. "It was an accident! An accident!"

I need to get him in the water and get that pollen out of his face.

Heaving my soaking dress up into my arms, I sprint over to him. "Ez, listen to me. It's Rosie. Come on, I'll help you." I touch his arm.

He staggers away. "Get away from me! I can't control it!"

"You're not hurting me," I say calmly. "I'm not in danger. See? I'm okay. Come with me."

"Stop, Kai, stop, I'm sorry, I'm sorry…" He slams a hand against his helm. "Get out of my fucking head!"

Shit, I didn't want to do it this way, but I might have to. I twitch my wrists, feeling for the briars at my command. "Ez, forgive me for this—"

The tearing of earth sounds, and I jump. At the edge of the willow tree, my thorns shoot up, growing and writhing. Someone is using them.

My chest heaves, and a strange smile appears on my face.

Caspian.

I should feel afraid, but instead I'm relieved. *He'll help me save Ezryn. I know he will.*

The briars fall away to reveal a figure.

Not Caspian.

A masked woman. Someone I've seen only once before in the Below.

The Nightingale.

52

ROSALINA

What relief I felt a moment ago turns to ash. I take a wobbly sidestep, placing myself between Ezryn and the intruder.

The Nightingale is dressed in similar armor to the last time I saw her: form-fitting, with jewel tones that change shade like a pool of oil. Her mask shrouds the bottom half of her face, revealing only her piercing blue eyes. Even with only that visible, I can tell she's smiling.

With feline grace, she glides away from the willow tree and chucks something through the air.

A seed. A seed just like the one Caspian gave us to grow a portal to the Below.

Light and darkness shimmer together as thorns burst up, forming an iridescent door. And through it charges hundreds of soldiers and goblins.

They form obedient ranks behind her, and she stands at the front, pride glittering in her eyes. The armored soldiers—the Dreadknights, she'd called them the last time—stand at attention holding blades and bows. She twirls a short and slender sword in each hand. Her goblins chitter excitedly at the back; thankfully, this lot isn't burning with green flame.

Though, I'm not sure that's going to make much of a difference right now.

The Nightingale steps forward. "Well, this could not be any more perfect. Your dear prince seems to be having a hard time. Perhaps he'd like to be put out of his misery?"

A thorn erupts beside me, "I'll never let you hurt him."

She throws her head back. "This is so fun! Here I was thinking we'd be playing cat and mouse all night. But your little thorn trick led me straight here." She gestures to the thorns I created to stifle the hallucinogenic pollen. "Now, I get to watch your face as I bleed your prince out, prick by prick."

My heart careens in my chest, and I stagger backward. Ezryn is completely oblivious to their presence, still trapped in his nightmare, pacing and muttering to himself. *Farron!* I cry out in my mind. *Help!*

Rose? His voice is faint in my mind. *Are you okay? We're heading up the mountain. Hold on—*

Hurry!

The Nightingale's sharp laughter interrupts my thoughts. "It really is my lucky day." She flicks a look behind her at her knights and the goblins. "Hold position. This one's mine."

I need to get us out of here *now*. I snatch my necklace and quickly, desperately, feel for my connection to Castletree. The air before me shimmers with pearlescent waves.

"Come on, Ezryn! We have to go home now!" I cry.

But Ezryn's fallen to his knees, staring up at the sky, a low-pitched keening coming from his throat. What is he seeing in the depths of his mind?

I run over and heave on his arm. "Come on! Come on!" But he's too heavy.

Thorns it is, then. Using my bracelets from Caspian, I summon a surge of thick briars to shoot up toward Ez—

An oily black vine smashes on top of them, pinning mine down.

What? The only people capable of wielding briars are me and Caspian.

"Not so fast," the Nightingale chides. "I'm not nearly done with you."

She bolts toward me. There's no time to do anything before I'm backhanded so hard, I collapse to the ground.

I struggle to my elbows to see her pacing over me. I can't even compare her to a predator because a predator is grateful for its prey. She instead looks down at me with such disdain, hurt blossoms in my chest.

"That necklace should not belong to you," she snarls. "You do not deserve it. Look at you. Soft. Weak. You disgust me."

"Yeah, well," I murmur, slowly sending one of my vines to creep up behind her, "I don't really want to be besties with you either."

My briars snag her around the waist and whip her hard against a tree. Despite that, she's standing within seconds. That playfulness gone.

"I will fucking kill you!" she screams.

Every maneuver Dayton taught me during our training flies from my brain. I turn and sprint, but she's so much faster, bowling me over despite her smaller frame.

I hit the ground, twist to my back, and she's right in my face, driving those thin blades down. I barely roll out of the way.

"Look at you, dressed like a little doll," she snarls, scrambling after me. "That's all this is to you, isn't it? Castles and dress-up?"

I duck around a tree and heave a burst of briars up to throw her back. "You forgot to mention the delicious food."

"You spoiled brat," she screams. With a roar, her own iridescent black briars surge up, destroying mine.

With a yelp, I take off running. What am I going to do? My portal to Castletree has closed, but even if I had a moment to summon one again, I can't chance this lunatic following me there. And if she can destroy any of the briars I make, I'm trapped here.

Ez, I cry out. *Please wake up.*

But he's still on the ground, head rocking back and forth. "I'm trying, I'm trying, I'm trying."

There's only one choice. I'll have to stall her until Farron and Dayton arrive.

And then hope the three of us can take on this bitch and her little army.

I shoot a blast of white fire out behind me, but her briars lift her up, projecting her over the flames. "The Golden Rose, they call you," she sneers. "I don't see any gold. Or roses. How can someone like you ever think themselves capable of saving anyone?"

I yelp as a briar wraps around my ankle and pulls. I slam hard to the ground, then am ripped backward. Her small hands are all over me, blades tossed to the side, as she shoves me on my back.

Then she's straddling my waist, clawing at my eyes like a vicious cat. "You can't even fight! You're weak! So weak!"

By some miracle, I catch her wrists and rip them away. The words are out of my mouth before I have a chance to think: "Why do you hate me?"

For a moment, there's silence in the clearing. "Because," she breathes, "you got him. And I got *nothing*."

Then briars lace around my wrists, pinning me down, and her hands are on my neck.

I can't move. There's nothing but the Nightingale. Tears fall from her eyes and land on my cheeks.

I gasp for breath, but can't take anything in. *Farron…*

I'm almost there, Rosie. Almost down the mountain. Hold on!

But I can't hold on. The breath is being squeezed out of me, and my mate will find my body here, and this fae woman who hates me for a reason I don't understand will kill Ezryn and he'll never know I forgive him for what he did in his past.

How I want to move forward with him into a new future.

My vision blackens at the edges. The Nightingale squeezes tighter, and she's sobbing now, full-on sobbing, but she keeps her hands wrapped around my throat. And I'm so sad. Because I never told each of them how much I love them.

Out of the corner of my eye, I catch sight of something. An eruption of thorns.

But these are different.

These are thorns frosted with ice.

53

KELDARION

"So, you still snore." A voice cuts through my haze of sleep. "I suppose you don't realize, as you spend most nights as that mangy beast."

The Prince of Thorns leans in the doorway, his black cloak covered in snow, moonlight glinting off his pink nose and cheeks.

I leap up, grabbing his collar and slamming him against the wall. "How are you here?"

"Oh, just thought I'd take a quick jaunt to the most miserable and cold place in all the Vale."

I snarl, drawing him closer. He must have traveled here from the thorns in the chasm. "I should rip you apart for what you did to Autumn. What you did to Farron."

Caspian slinks out of my grip. "Unfortunately, there isn't time for your empty threats today." He tosses me my warm jerkin and boots.

Keeping my eyes locked on his, I lace the shirt and tug on the supple leather shoes.

A sharp pain cuts through my bond.

Rosalina.

"Damn, she's fast," he murmurs. "You're going to need this."

From the folds of his cloak, Caspian reveals the Sword of the

Protector. *How did he get that?* I snatch the sheathed blade. But Caspian leaves his hand outstretched. "And you're going to need me."

"Rosalina is in trouble," I growl.

Thorns and shadows curl around his feet. Rosalina's terror grows through our mate bond. There's no time to question Caspian's game, to guess at his motives. There is no other choice. I take the Prince of Thorns' hand.

His smile is maddening. The familiar sensation of thorns whips me under the earth. I shut my eyes as my body ripples with power, ice crackling out in every direction.

We burst through the surface like breaking through water, an explosion of shadows and ice. Dreadknights, goblins, and Ezryn. My brother is lying on the ground, clutching his helm and screaming. But my focus narrows on my mate, pinned by another woman.

Rage like a winter storm, born from the depths of my magic, courses through my veins. I swing the Sword of the Protector, and a beam of ice explodes from it. It strikes the woman in the chest and sends her flying into her knights.

In a blur of shadow, Caspian brandishes a long purple sword made of briars and dispatches a goblin charging at me.

"Are you with me?" I ask.

A strand of dark hair falls across his face. "Don't see who else is going to watch your back when you go into a single-minded murder streak."

Dreadknights and goblins from the Below face us. Yet, he fights at my side. There's no time to question, not if I want a chance of rescuing Ezryn and Rosalina.

"Together," I say.

His eyes flash like stars. "Together."

54

ROSALINA

The Nightingale sails off me in a blast of ice, and I heave in great gulps of air, grabbing at my raw throat. My muscles ache. Through the haze of goblins, I see him. Keldarion. But even if I hadn't seen him, I'd know he was here. My mate bond blooms bright in my chest.

But strangest of all, he's not alone.

He's with the Prince of Thorns.

They stand back-to-back in the middle of the grove as a host of Dreadknights and goblins charge. I can't see the Nightingale through the throng. I wonder if Kel's blast killed her.

With gritted teeth, I force myself to get up. I need to get to Kel, and at the moment, he and Cas are the legion's entire focus. The two of them move with knife-edge precision. Though surrounded, not a single goblin makes it past their flanks. Magic—ice and thorns—flows perfectly with the strikes of their blades. It almost has the fluidity of a dance. A dance, I realize, they must have done many times before.

This isn't the first time they've fought on the same side. It's evident in the duality of their blows, the thorns covered in a dreadful frost as they penetrate the enemy, their feet moving in unison with each other.

A blur moves to the left, and I dodge as a goblin strikes out. Guess they're tired of ignoring me. I shoot a briar from my bracelets, and it wraps around the creature's torso, pinning it to the ground. Then I take off into the sea of bodies, letting my mate bond tug me to Kel.

He glitters white as snow through the chaos, swirling with Caspian's purple and black shadows.

At least, I'm pretty sure it's only leading me to Kel.

"Where do you think you're going?" A Dreadknight steps in my path, his iridescent armor glimmering in the moonlight.

I yelp and throw myself to the ground to avoid his grasp. He kicks me in the gut, sending me rolling into a goblin. A goblin who doesn't think twice before using its blade to strike me across the arm, leaving a line of sticky red blood. *If I don't get up, I'm going to die.*

"Rosalina!" Keldarion roars, fighting toward me, Caspian at his back.

"Kel!" I scream. Yearning fights through the terror.

The goblin moves to strike again, and I throw up a thick briar to block its attack.

Rosalina, hold on! Farron yells in my mind.

At the thought of my mate, my body burns. I stand and white flames explode from my hands. They sear the Dreadknight in front of me. He screams, falling back.

And for a single moment, I see a path to Kel. Once I'm with him, we can help Ezryn break free of his nightmares. Breathing rabid with fear, I run, darting around the confused Dreadknights and goblins. They say Caspian's name, voices tinged with confusion and ... anger.

He's betrayed them, I realize.

A goblin grabs at me from behind, ripping my dress, but I tug it free. Almost at Kel. Another goblin leaps in my path, chittering, blade outstretched. I don't have time to stop.

A large bramble grows beneath my feet, propelling me up, up, up in the air, just how I saw the Nightingale use hers. The thorn hurls me forward. I'm weightless.

Then I fall into Keldarion. He wraps his arms around me, pulling me close.

As if there was nothing else in the world, no goblins or knights, his lips crash over mine. It's every longing moment of our separation being released at last. Something no dream could replicate.

My body blooms and lights at his touch, his soft mouth pressing against mine. And I pull away long enough to breathe his name.

"Oh stars." Caspian rolls his eyes. "Do you two really need to do that now? Right now?"

Kel's kiss deepens, hands tangling in my hair, and I don't believe all the forces of the Above and Below could pull us apart now.

"Always surrounded by idiots." Caspian sighs, but as he does, a great barrier of thorns grows in a tangle around us, delivering a tiny moment of respite.

The chilling touch of Kel's body passes over me as I taste the snow and ice on his lips. Right now, I am safe. He pulls away and clutches my face. "You're hurt."

"I'll be fine. It's Ezryn. Those purple flowers spewed some pollen that trapped us in a nightmare," I explain. "I threw myself in the water and it seemed to help wash everything off."

"I'll get him," Keldarion says.

"Hope you turtle doves are ready," Caspian calls, voice straining as he attempts to keep up the briar barrier. "Because the goblins really want to say hello."

"Let them come." Keldarion shoves me between himself and Caspian, then unsheathes the Sword of the Protector. *When did he get that?* It was under my bed here in the Spring Realm.

Caspian lets the barrier fall. The enemy charges. His thorn blade pierces one, and it comes back sticky with black blood. "Where's your bow, Princess?"

"I don't usually bring weapons to a party." I duck under the swing of a Dreadknight.

"That was your first mistake." He spins, and there in his hands is a bow made of thorns. "I trust you remember how to make the arrows?"

I take it gladly. Cas nods for me to follow, and we keep a close tail on Kel, toward Ezryn's hunched form. He kneels in front of his mother's sword, silent but shaking.

Kel sheathes his sword, then gives a mighty roar, heaving Ezryn up and hurtling him into the lake. Water splashes on the shore, but there's no time to see if it works.

A host of Dreadknights surge toward us. I craft an arrow from my bracelet and notch it in the thorn bow. It flies, hitting its mark perfectly in a goblin's skull.

"Nice shot," Caspian purrs, striking a Dreadknight with his blade before kicking them.

Suddenly, I'm yanked back by a wet glove, and I'm face to face with Ezryn. His armor gleams with water, but there's a familiar stillness to him.

Kel takes my position beside Caspian, keeping the horde from getting too close.

"Rosalina." Ezryn's voice is rattling. Hoarse.

Tears brim in my eyes. "You're all right."

"You are not." Deep anger tinges his words. He quickly pulls off his gloves and puts one hand on my neck and the other on my scratched arm. Immediately, warmth passes through as my wounds fade away.

The shallowness of his breath, his shaking fingers ... Whatever those nightmare flowers did, it left him weak, and now he's using the last of his magic to heal me. "I'm all right." I pull away. "Really."

"Halt. All of you," a female voice says. My blood goes cold.

The Dreadknights and the goblins obey immediately. The four of us gather in a tight cluster, the princes all pushing me to the center. I strain to look through their tall forms. There's a sea of Dreadknights and goblins stretching so far, I can't see the end of it. And she brought them all here to kill one High Prince.

Might have succeeded if Keldarion and Caspian hadn't shown up.

Might still succeed.

The crowd parts as the Nightingale prowls forward. A chunk of her armor is shattered, the edges crusted with ice, leaving her shoulder exposed. And there's the slightest limp in her gait, another patch of frost around her thigh.

Though I can't say it leaves her any less deadly.

But it's Caspian's gaze she fixes on, and trilling laughter echoes off her armor. "I suppose they don't call you the Great Betrayer for nothing. Won't be the favorite after Mother hears of this, will you, brother?"

Brother. So, this is Caspian's sister, the one he told me about months ago in the Autumn Realm. But he doesn't seem inclined to answer her.

"Farron is close," I whisper.

"Even with him, there's still too many," Keldarion growls, reaching for his necklace. "I will not risk you. We have to retreat."

The Nightingale hisses like a cat. "Going to run away with your new family?"

"No." Caspian straightens. "They aren't my family."

He steps in front of us, violet cape catching in the night wind, and twists a palm to the sky. "But let me remind you who is."

From his hand sprouts a green flame.

55

CASPIAN

Sickening green flames glow along my fingertips, and I see the flash of fear in Birdy's eyes. *That's right, sister dear,* I think. *You've heard the rumors but never seen it, have you?*

"Cas—" Keldarion grabs my shoulder, and the flames flicker out. "Are you sure about this? Last time…"

Bloody giant arrogant idiot! Always having to ruin my moment. There's fear flashing in his eyes, too, but it's not the same as my sister's. Could this be fear for me? He's not afraid for Rosalina. Perhaps somewhere deep inside his cold heart, he knows that I'd *never* let anything happen to her.

"Last time," I snap, brushing his hand off my shoulder, "I granted your uncle his life's purpose. He should thank me, honestly."

Besides, I'm much more in control now. Grief, betrayal, anger … Those emotions caused more of an explosion. An explosion that caused a fissure to the deepest depths of the Below.

This is different. *Protection.* Rosalina watches me with that curious expression. Yes, this is easier to channel.

But I'd be lying if reaching for this all-consuming power again wasn't just a tinge frightening.

"Take your legion through the portal and leave," I tell my sister.

The Nightingale narrows her blue eyes. "Never."

Rolling my shoulders, I smirk. "Honestly, I was kind of hoping you'd say that."

I don't reach for my gift of thorns or the shadows my mother passed down. No. There's another legacy deep inside. Lying in wait. Hissing in my ear every day to bring it forth.

And every day I say no.

But not today.

I let the flames in. Power floods through my body, and every movement I make crackles with cosmic energy.

Energy not of this world.

Light floods my vision, and he appears in a flash. Grand and imposing, sitting on a massive throne with a sword of green flame and eyes the same color.

Oh, hello Father. Don't mind me, just going to use this corrosive magic to save the one fae who might have a chance at stopping you from ever making it into the Vale.

I quickly douse the thought, uneasy about how much it feels like he's a part of me when I let this power in. Or rather, when I give in to the power that's always inside of me. It's only when I let it out, when I use it, that he can truly see me.

Green flames writhe around my body, and I know the same color glows in my eyes. I fix my gaze on the goblins, then my sister's Dreadknights. Her pride and joy, the soldiers she's spent years training. An elite force, loyal to a fault, and adored by our mother.

I'm not sure Birdy will ever forgive me for this.

As for Rosalina...

This will only confirm for her the villain I am. But I told her I'd be her darkness, and if only a villain can save her, then so be it.

Power explodes out of me like a twisted storm. Torrents of green flames burst from my body. Like writhing specters, the energy surges out before diving to its targets.

The flames consume every goblin and Dreadknight in a single breath. Iridescent armor falls in a collective tinkle, almost reminiscent of spring rain.

The Nightingale stands stunned, one moment surrounded by a vast legion, now nothing. No one. Years of her world crumbled around her. *Do you see now why she favors me, sister? You shouldn't covet what you don't understand.*

Birdy lets out a heartbreaking wail and falls to her knees, clutching the cape of the nearest Dreadknight.

I release the magic, and my body feels empty. It takes everything in me just to keep standing. But I can't bear to turn around and see their expressions.

Rosalina's hand grips my arm, and I suck in a tight breath. *How can you even touch me?*

But her hand trails to mine and squeezes three times. She heard me.

"We should regroup at Castletree." Her brown eyes lock on to my own, and there's an expression there I can't read. But it's not the terror I expected. "All of us."

Ezryn only gives a stiff nod. I'm sure if he hadn't just been knocked out entirely by that pollen, he'd have more to say on the matter. And I can't bear to look at Kel.

But that great oaf grabs my face, his rough hand on my chin making me look up at him.

"You have a lot to answer for, Cas—"

Cas ... I always liked when he said my name like that. He's saying more, lips still moving, but my vision blurs around the edges. I shouldn't have used so much power, with most of my magic going to the briars holding up Castletree.

Rosalina pulls out her necklace and the air shimmers. Castletree. I won't be able to stay long before the rot takes over ... But maybe I can stay just a little while.

"Cas," Keldarion continues, "then—"

The Nightingale wails like a banshee. She rises, unsteady on her feet. And that's when I see it in her hand. That yellow crystal.

"Don't do it!" I shout, but it's too late.

She smashes the crystal on the ground. In a flurry of yellow light and vines, emerges Perth Quellos's monster.

56

DAYTON

My hands tangle in the fur of Fare's brown wolf, heart pounding. Rosalina is in danger. Farron is near rabid with terror as we race down the mountainside. He's following the pull of his mate bond. Even without my own mate bond, my whole body feels sick.

Or maybe that's from seeing the Prince of Thorns evaporate an entire legion with the flick of his wrist. We'd seen them from the mountain as we rounded a bend. Hundreds of Dreadknights and goblins—one moment they were there, and the next they were gone.

I can't even question why he's fighting for us or how Keldarion got here. My mind is still reeling, trying to comprehend that amount of magic. *And those green flames … Just like what Quellos harnessed during the battle in Autumn.*

The willow tree sways up ahead. "Almost there!" I growl.

Leaping off the wolf, I drop Farron's pile of clothes and draw my swords. Only one soldier still stands, the woman who tried to stop us from escaping the Below.

The Nightingale.

A crystal is shattered at her feet, and a noxious trail of yellow smoke curls from it. The ground rumbles. I stagger closer, and

Rosalina rushes into me as we hold each other steady. Kel and Ez give me a quick nod, tightening in around Rosalina.

But Caspian keeps his gaze fixed on the smashed crystal and growls, "Blades up, boys."

The yellow smoke expands, getting bigger and bigger, forming a strange shape with long wispy ends. Then it solidifies and falls to the ground in an earth-shattering rumble.

Before us stands a creature that defies the laws of nature. My heart quickens as I observe the amalgamation of a giant rat. Its fur almost entirely covered in rotten plant-life and moss. Thick, spurred vines wrap around its limbs. Sitting on its hind legs, the creature is over ten feet tall. Its tail is long with a pink spiked bulb at the end.

The Nightingale quirks her head, and though I can't see anything beyond her mask, the glint in her eyes promises a shit-eating grin behind it.

"What sort of cursed union is this?" I ask. "Whatever gets your dick wet, but by the gods."

"I don't think that thing was born." Farron runs up, a fae now haphazardly dressed. "It was crafted."

Caspian cast a quick glance over his shoulder. "The ice abominations that invaded Autumn were just the start."

"Perth," Keldarion growls. "So, he's in the Below."

The plant rat takes a step closer to us, a sinister grace to its movements. It opens its mouth, monstrous jaws unfurling thick petals that bare miniature teeth.

"This thing gets worse and worse," I say, tugging Rosalina tighter to me. Her knuckles are white around a bow of thorns.

The monster twirls, swinging its serrated vine tail toward us. Caspian shoots out his hands and a barrier of briars sprouts up between us and the ... the—

"What do you call a half-rodent, half-plant monstrosity?" I ask. "A rat-trap? Planty ratty? A rodent of unusual sprouting?"

Caspian grits his teeth, digging his heels into the ground. "I don't care what you call it, but I can't do this all night."

"It's just leaves and flesh," Farron says, his eyes blazing gold. "I'll take it down."

Caspian flashes a grin. "By all means, Autumn Prince, be my guest—"

The barrier of brambles shatters, and the serrated tail strikes, slashing across Caspian's arm.

"Caspian!" Rosalina screams, breaking from my grip and kneeling beside him.

The Prince of Thorns cries out, falling to the ground, clutching his shoulder that sputters blood.

"Look out," Keldarion growls. He leaps in front of them as the Planty Ratty lunges. He drives his blade—a brilliant, gleaming sword of ice, the godsdamned Sword of the Protector—right into its jowls.

The Planty Ratty hisses, petal mouth shaking in rage.

"Get away from my family!" Farron yells, and a great torrent of fire bursts from his palms. Flames engulf the creature. It thrashes, tail whipping back and forth. The fire consumes the creature in a blaze of brilliance, momentarily transforming the dark glade into brilliant light.

I glance at the Autumn Prince. The control he has now is impeccable. Not a spark flies off to the surrounding trees.

Keldarion backs up, standing directly in front of Rosalina, who bends and binds Caspian's shoulder with a ripped tatter of her dress. Yeah, let's make sure the stardamned Prince of Thorns isn't hurt. Not like he led an attack on the Autumn Realm only weeks ago.

But whatever the Prince of Thorns is doing here, I don't have the full story. He just saved my girl's life.

The hisses of the burning rat grow to such an intensity, a small part of me feels pity for it. Figuring the atrocities that have been inflicted on it, death will be the most peaceful escape.

Ezryn bumps my side, and nods past the creature to the Nightingale. Even though I can't see his face, I can read him as if he spoke the words. Once this thing falls, we're going after her.

The flames fall away, and charred marks line its body, seared chunks of burnt fur and plants fall to the ground. But the monster still stands. Its body shivers, then explodes, new vines bursting forth from some infernal center, tail splitting into two, mouth expanding with more teeth.

The Nightingale's laugh carries over the glade. "Even a High Prince's magic is no match."

But then Planty Ratty turns its gaze on her. Caspian looks up, strands of dark hair falling across his brow. "Birdy, look out—"

A gurgling sounds from the creature, and then it spews a spray of yellow slime toward her. She dodges, but a few drops land on her thigh. They sizzle and pop, working through the thick metal and down to her flesh.

So, it has no loyalty to any master.

She screeches, grabbing at her leg, then breaking into a run toward the lake. The monster darts after her, but Caspian jumps, spearing a thorn through its flank. I'm not sure who this woman is to him, but it's obvious he doesn't want her dead.

Though unfortunately, his little rescue attempt has set the creature's sights on what he had been protecting. Rosalina.

It lunges, petal mouth hissing. Keldarion grabs Rosalina around the waist and Caspian by the shirt and tugs them out of the way. The creature dives into the dirt.

Farron and I rush forward, magic on our fingertips. But Ezryn strikes first, driving his blade deep into the creature's mouth.

There's a terrible gushing sound. Ezryn pulls to retrieve his sword, but it doesn't budge. He cries out, dropping his hand, as Windscythe is eaten away by acid.

"He loves that sword. My father gave it to him," Farron pants, shooting a fireball.

The creature whips its tail and snares Ezryn around the waist, lifting the Spring Prince with great ease, and dangling him above its waiting acidic maw.

"Ezryn!" I yell.

A shadow swoops in from above, black cloak billowing. A sword smashes down upon the creature's back. It squeals in pain and drops Ezryn.

Kairyn lands in a crash and holds out his hand to his brother.

The brother whose life he just saved.

57

ROSALINA

The monster lifts its head, shaking off the blow Kairyn dealt. But if Farron's magic can't stop this thing, what can?

Kel releases his hold on Caspian and me. His sword moves at a rapid pace as he blocks a slash from the rat's tail. Blood seeps through my bind around Caspian's shoulder, but otherwise he seems unharmed.

"Can you do it to this creature?" I ask.

He blinks at me.

"That magic with the green flames?"

A strange expression flashes across his face as he says lowly, "Aren't you terrified?"

My hand closes over my thorn bow. "Right now, I'm more terrified of that thing."

Caspian gives a reluctant cough as black coats his lips. His eyes look hollow. Whatever source of magic he called on, it's now depleted.

Kel dodges another lunge from the rat and casts a look at Caspian. "You need to go back to the Below. And take her with you." Kel inclines his head toward the Nightingale, who huddles at the edge of the lake, clutching her leg.

Caspian shakes his head. "You don't understand. You won't be able to kill this thing, not as your magic is now. With Castletree so weak."

"And whose fault is that, thorn boy?" Dayton sneers, shifting a tunnel of water from the lake to strike the monster.

"You need to retreat," Caspian says slowly, and the intensity of the words fills me with an unsettling fear.

Ezryn holds one of Dayton's swords and slices the end of the tail. He whirls to us. "It's too close to Florendel. I can't risk it making its way there."

"I won't leave you," I yell back at him, standing. "And I won't leave the Spring Realm in danger."

"We stand with you, High Prince Ezryn," Farron says lowly, his eyes flashing as a column of fire singes one of the monster's front legs. But he can't burn it fast enough before the creature regenerates.

"I am always with you, Ez," Kel barks, then gestures at the bow in my hands. "Ready to show me what you learned with that thing, Rose?"

"Right." I draw my bow and pluck a crafted arrow from my wrist, nocking it. Slowly, I inhale, letting the breath flow through me. Then I shoot. The arrow sails true and embeds into the creature's left eye. It rears, shaking its paws and hissing.

"Stand together, fall together," Caspian says, coughing as more black goo trails out of his nose.

But he hasn't left either.

We surround the rat, keeping it at bay with our magic and weapons. Though this thing seems tireless, with all of us together, I know we can defeat it.

There's a shriek, and I turn. Kairyn has made his way to the edge of the lake, and he has the Nightingale held up by her throat, her legs kicking wildly.

"You almost killed the High Prince of Spring," he snarls.

She kicks violently, clawing at him like a wildcat.

"Don't touch my sister," Caspian growls, and weak as his magic is, a torrent of thorns sprouts from the ground. They strike Kairyn in the chest, spraying blood and hurtling him back against the bark of the willow tree. The rest of the thorns wrap around the Nightingale and drag her down in a familiar cast of shadows and briars. "Fly away while you can, Birdy."

"Kairyn!" Ezryn roars and rushes toward them. For a single moment, he pauses by the sword of his mother embedded in the tree. *Will he take it?* But he tightens his grip on Dayton's blade and charges.

Charges toward Caspian.

Of all the ...! My frustration grows. I throw my bow over my chest and let vines grow from my bracelets and burrow into the ground, feeling each one as an extension of myself.

"Enough!" I yell. The thorns sprout up, creating a barrier between Caspian and Ezryn. "We have enough problems with the giant rat!"

Something sharp grabs me around the waist, and I'm flung into the air. The rat's tail. I yowl in pain as the serrated edges rip my dress and pierce my skin. Blood blossoms from the wounds. The ground swirls until I'm hovering right above the creature's gaping maw.

"Rosalina!" five voices yell.

An explosion of magic hurtles toward me. Salt-crested wind knocks the creature back, followed by a whirl of fire, a slash to its gut —and then it's like we've been transported to the Winter Realm. A torrent of hail and ice spreads over the creature's tail. It shrieks and I fall.

Then a thorn wraps around me, holding me up. Gritting his teeth, Caspian leads the vine down toward him, and instinctively I wrap my arms around his waist, grateful to be on solid ground again.

I feel something beneath the folds of his tunic, the shape of a familiar notebook. "You keep this with you?"

He glances across the battlefield, gaze landing on Farron. "I never know when I need to add something to the 'Things That Make Me Happy' page. I was going to add man-eating rat weed, but—"

"Planty Ratty!" Dayton yells, slicing deeply into the creature's back.

"Well, now I'm reconsidering my stance on Planty Rattys." He smiles, and even crusted in black goo, it's a beautiful sight.

His gaze drops to my mouth, then to my wrist, and I realize I still haven't let him go.

"Now is definitely not the time or place," I mean to sneer, but it comes out a breathy sigh.

He raises a dark brow. "But battlefield kisses are your speciality. Must be the rot on my lips. Fear it may ruin your complexion?"

The ground shakes, and we fall apart. I half land in the lake. The creature has Caspian now, wrapped in its tail. The second tail that grew after Farron's flaming attack now has the Autumn Prince tight in its grasp.

Dayton's chest is smeared with blood. Ez and Kel fight side by side, holding the monster back, trying to rescue Farron and Caspian. And Kairyn has not risen since Caspian struck him.

My heart pounds in my chest, and I clutch my fingers into the soft earth. Where is my power? The power of the golden roses? It saved us against Lucas, it saved Dayton in Castletree, and it can save us now.

It would be great if I knew how to summon it. Every time, it's felt like exploding from within. The cries of the princes and horrible sounds of the monster fade away as I dig deeper and deeper and deeper. I grit my teeth, ignoring the call to the thorns on my wrist. There is another power within me. One that allows me to make briars of my own. To make the golden roses. If I keep reaching...

Darkness engulfs the grove, then the entire world. A darkness so immense it blocks out the stars and the light of the moon. It spirals inward, condensing into the shape of a woman.

Long, black hair drips down her back like spilled ink, and she wears a dress of night, tipped with spiked metal shoulder plates. Her beauty is like a moonlit graveyard, unsettling in its etherealness. There's no color on her pale cheeks, though jewels crest all the way up her long, pointed ears. Upon her head lies a dark crown with seven spikes.

My blood turns to ice and I go completely still, afraid to even breathe. She doesn't look my way. Instead, she walks toward the monster. Ez, Kel, and Day have all stilled their attacks, stepping backward. I see, in the careful movements, they're trying to make their way toward me.

"Sira," Dayton mouths.

Sira.

So, this is the Queen of the Below.

She tilts her head, regarding the situation with a look of benevolence. And when her gaze passes over me, I feel very much how a little mouse must feel when the shadow of a great owl flies above.

"Honestly, Caspian," she says, voice dripping with disappointment, "how embarrassing this must be for you, my darling baby boy."

Fear flashes on his face, more vibrant than when he'd stared at the monster. It's gone in a moment, replaced with a stony expression hidden by black-rimmed lips and eyes.

The rat monster lunges for her, but she sticks her arm into its mouth, as casually as one might slip a hand beneath an ocean wave.

The creature stills instantly, then convulses. Farron and Caspian wave back and forth in its tail.

Keldarion grabs me tight around the waist, his necklace in his hand. "The moment we get Farron, we retreat to Castletree."

Dayton has moved to the creature's other side, close to Farron, and I see Ezryn make his way toward his brother.

Sira's attention is only on the monster, but I have no doubt she knows exactly where each of us is. The plants forming the creature's legs ripple before disintegrating into black rot. Darkness sweeps the rest of its body in an instant, and the entire frame of the monster dissolves into a shadowy puddle.

Caspian and Farron fall to the ground. Sira shakes her arm, covered to the forearm in rot, and waves her other hand. A trail of shadows wraps around her arm before dissipating, leaving her skin clear.

She grimaces at Caspian, who sits up, gasping for air. "Take us to the Tower of Nether Reach." Her gaze lands on me. "The High Princes and their lady, too."

Dayton lunges for Farron. Kel tilts the mirror of his necklace, catching the moonlight, an iridescent glimmer before he shoves me forward.

But he's not faster than the thorns. They wrap around my legs, covering my body, and drag us under. With the last of my freedom, I urge one of my briars to wrap around Kel's sword and hurl it into the lake.

Then we are swept into darkness.

Down to the Below.

PART FOUR
EVERLASTING VOW

58

ROSALINA

We're in the Below. I know it in the way I know my own name or that the sky is blue.

But this sky is not blue. There's nothing above us but a gray, murky mist. A tight coil of thorns wraps around my body, and I'm pretty sure it's the only thing keeping me upright. Kel, Ezryn, Day, and Farron are all bound as well, and we form a circle around … Caspian.

The Prince of Thorns kneels, heaving up black rot. Standing above him is her. Sira. Queen of the Below.

My thoughts turn to Kairyn, left alone at the lake. He saved Ezryn. But there's no one who can save us down here.

Breath rattles in my chest as I struggle to get my bearings. A circular platform extends around us, surrounded by seven spiked pillars. As I peer down, I realize how high we are, surrounded by a land of darkness and shadow. In the distance, a lavender glow flickers like a distant candle, casting an eerie light upon the grim landscape. Cryptgarden, perhaps. I remember walking through the city on Caspian's birthday, looking up at the tower on which we now stand.

The Tower of Nether Reach.

"No," Farron whispers, eyes wide and shining. "My magic ... I can't reach it down here."

"We're too far from Castletree," Dayton mumbles. "It's too weak."

I feel for my own magic. It's distant, like an echo of what once was. But the thorns imprisoning us ... They feel vibrant, close. I can still use them, I know it.

Taking a steadying breath, I hone in on my control of the thorns, making sure I can grasp the ones around me. It takes me a bit longer to connect with the briars snaring my princes, but once I take control, perhaps I can get us home.

"So careless." Sira walks around Caspian, though it would be more accurate to say glides, as if she does not need to step at all. "What were you thinking, releasing that *thing*?"

Caspian sits back on his heels, wiping his mouth with the sleeve of his shirt. "The High Princes took out the Dreadknights and goblins. I was desperate."

"Risking your sister's forces instead of your own." Sira *tsks*. "I cannot decide if you are idiotic or brilliant."

"Oh, Mother." Caspian stands. The fluidity to his movements has returned. "You know, I always have a plan."

Mother? The Queen of the Below ... She's Caspian's mother. She raised him. *He truly is born of darkness.*

"And you can help with your sister's plan. Take their tokens," Sira says.

"As you wish, Mother," Caspian says lowly. He walks over to the princes one by one, ripping off their necklaces. The snowflake from Kel, the wooden rectangle from Ezryn, the golden leaf from Farron, chains snapping.

"W-wait," Dayton begs as Caspian stands in front of him. "It's just one of the shells. Don't rip the whole thing. They're important—"

"For stars' sake," Caspian grumbles, tapping his foot impatiently, but releases Dayton's hands from the thorns long enough for the Summer Prince to carefully untie his necklace and remove only the shell that is the token of the Queen.

"And her? What does she bear?" Sira asks, taking a step toward me. "Such a troubling little flower."

"Nothing important, I'm sure," Caspian says quickly and stands in front of me. His eyes burrow into my own. "Did your precious princes give you any jewelry to match theirs?"

I tear from his gaze, but my stomach roils at the thought of losing my necklace. The necklace with the moonstone rose that belonged to my mother, and the golden leaf I was gifted from the Autumn Realm.

"Take it," Sira demands.

He does, ripping it in a swift movement. Then he holds it up before his mother. "A little leaf to match her Autumn mate."

Sira shakes her head, as if the notion of mates and gifts is beneath her. Caspian didn't hand over my rose. What did he do with it?

"Very well then. I suppose today is not lost after all. Though I do not believe you received orders to assassinate the High Prince of Spring," Sira says, walking over to her son. He's taller than her, but somehow, she's able to look down on him.

"Thought I saw an opportunity," Caspian says.

Lie after lie. He's taking responsibility for everything his sister did.

"Still," Sira taps a pointed fingernail on the side of her cheek, "there are easier ways to kill the High Prince of Spring."

All the princes roar at once, but Ezryn's voice cuts over them all. "Then kill me and be done with it," he growls. "Make the High Princes bear witness to my death and your power if that is your will. But let them *live*. And know that with my death, you will face the full wrath of Spring and my brother's vengeance."

My world narrows to a frantic, singular purpose as Sira looks him up and down. "Don't you dare touch him!" I snarl.

She ignores me, instead gliding over to Ezryn and placing a finger under his helm, lifting it up so he stares at her face. "How very gallant."

Keldarion's voice is more roar than words. "Harming him will bring all the forces of the Enchanted Vale down on the Below, Sira."

Her red lips curve into a sinister smile, and she turns away from Ezryn to face Keldarion. "What forces, High Prince of Winter? Your people who have not had the strength of a leader in an age? Autumn? Those trembling folks were hardly capable of winning one battle, let alone an entire war. Or do you speak of Summer? Nothing more than a child's dollhouse. No. I do not think I will worry too much."

Shadows spill from Sira's fingertips, dripping to form two sinister serpents.

"Spring will never bow to you," Ezryn yells, thrashing against his binds.

Keldarion howls, the tiniest glint of frost gleaming on the edges of the thorns. But his magic won't reach here. The shadow serpents lunge from the ground, jaws unhinging to reveal inky black incisors.

"Ezryn!" I scream, and the thorns binding me fall away like waves rolling off sand. I stretch out my hand. Thorns from my bracelet strike at the shadow serpents. As they hit, the two snakes disappear into a cloud of smoke.

Sira turns to me, eyes flashing.

While holding her gaze, I try to reach for the thorns chaining my princes. If I could just connect with all of them, then we could escape.

"So, the rumors are true," Sira snarls. "How is this possible?"

Kel, Farron. I spread the magic further, reaching to connect with the thorns binding Ezryn and Dayton. A smile spreads over my lips. "I—"

"I made a bargain with her." Caspian steps in front of me.

Sira's expression contorts into one of fury.

There's a hard crack as she slaps her son across the face. "Fix this."

Caspian inhales a rattly breath. Shadows leach from Sira's fingers, wrapping over Caspian's thorns until they all shrivel and die. I feel the loss of the connection, like someone cut off my arm.

Then, like his mother, shadows creep from Caspian. "No," I gasp. The gloom forms shackles around the princes' ankles and wrists. Two inky black ropes shoot out and wrap around my arms, tethering me to the ground.

And Caspian's eyes are entirely void.

"Let me go!" I cry out, pulling at them, but they don't give. I have no connection to these like I did the thorns.

Caspian shrugs, dusting his shoulders, and the last of the shadows fall away from him like clouds, eyes returning to that dark purple.

Twice today I've witnessed Caspian wield magic I didn't know he possessed. I had noticed this gloom around his thorns before, but always thought they were connected. No, these shadows he inherited from his mother.

"Rescind the bargain," Sira commands, then shifts her gaze to me. "And I would not resist, girl, or you may find my mercy for the remaining princes short-lived."

Instinctively, I try to reach for the thorn bracelets around my wrists, but the shadows hold my arms taunt.

"What bargain?" Keldarion growls.

I can't bear to look at him, nor the rest of the princes. I should have told them. Now, my lie is out in the open.

Sira gives a light chuckle at Kel's obvious torment. "Well, darling, what are you waiting for?"

"I can't rescind the bargain." Caspian practically spits out the words, his usual musical cadence now clipped and short. "She hasn't fulfilled her end of it yet."

My stomach drops. I whip my head up, hair flying in my face, trying desperately to find Caspian's gaze. But he's not even looking at me. *No, no, no.* Certainly he doesn't mean now. Not here. Not in front of the princes of Castletree.

Sira waves an uninterested hand.

"Rosie," Farron calls out, eyes wide, expression frantic as he struggles against the shadows. "Rosie, what did you make a bargain for?"

"For this." Firm hands grab me, and suddenly I'm pulled flush against the Prince of Thorns. Then his lips are on mine. The kiss is rough and quick. He pulls away near instantly, wiping his mouth with the back of his hand as if to rid himself of the taste of me.

"We can consider the bargain fulfilled," Caspian says.

But I can't form words, my lips trembling. I'd barely been able to think about what a kiss with the Prince of Thorns might be like, but I had never imagined *that*. Like merely touching me disgusted him.

A distraught agony filters through my bond. I'm not sure if it's from Keldarion or Farron. It's Kel's gaze I catch first. Anger is clear on his face, but it's not directed at me or even Caspian, but at Sira. Ezryn is rigid as stone. Farron looks lost, confused. His eyes flash. "Dayton!"

"I'm going to fucking kill you!" Dayton snarls, voice low and feral. He surges forward and changes, body rippling into that of the golden wolf.

Shadows grab him from mid-air, sending him slamming to the earth hard enough to crack the stone. The Summer wolf growls and spits but cannot break free.

"Day," I gasp, my voice trembling with tears. What trace of magic had allowed him to transform?

Sira eyes him curiously. Is this the first time she's seen one of the beasts of the Briar?

"Save your strength, Daytonales," Keldarion orders, not taking his gaze from Sira.

The Summer Prince gives a low whine and submits.

Caspian rolls his eyes, then easily restrains the wolf in shadows. He leans in close to me, tucking a piece of hair behind my ear. "Say the bargain is fulfilled, Rosalina."

My gaze flicks to my thorn bracelets. Without them, I can't make my own arrows, can't protect myself. Can't save the princes. But what choice do I have? I can't even use them now, trapped beneath Caspian's shadows.

I meet the Prince of Thorns' violet-flecked gaze. "The bargain is fulfilled."

A jolt surges through me, and a burning sensation shoots along my arms. The bramble bracelets uncoil, then drop by my feet. A small, thin thorn falls from Caspian's wrist.

Caspian looks to the thorns, then back up to me. "Guess you're on your own now. Just like the last time you were here."

Unbidden tears slide down my cheeks at the loss of the thorns.

"I thought it would be quite amusing," Caspian runs a hand through his hair, "to bargain a kiss from Keldarion's mate. Didn't think she could get in too much trouble making a couple of extra briars, figuring the castle he keeps her in is already covered in them."

"The Golden Rose," Sira purrs. "Is that how she got the nickname? From using your magic, my son?"

"Those simple Autumn folk will turn anything into a song. Give them a rock, they'll call it a diamond. Give them briars, they'll call them roses."

"Hmm, you are certainly rash. You should have informed me of your plan from the start. But you've always had a clever mind when it comes to bargains." Sira snatches his wrist. "Like that perfectly wicked one you devised for the Prince of Winter."

59

KELDARION

Caspian looks at me, and his expression is so raw, it's like I'm back at Cryptgarden all those years ago when we first said the words of our bargain.

But those were words meant for whispered breath, not to be spoken aloud.

"A deep regret I shall suffer always," I growl, the frosted thorn bracelet on my wrist seeming to dig into my skin.

A twisted smile spreads up Sira's mouth. I'd always known that darkness ran in her veins, but for a while I'd hoped it had not passed to Caspian. But seeing them together, it's a wonder I ever believed that. The same inky black hair, the depth of their violet eyes, the grace of movement.

"You should have broken the curse when you had the chance, Kel," Caspian purrs. "Now you *all* belong to me, instead of just her."

Rosalina whirls, cheeks flushed and stained. "What do you mean?"

"She doesn't know?" Sira chirps happily, looking as pleased at this news as she did when she was about to set her shadows on Ezryn.

Of course, Rosalina doesn't know. I have never had the courage to speak of it to anyone, not even my brothers. The shame and stupidity were too great to bear aloud.

And the answer is so clear and so complex. To free myself without Caspian's agreement to rescind the bargain, only his death would do. Even with the High Princes' combined power, that would be a feat. How do you kill someone with his magic? *How can you bring yourself to kill someone who's lying on your bed, body betrayed by the air of the very world he wishes to conquer?*

My fists close at my side, bound by shadow. A magic he's always loathed to use.

"What was it again, hmm?" Caspian drums his fingers on his arm. "It was *so* very long ago now."

"Rescind the bargain," I growl.

"Oh, I remember now," he purrs. His voice takes on a dark purpose. "Let me take no other but you. If one day, my vow shall prove false and I lie with another, let them serve you in repentance until you tire of them as I did your heart. And if ever there is no love between us, let this bargain melt away like snow under rain."

There it is, the words hovering between us. I watch as they register with my brothers.

Ezryn roars and falls to his knees, shadow shackles still tight. "Kel, how could you?"

"All the fae that showed up at the castle," Farron says slowly. "Caspian didn't *want* to send them. They were forced to come after he lay with them. It wasn't that our magic wasn't strong enough to send them away. It needed to be Kel."

"It was you," Rosalina breathes, but it's Caspian she's staring at. "You were Kel's great love."

"Call it what you want, Flower." Caspian smirks. "It'll bring us together before long."

There's no anger on Rosalina's face, only a shocked understanding and sadness. "Let them serve you in repentance …" She echoes the bargain.

The way Caspian said it … So unlike how he'd said it all those years ago. The memory floods back to me in a rush. His hair longer, falling below his shoulders and into his eyes, which at the time were streaked with tears. When no words I said would convince him how I felt, would convince him he was *enough*.

"Then prove it, Kel. Prove it to me," he had said.

So, I'd spoken different words instead. "Then let us make a bargain."

And for the first time, his eyes cleared, and he sniffed, "You would do that with me?"

The magic of fae bargains is powerful and ancient. The only thing more so is the mate bond. I was not his mate, but this I could give him.

Back then, I had no notion of Rosalina. No notion that I would ever have a mate, or that I would be cursed into needing to find one. No notion that my realm and soul would rely on her love.

Every part of me had been convinced the broken and beautiful prince loved me. And that I loved him.

"Let me take no other but you," I had told him. "If one day, my vow shall prove false and I lie with another, let them serve you in repentance until you tire of them as I did your heart. And if ever there is no love between us, let this bargain melt away like snow under rain."

"No one but me," Caspian had echoed, as if he couldn't quite believe it. As if my choice to leave everything behind and join him in the damned Below wasn't proof in itself.

I spun him then, pushing him down to the sheets, so we were chest to chest. "Do we have a bargain, Cas?"

"Let me take no other but you," he gasped and kissed me wildly. Kissed me as he repeated the bargain. As our clothes fell away and we made love. It was not until later that I even noticed the bracelet on my wrist, the swirling twist of frosted thorns.

Scattered moments are still etched in my memory, clearer than any painting. The dusky lavender light hitting the sapphire silver circlet that rested on his dark hair. The pearl of moisture over his full lips. His elegant fingers stroking the newly formed frosted thorn bracelet over my wrist with a quiet curiosity.

"It's beautiful," he'd whispered.

"As long as it encircles your wrist, you'll know I love you."

"Or … I love you."

High-pitched laughter draws my memories away, and I feel raw and open as Sira's gaze rakes over me. "Even *he* doesn't know the truth of it, does he, my darling?"

Caspian raises a dark brow and smirks. "No, Mother. I never bothered to tell him."

Dayton growls low, and Farron watches me with a mixture of pity and horror. And Ezryn has removed his gloves and is clawing at the dead briars on the ground.

"Tell me what?" I ask.

"What I showed him the night before he made that little bargain with you." Sira claps her hands together. "Or what the Fates showed him."

The Fates. I had ventured to them only once. Ancient creatures that dwelled in the deepest depths of the Below. Perhaps they came from the Above like our ancestors, or more likely they've been here since the dawn of time.

Some described them as beautiful, others wizened and old. All I saw were shadows of time and space.

What had Cas gone to them for?

Caspian turns to Rosalina. "The Fates showed me you."

Rosalina doesn't say a word, but her eyes move between us. I know that look. She's thinking, always thinking. But there's nothing we can do. No way out of this. Perhaps I can find a means to petition for her safety. Why would Caspian even help me save her if this was his plan all along?

"What do you mean, you saw Rosalina? She wasn't even born."

Caspian shrugs. "The Fates show threads of the future. I saw your life with her. Your mate."

"So, you crafted a bargain to trap his mate," Farron spits out, face scrunched in agony. "You are despicable, Caspian."

I feel hollow, wrung inside out, my whole body numb. I know how it ended with him. His betrayal. But before that … The bargain…

Hadn't that been real?

I glance down at the frosted thorn bracelet, and I almost believe it will wither away.

"Oh, poor Keldarion." Sira worries her bottom lip. "He truly believed the lie."

"Idiots, all of them." Caspian smiles. "I told you, Mother."

"I *loved* you," I growl, lunging toward him. The shadows grow taut around my wrists.

"Sure." Caspian rolls his eyes in that infuriating way of his. "Believing that was your first mistake."

"There are so many mistakes regarding you."

Caspian prowls over, closing the distance between us. "And with this so-called love, you preached to your people how I seduced you, how I corrupted you and used all that dark magic of the Below to lure you into its depths. All so you could keep your precious throne."

"You betrayed me," I growl.

His eyes narrow to catlike slivers. "Who was the first one to bring an army into the other's realm?"

My gaze involuntarily slides to Ezryn, still clawing at the ground, but thankfully Caspian is too distracted to notice. "It doesn't matter. We both burned together, didn't we?"

"Speak for yourself, Kel. I'm not the one who hasn't had sex in twenty-five years. Was I really *that* hard to get over?"

I lunge, the shadows giving slightly, so I tower above him. "I would never subject anyone to the likes of *you*. Especially Rosalina."

"Oh, she looks like mine right now. All wrapped up in shadows."

Rosalina shrinks back, a look I haven't seen on her since she first came to the castle. "P-please, don't hurt us."

But in my mind, another voice filters through, strong and confident. *Keep him distracted, Kel.*

I don't risk a second look at her.

"It's you who can't let go, Cas." I spit out the nickname. "Haunting my castle. Obsessing over *my* mate."

"Of course, I would want to watch my greatest enemy fall. I've always loved a spectacle."

The air is cold around us, and the shadows tighten.

"You say I am powerless to let you go, Keldarion." Caspian's voice becomes a whisper. "Then answer me this. Why haven't you killed me? Why haven't you even tried? You never loved me, but you still can't let me go."

Power erupts from Ezryn, and all the decayed briars at our feet burst back to life as full, living vines.

Despite the distance to Castletree, he found a path to his magic. A path to save us.

"Rosalina!" Ezryn bellows.

My mate doesn't look scared or frightened. She just looks mad. Rosalina shoots out her hand and *screams*. The briars at my feet rustle and move under her command and wrap up around me.

And I've never been so happy to be tangled in thorns.

60

ROSALINA

Briars writhe beneath my touch, wrapping around each of the princes.

You're on your own now. It had taken me a moment to catch Caspian's meaning. But I understood when I saw Ezryn trying to revive the thorns.

The thorn bracelets helped me create briars, but I never needed them to control thorns that were already present.

And the last time I was in the Below, I could summon the magic, despite being so far from Castletree. Bits of magic had found their way through, changing Dayton into his wolf, letting Ezryn revive the briars. But my connection to the thorns feels stronger than ever.

Whatever the reason, may it be a blessing or curse, I'm taking my princes home.

Sira's gaze widens, and for a moment, the deadly Queen of the Below looks surprised. "It can't be."

"You wouldn't be the first person to underestimate me," I snarl.

My briars tangle around Dayton, then Farron, then Ezryn, then Kel, tugging hard enough to break Caspian's shadow binds with a puff of smoke. Whether it's because he's surprised or my power is that strong, I'm not sure.

The last thing I see before the briars consume us is Sira. Sira, with fury raging around her like a storm cloud. But it's not at me, or the princes of Castletree.

She grasps Caspian by his shirt. "You lied to me. How? How is she—"

And so, I make a decision. I curl the vines around him and *pull*. Then he's in front of me, and it's just us. Me and him in a world only the two of us understand. A place surrounded by swirling thorns and cosmic stars.

"Princess," he says, cupping my face, "I don't belong in your world."

"Why would you want to be down there with *her*?" I shout.

"She's my mother."

"She lied, didn't she? You struck that bargain with Kel without any knowledge of me, didn't you? You made it because you *loved* him."

An unreadable expression passes over his face. "No one knows the truth of that but me. But the Fates did show me you, Flower, all those years ago. I saw him leaning over you, saying the same vows of love he had once said to me."

I shake my head. "You're wrong about Kel. He *did* love you. Maybe a part of him still does. I can *feel* it. Otherwise, the bargain would be broken, wouldn't it?"

"Trust me. It's not Kel keeping this bargain alive," Caspian whispers. "You're clouded because he's your mate. He's never told you he loves you, has he? Maybe the Fates were wrong after all."

"It's like you're trying to make me hate you."

"Well, you should hate me," he snarls back. "And you certainly shouldn't trust me."

"I don't trust you." The briars have slowed around us, suspending us in this little world. "But I can't leave you either."

"Well, you'll have to."

But the briars aren't pulling him away. They're tugging us toward each other. Relief and fear soar through my chest as I'm wrapped up against him.

Is it my lips crashing against his, or his against mine? But his hands are in my hair, and I'm gasping in all the air he's willing to give me. This is wrong. Every logical thought is telling me this is wrong. Then why can't I let go?

Why can't I leave him behind? He's saved my life, again and again and again. And I can't let him go.

The briars draw us closer, cocooning us. Our kiss deepens. His hands are over my body, drawing my thigh up around his waist.

"Rosalina." He chokes out my actual name. Is this the first time he's ever said it to me? I'm not sure. "You certainly are a lot of trouble, aren't you?"

I swallow, head spinning. I'm not sure I would even know my name if he hadn't just said it. "Not as much trouble as you." A thought drifts through my starlit mind. "Cas, do you have my necklace?"

He tilts his head. "Yes. But they'll only take it from you again. You don't need it." He places a hand over my heart. "You have everything you need right here."

"But—"

"I'll keep it safe. I'll keep *you* safe." I think I catch a smile on his face between the speckles of light. Then he's kissing me again.

And I believe him.

Maybe here in this moment, in this space that doesn't really exist, it's okay to give in to the shadows. To submit to pure feeling and sensation and need. His fiery, desperate lips caress my neck. All sense of control is lost from both of us as I thread my fingers through his hair and writhe my body against his.

He kisses me again, softer this time. A kiss I know means the end.

He cups my face. "Goodbye, Princess. I think it'll be a little while before I see you again."

"Wait," I gasp, catching the edge of his shirt. "I have so many questions."

"And I have so many answers." His voice fades away as the briars swallow him up. I have the tumbling sensation of falling, falling, falling. I break through the vines, gasping for air, the foggy vision of Castletree's entrance hall swirling around me.

61

EZRYN

The thud of the hard ground reverberates through my armor. Thorns release from around my waist, and I steady myself on all fours, immediately taking in my surroundings. We're in the entrance hall of Castletree. Farron, Dayton, and Kel are collapsed beside me. My heart begins to blaze as I stagger to my feet and turn in a circle. The ground opens up again, and Rosalina emerges from a bramble bush.

Silence fills the hall, but blood rushes through my head, and my heart hammers.

Stay still. Stay in control. Stay grounded.

But when his eyes meet mine, there is no such thing as peace.

"How could you?" I roar, snagging Kel by his collar and slamming him against a pillar. "The bargain you made with Caspian has condemned us all!"

Kel grabs my wrists. "Do you understand now, brother, why I have chosen this path? Do you see me for the monster I truly am?"

"You are not a monster," I growl back. "For monsters have no reason, no responsibility. You are far worse. You are a traitor, Keldarion."

Pain riots through my chest, a wound that has no physical origin. I keep my grip tight on Kel to stop from falling to the ground. Year after year, I watched him throw his life away for Caspian. But for him to have made a bargain like this...

A bargain that now involves Rosalina.

Kel stares down at me with glazed eyes, a defeated half-smile on his face. "I own my betrayal. But let us not dance around it anymore. You betrayed me, too."

Breath tears from my throat. The thoughts in my head are raw with memories from the past, but they keep coming, assaulting me like arrows through the flesh. "Never. I never—"

"My army, Ez," Kel says softly. "You took my own army out from under me and marched it upon the Below."

"That wasn't a betrayal—" Even I can hear the doubt in my words.

Because wasn't that exactly what it was? *His own good, it was for his own good...*

Or was it for mine?

I'd known it from the moment he showed up at Castletree begging for sanctuary: Caspian had evil in his heart. He'd tricked Kel, charmed Dayton and Farron, and had all the realms bespelled by the hope of a single smile.

But I knew it.

Kel never believed me. Never *trusted* me.

When I discovered Caspian had been a spy for the Below all along, I knew it was up to me to save Keldarion from himself.

Keldarion and I had served as generals, side by side for decades. I was in Winter at the time I learned the truth of Caspian's plan, and my own army was still in Spring. But Kel's soldiers were right there. When I told his personal legion of Caspian's intention, they agreed to aid me.

Kel's Winter squadron were not only elite soldiers but dedicated to him. As was I. We would do whatever it took to free him from Caspian's possession.

More images flash before me: infiltrating the Below, goblins dying beneath our blades, breaking into Caspian's personal chambers, the objects he'd stolen from the realms above crushing beneath my boot.

Kel returned with me and the army. But his loyalty to Caspian didn't break.

At least not until after Caspian tore a hole in the world and all manner of ilk from the Below leached from the Great Chasm to march upon Frostfang.

"I did that to protect you," I force out.

Kel shakes his head. "I didn't need your protection, brother. I needed your trust."

Anger flares in my chest, and I grab Kel's wrist, yanking down his sleeve and revealing the bargain bracelet. "Look where your trusting nature has put us. Was your fucking love worth it?"

Kel rips his hand away and sneers.

I need to leave it. I need to stop. But the rage is too hot, cursed memories too fresh. I need someone to hurt like I'm hurting. I gesture behind me to Rosalina. "Look at her and tell me Caspian was worth it!"

Keldarion's eyes glitter and he opens his mouth. Closes it. Turns away from me. "One day you'll understand, Ezryn," he mumbles. "You'll understand what it means to shatter yourself for love."

The edges of my vision are black with rage, my breathing ragged. But when Kel turns away, the rest of the world comes back to me.

There's shouting. So much shouting. Rosalina is right under Farron's nose, eyes blazing with anger. Farron stands still, brow furrowed, and fists clenched. Dayton paces beside the two of them.

"I don't understand how you could make a deal with Caspian! Did you learn nothing from me? You know better!" Farron yells.

"That's exactly it!" Rosalina screams back. "I know. *I know*, Farron. There is good in him. Trust me!"

Farron stalks away, throwing a dismissive hand in the air. "That's what he does! He manipulates people. He offers them something, gains their trust, and then uses it against them. He did it to Kel. He did it to me. And he will do it to you."

"You don't know him like I do," she whispers viciously.

Farron gives a harsh laugh. "Listen to you! You've known him for less than a year. We have lived *centuries* with him. Believe me when I tell you this is all a game to him. He will take your kindness and turn it ugly."

Dayton grabs Rosalina's shoulders. "Rosie, I know you want to see the good in people. But Farron's right on this. He's not just dangerous. He's sadistic. It's *fun* for him to ruin people." Dayton's eyes shine. "Don't give him the opportunity."

She shakes Dayton off, pushing past him like he's a mere nuisance. Instead, she chases after Farron, grabbing his arm. "You're scared again, Farron. But you don't have to be. I can handle him."

"Can you?" Farron turns on his heel and holds her with a flaming gaze. "Did you forget what he did to me, Rosie? To my people? My history? He brought an *army* of goblins into Autumn to kill my soldiers. He used my beast against me and destroyed my realm's ancient texts." There's anger and hurt in Farron's voice like I've never heard before. "And Dayton nearly died because of him! Doesn't that matter to you at all?"

Rosie steps back, tears welling in her eyes. "Of course it matters."

"And you know why he did that?" Farron's voice shakes. "Because I ripped the damned little book you gave him. I ripped his book, and in return, he murdered and pillaged and *ruined*."

Lightning seems to cross over Rosalina's gaze. "You ripped it? That was *my* gift. You had no right!"

Farron's brow furrows. "You think you can change Caspian with compassion? Kel thought so, too. Look at him now."

We all turn to stare at Keldarion. A dark shadow has fallen over his gaze. His shoulders shake, but he stays silent.

Rosie looks down, eyes wide, chest heaving. "He hurts people because he hurts inside." She clutches at her heart. "I *feel* it, Farron."

Farron shakes his head. "I can hear what you're thinking. He's not your mate, Rosalina."

Silence erupts in the entrance hall. *Her mate?* The thought staggers me. The idea that Rosalina could be mated to someone with such evil...

My fingers itch for a blade. Freedom. There has to be freedom for her and Kel from this—

I turn to him. Of all of us, Kel would know—

He's staring at Rosalina, eyes glittering like sapphires. His expression … It's one of shock, but not disbelief. She stares back at him, as if finding a tether in his gaze.

"What the fuck?" Now, Dayton's voice is raised. He grabs Rosalina's shoulder and spins her to look at him. "You can't seriously think you belong with him. Not Cas. Anyone but fucking Caspian!"

"What do you care?" Rosalina speaks in a low, venomous tone. "You've got your little acolyte to make you pretty necklaces and fawn over you."

"That's not fair, Rosie," Dayton growls. "That's not fucking fair, and you know it."

Hurt flickers in her eyes. "Yeah, well, go cry on Wrenley's shoulder about the bitch of Castletree who's good for a fuck but not good enough to love!"

Anger explodes across Dayton's face. "Maybe I will," he snarls, "because why am I wasting my time here? You're not my mate, Rosalina."

She gasps and staggers back. Immediately, Dayton's eyes widen, and he blinks, dumbstruck.

Heat blazes, and fire licks up Rosalina's fingers. "Get out of my head, Farron. I don't want to hear your voice!"

"You don't want to hear Caspian's voice either, but that's what's happening," Farron yells. "It's only Kel's ridiculous bargain linking you two."

Rosalina looks shocked for a moment.

"Quiet, both of you," Keldarion growls, looking from Farron to Dayton. "You're both afraid. Not of Caspian. Of Rosalina. Of what she's capable of with him—"

"Shut the fuck up, Kel," Dayton snaps. "You're the one who sent her away! Don't pretend you know what's best now."

Kel storms toward him, and Rosalina starts screaming all three of their names, but I'm done.

"Enough!"

I stalk forward, standing between the four of them. Slowly, I pivot in a circle, hands extended, holding each of their gazes.

The anger is fading and there's only sadness.

"Enough," I say again, quieter. "We are family. All of us. And family doesn't turn against one another. Find somewhere in the castle to be by yourself." I take in a deep breath. "The night will pass. We have withstood each and every one so far. We will withstand this. Together."

Rosalina holds my gaze for a moment, and I see it thundering within: a Spring storm ready to rage over anything soft and fragile. A look both frightening and beautiful.

A rose covered in thorns.

The castle seems to take a breath. It will sigh or it will scream—

A small flutter sounds. I look up to see a bird made of paper flitting down toward us. It hovers right before Rosalina.

She reaches out and takes it, unfolding the little bird into a letter.

Her face turns ashen. "From Dom and Billy," she whispers. "It's my father. He's sick."

62

ROSALINA

When I was sixteen, a terrible windstorm swept through Orca Cove. Vancouver Island had reports leading up to it for weeks. Papa was gone, so I'd had to prepare for everything myself. I'd bought cases of water, canned food, flashlights, and extra batteries. And a hefty pile of books, as well.

When the storm started, I was terribly afraid. Our whole cottage shook with the might of the gale. Tree branches rapped on the windowpanes like an unwelcome guest. I'd called Papa before the power went out, but it went to voicemail as usual. Then I'd tried Lucas, begging him to come over or bring me to the lodge. He'd told me I was being inconsiderate; a falling branch could scratch the truck his parents had just bought him. Also, I was sixteen and I should stop being a baby.

I was afraid. So, I wrapped myself in a blanket and crawled under my bed, so sure the little cottage would topple in on itself or the whole thing would fly me away like Dorothy. I spent the night like that, listening to the roof rattle and the whine of bending trees, and I thought the storm would never end.

But when I woke up in the morning, slipped on my gumboots and stepped outside, everything was calm. Yes, the path was scattered with twigs, and my lawn chair was down the road, but the little pond by our house barely rippled.

Then I'd seen my father's tall frame coming up the path, backpack smeared with dirt. "Came back as soon as I got your message!"

"Missed the storm," I'd said lightly. It seemed so strange to me, after the turbulence of the night before, how there could barely be a breeze.

Papa smiled warmly. "Eh, the storm always passes."

The storm always passes. That's what it's like now, morning light filtering in through the windows of Castletree. Last night had been a storm. We'd blown and blustered and raged. *I'd* raged.

But now my room is so silent, I can almost hear the soft brush of the cherry blossoms hitting my floor. After I got the letter from Papa, I'd told everyone to leave me alone. Farron went to the library, and the rest of the princes went to their respective chambers.

My heart aches for each of them, for the sorrow in all the things we'd said.

A chill passes over me, and I pull my blankets up to my nose. Then I see the ice cracking beneath my door.

"Kel?"

Slowly, the door opens and the Prince of Winter stands in the entranceway.

"Come in," I say.

He does.

"Are you all right?" I ask.

"I'm managing," he says, then his icy gaze narrows as he takes me in. "But you're not."

"I'm ... I'm..." I start, but I can't even get the words out before a sob rips from me.

Kel lies down on the bed, and I clutch at him as he wraps me in his strong embrace.

I'd told them I needed to be alone, but the solitude had only turned me numb. Kel pats my hair as tears cascade down my cheeks. Not soft, delicate tears, but a full-out ugly sob. I curl into his chest, hands clasping his shirt, staining it with my tears.

And I let his words, spoken in that deep, gravelly voice of his, sink into me. "Your father will be okay. As soon as we get the news that Dom and Billy have brought him back to Coppershire, we can visit him."

"Knowing Papa, he probably overindulged in some strange fae berries or something," I mumble when I find my voice again.

Keldarion gives a light chuckle. "If his spirit is half as strong as yours, then he will be fine."

"Where do you think I got it from?" I say, a smile forming on my lips.

He tilts his chin down, tangles of white locks falling across his brow.

"I've made a right mess of your shirt," I say, patting the tear-soaked fabric.

He grabs my wrist and brings it to his lips. "Don't trouble yourself."

A flutter runs through me at his affection, and I hate that I'm not sure how long it's going to last. We've both been trying to keep our distance, but we've fallen back here, in each other's arms.

But now I know the truth, why he's kept away from me. My fingers slip to the V in his shirt. The absence of his snowflake necklace is startling.

"Is Sira going to come for us?"

"I don't think so. Even in the Below, she wouldn't have dared to kill all of us," Keldarion says. "She could not hold all the realms presently. Though her intent is clear, if the others don't break their curses soon, we may not have the strength to protect Castletree. And now you understand why I cannot."

"I won't say you should have told me," I whisper. "Some secrets are so close to the heart that it feels like we have to rip the entire thing out just to bear them."

"Like the scars on your arm," Keldarion says lowly.

I nod, feeling new tears well. "When you first saw my scar, I felt the pain of it all over again, every mark Lucas made. I can't imagine what it must have been like for you, Kel. I'm so sorry."

He takes a long breath. "No, you should have known. I should have told the others years ago, but—"

I press a palm to his cheek, rough with stubble. "I'm here if you want to tell me more about it. I don't expect all your truths, but please do not lie to me."

"One day, I'll tell you everything, all about Caspian. I did love him. I trusted him, and in the end, it almost destroyed my realm." Keldarion closes his eyes. "I never lied to you, Rosalina."

I wrinkle my nose. "What about when you said being mated to me was—what did you say again? Utter torment."

There's a low growl in his throat. He pulls me on to his lap. "Because it *is* utter torment. To have the most beautiful and kind and *strange* woman as my mate and not be allowed to do more than look upon her."

"Strange?" I reply, flicking him on the nose.

"I would not have you any other way."

We stare at each other, and I let myself enjoy this quiet moment in his presence amid the turmoil of last night. Finally, I open my mouth to speak and Kel silences me with a quick shake of his head.

"Don't say it."

"You don't even know what I was going to say."

He raises a dark brow. "That I should make love to you, forge our bond, break the curse, and you would be *just fine* in the Below."

I stick out my bottom lip and cross my arms. That was what I was going to say. "I would be fine. I've escaped the Below twice already."

"Yes, but the bargain doesn't send you as you are. You would be enthralled to him. Think of the woman who showed up here, how desperate she was to see me. I never imagined that horrific result because I never imagined the bargain would be used in such a way."

"Caspian wouldn't..." I begin, but even I can't be sure of exactly what the Prince of Thorns would do. He wouldn't hurt me, but I'm less and less sure of his ability to protect himself in the Below. And he's certainly not willing to help us, otherwise he would have rescinded his bargain with Kel ages ago.

But can they even break it? Or does the wording forbid that?

"Caspian wants you there for some reason," Keldarion continues as if reading my mind. "He wants you there under his control, as *his*. I can never let that happen."

I sink into Kel, my lips falling to the crook of his neck. "Wouldn't it be worth it, though? One woman to save your entire realm?"

"It wouldn't be worth it for me." Keldarion grips my chin and makes me look at him. "If that brands me as a terrible leader, then so be it. But there is nothing I would not do for you. There is nothing in this world I would not sacrifice for you."

I cannot argue it because the same devotion runs through me for all the princes of Castletree. "Kel." His name falls from me, dripping with need.

With his hands in my hair, my face an inch away from his lips. His warm breath caresses my cheeks.

"And there is nothing I would not give to both of you," a deep metallic voice says from the door. Slowly, we turn, barely moving away from each other. Ezryn leans against the doorway. "May I come in?"

A smile quirks on my mate's lips. "Always."

63

ROSALINA

My bed sinks with the weight of Ezryn's full armor. I slide off Kel and cuddle between them, feeling a strange bubbling happiness at being boxed in.

Ezryn tilts his helm down, running a gloved hand along my cheek to tenderly caress the pointed tip of my ear. He looks at Kel.

No words are spoken between them, but I sense an understanding.

"I was telling Rosalina I am glad she is aware of the bargain now," Keldarion says slowly. "As I am you."

Ezryn makes a dismissive noise. "I would have stood by you, Kel. I will always stand by you. And I agree with your decision. You cannot fulfill your mate bond until we figure out a way to break your bargain."

"Of course you would agree with him," I say, sneering. But Ezryn pulls me close, and I melt against him, feeling the hard metal planes of his body through the thin layers of my nightdress.

"I'm glad you're all right," I whisper. "I was so worried about you, caught in that terrible dream."

"It wasn't just a dream," Ezryn whispers back. "The pollen brought forth my memories. But you already knew that, didn't you?"

"I did."

"So, now you are aware of both of our greatest shames," Ezryn says. "Only a few know the truth of the day I received Spring's Blessing, Kel included."

All this time, they've both been hiding so much pain.

"It is no great shame to love someone, to want to prove your devotion." I run a hand along Kel's jaw before rolling back to Ezryn. "Ez, you may have been told this before, but let me say it once more. I felt you in that memory. It was not your fault; I don't understand the magic required during the passing of a Blessing—"

"But if I had—" Ezryn shakes his head.

"There was nothing else you could do. It was an accident. It doesn't mean you didn't love your mother. The fragility in which you hold me, the tender care in which you use your magic now, is all proof of that love for her."

Ezryn shivers beneath me. I cannot imagine what he's been going through, to carry that burden for so long.

"Ezryn, you have my forgiveness, but you don't need it. Only you can offer the forgiveness you seek." Gently, I touch his helm, then place a light kiss where his lips would be. Cold metal prickles my mouth.

Ezryn holds me around the waist. "Petal, I do not know if the day will ever come where I am able to do that."

The bed moves as Kel slides an arm over me, clasping Ezryn's forearm. "But we keep trying. Each time we fall, we rise again."

Ezryn nods. "Tomorrow, I will return to Florendel. I will need to reopen the way between Castletree's main door and Keep Hammergarden. With the loss of our tokens, we will no longer be able to use the mirror to travel anywhere in the Enchanted Vale."

I know the loss of the necklaces is a terrible thing, but the idea of opening the ways between Castletree and the realms feels like hope. We've already opened the way connecting Castletree to Autumn. Kel opened the one to Winter for his own personal use, and now we'll open Spring. Only Summer remains closed.

"We will retrieve them," Keldarion says. "Though, I cannot fathom what the Below wants with the tokens. Only the High Ruler can use their realm's token to travel to Castletree."

I could use my moonstone rose as well, but there's no Blessing inside me.

"We must be wary of that assassin. The Nightingale," Ezryn says.

My body goes cold thinking of her hands around my throat. "She could summon and control thorns like Caspian."

"That's what those other thorns were in the grove," Ezryn says. "I knew there was something different about them."

"Kel," I say, "you told me that *only* Caspian could control the briars. Well, both her and I can, too."

Keldarion shakes his head. "Your magic is a mystery. Those of the Below may use it for evil, but I promise we will unravel your secrets together, Rosalina."

Ezryn turns to us. "Once I'm in Spring, I must ensure my brother and father's safety and rid Spring of these toxic weeds. Who knows what effect they've had on others? My realm has been unattended to for too long."

I curl closer at the thought of him leaving.

Ezryn looks down at me. "I'll also send word to Autumn to have your father transported to Spring. We have the best healers in the realm, and I'll personally take charge of his care."

"Then I'm going with you," I say.

"Rosalina," Kel says.

"I want to help prepare for my father's arrival and be at his side while he's healing. Kel, you and the other princes need to restore magic to Castletree. Besides, Astrid and Marigold are still in Spring."

"Keep Hammergarden is well fortified," Ezryn says. "We will be safe there. You know I would sooner cut out my heart than let harm befall Rosalina."

"I suppose you're right," Keldarion grumbles.

"And also, I have to get your sword," I say, suddenly remembering.

"I assumed the Below took it," Keldarion says.

"No, I threw it into the lake so no one would find it," I say. "But you'll have to get it before you go back to Winter. That's your plan, isn't it?"

Ezryn tightens his fists. "Do you still intend to pass on your Blessing?"

What? How could Kel consider such a thing?

"I do not know," Keldarion says. "First, we must replenish Castletree's magic, then devise a plan to retrieve the necklaces. I will not pass on the rule of Castletree in such a state."

I run my fingers along his rough knuckles. "Think carefully about this, Kel. You were meant to be High Prince of Winter."

He gives a low sigh and kisses my hair. Sleep begins to take me, even though it's morning. "Please stay," I mumble. "Both of you."

64

KELDARION

"You can sleep," Ezryn says. "I'll keep watch."

Drowsiness pricks at my consciousness, but I won't let it take me. "I don't want to miss a moment of this."

Rosalina lies huddled between us. Her head rests on Ezryn's arm, her back pressed against my chest. She's deep in sleep, body twitching every so often in dreams. Lying here with my mate and my best friend, with the afternoon light drifting in through the curtains, is a relaxing respite I have not felt in an age. "I thought you might have been asleep yourself," I whisper to him.

"No," Ezryn says.

I chuckle. "Should have known. Your whole body would rattle with your snores."

Ezryn gives a quiet laugh, and I'm struck with the bitter edge of sadness that I do not remember the last time we laughed together.

He regards me, and I can tell by the tilt of his helm, it's something serious. "I know why you didn't tell me about your bargain with Caspian."

"I was ashamed."

"More ashamed than me for what I did at my Blessing? Your parents—*you*, Kel—were the only ones I could tell. Your family sheltered me against myself. Shame has never been a barrier between us."

"Ez ..."

"After you defied your father and they banished Caspian, I begged you not to follow him. But you confided in me that you were going to Cryptgarden anyway. It was later that I discovered the truth of his plots, how he was working for the Below the whole time. One of his very own minions betrayed his true intentions to me. And when you didn't return from the Below, it forced me to retrieve you with your army. The army you told Caspian came at your order."

"If he found out you led that army, he would have killed you."

"He tried to kill *you*."

"I knew I could survive it." I massage my wrist, still unsure if I have.

"That was the last secret you ever told me."

I swallow in a dry throat. He's not wrong.

"You didn't tell me of your bargain with Caspian, nor when your own mate walked through these very castle doors." He gives a long sigh. "You lied to him for me, Kel. But you never forgave me."

I stay silent because he speaks the truth.

"Even though I have been proven right again and again, you will not forgive me."

There are no words, because again, it is the truth. So often I have wondered what would have happened if Ezryn had not followed me to the Below that fateful day. Had he not harmed those Caspian held dear. If I had not taken the blame for it ... Would things have been different?

No, you idiot, I chide myself. Of course, they wouldn't. We had already made our bargain, and by Sira's account, that had been another one of his schemes. Maybe that hurts more than the later betrayal. I'd always blamed Ezryn, thinking that his actions had caused Caspian to switch sides. To betray me.

But like the Prince of Thorns had told me when he left me on the side of that mountain, he'd been planning the betrayal from the moment he knocked on Castletree's door, seeking refuge.

"I'm broken, Ez. You know that."

The Spring Prince snatches my wrist, baring the twisted frosted bracelet. "Your bargain stated it would break on its own if there was no more love between you two." His words are hushed so as not to wake Rosalina, but still cutting as a knife "It is clear the Prince of Thorns holds no love for you, so tell me why you cannot let him go. For Rosalina. For your people."

"I wish I could, Ez. Long nights I have thought every vile thing there is of him, and the list is staggering. I have stared daggers into the bracelet, yet still it remains."

Ezryn swears something under his breath and tosses my wrist away. Rosalina stirs at the sudden motion and curls into Ezryn, despite the hardness of his armor. Her bottom and long legs drive into me, as if she's determined to be touching us both at the same time.

"She is very fond of you," I say.

He runs a gloved hand through the locks of her chestnut hair. "And I of her."

"I never thought of myself as one to share a lover, but there is great joy in seeing the pleasure she gets from all of you. And great contentment in knowing the protection you offer."

"Or the protection she offers us," Ezryn muses.

"That seems to become more and more true by the day." I run a delicate hand along her brow. "You've saved us so many times, my Rose."

She gives a little smile, then begins to sleepily paw at her clothing.

"Silly girl fell asleep in her heavy robe," Ezryn says.

"That can't be comfortable." I eye my brother across from me, and we both shift. The thought of undoing Rosalina's clothes sets my body blazing.

Ezryn delicately unties the knot around her waist. She rolls to give him better access, murmuring a sleepy, "Thank you."

"How long have you been awake?" Ezryn asks.

"Not long," she mutters without opening her eyes. "Just dozing. This was too hot."

"Of course. Is there anything else you require?" I ask as I pull the robe off and toss it away, leaving her in only a thin pink slip.

"Thank you," she mumbles, rolling around in a dramatic display to get comfortable before finally deciding to burrow her head into my chest and press her hips against Ezryn's.

"Just when I think she can't get any cuter, she does things like this," I growl under my breath.

Ezryn makes a low sound. "I don't think cuteness is her objective right now."

He pulls the blanket down over her hips to reveal her slip ridden up to waist height, revealing her milky white thigh draped over Ezryn's leg. He runs his hand over the skin, causing her to shiver—and press her soft chest into mine.

And I know exactly what he means.

"Did I ever tell you about the time she sat on my lap and almost came on my thigh?" Ezryn growls.

Rosalina shoots her eyes open. "No! That's way too embarrassing!"

"Embarrassing enough not to do it again?"

Rosalina gives a little peep, and he tugs her harder against his leg. Her eyelashes flutter as she begins to writhe against him. My heart increases as I watch them move together. How he seems in tune with exactly what she wants.

"Though you didn't have this barrier last time." Ezryn pries a finger beneath her panties.

She wiggles, legs spread on either side of his thigh. "Off. Take them off." Then her brown eyes widen. "If that's all right with you, Kel."

"Watch your mate's face as she comes," Ezryn says. Not a question, but a demand. One I am happy to obey.

"I have seen her face in such a way only once, and that was simply beautiful," I say. "You must not touch me, Rosalina."

"Yes, Kel." She nods sadly.

"Then we agree," Ezryn says. With a quick efficiency, he yanks off his gloves then strips Rosie of her clothing.

"Fuck," I groan. Watching him touch her, I can't help but shove my own hand beneath the blankets to grip my cock.

The sight of them is staggering. Rosalina, completely naked, her rosy skin writhing against the silver metal, every part of her soft: her delicious curves, her full breasts, all squished against the hard and imposing Prince of Spring.

His large hand captures her entire breast and squeezes. She cries out, grinding against him.

I massage my cock, feeling as though I may come undone at any moment.

"Show me, Kel," Rosalina gasps. "I want to see you."

I throw the blanket off my heated body. My shirt has risen up, leaving my chest exposed. I slide my pants down to my knees and give my hard length a stroke.

"Fuck," Rosalina gasps. "That is a nice cock."

"There's such a naughty mouth on you sometimes." Ezryn shoves a finger into her mouth.

"But you have to agree," Rosalina mumbles, saliva running from her lips as she sucks Ezryn's finger. "It *is* a nice cock."

Ezryn tilts his helm at me. "That it is." He drags his hand down her stomach, then rubs her clit. "And one day, he's going to fill you with it. Would you like that, Baby Girl?"

She whimpers something, eyes fluttering closed as she grinds faster and faster on his leg, gripping his arms as he works her. "Yes. Both of you."

He chuckles lightly. "Perhaps."

The thought of truly having her, of sharing her with my brother, sends me nearly over the edge. And I may not be able to touch her, but I can *feel* her—the waves of her pleasure cresting higher and higher.

"Kel," she whimpers, sensing my urgency, eyes wide. "Over me. Over us."

I grit my teeth, pace increasing as I angle myself. Roaring, my release explodes from my cock, splattering over her.

Rosalina cries out, body writhing as Ezryn works her clit in circles. Her pleasure erupts around him. Her fingers grasp his armor for purchase, and I watch her sigh with ecstasy before she falls boneless in his arms.

"Magnificent," I say. "Both of you."

AFTER WE CLEAN UP, we take an early supper, where Rosalina practically falls asleep at the table. I'm not sure where Farron and Dayton are, but my connection with the former lets me know he's all right. Content, even. They must be together.

As we push away the last of the supper, Ezryn scoops up Rose in his arms.

"I'll have her sleep in my room tonight," I decide, unwilling to be parted from her, knowing she will leave for Spring in the morning.

Ezryn nods and we head through the halls to the Winter Wing.

"Tell me it wasn't just us who enjoyed that." I bump his shoulder with my own.

Ezryn gives a light chuckle, handing Rosalina over to me. "I am a man of flesh beneath this armor. She is not so easy to resist."

I place a hand on his shoulder. "I've always trusted you with my life, but now I trust you with my heart as well. You'll keep her safe in the Spring Realm."

Ezryn nods. "It's almost night. I plan to clear the Briar before I depart tomorrow."

I don't remove my hand. "Stay with us."

He tilts his gaze down to Rosie, who nuzzles into my arms. "You may stay a man at night, but her touch will not stop my change."

"Why should it matter? The bed is large enough for us all." At his silence, I continue, "If I was granted one wish, it would be that you were her mate, as well."

He laughs as if the concept is ridiculous. "Come on, Kel. I thought we stopped wishing on the stars when we were children."

Ezryn steps down the main staircase, then pauses. "Kel, you know the bargain you made? It mentions giving in to your own pleasure. However, it doesn't mention anything about giving to another."

"What are you saying?"

"I watched Caspian at the party. The bargain takes no heed of your lover's release ... If you feel you could restrain yourself."

"I could touch her."

He only nods his head, then descends the stairs.

65

DAYTON

I t feels like even the castle is tiptoeing around. Not only have the staff hidden away, but the bits of magic that lace through the wings—a breeze rustling the leaves in the hall or the smell of a campfire with no origin—have disappeared.

Castletree is disappointed in us.

And I can't blame it.

But I'm an idiot who doesn't like to leave anything alone, so I find myself wandering down the leaf-strewn hallway to the library. Even in the corridor, I hear his voice.

"Useless! Stupid, stupid! Arg!" A crash sounds, and I heave in a breath before pushing open the doors.

Farron's hunched over a table, papers and books spread before him. His hair is stuck to his forehead, eyes wild, clothes wrinkled.

He doesn't even look up when I walk over to his table.

"What is all this?" I murmur. There are open books on everything from botany to fables to human culture.

"It's nothing!" Farron shouts, chucking a book across the room. He digs his hands into his hair. "It's all fucking useless. I'm the High Prince of Autumn and I can't figure anything out."

"Tell me what you're trying to do," I say slowly, sternly.

"Everything! Nothing!" He scrubs his face. "I'm looking up medicines for George. And mate bonds to break yours and Ez's curse. And I'm trying to figure out how I'm going to get fucking Caspian away from Rosalina before he does something—"

"Fare." I grab his shoulders. "It's too much, even for you. Let's take it one step at a time. Together. I know Ez, Kel, and I haven't been the best these last twenty-five years, but we're in it with you now."

Farron squeezes his eyes shut. "Something terrible is going to happen. I can feel it."

"Take a breath. George is with your family—they'll look after him. Me and Ez? We're going to be fine. I promise. And Caspian … He did save our fucking asses. He doesn't seem to want to hurt Rosie."

Defeat clouds Farron's features. He shakes his head and steps away from me. "Didn't you see how he looked at her?" He sighs. "It was exactly how he used to look at Kel."

"Yeah, well, Rosie's a lot smarter than Kel."

"It doesn't matter." Farron grabs the side of the table, knuckles white, body shaking. "You don't understand what we saw, Day. Caspian has been holding back on us all these years. He *harnesses* the Green Flame. He's not like the goblins or even that power-hungry vizier. If he desires something, he can take it." Farron looks back at me, eyes wide and shining. "We know he wants her. It's only a matter of time."

"I won't let that happen," I growl.

"You can't stop this!" Farron cries. "What are you going to do, Day? You haven't even broken your curse. And when you do, Rosie won't matter to you anymore. *I* won't matter to you anymore."

I lurch forward and wrap my arms around Farron, holding him tight. "Listen to me, and listen to me well, Pup. You are mine. I am yours. And she is ours. Until either of you say otherwise or force me away."

Farron takes in a shaky breath, his body quivering against mine. I keep my arms like a vice around him. "I know I haven't always been good to you, Fare. I took your love for granted. It wasn't right, and I'm a bastard for doing that to you. But everything changed when Rosalina walked through those damned doors. She taught me there are things worth fighting for. And no mate bond, no curse, not even Caspian himself, will stop me from fighting for you."

Farron's voice is a shaky breath. "I would rip it apart—the cosmos, the threads of life—if I could bind you to us."

I spin him and push the hair off his brow. "I know you would. But even the brilliant High Prince of Autumn has his limits." I lean in, brushing my lips over his. "So just love me instead."

Something shifts in Farron's eyes, golden and predatory. He pulls away from me and shoves the papers off the table. They land in a clattering heap. Then he takes my shoulders and pushes me on top of the mahogany. "I'm going to do more than love you, Daytonales," he says. "I'm going to take you."

66

FARRON

Somehow, we find our way to my chambers, a trail of clothes in our wake. Everything else is lost to feverish kisses, hands in hair, and the drum of my heart against my ribs.

Dayton slams my door shut with his foot, his fingers busy on my face, then my neck, then my ribs. My chamber is lit with orange glowing orbs that hover in the corners, casting dusky light throughout the room. The true fading sunlight is concealed by heavy curtains.

We've both lost all our clothes by this point. I run my hand over his sun-kissed skin, marveling at the patchwork of scars over his chest, how they only make him more beautiful.

The bed is too far, so we collapse on my large chaise, the one right beside the bookshelf. Rosie and I have spent several nights cuddled up on it together, forgetting the world.

And that's what I want to do now.

Forget all the things that tear at my mind, that steal the joy and replace it with fear.

I won't let that happen to me tonight. Dayton won't let it.

He collapses on the chaise, arms spread over the back and legs far apart. He grins up at me like a king. His cock bobs triumphantly.

A growl rushes up my throat, and I slam my body against his, pressing our cocks together. His salty sweet skin is as addictive as a drug, and my teeth nip at his throat.

He laughs and pulls me back by my hair to steal a kiss from my lips. "Tell me what you want, Pup," he murmurs when we finally pull away.

"I want to take you in a way no one else has," I breathe.

His eyes shine. "I want to give you that."

Elation surges through my chest, and a genuine smile appears on my face. This … This is safety. This is home.

"Let's take it slow, yeah?" Dayton says. "I want to enjoy every piece of you tonight."

We fall back together on the chaise, me on his chest, and we take it slow. Kisses long and languishing. Hands feeling skin as if for the first time. His hard length presses against my stomach, and bursts of nervous anticipation bubble through me, even though it's Dayton. My Day.

We spin so we're both lying on the chaise, arms wrapped tight together. Needing to be closer, I press my leg over his hip. I can see it all in my mind's eye as we kiss: the sand and sea, long days spent in the Summer Realm, that cocky grin that turned so serious when I showed him too much of my heart. *I knew it,* I think. We've always been that special time between the turn of summer to fall when the leaves change as bright as the beaming sun that hasn't yet been chased away.

How'd we end up here? A cursed castle, our realms in disarray, a demon lurking at our doorstep.

And yet … Would I trade it? It brought him to me. Brought me Rose.

"Doesn't it matter to you?" he says slowly.

I turn to look at him, his blue eyes shimmering like a sea before a storm. So much emotion bubbling beneath the surface. I graze his jaw with the back of my knuckles. "What matters, Day?"

"That Rosie and I aren't mates. She was… disappointed, I think. But you haven't said anything."

"Who says you're not mates?"

He gives a humorless chuckle. "If there was a bond there, it would have awoken already with how much we've been through. With how much I—" His voice cracks. "With how much I love her."

I sit back and stare at the man below me. A year ago, would I think this man a stranger? Physically, he's the same, long golden hair splayed around his chiseled face, the cord of muscles in his chest, those plush lips. But the vulnerability etched into his features, the words of love so easily offered on his lips... That is all new.

No, I decide. I would know him anywhere. I always knew this version Dayton lived within him though he only showed me fractured glimpses of it through all the long years.

"No, Daytonales, it doesn't matter to me."

He shakes his head. "Why not?"

"Because this is something I can actually prove. When we make love, when we made love with Rosie, when Rosie speaks of being with you—it's different than anything I've experienced before. It's magic. It's enchanted. It's golden."

Dayton doesn't say anything, but shimmering tears pool in his eyes.

"You've always been mine. Mine to chase. Mine to love. Mine to lose." I kiss him softly. "And I'm not going to let that happen. I'm never going to lose you."

"Fare," he says, "we can't control the fate of the stars."

"Who says we can't?" A growl ripples through my words. "I know in my heart, in everything I am, that you belong with Rosie and me. And damn, I hope the stars are watching because I'm going to show them how much."

He pulls me into a devastating kiss. "Finally, something I know how to do."

He grabs for my cock, running a firm thumb from base to tip, then sits up, dragging me with him.

I suck in a deep inhale and emulate his stance from before, arms out, legs spread. He sinks to his knees before me. I'm reminded of the legend of sirens peering up from the ocean, ready to ensnare sailors.

I would gladly sink to the bottom of his sea.

"Oh Day," I say, a rough edge to my voice that sounds foreign to even me.

Dayton never takes his eyes off me as he engulfs me entirely. I groan, hands grasping for purchase on the chaise. Ecstasy ripples up my core.

He pulls back, and I expect to see that self-satisfied look on his face. But there's something else.

Devotion.

So slowly, he laps the head of my cock, his teal gaze shining. His tongue runs over my pearling tip, and he groans. I close my eyes, the sight too fucking beautiful to bear.

"Deeper," I grunt. I feel his mouth curve into a smile. "Good boy."

Fire shoots through my body as he sucks me into his throat. I grip his hair and rock my hips. His mouth is so fucking good, it would be easy to lose myself here.

"Hold on." I push on his forehead, so I don't accidentally fill his entire mouth.

Now, that arrogant grin is back. He cups my balls and gives them a playful tug. "Are the lips of the Summer Prince too much for you?"

I grab his chin and pull him up to eye level. "Yes. And I'm saving every last drop of cum for your ass."

A flush colors Dayton's cheeks. "Yes, sir," he purrs.

"Go get the oil. You know where it is."

I stroke my cock slowly as Dayton gets up and walks to the end table. The view of his round ass is positively exquisite.

When he returns, I kneel down at the end of the chaise. "Lie down before me," I order. I'm not sure where this person came from who freely orders the Prince of Summer around, but I like him.

And so does Dayton. He bites his lower lip and cups his balls up toward his huge cock, then lies before me, facing up. He's like a slab of marble, and I can't wait to start carving.

I dip two fingers into the vial of oil then gently spread Dayton's legs, revealing his glorious cock and entrance.

"We'll take this easy. You'll lead the way—if it gets too much, say the word and we stop," I tell him.

Dayton raises an eyebrow. "I'm a gladiator of the Sun Colosseum. I can take anything you give me, Pup."

"We'll see." I grin back at him. My slick fingers rub circles around his entrance, and he groans. His hips buck upward as he pushes against my hand, asking for more.

"Slow down," I chide. "We're taking things slow, remember?"

His smile is like the sun. "I've never had any control around you, Fare."

I smile back, but it's not the truth. He's had lots of control around me: every night he left to sleep alone, all the times he kept his feelings hidden.

But now, he's fully giving me his trust.

My fingers slowly begin to dip in and out of him. "You feel so good, Day."

He only moans, arching his back and vigorously pumping his cock a few times. The sight makes my own length twitch with need.

I slip one finger in deeper now, getting him used to the feeling of fullness. "How is that?"

"More," he groans. "I want more of you."

I suck in a breath and inch my other finger in. Fuck, he's so gorgeous, this gladiator with my fingers curled in his ass, holding him at my mercy. His eyes shine with a taunt. I begin to pump my hand in and out, in and out.

"Fuck, yes, Fare. Fuck."

I grip his length with my other hand, simultaneously pumping cock and ass.

"Does this feel good?" I ask, my voice a raspy breath.

He pushes hard against me. "You have no idea."

"I do, actually." I laugh.

Then he sits up on his elbows. "I need you now, Fare. Fuck me." Then he smiles. "No ... Make love to me."

I can barely breathe, my heart near beating out of my chest. I pull my fingers free and lean over him, capturing his mouth in a kiss. Then I position my hardness at his entrance. "Ready?"

"So ready," he says, and it seems to mean so much more than just this moment.

Inch by precious inch, I drive into Dayton's ass. His body feels made for my cock, hugging me so tight, each movement has me shuddering with ecstasy.

Dayton grabs my hips and guides me further, deeper. My name is a helpless moan on his lips.

When I'm fully sheathed inside him, we blink at each other. "Well?" I whisper.

"I told you," he says. "I'm yours."

And so, I take him. Our bodies move like a single entity, rocking together as if we've done this a thousand times before. And yet my heart sings in a way that celebrates this as the first time. Something Dayton has gifted me alone.

"How are you doing?" I manage among my pants and groans.

"You've got the cock of a god," he growls. "I love being stuffed full of this godly cock."

His praise makes me fuck him harder. I lift his leg over my shoulder, revealing a glimpse of his plump ass cheek. I smack it. Dayton half-growls, half-laughs, then grabs my hips and plunges me deeper into him. We both cry out.

Then with a roar, he flips us over so I'm on my back. He positions himself on top. With a hungry gaze, he drives his ass down on to my shaft, plunging me deeper in him than I've ever been. My mind turns to haze, clouds of lust and elation falling over me.

"This is your ass," Dayton says, voice gravelly. "I'm giving it to you. Watch your cock fill me up."

He pops himself right to the tip of my shining head, then slowly inches himself down. His scorching tunnel engulfs my entire length, all the way to my balls, and I can hardly keep my eyes from rolling back into my head.

Dayton grips his base, squeezing. "You're too much, Fare. I can't take this much longer."

I run a hand down his chest, voice pleading. "Come with me."

"Where?"

"All over me," I breathe.

A feral glint possesses his gaze. "Are you ready to fill my ass, Pup? I want your cum dripping out of me. Hold nothing back."

"It's all for you."

He closes his eyes and smiles. And then he moves like a man driven to madness: his ass bounces up and down on my hardness as if getting my cum is his only mission in this world.

And maybe for this moment, it is.

His warm sheath tugging against my head is enough to send me spiraling. I cry out, "Come with me!" Before entirely losing myself. My release spurts out of me as my cock contracts. Dayton's ass tightens around me, and he groans. Cum gushes from his cock, painting my chest.

My orgasm roils through me a moment more; faults in the earth, cracking before settling anew. Dayton collapses on the chaise beside me, arm thrown over my belly.

"We should have done that ages ago," he murmurs.

I play with a strand of his hair. "You weren't ready."

Our gaze meets, and he offers me a smile. "I'm ready now."

Again, it feels like so much more.

We take our time cleaning up. As I emerge from my ensuite bath, now dressed in a fluffy robe, a part of me wonders if Dayton will still be here.

But he's waiting for me on the bed, hair wet, and that same smile on his face. Not the arrogant one, but the other one. The devoted one.

And I realize … I'm not surprised he's still here.

I knew.

"It's almost night," he says.

I drop my robe, and feel for that reserve of magic, that one that now has a permanent spot within me. The one that guides and protects. My body shifts until I'm on all fours, now in the shape of the Autumn wolf. "I know."

Dayton stands. His body shimmers. Those blue eyes stay, but the rest changes into the golden wolf of Summer.

I trot over to him and nuzzle against his snout. "Are you going to leave?"

"No." He lies down, but his gaze stays trained on me. "I met a couple people who taught me to stop running away from everything."

I nestle beside him. "They must be really great."

"Yeah." His voice grows low and sleepy. "They're pretty much the best people I know."

And as Dayton drifts off to sleep, I hope he knows: *I think the same about him.*

67

ROSALINA

Strong arms clasp around me, and I'm enwrapped in Keldarion's scent. I snuggle deeper into his embrace.

"I'd give you space, but then you'd be beside something much more furry," Keldarion says lowly.

"You're already pretty furry." I run a hand down the hair on his chest. He's not wearing a shirt, only loose sleep pants. And I realize his shirt is on me. I must have passed out at dinner. "What time is it?"

"It's still the dead of night. Go back to sleep."

I peek over his massive body to catch a glimpse of the moonlight dancing through the window. Kel gives a low grumble. "You see, this is what happens when you sleep all day. You're wide awake in the middle of the night."

I grin sheepishly. "It's okay. I'm perfectly happy to lie here with you."

He bends to kiss the top of my head before pulling me into a tighter embrace.

"Kel?" I whisper. "What did Ezryn mean when he said he marched your army into the Below?"

Kel gives a low groan and flips to his back. "So, you heard that?"

I lie half my body over him, resting my cheek on his chest. "I did, but you don't have to tell me."

"Seeing as you can't sleep, perhaps I should."

"I want to know," I say.

He takes a deep breath, then begins. "I'd always known of the Prince of Thorns. Sira's son who could control shadows and briars. His name was whispered amongst all of us. We'd glimpsed him from afar. I swear I even met him as a child. But it wasn't until the Rainbow Eclipse Festival at Castletree that I truly knew him."

I snuggle closer to my mate as he recounts the tale, burning with questions but letting him be as sparse or as detailed with the information as he needs to be.

"Caspian came to Castletree seeking refuge, claiming he'd barely escaped the Below. No one trusted him. My father took him prisoner and threw him in the dungeons of our Keep," Kel says. "However, I, in all my perfect wisdom, thought of this as a great opportunity. My parents had spent decades in battle with the Below. They'd even commanded a dangerous mission diving into the depths to retrieve a great power said to have come from the Above itself."

"A great power?" I whisper.

"A heavenly flower plucked from the Gardens of Ithilias. Sira used it to create the goblins. My parents theorized if they retrieved it, her army would dwindle. However, during the operation, the heavenly flower was lost to both the surface realms and the Below. Long had our forces searched for it. And my ambitious mind immediately thought Caspian was the perfect tool. With his knowledge of the Below, of the deep magic, he could help me find this great power. And he was my prisoner. I was so foolish."

I clasp his hand as Kel explains how Cas cooperated with the Winter Realm as they planned an expedition to the deepest depths of the Below to retrieve this mysterious power. During this time, the two of them grew close, and in turn, Caspian befriended the other princes.

"And Cas and Ez started their board game rivalry?" I ask, smiling.

"Indeed." Kel lowers his voice. "I was also engaged at this time. My parents wished for me to be wed before I took the mantle of High Prince."

"I met Tilla. She works at Draconhold Forge. Gave me my own Spring steel bracer."

Kel raises a dark brow. "You could charm a bard of his fiddle."

"I wasn't charming anyone," I say. "Though she told me she didn't think you ever loved her."

"I didn't. But the wedding hurtled ahead like a tidal wave until I was standing across from her and somehow knew saying that vow was wrong. Wrong all the way through me. So, I fled. In front of my entire realm, I fled. It was Cas who helped me escape. He used his thorns and took us all the way to the edge of the Winter Realm.

"And there we fought. I can't recall how it began, only that he was always getting on my last nerve, and all the anger I felt about the wedding, our mission, cropped up. We screamed at each other so loud, I thought we'd shake the snow from the mountain. But then suddenly, we weren't screaming anymore. My mouth was over his, and I don't remember why, only that it was me who did it, and maybe it was the only way I thought to shut him up. I had never kissed a man before, didn't even realize I wanted to."

I feel it through Kel and can almost see the memory like a dream lost upon waking: Caspian with windblown hair, flecked with snow. And oh, how well I know the darkness behind those lips.

"We didn't leave that mountainside until the next morning. When we returned to Frostfang, we found it had been attacked. And all the signs pointed the blame to Caspian."

"But he was with you all night," I said.

"Yes, but I couldn't very well admit that. Not without the shame it would bring to me, my family. He told me to keep it a secret. So, I let them banish him away, even after all those months of work to help us. And I said nothing.

"Once he was gone, I found I could not let him go. I followed him all the way to the Below. And it was there I decided to stay while we continued our mission to search for this power. Much to the dismay of those above. And to Ezryn."

"That's when you resided in Cryptgarden," I say.

"Yes. Ezryn came down a few times, and I assured him my personal army was awaiting my order if I ever needed assistance. But after months, Caspian and I finally found the power, a heavenly rose plucked from the Gardens of Ithilias itself. That night, in the haze of victory, we made the bargain, planning the next morning to attend a celebration in the surface world."

I trace the frosted thorns around his wrist. "Go on, Kel."

With shaky words, he tells me of awaking alone, of Ezryn storming Cryptgarden with the Winter army. "He believed I was in grave danger, stating Caspian was a spy all along. In the raid, many of Caspian's personal guard were killed. Among them were a few friends whom he was very fond of. Parts of Cryptgarden were destroyed, including some of his most treasured places. I knew if Caspian learned it was Ezryn who led the army, he would hunt him down. And that would end with either my best friend or the man I—with Caspian dead. I thought if I said the army mistakenly came down at my command, he might understand."

"Did he? Understand?"

"When I found him, he barely spoke. But he still agreed to come to the celebration. But it was there he betrayed all of us.

"In his anger, the Prince of Thorns created a great chasm that bled from Winter to the depths of the Below. And all of the Below's terrible and ancient creatures flooded out into my realm. They marched over a frozen wasteland to the capital, Frostfang. And the Prince of Thorns attacked with such a force that the people of Winter had no choice but to retreat to Autumn for refuge. The goblins pursued, and a great battle was waged on the fields outside of Coppershire."

The chrysanthemum fields with the grave markers ... The fallen from that battle became the army I saw Perth raise only months ago.

"My mother was lost in the siege of Frostfang," Kel continues, and his throat bobs. "And I did not escape. Caspian took me prisoner, left me hanging on the side of a mountain to die."

"Kel," I whisper.

"Don't fret." He runs a finger down my nose. "Ez climbed the whole thing, hand over hand, and freed me.

"After I returned, the forces of the four realms were able to rally and take back Frostfang. Ultimately, we defeated the Below, though many were lost. The heavenly flower we had spent so long searching for was destroyed in the fight."

"I can't believe you lived through all of that," I say. My mind reels trying to place each of my princes in this sordid history.

"Now you know my greatest shame and why I was cursed. My father died during this War of Thorns, and I became High Prince. It was not long after, that the Enchantress came to Castletree, cursing us forever. Only days passed before Caspian began to wrap Castletree in his thorns and start siphoning the magic from these hallowed branches."

I hold tight to him, not only to keep him fae, but because he needs it. A light sweat covers his body, and he shivers.

"Thank you for telling me. I'm glad to know your past and all you faced." My mind spins with the new information and trying to make sense of Caspian within it. *Was that what you wanted, Prince of Thorns? Did he love Kel all along, or is it as the Winter Prince believes and a plot of betrayal? Why the thorns and lying to the princes about the nature of it? Why save* me *time and time again?*

"There is, of course, more than I have said, and you may ask me any of it."

"I will," I say, nuzzling into his neck. "For tonight, this is more than enough. But there's something I need to tell you about Caspian."

Kel tilts his chin. "Is it how you told Farron you think he is your mate?"

"Caspian spoke in my mind, Kel. Only you and Farron have done that and ... I don't know. Farron believes it's a side effect of the bargain between you two."

The muscles in Kel's jaw twitch, but there's no anger at this mention. "If he feels a connection, it would explain some of his actions. His ... preoccupation with you."

"I don't really understand it," I admit, "only that I know Caspian has done terrible, unforgivable things, but a part of me believes there is still good in him."

"I want to say you're wrong, but if I truly believed that, then these thorns around my wrist would be gone. Because I've seen it. Seen him in a light many others haven't. When he's sad, with tears running down his cheeks. Or nervous before a party, desperately trying to smooth down his hair. I've seen him blissed with pleasure and hysterical with rage. I've even seen him laughing so hard he cried."

"I hardly believe that," I say.

"It's rare, but true. And to think all of that was just an act? A part of me still can't make sense of it."

"What about that blackness he coughs up? He called it 'the rot'."

"Caspian is a creature entirely of the Below. He is made of a magic not of this world," Keldarion says lowly. "He never told me the details, but from what I gathered, it had to do with the circumstances of his birth, how Sira bore such a powerful child. There is always a cost for such magic, and for Caspian, it means he cannot survive on the surface. Though, he used to be able to spend months up here before returning to the Below. I would think he is even more powerful now with all the magic he siphons from Castletree."

My gaze drifts to the thorns snaking up the room, and I desperately want to tell Kel the truth. But Caspian made me promise not to. But I can tell Kel *my* truth.

"I can feel the thorns," I say. "And they're not siphoning magic."

"Are you sure?"

I take Kel's hand in my own and press it over a thorn above the bed. I close my eyes and let myself feel. "When you tore the vines in High Tower and when I tried to remove them in the dining room, Castletree crumbled. Look how they curve along the walls … I don't believe they're hurting Castletree."

"Why would he offer strength to his enemies?" Kel gives a low breath. "Perhaps that's why he's so sick."

I hadn't thought about it like that. How much magic is he using to keep Castletree standing?

369

I shake my head. "Why does Caspian do anything? I mean, he kissed me, after all."

"I saw."

"No, when we were escaping. I tried to pull him with us, and we were alone amidst the thorns. We kissed again." I clutch Kel close and remember the way it felt to be held in Caspian's arms. The memory is so vivid, I know Keldarion can see it, too.

He says nothing, but his gaze is soft with a flicker of confusion. "We have to be careful around him, Rosalina. Our hearts are not always trustworthy."

"I know," I say. But I know that there is at least one part of my heart that shines with the utmost honesty: the part that binds me to Kel, that says I can tell him anything.

A sly grin crosses my face. "I have one more question, if it's not too bold to ask."

"And that is?"

I rise on his chest. "What is it like to bed the Prince of Thorns? That woman who was sent to Castletree said it was quite lackluster."

Keldarion chuckles so loudly I bounce up and down with the movement. "Shouldn't you be seething with jealousy at the thought of my former lovers?"

Honestly, I ought to, shouldn't I? Yet the idea of him with Caspian stirs up a different feeling within me altogether. It's as though I can almost picture Caspian appearing in my thoughts and playfully teasing me about it. *What happened to you after we escaped?* I wonder. *After you kissed me?* "I'm curious."

Kel raises a brow. "He was much as he is now. Passionate, cunning. Extreme. Sometimes it felt like my whole chest was on fire."

"That's interesting."

"Though I do not think he would be the same with you, based on that kiss you shared in my mind."

I inhale sharply. "Shouldn't you be seething with jealousy at the idea of me with him?"

"I should be, shouldn't I?" he says. "And a part of me is very angry at the idea, and yet—"

"And yet?"

"I cannot stand the idea that he was the last one to kiss you." Suddenly, Kel's lips are over mine.

I can't control my desire for him, deepening the kiss.

"Damn, you even taste like him," Keldarion growls, hands gripping my hair as his tongue explores my mouth.

"Make me taste like you," I plead.

"Somehow, I don't think my story has tired you out enough."

My leg slips between his. "Kel..."

"You heard what Ezryn said, didn't you?" Something dark and predatory lingers in his voice. "May I pleasure you?"

A shiver runs through my entire body. "Wouldn't that be terrible for you? To receive nothing in return?"

"Oh no, my Rose. Your body is all I have dreamed about since you walked through the door of Castletree. Will you let me touch you? Touch all of you?"

I press down on his chest, eyes blazing. "I'm yours, Kel. But let's get something straight."

He narrows his eyes in a catlike way.

"I want this always: your heart open to me. Don't shut me out again. No more lies." I say, determination lacing my voice. "And I will hear no more about you fucking every man and woman in the Enchanted Vale. You belong to me, Keldarion, Prince of Winter."

He smiles. "Is that all?"

"Close me out again, and I'll chop that perfect cock off with my thorns." I take control of some of the ones from around the room for emphasis.

"I do not doubt it." He rises, takes my face between his palms. "I have always and will forever be yours, my Rose."

I drop the thorns and kiss him lightly. "I'm yours, Kel. You know I'm yours."

He grips me around the waist and tugs me over his hips. "Then hold on to the headboard and sit on my face."

68

ROSALINA

I blink at him, stunned into stillness. "Kel."

"If you do not want this, then tell me now." He runs a thumb along my lips. "Because I have been dreaming of the taste of you for so long."

I've dreamt of this, too, I think, but I won't be able to reciprocate.

He kisses the side of my neck. "Rest assured, being able to touch you, to watch you come apart under my care alone, is all the pleasure I need. Lift your arms."

I do, and he removes my shirt. My whole body quivers with anticipation. He's only ever given me fleeting touches. But he means to have me. All of me.

Rough hands glide down my body.

"So perfect," he says, a surprising lightness to his voice. "Long have I ached to touch these beautiful breasts."

My laugh turns to an almost feral moan as he kneads at me, thumb flicking over my pointed nipples.

"And these hips, your stomach, these gorgeous, long legs." His eyes roam over me like a fire. "By the stars, I could gaze at you for an age."

I tuck a strand of dark hair behind my pointed ear. "I might be fae now, but even I'm not that patient."

He slides back down on the mattress, eyes narrowed. "Then, my Rose, do what I said. Grab the headboard and sit on my face."

I reach forward and grip the white wood that makes up the back of his large bed. Then I lift my hips and gingerly hover above his face. He grips my thighs with his hands, rubbing his rough stubble along the sensitive skin. My inner muscles clench with the sensation, with the warmth of his breath.

Then he guides me lower, and as he lightly brushes my aching center, all I can do is sigh. But it's his sounds—so purely male, so eager —that make me wet with anticipation. His touch is delicate and careful, like slicing the tiniest piece off an expensive dessert to savor each bite.

He's savoring me.

My fingers curl, gaze focused on the ripples of wood, as he continues the light kisses between my legs. Light like butterfly wings fluttering against my skin.

"You're holding yourself up." Kel's rough stubble scratches the inside of my thigh. "I mean for you to use the headboard to push yourself down."

"I'll suffocate you," I whisper.

He makes a dissatisfied sound. "What need do I have for air with your thighs around my head?"

And with that, he grips my hips and pulls me down. His tongue drives into me. All sense of delicacy gone, he works me with the furious passion of a man long starved. Licking, sucking, nipping at my inner thigh until he remembers he is indeed mortal—or near enough to it—and needs to breathe.

All I can do in response is babble an incoherent sob and clutch the headboard as the glorious sensations threaten to overtake every sense of my body.

Eventually my hips find a rhythm of their own, rocking and grinding against his lips, the roughness of his jaw causing an even greater thrill. "Kel," I cry out his name, along with more senseless prattle, as my pleasure builds and builds. My palms grow slick on the headboard, but I do as my mate instructed. I push down, desperate for more of him.

I'm rewarded with an absolutely pleasurable growl as his tongue works. "Kel, I'm—I'm—" I explode into a series of spasms, muscles convulsing.

"Fuck yes, Rosalina," he growls, continuing to lap at me as I come, rough tongue massaging my aching and tender core. "Come, Rose. Don't stop. Give it to me."

My pleasure crests out of me with a tiny whimper, and my fingers fall limp off the wood headboard. My legs feel like jelly. Kel lays me flat on my back. My vision spins as he kisses me, and I taste myself on his lips.

"Do you know how tortuous it has been?" he growls. "To feel you come for the others, to know they get to taste you, to watch you writhe and moan? Until dawn, Rosalina, you are all mine."

I grip the back of his neck, fingers threading the white strands of his hair. "All yours."

"Do you trust me?"

A nervous flutter weaves through me at the taunting tone of his voice. "Yes."

"Good." He runs a hand along my bare stomach. "Then trust me when I tell you that this will feel—"

A cool, prickling sensation runs down my belly, and I jam my leg up, kneeing him in the face. He jerks back, a small shard of ice flying from his hands, and cups his nose.

"What was that?" I cry.

He drops his hand and grins. "I was trying to be sensual. Do you think you could refrain from attacking me?"

I bite my lower lip. "I suppose."

He twirls his hand, and another thin shard of ice appears between his fingers. "Good. Then lie back."

He drags the ice along my upper ribcage, leaving a trail of water. The chill causes goosebumps to prickle all over my body, and my core clenches at the strange sensation.

"A bit of cold can be pleasurable," he says, dragging the shard along the soft mound of my breast. When he drags the ice in circles around my nipple, I dig my heels into the mattress, straining, and try not to move. The points grow hard and aching, and the Winter Prince smiles deviously.

"You're enjoying this," I gasp out, wanting to swat his hand away while simultaneously telling him to never leave.

"Of course," he continues until the whole shard is near melted under the combined heat of our bodies. "I am only just beginning to explore you, to see what makes you smile, makes you gasp."

Then as the last of the ice melts, he replaces his hand with his mouth, the warmth such a contrast to the cold. I arch my hips, gasping, clawing at his back. He laps up the cold water around my nipple before swirling with his tongue and sucking.

Unable to help myself, I shoot a hand between my legs, wishing I could reach for him instead.

His free hand goes to massage my other breast, and I cry out at the cold points of his fingertips. The icy bastard doesn't even need to make ice—he's bloody frost itself. But I don't have time to launch a complaint before his hot mouth replaces the cold.

"Oh fuck, Kel, I hate you. I hate how good this feels, you stupid, icy prick."

He laughs and sits up, spreading my knees and clasping my wandering hand with his own. Then, with a wave of his palm, soft snow begins to fall, the flakes landing and melting almost instantly on my heated body. I sigh in pleasure at the sensation.

"I have one more thing." He grins wickedly, then holds up a new object made of ice.

I raise myself on to my forearms. In his hand is a large icicle, but with a rounded tip. I suddenly realize what he means that for. "It's too big. Kel, that's—"

"It'll melt inside of you," he says plainly.

"Even if it melts a little, that's still—"

"You've had both Farron and Dayton's cocks."

I cross my arms. "That's different. They can't control the size. This you're purposely making … monstrous."

He grins and bites the lobe of my ear. "You've seen my cock, Rosalina. You know this barely compares. One day, I will fill you. And it's best to be prepared."

Slowly, I let my knees fall to the side, unable to say that his prowling look and his words weren't making me a little curious.

"All right," I say. "But I'm telling Day you made an ice dildo, and you'll have to deal with his reaction. He'll probably want one for himself."

"Fair enough." Keldarion chuckles lightly, propping the cold object at my entrance. "But that is considering you still have a voice tomorrow and have not lost it all screaming."

"Kel—" His name fades to a moan as he gently slides the ice inside me. The shock of the chill, of the size, has me throwing back my head and writhing. "Oh god!"

His eyes blaze, hand tight around the shaft. "Long have I dreamt of slipping inside you. This will have to do for now."

I squirm on the object, wishing it were truly him, but euphoria seizes me regardless. He drives it deeper and deeper until I feel his fingertips at my entrance and the most wonderful full sensation.

I grasp his shoulders, pulling his chest against mine. "Say it will be so one day, Kel. Say it because I don't think I can bear it if it can never be. One day. One day, we'll be together."

Salty tears flow down my cheek as he bends to kiss me. "One day, my Rose. One day, I will have you unbound. I will sheathe myself inside you and never leave." His hand glides up to my stomach. "And I'll fill you with my seed as many times as it takes."

The thought has me whimpering with sadness and desire all at once. "Yes, yes. *Yes.*" My words descend into chaos as he moves the object, slowly at first, letting every cold inch touch my inner walls. But his speed increases as I adjust to the size, and the length of it slides in and out in the most delicious rhythm.

"How are you not …" I gasp, tears streaking down my face. "God, Kel, how am I the only one coming undone? You've untethered me from the earth."

He keeps pumping the icicle in and out, my whole body thrashing. His eyes flash as he growls, "Trust me, it is not without great difficulty. But my will to watch you come in my arms is strong."

The bed is soaked between us, from the melting ice and my own warmth. He pulls his hand away, the ice dildo diminished. He raises a brow and tosses it to the floor. "I could remake it, but I think I'd rather feel you writhe around my hand."

With that, he shoves two fingers inside me. "Oh, yes, Kel. Yes." The heat of his hand compared to the ice has me seizing. I grip his face madly, seeing the passion in his features.

I'm yours. The thought explodes through our bond. It's so much stronger now that I know his truth. Know why he kept himself away. But this thought has always been there: *I'm yours, I'm yours.*

He pulls me into a kiss. "My Rose, my love."

My storm crests in a cascade of pleasure, muscles clenching around his fingers. He softly strokes me through wave after wave of it.

We fall together on the bed, and he clutches me tight to him. "You're still here," he murmurs. "I knew Ez was right, but still I worried the pure euphoria of my pleasure would be enough to trigger the bargain, even without a physical release."

I can't help but laugh in his arms while the starlight still flickers through me. "Fae bargains, so dramatic."

He brushes the hair from my brow and kisses my forehead. "Now that I know what we're capable of, Rosalina, it is only the beginning."

I grasp his hand. "Until one day."

He squeezes back. "One day."

69

ROSALINA

T he sun is shining through Castletree, and it seems a mockery
of the sadness that gripped it two nights ago. Ezryn's
waiting for me in the entrance hall so we can return through
the mirror to Keep Hammergarden.

But I can't leave yet. Not with the way things are.

My mind has been eerily quiet. I know it's Farron giving me the
space I asked for, but I can't stand it anymore. Can't stand the pain I
put him through or the pain he put me through. Our words have
always been weapons; I just never thought we'd wield them at each
other.

I open the door to the library and peer inside. Farron's sitting at a
desk, examining a stack of papers. Dayton leans near him, wearing
only trousers.

You're not my mate. The words had edges, gouging me open. But
he's right. I was so angry, it was easy to find something to be angry
about. And my jealousy—my grief at losing Dayton to someone else
—was so close to the surface. I can't blame Dayton for telling the
truth.

They both look up at me as I enter. Dayton slaps Farron on the
back and mumbles something to him. Then he heads my way.

He moves as if to pass, but I reach out and snag his wrist. Our eyes meet.

The air ripples with the unspoken words. *I'm sorry. I'm so sorry.*

But instead, I say, "You know."

"I know," he responds, voice a low rumble. "And you know."

"I know."

Taking a deep inhale, I let the moment ripple through me. This is how things are with Dayton. Never said, always felt.

He smiles. "Give him hell, Rose. He's less fragile than he looks."

I snort, but Dayton's soft expression sends a jolt of energy through me. I turn to watch him walk from the library.

Farron stands up, hand on his neck.

He looks so beautiful bathed in the morning light. I think back to when I first fell in love with him all those months ago: our long days together, the stories we shared, how he felt like the first person in my life to understand me to my core.

And that's why I understand him so well.

Understand his anger. His fear.

Can we have a do-over? I say in my mind.

His golden eyes flick up at me. *Anything you ask.*

The space between us disappears in a moment, then his hands are on my face and my fingers are tangled in his hair, and his mouth is on my neck, my jaw, my lips.

"I'm so sorry, Rosie," he murmurs against my skin. "I trust you. You know I do. And I know better than anyone that us princes have no right to cast stones."

"I'm sorry, too. I want you to know that I understand how much Caspian hurt you. Hurt Kel. I'm not apologizing for him."

Farron pulls back and wipes away the tears I didn't even realize were falling down my face. "I wish I had your optimism about the world."

"And I wish I had your sense of self-preservation." I force a smile, and we both laugh.

He wraps his arms around me and pulls me tight to his chest. "We'll figure this out. We always do."

I breathe him in, letting his scent calm me. "You know I want to protect you as much as you want to protect me, don't you, Fare? I want to protect all of you. I won't let him hurt Kel again."

"That may be your intent, Rosie, but none of us can control the Prince of Thorns. Even if you're right, even if there is some good in him, he's still in allegiance with Sira."

But what if he doesn't have to be? This thought I keep to myself. For now. "Did you really rip his book?"

Farron shrugs.

My thoughts drift back to Caspian's birthday party, the indifference in which Caspian regarded my gift to him. But beneath that indifference, I'd felt something else. A spark of joy. "Hatred doesn't cure hatred," I whisper.

"I know." Farron closes his eyes and leans his forehead against mine. "I don't like myself like that. I don't *want* to be that person."

"You aren't that person, Farron." I place my hand on the side of his face. "I know your heart better than anyone. The anger there. The sadness. But your goodness will always win."

A roguish grin crosses his face. "Well, I can be a beast when I want to be."

I lift up on my toes to kiss his mouth. "Don't give me that look, or I'll never leave."

"Ez better take good care of you."

Regretfully, I pull away from my mate's strong embrace. "Don't worry. We'll be back before you know it."

Something shifts in Farron's gaze, a look of longing. *I love you,* he says in my mind.

In the starlight way, I say back.

Be safe.

I promise.

I force a smile as I leave the library, knowing in the world of the fae, this is never a promise I can keep.

70

ROSALINA

The humidity hits me as I enter the conservatory. It's built at the back of Keep Hammergarden. The air is alive with the delicate flutter of wings as butterflies in every shade of the rainbow flit from flower to tree to fern. I inhale the sweet fragrance. Despite all the turmoil of the last few days, I've missed the Spring Realm.

Ezryn and I arrived at the keep only an hour ago. Astrid and Marigold found me right away. Thankfully, they're all right—besides their worry over me and the princes. I assured them that Ezryn and I were fine, and Kel, Dayton, and Farron were safe at home, using their magic to restore Castletree. As much as I wanted to fill them in on everything, I had noticed Ezryn wander off, his usual silence especially heavy this morning.

We never talked about what happened by the lake. Even though I'd only glimpsed the pollen-induced vision of Ezryn's nightmare, the memory still shakes me to my core: Princess Isidora's keening cry as she sunk to her knees and Ezryn's body shaking with uncontrolled power.

I can't imagine what it's been like living with that for so long.

The room is bright, sunlight filtering through the glass ceiling and over the translucent wings of the butterflies. I feel like I'm walking through a tropical oasis. Extending my hand, the velvety touch of a butterfly whispers along my fingertips. Its tiny feet tickle my skin. I bring it closer, examining the myriad of pinks and reds that make up its wings.

It flits off, dancing further into the conservatory. I follow behind. At the very back of the room is an elevated pond bordered by rocks that shine with the opalescence of a pearl.

Most magnificent of all is the man who sits on the edge, as straight-backed and still as the stone itself. He's so calm, the butterflies have flocked to him, landing on his armor. There's so many of them, it almost appears as if he's made of butterflies.

As quietly as I can, I take a seat on the edge of the pond beside him. I inhale and try to match his stillness and posture: hands on my knees, shoulders back. One of the butterflies flaps over from him and lands on my knee.

"You found me," Ezryn murmurs.

"Marigold said you might come here."

His chest rises and falls, the butterflies across his torso fluttering with the movement. A couple more flit my way. "I need to make a decision on how to best guide Spring. My mother used to sit in here before she ever settled on her course."

A part of me thinks I should leave him to his own thoughts. But isn't that what he's had to do all these years? Process everything on his own? "Ezryn, we need to talk about what we saw by the lake."

His chest stops moving.

I turn to face him square on, scattering the few butterflies I've collected. "Some of the hallucinations were memories, weren't they? The one we saw together ... That was your past."

"I wanted to tell you the truth," he says. "I was going to explain everything that night. That's why I took you to the lake. You're right—what we saw wasn't some nightmare. It's my history."

The moist air fills my lungs with each breath. "I'm so sorry. I can only imagine how hard that was to relive."

"Do you understand what happened there, Rosalina?" Slowly, he tilts his head to me. None of the colorful butterflies leave. "Everyone in Spring thinks my mother died when she passed the Blessing to me. That's not true. She was alive and healthy afterward. It was *me* who ruined it."

"Ezryn—"

"As soon as the Blessing came to me, I knew it was wrong. I was powerless to control it. Imagine if a maelstrom exploded from your chest—that's what happened. I couldn't leash it. Everything felt violent and unstoppable." His hands clench into fists. "It wasn't the passing of the Blessing that killed her. It was *me*."

"No." My voice is a breath. I caress the side of his helm, the whisper of the butterfly wings falling over my skin. "You didn't mean to. It was an accident."

"It doesn't matter. She died because I couldn't control my own power. Because there is something broken within me, and the Blessing knows it."

He looks so gentle right now, dressed in sunlight and color. His every movement is slow and careful so as not to disturb the tiny creatures around him. It reminds me of the many times we've been together when I was fragile and afraid. "When we stood on my balcony in Coppershire, you told me you were dangerous. Is this what you meant?"

"I didn't just kill her, Rose. I destroyed my father and brother's lives. If that were ever to happen again ..."

"I'm so sorry," I say. "There isn't anything wrong with you, Ez. It was a horrible accident, but that doesn't mean you're broken."

He shakes his head. "Kel, Dayton, and Farron have never lost control of their magic like that. Farron was passed the Blessing in the same way with no repercussions. And when you two mated ..." He stares at me. "It awakens great power in a fae when they accept their mate bond. At no point, even with this influx of magic, did Farron ever lose control of himself."

The image of Farron's body glowing plays in my mind. I'll never forget the moment in the Emberwood when our souls laced together. Even I had felt the energy radiating off of him.

I tuck closer to Ez. "You can't blame yourself for losing control of your Blessing any more than Farron can for losing control of his wolf." I look down at my hands, thinking of the golden briars that sprouted from me once, but never again. "This magic is bigger than all of us."

"But Farron did control it in the end," Ezryn says.

"And so have you." I take his hand and pull off the glove, lining up our fingers. "Your magic healed me. It faded a scar that was not only etched into my skin, but my heart. You learned to wield fire to cauterize Dayton's wounds and saved his life."

His voice begins to shake, and I tuck his hand into both of mine. "But don't you understand, Rose? What if something happens and I just ... break again?"

It's all so clear to me now, why every time things get hard, Ezryn leaves. Losing himself in the Briar, killing goblins—it's a way for him to feel in control of himself. I sigh and scoot close to him, leaning my head on his shoulder. "Then I'll put you back together."

His helm tilts against my forehead. "I can't help but think the Blessing would have been safer if I had passed it onto Kairyn."

"Your mother wanted *you* to lead Spring. Not him."

"But—"

I slip to the ground, sliding between his feet, and look up at him pleadingly. The action causes the butterflies to take flight, bursting from his chest in a cloud of color. "You are the rightful High Prince of Spring. I understand how hard things have been. You didn't just lose your mother; it was like you lost your entire family. But you made the right choice fighting for yourself in the Rite. Now, both you and Kairyn are back home. Wouldn't it make your mother so happy to see her sons working together?"

"You're right. That would make her happy." He stands and pulls me to my feet. "Thank you, Rosalina. You've given me the courage to do something I should have done a long time ago."

I wrap my arms around him. "You know she would want you to forgive yourself."

"I know," he murmurs. "I'm trying, Rose. I promise, I'm trying."

71

EZRYN

I find my brother in the Healing Gardens on the western corner of the keep. The open-air space is filled with rocky water features, green shrubs pruned into the shapes of mystical creatures, and aromatic herbs that fill the air with sweetness.

Kairyn sits on a stone bench beside my father, who is bundled in a thick blanket, helm lolled to the side, dozing.

My brother's right arm is in a sling, and he wears no metal besides his helm, merely dressed in a black long-sleeve tunic and pants. Even without the armor, his size is impressive, shoulders broad.

He stands as soon as he sees me. "Brother. I sent search parties out —I wasn't sure what happened."

"All is well. The other High Princes and I made it back to Castle-tree mostly unscathed thanks to Lady Rosalina."

Kairyn shakes his head. "Everyone is all right …"

"And thanks to you." I touch his good shoulder. "You saved my life."

"I-I was not strong enough,"

"Do not disparage yourself, Kai. None of us were strong enough to defeat that creature, not even with our Blessings. There's nothing you could have done."

Kai turns away from me and stumbles back to where our father sits. He pulls the blanket tighter around him. "There is so much I could have done."

Sun beams off my father's magnificent helm, and I have trouble reconciling this version of my father with the one from my childhood. The imposing man with a voice as powerful as a bellowing forge. The skilled swordsman who spent hours sparring with our mother in the gardens. The mated fae who loved our mother with such ferocity, it sometimes seemed like there was nothing left over.

When she died, she took all of that love with her. Father had been a husk then, too, but one that could feign conversation. With Eldy's help, he had been able to rule. But now...

"Our healers still have no idea what's causing his affliction?" I ask.

Kairyn shakes his head. "They suspect his heart could not withstand so many years of pain."

Though outwardly Kairyn says nothing more, I hear his voice like a roar in my head: *See that? You've not only killed Mother. Your actions are killing Father, too.*

Squeezing my eyes shut, I take in stuttering breaths so the memories of the hallucination do not cloud me again. I should have admitted everything to Kairyn years ago. Without his forgiveness, how will I ever be able to forgive myself?

I need to do right by this Kairyn to stop the one in my head from tearing me apart.

I put my hand on my brother's arm and guide him to look at me. The owl helm turns, and for once, it does not appear furrowed or vicious. Perhaps it's the glint of the sun, or the gentleness with which he tends to my father, but my brother only seems ... sad.

"Kairyn, I must do what I should have done long ago." My voice is shaky, but I think of Rosalina. Of what her heart spurs my own to do. "I came here today to ask you something."

Kairyn says nothing, but I hear the heavy reverberation of his breath through his helm.

"I ask not for your forgiveness, for this is not something I have yet earned. But I ask that you give me the opportunity to earn it from you.

I never admitted the truth to you, even when you saw it with your own eyes." My hands shake on his arm. "When Mother passed the Blessing of Spring on to me, the magic overwhelmed my body. I could not control it. And she was killed in the collateral."

Still, Kairyn says nothing. I see now how long his hair is, black strands poking out from under his helm. It reminds me of the young boy, eyes so dark they were nearly black, a slightly crooked nose with a crooked smile to match.

I have not seen my brother's face in decades. I wish more than anything I could see it now.

"You did what you felt you needed to do when you challenged me to the Rite," I continue. "I had the choice to unhelm or kill you. I thought banishment to the monastery would give you purpose, meaning. In a way, perhaps it has. But I see now all it truly did was fracture us from what we both needed most: each other."

I know in my heart this is what I need to do for both of us to heal. We might still have a chance at the brotherhood we never had in our youth.

I clasp the side of my brother's helm and stare into his visor, imagining those dark eyes from his boyhood. "In my absence, you have accomplished great things in Spring. Though we may disagree on the method, I know our hearts beat toward a common goal. We have much work here. Our people are sick. Our enemy wields our greatest resource. Even Spring's bounty turns against us, for a dangerous plant has grown in our most sacred space. But you and I can see our people through the tribulations." I intake a deep breath. "Consider this my formal approval of your permanent position as my steward. Let us lead Spring into a time of peace and hope together."

A heavy moment passes. Then Kairyn stumbles forward, helm falling to the crook of my shoulder. "Long have I desired to hear you speak these words to me," he says shakily. "All the years in the monastery, I only wanted your approval and the truth of what happened."

"I should have come sooner," I admit. "My mind was so clouded with grief and anger."

Kairyn straightens, his frame blocking out the sun, drenching me in shadow. "I see so clearly now what I must do. I've known it all this time, but I was too afraid to act. There is no other path forward for me now. I know now where my loyalty truly lies."

"Then you accept the role of steward under my service?"

"I do," he breathes. "And I shall see this realm elevated."

72

ROSALINA

"Couldn't sleep a wink the night of the full moon," Marigold cries as the three of us reconvene in my bedroom.

"I know," Astrid grumbles. "I'm in the room beside you."

Marigold puffs out her chest. "Well, what else were Eldy and I supposed to do? We had to trust that you'd all look after each other."

"We did," I say, smiling. And I'm happy to hear that some old wounds between her and Eldy seem to be mended … She's got quite the twinkle in her eye and has laced her corset so tight, I think she might well pop out of it.

We've been huddled on my bed for an hour now as I've caught them up on everything that's transpired: the assassination attempt, by the Nightingale, Sira's appearance, and the letter I received from Dom and Billy.

I clutch it, the paper wet with my tears. My father has always been so strong, so determined. I can't imagine him sick or bedridden. My only solace is knowing Farron's family will look after him like he's one of their own. Once I get word from Coppershire, I'll travel straight to his side and see he makes it safely to Spring. Ezryn promised his realm's best healers would look after him.

The door knocks and creaks open. Eldy pops his head in. "Apologies for interrupting, ladies."

"I'm happy to see you, Eldy," I tell him genuinely.

He looks to Marigold and the biggest smile appears beneath his mustache. She blushes and smooths her perfectly pressed skirt. Quite the difference from the two squabbling staff they were when we arrived. I wonder if Marigold is tempted to tell him about her curse. Probably not. She's so loyal to Ezryn and the other princes. But hiding the truth from her love … It must be killing her inside.

Pain laces through my chest, and I rub my heart.

If only Ezryn could find his mate.

"Why are you here?" Astrid says sharply, bringing everyone back to focus.

"Oh! Hem. Yes." Eldy straightens and places a wooden chest on the end of the bed. He clicks it open, revealing many small bags, vials filled with plants soaked in liquid, and dried herbs. "Ms. Marigold told me of your father's illness, Lady Rosalina."

Astrid gives her a glare, but she just shrugs. "It was when I was fetching us tea!"

"I'm sure he'll have excellent care in Coppershire, but I thought I'd put together some of our most potent and rare treatments until he can be transferred to see us here in Spring. See, this one here is a powdered stardrop. They're quite a plentiful resource, found up in our mountains. Sprinkle a little on his tongue to neutralize any toxin. A healer will know what to do with all of these," Eldy continues. "Consider it a gift from the Spring Realm."

I get up, placing the letter on my end table, and grab Eldy's hand. He blushes but doesn't pull away. "This is so thoughtful. Thank you for all the hospitality you've shown me." I look back at Marigold and Astrid. "Thank you all for everything."

"Whatever you need, Rosie, we'll be here," Astrid says, grabbing my arm.

Another knock sounds, and Eldy opens the door. Wrenley stands there dressed in her gold and white robes, arms filled with beautiful red flowers.

Her gaze shifts around the room, taking each of us in, before she steps inside. "Forgive the intrusion."

"Not at all. What can I do for you, Wrenley?" I do my best to sound genuine, but I can't help but feel jealous at the sight of her, remembering how she and Dayton had laughed and danced at the party. And the bitter words I'd said about her. She's been nothing but nice to me. It wasn't like this when I saw Tilla. *Because I know Kel is mine, and Dayton ... Dayton isn't.*

"I ran into Prince Kairyn, who informed me that you and High Prince Ezryn had returned to the keep." She smiles. "Prince Kairyn told me to bring these flowers to your room."

"Thank you. That's very kind." I wave her in.

"Majordomo, your boutonniere has wilted." She offers Eldy another one of her sweet smiles and plucks the white flower from his breast pocket. She replaces it with a blooming red one.

"Ah, is red the new fashion? Hard to keep up with you young things." He straightens the flower. "Thank the stars. It was such a trek up the mountain to find these little stardrops."

"I'm up there all the time," Wrenley says, touching her own white flower.

Eldy looks back at the trunk. "All right, Miss Rosalina, let me explain some of the ingredients."

Marigold and Astrid gather around as well, and we all listen attentively as he describes the healing components. Out of my peripheral vision, I watch Wrenley tossing the old flowers in the vases and replacing them with the new ones. An uneasy feeling settles in my stomach. *Stop being ridiculous,* I chide myself. Disliking her because Dayton doesn't is selfish.

Turning away from my friends, I face Wrenley only to see her bent over the letter on my end table.

"Excuse me, that's private." I hurry over and snatch the letter out from under her.

"Apologies, my lady, I meant no offense." She leaps back, blue eyes wide. "I didn't mean to invade. I only caught sight of a few words and became concerned. Your father ... He is ill?"

I take a deep breath. It's not really private, figuring the three of us were all talking about it. "Yes, he was on an excursion in the Autumn Realm but has grown weak with malaise. The healers in Coppershire will examine him, and then Prince Ezryn will have him transported here."

She blinks at me. "Your father is coming here?"

"Yes. Ezryn said Spring would be the best place for him to heal."

Wrenley stares at me intently. "You're concerned for him." It almost sounds like a question.

"Of course I am," I snap, my voice harsher than I intended it. "He's my father."

She steps back as if struck. "Apologies. I haven't seen my family much since coming to the monastery."

Immediately, guilt floods my chest. I sigh and place the letter back on the end table. "I'm sorry. I didn't mean to snap at you. The worry is getting to me, I guess."

Her fingers drift over the letter lightly, curiously. "This is his writing?"

"Yes. Explorer's scrawl, he would call it. So messy you can barely read it."

"I can read it," she says quietly.

There's a flash of emotion on her face, and I wonder if my story strikes a chord with her. "There were times when my father and I had some distance between us," I say. "But we've reconnected recently. There's so much we still have to learn about each other. So much I have to tell him."

"I understand."

"Are you close with your father?"

Her gaze shoots up from the paper, and a grin spreads across her lips. "Oh yes, very close. My father loves me very much, more than anything. He's a cartographer in the Summer Realm. Travels a lot, making maps."

"That sounds fascinating," I say. At the party, I'd sworn she'd said her father was a vendor. Maybe I misheard, or it was before his mapmaking days.

Wrenley grabs my hand and squeezes it tightly. "You've been blessed with much throughout your life, Lady O'Connell. I will pray to the Queen that such blessings do not run out."

I stay rooted to the spot as Wrenley steps out of the room.

I walk back to my friends and engage with their conversation, but my heart is stuck on Wrenley's words.

There have been so many blessings in my life, and I've had to fight for each one.

Nothing, not even the Queen herself, will take them from me.

73

ROSALINA

I must go up the mountain.

The thought strikes me slowly, creeping through my mind as I attempt to follow Eldy's words. I'm still standing in a circle with him, Marigold, and Astrid in my bedchamber, and we were having a conversation about something, but this thought keeps creeping in.

I must go up the mountain.

"Up the mountain! Come on, darling! Up the mountain!" It's a woman's voice, light and ethereal, calling to me through the door. Well, I can't keep her waiting. Whoever she is, I know she's important.

I open the door and walk out into the hallway. Distantly, I notice my friends walking beside me.

"I must go up the mountain," Marigold says.

"Indeed. Up the mountain," Astrid responds.

Eldy nods. "Up the mountain. Up the mountain."

Oh good. We're all going up the mountain.

We walk out of the keep and past the guards.

"Lady O'Connell!" one calls. "High Prince Ezryn requested you have an escort if you leave the keep."

"Up the mountain," I tell her.

The guard looks around. "Majordomo, shall I call for an official escort?"

Eldy's eyes stare straight ahead. "I'm going up the mountain."

The guard places a hand behind her head. "Well, if you're together, then I suppose that fulfills the High Prince's request."

We leave the keep behind, shuffling forward. Florendel is huge, but I know the way. Distantly, I think about how I rode up to the monastery on an ibex. But that doesn't seem necessary now. I'll crawl to the top if I have to.

"Hurry, Rose! We're waiting!" a different voice calls to me.

Papa! It's Papa! He's better! He must have decided to surprise me.

I can't wait to get to the top of the mountain to see him.

I want to move faster, but my legs seem in their own determined rhythm, one step in front of the other. My friends are still with me, equally excited.

We start upon the trek leading up the mountainside. Within a few minutes, my lungs feel on fire and my legs are sore. I'm wearing slippers and a dress with two petticoats. Silly clothing for trekking up the mountain, but there was no time to change.

Far, far ahead, I see the silhouette of two people waving at me. It is Papa! I can tell by his height, the width of his shoulders, the curve of his face. He has his arm around a woman.

"Hurry, Rosalina," she calls. "We will finally meet. But you must come to the top of the mountain."

"Mother?" I whisper. "Mom, is that you?"

Excitement bubbles in my chest. Now, I truly want to go faster. Nevertheless, I can't get my legs to change pace. And actually, I could use a moment to catch my breath. I realize now I'm heaving and sweating, the trek strenuous. But my feet won't stop. Beside me, Marigold's face is bright red, and Astrid's white hair is plastered to her forehead. Eldy's panting.

We should take a break, I think.

"Up the mountain," my mother growls. She's so far away, just a silhouette on the horizon, and yet I hear her voice roaring in my ears.

All right. Up the mountain.

Up the mountain.

We trek further up until Florendel looks like a collection of doll-houses below. The monastery looms at the peak like an impossible goal. But not impossible because I won't stop until I reach the top. Beside us, the river that carves down the mountainside roars with white water.

Water.

Water is important. I'm thirsty. Water is important because I drink it.

Yet, it is important for another reason as well.

I think it's because—

"You're almost there!" my father cries. I don't see him, but that's because he's at the top of the mountain. And we're almost there.

The sun shifts on the horizon. I don't know how long we've been walking. Minutes, hours, days, forever. My body feels like it's going to collapse in on itself. There's blood oozing through my slippers from where rocks have dug through the thin fabric. But we're almost there. The monastery is up ahead.

But we're not going to the monastery. We're going up the mountain.

Astrid's a few steps away from us. She turns, a huge smile on her tear-streaked face. I can barely hear her voice over the roar of the river so close. Wind howls, and I think I'm cold. We're so far up, there's no more 'up' to go. "Up the mountain!" she exclaims.

Now, she's moving faster than the rest of us. How does she get to do that? She's walking straight ahead. But there's no more path to trek. No more up.

There's only off.

Watch out for the cliffside, I try to yell. But Astrid doesn't seem to care. She's heading straight for it.

And now Marigold and Eldy are heading that way, too. Eldy brushes past me. I can't seem to move my arm, but somehow, I hook my finger around his shirt and tug.

He looks back at me. "Up the mountain," he says sternly.

This is what we're supposed to be doing. Yes, yes, I must go with them...

"Come on, Rosie, darling, I've been waiting ever so long." The woman's voice. My mother's voice. She's standing with my father at the very edge of the cliffside, right where Astrid's heading. Beautiful stardrops dance beneath her feet. Her body is a dark shadow, hidden by the beaming sun behind her. "All you have to do is follow."

And then she and my father turn to each other, clasp hands, and step off the edge. A cluster of white flowers sways with their movement, the pollen breezing toward me.

It must be all right, then, if they did it. Off the mountain, we must go off the mountain—

Except my father would never leave without me. Not by choice.

And my mother isn't here.

And Astrid's nearly at the cliffside...

And this is all wrong.

Suddenly, I feel the beating of my heart against my chest, a wild drumming. But the voices are so loud, screaming at me, and my legs won't work.

I need to get out of this. But I can barely hear myself think over their shouts, the wind's howl, the rushing river—

The river. Water.

Something happened to me recently, and water saved me.

I need my body back.

Inner fire blazes through my chest; I picture the chains lacing around my arms and legs snapping, and then, with a roar, I throw my body to the side.

I smack into Eldy, and we fall, tumbling on the ground until we both splash into the white water of the raging river.

74

ROSALINA

Cold water pounds my head, my face, down my throat. But my thoughts return to me with shocking clarity. And there's one thought raging above all the rest.

I kick to the surface. The water rushes so fast, I'm already carried away from precipice of the cliff. But I can still see Astrid and Marigold, dangerously close to the edge. I throw my hand out of the water to shoot a tangle of briars to trap them—

Nothing comes.

My bargain with Caspian was rescinded, my bracelets are gone. I have no power to create briars anymore, and there's none around for me to take control of.

I can't think about the shocking cold or the water splashing down my throat or the rocks smashing against my legs or even Eldy floundering beside me. I need to break Astrid and Marigold's enchantment before they throw themselves off the cliff. But how?

Magic—it's inside of me. Fire comes as easily as breathing, but that's not the only thing I've summoned. I think of the training grounds, of Dayton's hands on my shoulders, of the water arrow shooting straight into the target.

I don't have to summon water from nothing—I only need to take control of it. My human self grew up in rainstorms and trees that dripped with dew. I survived the icy cold of a lake, and I rescued my mate from the depths of a frozen river. My fae body remembers everything. It lives in my bones and blood. Not just my own experience, but that of the rain, the trees, the lake, the river. I have been reborn a part of the natural world.

And I will make it answer me.

The numbness and pain dissipates, replaced by a rush of power. Catching sight of Astrid and Marigold, I channel that energy out of my body and into the river.

Tendrils of water reminiscent of thorned vines surge out, rushing over the two fae women. Astrid falls away from the edge of the cliff, slamming into Marigold. They both collapse on the ground. More tendrils of water splash over their faces.

I catch sight of Astrid shaking her head and coughing before the river sweeps me away.

Kicking, I keep my head above the water, trying to find purchase. But the riverbank is slick rock, the river too deep to stand. Again, my useless hand flicks out, attempting to throw a briar at the shore. But there's nothing.

A flash of gray hair bobs beside me. Eldy sputters before dipping under the surface. He pops up a little ways away, eyes wide and frightened, mouth agape. "I-I can't swim!"

"I'm coming—" I try to say, but white water rushes over my head. For a second, there's nothing but bubbles in my vision, and I'm afraid I've lost what is up and what is down. But somehow, I find the surface and gasp in a breath.

I've got to get Eldy out of here. The water still feels close at my command. I force myself to concentrate on Eldy, channeling the water to rise around him, lifting him to the surface. For a moment, he bops up in the swell, but the river's too fast, too vicious. It sweeps him back down.

"Eldy!" I swim forward to grab him and snag a fistful of hair, yanking his head out of the water.

He struggles to suck in a breath before another surge of white water charges over us.

Fuck, fuck, fuck, I have to do something! What power do I have to get him out of the river? I have to try!

My magic is like a livewire inside of me, sparking off my edges. I grab Eldy's head, holding him out of the water with all the strength left in me. His eyes shimmer with fear.

The words come out of me like a prayer and a plea, born from something deep, buried underneath the rest of my magic: "Fly. Fly away."

His body shifts beneath my fingers. Skin grows feathers, arms shrink to wings, and then I'm careening down the river, hands held aloft, cradling a tiny bird.

Fear overtakes reason as I toss the bird into the air. It beats its wings above me. The eyes...

The eyes are the same.

"Eldy!" I scream. "Get Ezryn!"

The last thing I see is the little bird flying away before I plunge under the water and slam into something hard. The breath falls out of me and then there's only blackness across my vision and fire in my lungs.

75

EZRYN

I leap to my feet.

Kairyn tucks the blanket tighter around my father's shoulders and quirks his helm. "What's wrong?"

"I ... I don't know."

But something is terribly wrong. I feel it in my chest, as if my heart has lost its cadence. Squinting my eyes close, I rub my armor, wishing I could feel my skin. A chill runs through me and my lungs feel like they can't get enough air.

"Brother?" Kairyn stands and puts a hand on my shoulder. "Sit back down. Your erratic movement is disturbing Father."

A flutter sounds through the air. A small wren flaps its wings desperately, swooping back and forth as it speeds into the open-air healing garden. It heads straight for me; its flight is so off kilter, I snatch it in my hands.

The bird opens its beak. "Your Highness!"

I jolt, nearly dropping the thing. As familiar as I am with talking animals, I've never seen one do so during the day. And that voice...

"Eldy?"

"There's no time to explain!" the bird cries. "It's Rosalina! She fell into the river! She's drowning, sire!"

Not a single moment passes before I've dropped the bird and sprinted across the healing garden. This feeling in my chest...

It wasn't my fear. My pain.

It was hers.

Sounds fade away. My brother calls after me. Something about summoning the guards to find her, but I can't stop.

"I'll lead you to her!" the bird cries, but I'm faster than its tiny wings.

I don't need him, anyway.

My heart knows the way.

I run faster than I've ever run before, surging through the keep, shoving guards out of the way. My boots pound against the stone, as fast as my heart against my ribs. How could this have happened? She was in her room when I last saw her. She was with Astrid and Marigold. Eldy said he was going to look after her.

I *promised* I would keep her safe.

Sickening bursts of fear course up my body, but I can't give in to it. Not now. I'm out the gate and sprinting through the streets within seconds. The city streaks by me. The river ... It runs down Mount Lumidor and empties out into Sylvanita Lake.

Empties via a waterfall.

I have to get Rosalina before she plunges into the rocks.

Hold on, I cry in my mind. *I'm coming!*

I'm not sure what I was expecting, but there's no response.

The city gives way to the mountain trail. Every muscle feels alight as I push myself beyond any speed I've ever run before. The river rages beside me, white and spitting. I jolt to a stop at its shore, looking up and down.

West. My heart thunders the word, and I follow the river at its command.

"Rosalina!" I yell. The water is nothing but bubbling swells and slick rock. "Rosalina!"

She's here, I *know* it. I must be faster than the river to catch her.

The wind seems to answer my call, pushing on my back and sending me forward. My feet fly over the craggy riverbank.

"Rosalina!" I cry again.

And then I see her. A slip of pink roiling in the waves. Her head is tilted out of the water but her eyes are shut, hair spread like tendrils. She looks like a ragdoll being smashed from rock to rock.

"Rosalina!" Catch her. I have to catch her. The river widens up ahead and the roar of the impending waterfall booms like war drums.

Down below lies Sylvanita Lake, the death place of my mother.

I will not let it be Rose's, too.

The ground lifts beneath me, my magic working subconsciously, raising the earth to shoot me forward. I'm not running—I'm bounding, the earth propelling me toward her.

I won't let anyone, or anything take her from me. Not the monsters that prowl the Briar or the demons that masquerade as men. I will be damned if my own land steals her away.

Breath rages through my throat—precious breath that she must have so little of. A few more bounds, and I'll be beside her.

One step. Two. Three.

I throw myself to the ground and stretch out my hand. Water spits up and splashes into my helm, blurring my vision. My arm strains so much, I think my shoulder may have popped out of the socket. But she's drifting past me. My fingers catch the strap of her dress—

Her legs smack hard against a bulging rock, and she rolls under a swell. The strap pulls free of my fingers, and she's gone. Tumbling away to the middle of the widening river. Ahead, the waterfall roars.

All I can do is watch her sail away from me. If Rose goes over that waterfall and breaks against the rocks, I will break with her.

I have been a dead man walking for longer than my cursed twenty-five years. Asleep to the joys of the world, to the wonders that were screaming at me to wake up.

She brought me back to life.

And for the first time in centuries, I've found something worth losing everything for.

My gloves are off first. I fling the breastplate to the side as I'm sprinting to the water's edge. The boots are next, and I'm able to unhook my greaves without stopping. By the time I reach the last piece of land before the waterfall, the only piece of armor left is my helmet.

She's in the very middle, too far for me to grab or to reach by swimming. I bounce on my toes, sucking in a deep breath.

You are an idiot, Kairyn screams in my mind. *You think you can save her? Fool! You'll only kill yourself.*

"Then so be it," I murmur.

And at that moment, Rose is sucked into the swirling vortex and plunges over the waterfall.

I leap after her.

Air and water rush past me. I keep my arms pinned to my side, legs tight together. The world blurs in a spray of cold water. Beneath me, Rose's body is limp, her hair and limbs flinging out.

I will never break my promise. The space between us vanishes, and I wrap my arms around her waist. With all the momentum I can muster, I twist our bodies so she's tight against me, and my back is to the rocks.

I didn't think much further than this. There's about two moments before we crash against the jagged rocks below.

For the first, I clutch her tighter to my chest, reveling in the feel of her skin one more time, the beauty of her delicate face even now.

For the second, I pray to the Queen who abandoned us that there's something growing among the rocks.

I stretch out my hand, feeling for the veins of life within the lake: the glowing threads that run through all living things, be it fae, humans, animals, or plants. Then I snag the closest one: a cluster of lily pads.

Thrusting my power out, the lily pads grow ... and grow. With a roar, I yank those threads closer.

The fall ends. But instead of rock, we bounce against the gigantic green pad, sailing off into the lake. I hit the water with a smack, and Rose flies out of my arms.

Water pools in my helm, but I kick upward until I'm at the surface, the cold water dripping away from my eyes and mouth. Rosalina floats like a corpse nearby.

"Rose!" I splash over to her.

She's not breathing.

I can't think about that. I flip her over, grab her under her arms, and swim on my back to the shore. The sound of my breath and blood rages through my helm.

Finally, I reach the shore and drag her out. Her dress is plastered to her skin and heavy with water. Soaked tendrils of hair stick to her face. I quickly brush them away and put my hand to her mouth.

Nothing.

"No, no, no." My own chest heaves, and I feel the panic rising. "Rose, wake up. You've got to breathe. Come on, Rose."

I grab her wrist. She's got a pulse, but it's weak. Breath. I need to get her breath started. I put my hands on her sternum and push down hard. "Come on, Baby Girl. Breathe for me." Again and again, I compress her chest. Water streaks down my face, and I don't know if it's the lake water or my tears. "Breathe!"

My compressions get harder, and I think I may crack her ribs. She's still not breathing. I look around the grove, desperate, as if someone might appear. "Help me," I whimper. "Someone, help me."

But there's nothing.

She's *dying*! I promised to protect her.

She promised to protect me.

I stop the compressions. A sob escapes me, and I grab her in my arms, clutching her to my chest. She's so limp. I stare up at the sky and howl. "You can't do this! You can't take her from me!"

My hands run through her hair, and I clutch her face. She's so pale, the life leaving her with every one of my wasted breaths.

My breath.

I can give her my breath.

Every piece of me belonged to her the moment I saw her climbing out of Castletree, anyway.

She was so ungraceful, it's a wonder I ever suspected she was a spy. Not just ungraceful but unmannered, throwing bread rolls at Kel when we sat together at dinner. And the way she squirmed when I first healed her, nervous as a doe.

And yet ... She is fierce. She made bargains with fae, rescued a realm, rescued *us*. She laughs with abandon and loves without judgment. She leaves every path she crosses more beautiful.

There is no one more deserving of breath.

And it will be the honor of my life to give her mine.

I lay her back down, then shakily grab the bottom of my helm.

If this works and she awakens, you will have broken your creed, Kairyn sneers in my mind. *You will have abandoned everything you've ever stood for! You will bring shame to the throne of Spring!*

"I know," I whisper. "And I choose this path, anyway."

You can't do this! Ezryn, stop!

I lift the helm off my head and drop it to the side.

The air makes my wet cheeks cold, and a breeze plays at the ends of my hair. It's been so long since I've bared my face in nature and not only in the privacy of my chambers.

"I seek no forgiveness, nor ask for understanding," I whisper to the wind, to my people, to the ancient fae of Spring. "This is my will, my choice. I offer Rosalina O'Connell the breath of life."

I lean down and place my lips against hers.

76

ROSALINA

A wind blows through my lungs, quelling the fire that's blazing. My ribs ache with pressure, and water billows up my throat. Then that wind flows through me again.

Come back to me, a voice cries within my mind.

That wind … It's pushing me out of the fire. But I'm so tired, it would be so much easier to lie down and burn.

Come back to me, the voice growls again, commanding and insistent. *I give you my breath of life. Come back to me!*

The blackness clouding my vision wavers, but I still can't see anything. The voice is right beyond it, I'm sure of that. A beam of light shoots out, disappearing into the gloom ahead.

Come back to me.

I suck in a breath of cool air. The shred of light tremors with each beat of my heart. I want to follow where it leads. *I'm coming. I'm coming back to you.*

I run through the darkness in my mind, using the light as a guide. The wind and fire and water swirl around me, but I push them away. *I'm coming!*

Because this thread is familiar; it's been dormant in my heart, waiting for its moment to bloom. No longer stuck in hibernation, waiting. This part of me has been patiently anticipating its season.

Waiting to be forged into something greater.

The darkness shifts, storm clouds cast away by a breeze. An image wavers in front of me. I blink my eyes, trying to clear my vision.

There's a face. Someone's holding me in their arms. A man.

It's a stranger ... I don't recognize him. But he seems concerned, his dark brow furrowed, mouth trembling.

This stranger is beautiful, in a rugged way. Stubble covers his firm jaw, his upper lip shaded by a mustache. His tawny skin drips with water. His dark hair falls in short waves around his pointed ears.

"Who are you?" I manage to ask, throat raw and raspy.

He flicks his gaze up, eyes meeting mine. They're the deepest brown.

And familiar.

Eyes I've never seen, only felt.

Suddenly, it hits me like an arrow to the heart. This face isn't unknown to me at all; I've seen flashes of it within myself and only now have the clarity to understand.

"Rosalina," the fae man says. His voice sings within me. I recognize that voice. It's different without the reverberation of his helm, but it's still unmistakable.

"I know you," I whisper, raising my hand to lightly touch his jaw. The feel of this skin beneath mine is like coming home.

A hesitant smile breaks across his face, and it's more beautiful than anything I've ever seen. His eyes crinkle as he looks me over, taking in my heaving chest. "I know *you*," he whispers.

"Ezryn." I fling myself upward, wrapping my arms around his neck. He grabs me back, burrowing his face into the crook of my neck. Tears fling from my eyes as I rake my nails across his skin, then tangle my hands in his hair; every bare piece of him feels like magic.

"I thought I lost you," he murmurs.

Pulling back so I can stare into his eyes again, I say, "I'm not going anywhere without you."

His expressions are all new, and yet it's as if I can match them perfectly to the tilts of his helm. Relief and joy bloom in the warmth of his smile, the shake of his head.

Something glints beside us: Ezryn's helmet. "Ez," I gasp. "Your helm! You're showing me your face."

Now, his expression shifts to one I've never seen before. He stares deep into me as if he could see the whole world in my eyes.

And it's funny, because I swear, I'm seeing the whole world in his.

"Do you know why I didn't kill you that very first day in Castletree when I thought you were a spy?"

"Because I was an innocent human?"

He shakes his head, a soft laugh bubbling up his throat. "Why I put you up in the Spring Wing instead of letting Kel imprison you?"

"Because Kel should clearly not be allowed to make decisions?"

Now, his smile is so big, it's caught me too, and I'm laughing with him. "Why," he continues, "I have sworn to myself a thousand times over that I will do anything and everything to ensure you are safe and living the beautiful life you deserve?"

I sit up on my knees before him and grab his face. I know what he's going to say. My heart is crying out with it. My chest feels like it's glowing, invisible beams of light radiating toward him.

"I know, Ez," I say, tears flying down my face. "I know because I know you."

"Rosalina O'Connell," he says, lips trembling, "you are my mate."

A smile breaks across my face like the first rays of dawn. "And you, Ezryn, High Prince of Spring, are mine."

77

ROSALINA

I remember how I felt months ago when Ezryn and I stood on the balcony over Coppershire and he took my wrist in his hand, fading the scars of the past. My wrist was fiery red, the skin fresh, raw, fragile.

That's how I feel right now, all over. Like the blooming of my mate bond has been a thunderstorm, washing away all the jagged and broken pieces of me. I am brand-new. Reborn.

And ready to be marked by him.

Ezryn drags a hand through my wet hair and cups my face with his other. His eyes shine with a question.

"Kiss me," I command. "Kiss me and claim me."

He does.

I'm on my back, the full weight of his body over me before his lips cover mine. Our tongues tangle, the kiss fierce and hungry. All the months of longing looks blocked by metal are unleashed in this moment. I tug him closer, not wanting to waste a second away from his lips.

Deep inside, I *knew* that the High Prince of Spring belonged to me. I just couldn't comprehend how someone like me could have one mate, let alone three. Kel and Farron drift into my mind. *Can you feel us together?* I can only imagine Kel's joy when we tell him the news.

Another face flashes in my mind. Dayton. Maybe we were wrong earlier—

Ezryn lightly sinks his teeth into my neck, and I'm torn from my thoughts. Heat explodes in my core, a different type of fire. One that makes the wet clothes sticking to Ezryn's skin an object of derision.

I push him up and make quick work of the tight black shirt, the kind he always wears under his armor. I begin to wonder where the rest of it is, but I'm distracted by the chiseled lines of muscle along his chest, the thick thatch of hair.

But I've seen—and felt—his body before. My eyes drift back to his face. "Ez," I breathe, "you are so fucking hot."

He raises a brow and laughs. "Would you have been upset to be mates with me if I were hideous?"

I crawl on to his lap and try to ignore the iron-hard press of his length against my belly so I can be serious for a moment. Tracing my fingers along the rough line of stubble on his jaw, I hold his gaze. "I fell in love with you when I could only ever dream of the color of your eyes. I would have stayed in love with you even if you were clad in metal for the rest of my life. And I love you now because of who you are." I bite the lobe of his ear and whisper, "You being a total hottie is just a plus."

I thought that would get another one of those glorious laughs from him, but he shifts so we're staring at each other again. "You love me?"

"Isn't it completely obvious? Of course I love you, Ez. You stood by me from the very first day we met. You trust me when I doubt myself. You watch out for your family no matter what. And when there seems to be not enough hope to even stand, you raise us up and keep us going." I'm crying again, quiet tears dripping over my lips. I'm smiling too. I can see in his face, he can't believe what I'm saying. "You might not trust it now, but that's okay. I'm not going anywhere. I'll spend every day proving it to you if I have to. And you know how stubborn I can be."

That at least gets a little smile out of him. "You love me," he whispers.

"I do." I trace the curve of his nose, the lines of his lips. "Trust what I say. You know me." I say the words like an offering.

"I know you," he repeats. Then his eyes lower, taking in my wet dress, hugging tight to my body. "My mate..."

"Yours."

A growl rushes out of him, and in one swift movement, I'm on my back with him leaning over me. "My mate," he says again, and his hand trails down my jaw to lightly land on my throat. "My mate, whom I love."

In this position—pinned beneath him, at the mercy of his huge hand on my neck—a desperate need surges up my body. My core pulses. "You've shown me your love every single day we've spent together. I know your tender heart. But I want every part of my mate. So, fuck me, Ezryn. Unleash yourself on me."

That beautiful face shifts. Something feral glints in his eyes, and his mouth twitches, revealing gritted teeth. "You don't know what you're asking for, Baby Girl."

"Try me," I breathe.

He leans down, lips to my ear, voice a low growl. "Your word is 'mercy'. Unless you say it or mouth it, I will give you none."

I suck in a shaky breath. "I understand. But you have to do something first."

He raises a brow, and I push myself up on my forearms and look around. We're on the soft, grassy bank beside the lake he took me to the night of his welcome home jubilee. The willow tree's branches drift softly in the breeze.

"As your mate, it is my right to bear witness to your face," I say, unable to stop myself from stroking his cheekbone. "But I don't want someone to wander in here."

"I'm not waiting to take you," Ezryn growls. "I've waited my entire lifetime."

"Then do what you do best. Shelter me."

Understanding clicks, and he smirks. The earth shifts beside us, a cluster of rocks jutting up from the grass, gating us in on all sides. The rocks form a natural wall, beautiful in their own right, with bits of moss clinging to them.

"This will give us enough protection if anyone dares wander in here while I am busy with my mate," Ezryn says, grabbing the edges of my dress and pulling it over my head. "Now, Petal, let's hear that pretty mouth beg."

78

EZRYN

My mate has never looked so gorgeous as right now: soaking wet, naked, and on her knees looking up at me. I stand above her, my own trousers dropped. My cock bobs before her beautiful face, and I give it a long stroke. Her eyes track my every movement, a wildness in her gaze like I've never seen.

"I need you, Ezryn," she begs. "I need you to claim me and make me yours. Fuck me so hard, I can't remember a time when I didn't belong to you."

I hold her chin in my hands. It's requiring all my willpower to avoid seizing her hair, flipping her on to her stomach, and mounting her from behind like a beast. "Such a good girl."

Her mouth trembles, and her hands crawl up her thighs. Her eyes dart to my cock, so close to her mouth. "May I?"

I suck in a breath. Her mouth looks so fucking tantalizing. How easy it would be to wrap her hair around my hand like a rope and stuff her throat with my cock. To watch her eyes roll back in her head, to hear her gag. *There is time for that*, I tell myself. For Rosalina is my mate. I have centuries to fuck her into oblivion in every way we could possibly imagine.

But for now … Now, I will show my mate depths of pleasure I have never been able to before.

I will claim her as she asked.

I drop to my knees. We are skin to skin, and I press my hardness against her so she can feel exactly what she does to me. She moans and reaches for my cock. I snatch her wrist. "Not until I tell you."

She runs a tongue over her top lip that seems to say she's going to put me to work.

A growl rumbles through my chest. I can't believe I'm finally staring at her—all of her—with my own eyes. Her breasts are even more beautiful without the tint of the visor.

Gently, I place my hand on her throat. She grabs my wrist and drives it harder against her skin. I laugh, but give her what she wants, pushing her down to the ground as my grip tightens. She inhales sharply, throat bobbing deliciously against my palm.

"Look at you," I murmur. My other hand drifts over to her breast, and I run my calloused hand over her softness. "So pretty under me."

Her breasts are too addictive, so I let her throat go. She gasps out, that feral light flashing in her eyes. She lifts up, snagging me around my neck. "Fucking kiss me."

I pinch her nipples to bring her even closer. "My pleasure."

She cries out against my mouth, and I capture her voice in my kiss.

"Now," I murmur, "bend over and show yourself to me. I want to look at my pussy."

Pink flushes over her face and she bites her bottom lip. Something about her shyness sends my cock pulsing. I snatch her chin. "Do what I say, Petal."

Rose nods, then turns around on all fours. Her voluptuous ass points straight up in the air, revealing her pink entrance. The whole sight—fucking glorious.

"Mhmm." I come up behind her, stroking my hands down her back and massaging the space between her shoulder blades. "You are such a good girl."

"Ez," she moans. "Please."

"Please what?" I reach around to cup her hanging breasts. The points of her nipples, against my palms, makes my balls tighten.

"Please give me your cock," she begs. "I-I've been good."

"So good, Baby Girl." I give her round ass a pat. "But you're not getting anywhere near this cock until you're already a quivering mess."

She lets out a hiss, and I respond with a firm smack. Her ass bounces with the force, and I need to clench every muscle in my body to keep from painting her with my cum. A moan escapes her. I lean forward to place a kiss on her neck.

"Now," I say quietly, "show me how a good girl comes, Rosalina."

She sighs, a sound of ecstasy. "Yes."

I stroke up her glistening center. "So wet already." My fingers shine, and I can't help myself. I lick them clean, moaning.

She turns around to watch me. "Fuck, Ez."

I take my time, the taste of my mate aphrodisiacal.

"Ez!" she cries out, but I pretend to ignore her whining. She'll get what she wants. The waiting only makes it sweeter.

When I'm finished, I meet her gaze. "We're ready then."

I drive two fingers into her. Her voice breaks, a magnificent sound. Her warm wetness hugs me, and I turn my wrist to curl into her.

She clutches the grass and bucks back against my hand, begging for more. I pump harder in and out. My other hand grabs the base of her hair and tugs, revealing her gorgeous long neck.

"God, you are driving me crazy," she moans.

I pull my hand out to gently rub her clit. "Don't think about what it will feel like when it's my hard cock fucking you."

"I can't help it—" I interrupt her by plunging my fingers back inside. Her words turn into a cry.

"Don't think about what it will feel like when your beautiful pussy makes me need to come." My voice is raspy. My senses are alight: her glorious body, the slap of my hand in and out of her, her soft hair wrapped tight around my palm, the taste of her cunt still in my mouth from when I licked my fingers clean, all bathed in the sweet smell of my realm. I knew I would take her here.

"Fuck, Ez, I'm going to—"

But she doesn't need to tell me. I can feel it: her walls tremoring against my hand. I curl my fingers again, and it's all she needs. Her delectable scream erupts over the lake as her orgasm ripples through her.

My heart hammers in my chest. Slowly, I pull out of her. She shakes, arms barely able to hold herself up. But she doesn't need to do that. I hold her in my embrace, cradling her against my chest, kissing her neck, her jaw, her pointed ears. A tear trembles down her face, and I kiss that, too.

"Holy fuck," she whimpers. "That was amazing."

I take her hand in mine, massaging her palm, then kissing her knuckles, the soft skin of her wrist. "Now, darling, I'm going to fuck you like you deserve."

Rosalina looks up at me through her dark lashes, the softest smile. She crawls from my lap and lies down in the grass, tracing her fingers over the soft blades.

I place my hand over hers, channeling my magic. Little daisies bloom up around her.

She lets out a small gasp. "It's beautiful."

I stare at her face. "I know."

"I'm ready, Ez." There's the most genuine look of happiness on her face.

I've seen Rose laid out before me in the past, but this is different. This is more than the gift of her body, more than any sort of base fun.

This is something sacred. Something forged in the story of the stars.

I hold her head and position myself. Her chest heaves beneath me, and I wonder if she's nervous.

I wonder if *I'm* nervous.

There is no doubt in me that I will show my woman the furthest reaches of pleasure, but I'm nervous about something else. For how this changes who I am. I've always known there was darkness living inside of me ... That I brought pain to those who got too close. What does it mean for me to—

Rosalina softly smacks my cheek, and I focus back on her. "Stop it," she says fiercely. "Stop thinking and just love me, Ez. That's all I want."

Just love.

I can do that.

I can do that.

My mate captures my mouth and my mind, and I enter her body and into oblivion all at once.

It's like no feeling I've ever experienced before. This ... This is what life is. Her warmth around my cock, fitting me like we were crafted in the same forge. She wraps her legs around my hips, dragging me deeper.

Most glorious of all is her face, her eyes shining, mouth in a trembling smile. How of all the fae in the realm do I deserve her? My chest feels heavy and light all at once, a bursting sensation that simmers like coals and burns like fire.

I lean down to suck her breast into my mouth, reveling in her moan of pleasure. She rakes her fingers into my hair; how wonderful it is to be touched, to feel her skin against my face. Is this what it is to be seen? Is this what it is like to see for the first time?

We twist so I'm on my back and she's riding me. My mate. My beautiful, funny, strong, kind mate who sits upon my cock like it's a throne.

"Ezryn," Rose breathes, dragging her hands through my chest hair. "I love you."

"I love you too, Rose." I'm holding tight to a semblance of restraint, my cock thoroughly ravished by the up and down movement of her pussy.

She bucks hard, her hips grinding down. Her breasts bounce, and I have to squeeze them before I lose my mind. "Your cock is so good," she sighs.

"You take it like a queen."

Her breath is ragged and stuttering now. "Then worship me," she growls. "Give me your cum."

"Anything for my mate," I say lowly. "And you're going to come with me."

I grab her hips, lifting her to the tip of my cock before plunging her down. A breathless plea escapes her, and her eyes ignite with a sultry flame. I don't stop—and she doesn't, either. She meets me stroke for stroke. Our gazes never leave each other, and it's an unspoken connection—we will find bliss together.

I know you. Her sweet voice is a caress in my mind.

I know you. And as I say the words within her, my body responds. Light streaks across my vision as I explode. A roar breaks out of me, and her cry is equally feral, fingernails raking down my chest. I feel her tighten and pulse around my cock, only making me come harder. My seed erupts deep within her.

A beat passes. Our gazes never break. Tears stream down her face, but she's smiling.

Smiling at me.

And I know something has happened—something greater than even the sealing of a mate bond. We have forged this bond so tightly that nothing will ever tear us apart.

79

ROSALINA

The air around me seems to sparkle. Flower petals float from the cherry blossom trees, a warm breeze blowing through its branches. Lazy clouds drift by, and the sun's rays feel like kisses over my skin. I lie in the grass, encased by the rocky wall, gazing up at the sky and wondering how my ordinary life could be so touched by magic.

My mate lies beside me. Our clothes were nearly dry, so I pulled on my dress and Ezryn's wearing his pants, but he's shirtless. Staring at his carved chest, the bob of his throat as he breathes, makes me want to leap back on top of him.

But that will come. What happens next is most important. My heart bursts with excitement. I sit up on my elbow and peer over at him.

He smiles up at me. I can't believe this face has been hidden from me for so long. But now it's mine forever. "Ez?"

"Yes, Petal?" He caresses my cheek.

I can barely contain my smile. This is it. I can *feel* it, my heart bond singing out in a chorus. A familiar feeling that reminds me of a rainy afternoon underneath a canopy of fall leaves, and yet something new all together. "I meant what I said earlier. I see who you are. Whatever life you've lived in the past, whatever you've had to do to make peace with yourself, it doesn't matter to me. Because I know this heart." I place my hand on his chest. "It beats with strength and goodness and love. You are more than your beast. You are everything to me."

He sits up, hand tightening on my face. His brown eyes swirl with emotion. "I was born and raised to be a great leader for Spring. And at every turn, I have only let my people down. Destroyed the hopes and trust of those who love me." His gaze drifts up to the willow tree. "There's always been something wrong with me, Rose. Something jagged and broken. I thought I kept it at bay by killing ... by falling into malice. I never thought I could leave it behind." He sucks in a breath. "But there must be some hope for me if I have earned your love."

"There is more than hope." The air sparks and light shines beneath Ezryn's skin. "The world needs you, Ezryn."

"For you, Rosalina, I will be better," he breathes. "For you, I would do anything."

I recognize the shimmer from Farron's skin months ago. I can't help myself, crying out and wrapping my arms around Ezryn's neck. It's happening.

Ezryn's curse is breaking.

"Look, Ez!" I cry. Finally, Ezryn will be rid of the monster that he swears he is. And all of the Spring staff will be free. Marigold can reunite with Eldy without fear. Ezryn's power will grow. We can protect Spring. Everything is going to be okay—

"Rose?" Ezryn pulls away from me and gets to his feet. "Rose, you need to—"

"It's okay, Ezryn!" I smile up at him. "It's your curse breaking!"

Light beams bright and the silhouette of a wolf begins to form behind him. Something is wrong though. Farron had looked curious, hopeful. Ezryn looks terrified. And the shadow of his wolf thrashes, clawing at his back.

"It's okay, Ez. Just relax. Let it happen," I breathe.

Ezryn doubles over, clutching his skin. "No! It's too much. I can't hold it. Rosalina, you need to go."

I stumble up, backing into the rock wall. "What's happening?"

Ez cries out again, his skin looking like a star about to combust. The wolf's silhouette howls, a mournful, anguished sound. This is wrong. This isn't the way it's supposed to go.

"I won't let it happen again," Ezryn growls.

It's like he's fighting his curse breaking, pulling the beast back into himself. "Ez, stop! You need to let your curse break!"

"It's too much power," he grits. Then he jerks his head up, eyes glowing like a beast.

I gasp, hanging on to the rock wall to steady myself. Farron told me when his curse broke, his magic grew. And the last time Ezryn had a great influx of magic...

Was when his mother passed on the Blessing of Spring.

When he accidentally killed her.

"Rosalina," Ezryn snarls. But it's not his own voice, but that of the beast. "Leave. Now."

80

EZRYN

I have to suppress it. I can't let it out.

Magic roars through me, making my blood swell and my heart feel like it's about to explode. I clench my hands into fists to try to hold it in. Something's tearing out my back, trying to escape, but I can't let it.

No more magic. I can't control it. And last time…

The image of my mother's body flashes in my mind's eye. Her armor caving in, the helm crumpling—I let out a scream.

"Ezryn, I'm not going anywhere." Rosalina's voice. "Your curse is breaking. You must let it. It will be okay. You can do this."

No, no, no. She doesn't understand. She's too close. If I let the curse break, this trapped well of magic will bubble over, explode out—

The thought makes me panic more. I claw at my skin, unable to shake the vision of my mother's blood seeping into the earth. "Get away from me!"

"You won't hurt me," she says. "Let me help you."

She touches my shoulder. It feels like static before a storm. "NO!"

Power floods through my arm, and there's nothing I can do. I thrust my hand out, and a jolt of electricity surges from my palm into the rock wall. It smashes apart, and Rosalina screams, ducking away from the debris.

She's afraid of me. I told her the truth, but she wouldn't listen. Now, she sees.

Now, she truly knows.

A beast's howl erupts through my chest. I can't hold back the magic anymore. Another shock of electricity bursts from my body, shattering the rest of the rock wall I created. The grove opens up. Sunlight streams down over the crystalline lake. It's too bright. My entire being is brimming with energy, my eyes burning.

"Ezryn, please stop this," Rose begs. But there's nothing I can do. I'm not myself, not even the beast. The magic keeps filling me, and my wolf wants to escape.

I must stop him. For if he leaves, the magic will take me over completely. All the power trapped by the Enchantress's curse will be unleashed.

Sinking to my knees, I dig my hands into the earth. The grass dies beneath my touch.

"Ez, stop! The trees!"

Rose keeps screaming at me. But I can barely hear her over the rushing of blood in my head.

"Ezryn, STOP!"

But I can't.

More sounds clatter. The clink of armor, men shouting.

I force my eyes open. Black veins of decay slither across the ground, leaking from my fingertips.

"Y-your Highness?"

I look up. Standing at the edge of the grove is a cluster of Spring Soldiers.

They're staring at me.

Witnessing me.

My helmet ... Where is it? No, no, no.

"No!" I howl, and the decay shoots out further, leaching into the lake. A black ooze like oil slicks over the surface.

Rosalina runs up beside me and moves as if to touch my shoulder but pulls back.

"That cannot be the High Prince," one of the guards says. "Prince Kairyn said he may be here. But it cannot be."

"The fae woman said his name," another says urgently. "And there, on the ground! His helm!"

Rosalina holds her arms up to them. "Please, you have to get help. You must send word to Castletree at once—"

"The High Prince has broken his creed," the guard interrupts. "He's using his Blessing to destroy our sacred grove."

Another raises his spear high in the air. "Arrest him!"

I ... I have broken my creed.

The thought tears all the energy from me. But the decay doesn't stop. Black lines run up the willow tree. The catkins turn to ash, blowing toward us as charcoal petals.

Suddenly, a glowing white light appears before me. A bonfire. But it's a person. Rosalina's skin flickers with flame, her hair blowing in bursts of embers. She stands in front of me, blocking the soldiers' path. "Touch him and die," she snarls.

The guards balk. But one steps forward, raising his bow. "The High Prince has broken our most sacred creed. Step out of the way or I will do what I must."

"You will leave this place," Rosalina says, her voice like a thunder-clap, "and tell no one of what you saw. I am the Golden Rose. I will crack your bones with fire if you so much as move against him."

Rosalina doesn't understand. To the people of Spring, the creed is as sacred as life itself. There is no other way.

"Run!" I cry and move to leap in front of her. But I can't—my hands are stuck into the dirt, the decay no longer just lines but great waves spreading all over the shore, the treeline, the lake. "Run, Rosalina!"

It's too late. The archer looses his arrow.

Rosalina's fire flickers once, twice, before she falls to the ground, a shaft sticking out of her shoulder.

I implode.

The sound that escapes me is more than a man or a beast, but a monstrous roar. I tear my hands free from the earth and jerk them toward the guards. I have been a healer, a maker of storms, a shepherd of growing things.

Now, I am a taker. I leach the life and power from everything in my path. It funnels up into my chest, mixing with my own storming magic, strengthening me. The grass shifts to brown. The willow tree turns into a bone-white husk, branches swaying like skeletal fingers. Fish float to the surface of the lake, bloated and rotten.

I have stopped the curse from breaking, stopped that onslaught of power. This is different. This is my own magic that I've always kept caged away. But now, there's no stopping it. My heart rages with hatred. They *hurt* her. I don't need new magic to destroy them all.

I smile as I suck the life from the guards. Their faces pucker, their skin becoming tight around them, their eyeballs drying up to reveal empty husks.

"Help me," one of the guards whimpers as he collapses to the earth before all the water in his body is sucked out.

Power shivers through my bloodstream as I stare at the corpses before me. They hurt her.

I obliterated them.

And I would do it again, do *anything*, to keep her safe.

I turn to look at Rosalina.

She's lying on the ground, writhing. The arrow shaft still sticks out of her shoulder. But it's her skin ... sunken, ashen, her eyes bulging from their sockets.

"Ezryn," she whimpers, reaching for me.

I haven't saved Rosalina.

I'm killing her.

81

DAYTON

My breath runs ragged as I explode out of the Castletree's door into Keep Hammergarden's throne room. Keldarion and Farron are right in front of me, their eyes filled with matching terror.

It had happened so suddenly. One moment, the three of us were in separate wings of Castletree. The next, both Farron and Kel were sprinting for the magic mirror in the entrance hall, yelling at the top of their lungs.

At first, I'd thought it was a goblin attack. If only it had been so.

Farron had stared at me, his whole body shaking, eyes like pools of amber. "It's Rosalina," he'd breathed. "She's..."

I knew the mate bond was harder to feel when they were in different realms. If Farron—if Kel, even—could feel something was wrong...

Then something was very, very wrong.

The imposing Vernalion Hall greets us as we spin in a circle, catching our bearings. Kairyn runs in, surrounded by a host of soldiers and a few of his acolytes. Wrenley's with him, and she catches my gaze. Her brow is furrowed with concern.

"Keldarion," Kairyn breathes. "Farron. Dayton. What are you doing here?"

"Where is she?" Kel growls, storming toward the armored prince. "Where is Rosalina?"

"She's in danger," Kairyn says. "Word came she fell into the river. Ezryn went after her. I'm assembling a host of guards and healers right now to find them and assist in any way I can."

Kel unleashes a growl. "Farron!"

"This way!" Farron cries and takes off, running out of the hall. "I can feel her."

If he can feel her, it means she's still alive. I take hold of that thought and don't let it go. I can't even think about the possibility that—

Stop it, I chide myself. *We're here now. It's going to be okay.*

Kel and I follow right at Farron's heels as we sprint out of Keep Hammergarden. I notice we're not alone—Kairyn's kept up with us. Stars, he's got incredible stamina and speed given all that armor.

And it's not just us—Wrenley's here, too. Her long robes flow behind her, a desperate look on her face.

We run through Meadowmere Forest where Rosie and I had danced—and made love. Happy memories that seem so far away. *Has Ezryn found her? Is she okay? Is he okay?* I can't think about any of it right now—I have to keep moving.

A flash of light cracks in the sky ahead, and then a boom rattles the trees. A thunderstorm. But the sky is clear.

"Up ahead," Farron says.

Toward the storm. Of course.

We break out of the treeline to an open grove, where a waterfall spills into the lake. Except ... the place is destroyed. Dead fish and an oily film mark the water's surface. The grass is dry and brittle; even the dirt looks covered in decay. And the trees at the very edge are no more than white bones.

In the middle of the grove is a tempest. Dark clouds swirl with a cyclone, carrying branches, rocks, and logs. Lightning cracks, splitting the earth nearby. There's something in the eye of the storm. A man.

"She's here somewhere," Farron croaks, whipping his head back and forth.

Keldarion grabs Kairyn by the cloak and lifts him an inch off the ground. "What the fuck is happening here?"

"I don't know," Kairyn growls, breaking free. "Ezryn went after her."

I haven't been able to tear my gaze from the man sitting in the center of the storm. He's curled over, hands dug deep into the earth. But there's a stillness to him ... Something familiar.

"I think," I murmur, "I think Ezryn is here."

Wrenley steps forward. "The High Prince of Spring has caused this storm. He's destroyed the grove." She turns to Kairyn. "And he has broken his creed."

Kel, Farron, and I look at each other. No words are needed. We all feel it. That man is our brother.

And he's in trouble.

A clatter sounds as Spring's guards enter the grove, weapons drawn. "Prince Kairyn! What are your orders?" one says.

"Stand down," Kairyn growls.

"He'll destroy the entire grove if he's not stopped," Wrenley urges. "Your Highness."

"I will stop him," Kairyn says and looks into the storm.

Kel grabs my shoulder, then Farron's. "Find Rosalina. Do whatever you must to save her." His gaze shifts to the tempest. "I will stop Ezryn."

I turn to Farron. "Lead the way."

Farron nods, then closes his eyes. I can tell he's going inward, feeling for the bond that weaves him and Rosalina together.

Kel walks up beside Kairyn. The owl's mask tilts toward the High Prince of Winter as Kairyn says, "I am going into the storm to save him. I'm his brother."

Kel sucks in a breath through his nose, then marches into the wind. "We both are. Now, come on."

82

FARRON

The turmoil encircling me fades away. The tempest raging
through the grove could be no more than a spring breeze,
the clatter of guards distant and unimportant. All that
matters is the pull to Rosalina. I run away from the lake, from the
torrent of wind spiraling around Ezryn, and toward the base of the
huge willow tree.

"She's here!" I call to Dayton.

My bond cries out within my chest. She's *here*, but where? I can't
see anything but churned earth, cracked branches, and a rusted sword
in the sickly trunk of the tree—

"There." Dayton rushes forward then slides to the ground,
reaching toward a pile of broken boughs and ragged cloth.

From that pile, he lifts my mate on to his lap.

"This isn't happening." I fall to my knees beside them, grabbing
her face. I hardly recognize her; she looks so small, her skin sallow
and limp, as if all the moisture has been pulled from her. Dark bruises
encircle her eyes, and her lips are cracked, cheekbones too prominent.

"What's wrong with her?" Dayton cries.

"I-I don't know." I feel her pulse—weak—and her breathing—

barely audible. "She doesn't seem injured. It's like the life has been sucked out of her."

Dayton casts his gaze around the grove. "The same as the rest of this place." Then he stares at me. "Fix her, Fare."

"Me? I'm no healer." Panic rushes up my chest. Suddenly, I'm back on the fields outside of Coppershire, holding my mother in my arms as her blood runs over my hands.

"You've been training with Ezryn." Dayton's blue eyes are relentless, burrowing into me. "She is your mate. Do something. Do *anything*. Just save her."

It's so simple in his eyes—save her. Just do it. But he doesn't understand. Doesn't feel what I feel: the panic rushing through me, the crying out of my bond for hers, each of her weakening heartbeats sounding in my own chest, the image of my mother's open-eyed stare.

"She needs you, Farron." Dayton's voice cracks. "*I* need you."

I close my eyes. Rosie needs me to save her life. Dayton needs me to protect the woman he loves. Kel needs me to keep my promise that I will do anything for her. Ezryn needs me to save him from a life of guilt.

And I need to stop thinking and just *do* this.

I will not bear witness to any more final breaths.

I place my hands on Rosalina's face, bringing my own body tight to Dayton's. Wind bellows around us, carrying both a man's cry and a wolf's howl. I seek inward for my magic reserve, for the new knowledge I've learned since studying with Ezryn. Tendrils of orange power spark out from me, dusting over her figure.

There are no bones to be mended, no skin to be sealed. No blood to redirect back in the body, no oxygen needed to inflate the lungs. She's simply … empty.

I don't know what to do here. Even with my healing magic, what is there to heal?

"It's her life force," I whisper. "Everything's been sucked into that huge storm. We need a way to replenish her."

Dayton's jaw twitches. "Okay, then."

Panic surges through me with each pump of her weakening heartbeat. "Okay, then? *Okay, then?* Day, we need to do something *now*—"

"Use me." He smiles softly. "My magic is at your disposal, Fare. Siphon my life force into her."

"Day …"

"Our bargain. Through every storm and every season." He grabs my upper arm, touching the gold and silver cuff. "There's no time. Take my magic and use it to save her life."

"I-I don't know what I'm doing. It could kill you—"

His blue eyes flash. "Then kill me."

"Dayton, no!" a high-pitched voice cries.

I turn to see a fae woman hanging on to one of the dead tree trunks, wind tearing at her short brown hair and robes. It's the acolyte Dayton saved from the river, Wrenley.

She rushes forward and grabs Dayton's arm, trying to tear it off Rosalina. "You can't, Dayton! It's too late to save her. She's gone. Don't throw yourself away."

Dayton shrugs her off. "I've never been afraid of death." He looks up at me and smiles. "And there's no one I trust more."

In this moment, I feel his faith in me. And I trust myself, too. Because I won't let the world take him or Rosie from me.

Ever.

Ignoring the acolyte, I hunch over Rosalina and place one hand on her chest and one on Dayton's.

"I'm going to start by funneling your magic into her," I explain. "If I have to, I will also siphon your life force. Hopefully, a little will be enough to stabilize her."

A guttural sound emits from his throat. "Everything I am belongs to her, anyway. Take it."

I close my eyes and go inward. Not to myself this time, but into them. Fragments of my self spread out through my magic, seeping into theirs.

With this oneness between the three of us, I begin to weave the threads of life together.

Like I thought, Rosalina's light is dim, barely visible. Dayton shines like sunlight on a turquoise ocean. His magic is familiar to me: he gave it to me once before, on the field outside of Coppershire, when he fought by my side to protect my realm. This I shepherd into Rosalina, feeding her with wind and sea spray and strength.

Dayton's magic will replenish when he returns to Castletree, so I take it all, every drop, every spark. He will be okay without such power; I will watch out for him, as he has done for me for so many years. The only thing that remains is the slumbering beast within him, for that is his alone.

Rosalina's light brightens, fed by this magic. But it's not enough.

Now, I must take blood and breath.

I grit my teeth, feeling my own body weaken under this channeling. But I can't stop. Not yet.

I'm sorry, Day.

He's strong, I know he is. And so is Rosalina. She has always flourished on so much less than others.

Dayton cries out beside me, but I don't dare open my eyes or tear myself from this inner space. His light flickers, but hers is growing...

Blood and breath and bone and water. Fires within, one I stoke and one I dim.

Just a little more...

"S-stop."

A weak voice, but one that sends my bond bouncing through my chest. I tear myself out of our inward space, blinking against the light.

Rosalina pushes herself up from Dayton's lap. Her face is too pale, eyes rimmed with dark circles, but she's herself again, awake and alert. Dayton wavers, all color has drained from his face, and his hands tremble.

"Dayton," she breathes, falling off his lap and letting him collapse against her. She turns to me. "What did you do?"

"He stole Prince Dayton's life for yours," Wrenley whispers, staring down at us.

"Farron," Rosalina says, "is this true?"

"Give me a minute," Dayton groans. "I'll be ready to kick ass as soon as I catch my breath."

I give a shaky breath of relief. That was too fine a line to walk.

Rosalina touches my face. "You're here."

"Always."

She smiles at me, then props up on her knees, looking deep within the tempest. "Ezryn? Ezryn!"

I grab her arm to stop her from running straight into the storm. "Rose, wait. What happened?"

"It's Ezryn," she cracks. "He's my mate. And he's fighting the breaking of his curse."

83

KELDARION

Wind and debris tear at my hair and clothes as I take another step into the storm. The air spirals in a vicious circle around Ezryn. Pieces of the grove have been torn into the cyclone: logs, branches, rocks, and chunks of dirt fly through the air. I hold my hand up to shield my face.

"The storm's too strong," Kairyn grunts beside me. "We'll never get close enough to him."

I wrap an arm around Kairyn's shoulder. Somehow, he's become even taller than me. His black cape snaps in the wind, and a rock *tings* off his helmet. "Keep going. Ezryn needs us."

We both take another shaky step forward, fighting the gale. Shrouded by the flying rubble, I can see to the eye of the storm. Ezryn sits on his knees, hands in the earth. What is happening inside of him to trigger this? He would never destroy his home on purpose. Never hurt Rosalina.

I grit my teeth at the thought. The only thing keeping me from rushing out of the storm and finding Rose is my trust in Farron. He is mate of my mate. I know he will do what he must.

And there is one other thing.

Ezryn may not be my blood brother, but he is still my family. He came for me in my darkest hour, when all hope had abandoned me. I will not let him suffer alone.

The wind screams in pain, a sound strangely familiar. Step after step, Kairyn and I fight through the storm. Each movement brings us into harsher winds. Little pieces of earth rip at my flesh, and warm blood streaks across my face. My clothes rip as sharp rocks snag fabric. But I don't stop.

"It's too much," Kairyn cries. "We must turn back."

I yank hard on his arm. "No!" This boy does not yet understand sacrifice, pain. He does not fully understand what is at stake.

"Together!" I roar. We move in unison, left foot raising, finding purchase, then the right.

I can barely open my eyes now; the wind is too strong, hail mixing with debris. A huge chunk smashes against my brow. I hiss in pain but take another step.

Kairyn stumbles backward. I twist and snag him by the front of his breastplate. He nods in thanks.

I turn back around, but Kairyn cries: "Watch out!"

A rotten log sails through the wind. I don't have time to react before it strikes both of us. We roll, tumbling over one another. Armor and ground and debris crash into me. I completely lose orientation of up and down. An attempt to stand only sends me spiraling to the ground. The gale is too strong. I force my eyes open and see Kairyn a little behind me, lying on his stomach.

"Kai!" I yell.

He quivers and pushes up to all fours before staring at me. A huge crack runs down the front of his helm. Though his face is still shrouded, I catch the barest glimpse of skin along his forehead.

I stretch my whole arm toward him. "Take my hand!"

Somehow, fear seems to flicker across the cracked owl's mask. "We must turn back. There's no getting through the storm!"

"He's your brother," I call.

Kairyn shakes his helm. "It will be the death of us."

I hold the gaze of the owl helm, my own pleading. "Kairyn! Take my hand!"

The boy quivers, frozen in place. *He's terrified.* Terrified of his own brother.

But I will not bend to any maelstrom, and I shall not let Ezryn face it alone. My expression transforms into a sneer as I turn away from Kairyn. "Then so be it."

I leave Kairyn behind, now crawling forward. I cry out with the wind, letting it rip my clothes, my hair, my flesh. It cannot tear my resolve.

The eye gets closer, Ezryn's huddled form visible between the breaks in flying wreckage.

"Ezryn!" I yell. "Stop this!"

He doesn't even look up, doesn't move.

With a desperate cry, I throw my body forward, rolling between two flying logs and landing within the eye.

It's ... so calm. Around us, the wind cyclones, but here, it is deathly quiet. Even serene.

I stand on shaky legs and approach the fae man huddled in the center. It doesn't look like my brother; my brother is hard and metal and unreadable. This person has wavy brown hair that falls around his pointed ears. And when I crouch before him and gently lift his head, there is so much pain in his dark brown eyes that I feel it myself.

"Brother," I breathe. "I'm here."

"Kel?" Ezryn's voice trembles.

I gesture to the storm. "You don't need this anymore. I'm going to look after you."

"It was too much, Kel. Too much. I couldn't ... I hurt everyone."

I take his face in my hands. A shock passes between our skin. Never did I think our eyes would meet with no barriers. Never did I think I would need to save him.

"We're going to figure this out together," I tell him. "Trust me, Ez."

Ezryn curls over, a keening sound prying out from him. "I stopped it. I stopped it from happening."

"Stopped what from happening?"

He looks up at me, and tears streak down his face. "I stopped my curse from breaking."

I suck in a breath, eyes widening. If his curse was going to break...

Rosalina.

Of course.

Of course she would save us all. My Rose's eternal love has no limits.

I don't understand the implications of Ezryn not allowing his curse to break or what it means that I have witnessed his face.

But I do know one thing.

I will weather this storm with him.

Kneeling beside him, I place my hands on his jaw and bring his forehead to my lips. A kiss of honor. Of loyalty. Of brotherhood.

"I'm not going to let you hurt anyone, Ezryn," I say against his skin. "This, I vow."

His body shakes, then stills. A howl sounds from somewhere both close by and far away, then drifts to silence.

The storm rests.

I breathe in a sigh of relief, collapsing my forehead on his shoulder. He's safe—

"Kel! Watch out!"

Rosalina's voice. But it's too late. Rough hands snatch my shoulders, yanking me away from Ez. I growl and thrash. Two Spring soldiers hold me back. I could easily freeze their bones to brittle, but they're still Ezryn's men. "Let me go."

The rest of the force surrounds Ezryn, weapons pointed at him. One steps forward, clinking manacles on his hands. "High Prince Ezryn, you are hereby under arrest for the breaking of our ancient creed and the murder of three members of the Spring Realm guard."

"Stop!" Rosalina cries. She bolts out of the treeline, movements weak and stumbly. The princes follow, with Dayton being mostly supported on Farron's shoulder.

I pull free of the guards and search for Kairyn. He's standing motionless behind the soldiers.

"What is the meaning of this?" I run to him, grab his breastplate and pull us face to face. "Call them off."

"There's nothing I can do, Keldarion. You know it as well as I." His voice is a deep rumble. "My brother's face has been witnessed by others outside of kin or mate bond. This is the creed in Spring. Ezryn must accept the fate of his actions."

"There has to be something you can do."

"Look at him." The owl's helm drifts from me to Ezryn, kneeling quietly amidst the ring of soldiers. He allows himself to be jerked forward, for his arms to be bound behind his back. "Ezryn would never forgive us if we dishonored his own commitment to the creed."

I snarl and shove Kairyn away.

Rosalina doesn't stop running. She barrels into the nearest guard, pulling at his arm. "Stop it! Get away from him!"

The guard shakes her off, then pushes her to the ground. "Stay back or you'll be next."

Icy rage coils up my body, and I've crossed the space between them in less than a second. "Place a hand on her again and I will remove it."

The guard sneers at me. "This doesn't concern you, Winter Prince. These are matters of the Spring Realm."

Rosalina clutches me. "Kel, we have to do something!"

At that moment, Dayton and Farron reach us. Their eyes are equally pleading. They're going to follow my lead.

My chest heaves with breath as I shift my gaze from my mate to my brothers to Kairyn. Then finally, I look to Ez.

Our eyes lock and ever so slowly, he shakes his head.

Pain cuts through my heart. It would be so easy to dispatch each of these guards and rip off his binds.

It is so much harder to understand why I must let this happen.

I lace my fingers through Rosalina's and step back. She turns her gaze toward me, her expression filled with questions. "Kel?"

"We can take them," Dayton growls. "What are we waiting for?"

The guards drag Ezryn to his feet.

"Are we really not going to stop this?" Farron whispers.

"This is Ezryn's will," I respond. "His honor demands he answer for breaking the creed."

Rosalina tears from my grip and runs to the line of the guards as they begin to march Ezryn through the grove.

"Ez," she cries.

He doesn't—can't—meet her gaze. "Let me go, Rose," he whispers.

Kairyn follows the troops at the back. I grab his arm as he passes. "Remember," I growl, "Ezryn showed you mercy once."

"I am all too familiar with Ezryn's mercy," Kairyn says. "I've had to live with it."

The guards, the Prince of Spring, and the High Prince turned creed-breaker march from the grove, and I am left among the wreckage.

84

ROSALINA

"Hello! Are you listening to me? There's something wrong with the flowers!" I bang louder on my chamber doors in Keep Hammergarden. "Hello! I need to speak to High Prince Ezryn, or even Kairyn! Just for a moment."

I growl, white flames licking up my palms. I'll burn this place down if it comes to it.

The door creaks open, and I immediately stagger back as Marigold trots in, rolling a trolley of coffee and cookies. She casts a withering glare at the row of guards outside my room. Eldy and Astrid toddle in behind her, then close the door.

"If I'm a prisoner, Kairyn should show the courtesy of putting me behind bars." I scowl at the closed door before slumping into a plush white chair beside the window. Outside, the late afternoon sun glows a soft pink, and cherry blossoms and petals float in the breeze. It's too peaceful, too pretty and bright.

Moments like this would make a lot more sense when surrounded by a storm.

"I usually say there's nothing a hot cup of tea can't fix. But I … Well—" The delicate cup shakes in Marigold's fingers, sloshing liquid on to the floor.

"Here, let me," Eldy says, taking the cup and placing it on the table beside me.

He's a fae again. After he warned Ezryn of my drowning, he said he'd landed and focused on returning to his prior form. The spell had ended, and he'd shifted back into a fae. Apparently, it was quite the start to some of the Spring staff, seeing their naked majordomo running through the halls.

After that, he'd arranged a party to rescue Astrid and Marigold from the top of the mountain. They were already heading back down, cured of their hypnosis thanks to the water I'd doused them in. Thankfully, no one was seriously injured, my own wounds healed when my mate bond awoke.

Whatever had happened to us was eerily similar to the condition that had afflicted Ezryn and me after the jubilee. That incident had been caused by the purple flowers, but there hadn't been any of those in my room. Though there was a vase of red flowers, brought fresh to my room by Wrenley. Kairyn had instructed her to do so. *Does he know? He can't. He wouldn't?*

My mind spins with thoughts. There are red flowers all over the city and in the throne room. The townsfolk talked of a sickness going around. *Could it all be connected?*

Even if I'm on to something, not a single person is listening to me. I made sure my room was clear of flowers. The red ones were already gone, replaced with daisies, which I promptly threw out the window.

Above all else, I have to make sure Ezryn is all right.

My mate.

A new mate, the flowers, the power of change. Everything has happened so fast, and I don't know how to process it.

"It'll be all right, Rosalina," Astrid says, sitting on the edge of the chair and wrapping her arms around me. "We'll get through this."

"Astrid is right," Marigold says. "We have faith that Kairyn will provide a fair trial for Ezryn, considering the situation and..." Her lip quivers and Eldy wraps a comforting arm around her.

Something blooms bright in my chest and loud arguing sounds from outside my chamber. The door whips open, and I hear Kel's voice growling low and dangerous, "Get your hands off me," before storming inside. Farron clambers after him, a bundle of books and scrolls in his hands.

I leap up, and Kel gathers me in his arms. "Rose, I've negotiated with Kairyn for free run of the keep. They never should have locked you up."

"Indeed," Farron says, golden glasses low on his nose. "The law is very particular. The person who saw the face is not held responsible at all. The blame falls solely on the royal."

"What are all those books, Farron?" I ask, peeking out from Kel's strong arms.

"Laws and writing on the Spring Realm creed. I was looking for a loophole, something to help Ez, but from what I've read so far, this rule is ironclad. Day's carrying up a few more texts from the archives, but I don't think there's anything I can find that can help him."

"It wouldn't matter if you did." Marigold steps forward, shaking her head. "The creed is bred into that boy's bones. He will follow it as he knows it."

Farron throws the books and scrolls down with a long sigh. "Right as usual, Marigold."

My gaze drifts to the chief majordomo. I transformed him … into a *bird*. Everything's happened so fast, I haven't even had time to think about it. What well of power did I draw from? It's unlike anything I've ever done before.

But then again, I did transform the arrow into seawater back at Castletree. There's only been one other fae documented to transform matter like that. My hand drifts over my heart.

How is it possible that my magic resembles the Queen's?

"Is everything all right?" Eldy asks me.

I give my head a shake. "Huh? Yes, I'm fine. Sorry for turning you into a bird."

The room fills with silence, and I look around to notice everyone is staring at me.

"How *did* you do that?" Farron asks slowly. He drifts over to Eldy and grabs his arm, examining it.

"Excuse me!" Eldy pulls away from Farron and turns to me. "Your apology is quite unnecessary. That incredible feat of yours saved my life. Besides, I made quite a dashing bird, if I do say so myself. Though not so dashing, I'm sure, as a fair raccoon." His face flushes as he looks down at Marigold.

"So, you know of the curse, then," I say.

"I filled him in as soon as we arrived back at the keep," Kel says. "Figured now that he's been turned into an animal himself, he ought to know about the rest of us."

"I knew our Rosalina was a special one the moment I set eyes on her," Marigold says. She takes Eldy's arm. "You know, Ezryn's mother used to say that there's deep magic in the world, more than we could possibly understand. It wakes up when it's ready to."

"Maybe this magic's been asleep for five hundred years," Farron says.

"Farron, what are you saying?" I ask.

"The realms were crafted of the four seasons to keep the Vale in balance, but the world has been anything but balanced lately." He shrugs. "Maybe her magic found a way back to us."

"I don't know." I rub at the space over my heart. It doesn't feel like the magic found me.

It feels like I found it.

Kel holds me tighter against him. "If anyone has a chance of restoring harmony to the Vale, it would be you, Rose."

"That's a lot of pressure," I mumble.

Marigold squeezes my hand. "We should let you all get some rest." She gestures toward Astrid. "We need to get to our own chambers before nightfall."

She and Eldy leave the room. Astrid gives me a quick hug before turning to follow them.

"Wait, Astrid!" I grab a letter off the nightstand and give it to her. "Can you make sure this gets to Farron's brothers? I need them to keep my father in Coppershire." My throat tightens. "I don't want him brought to Spring until we know what's going on."

She kisses my cheek. "You can count on me." An exhausted sigh fills me as she leaves, and I'm left staring at my hands. I wish I could talk to Papa about everything. Maybe something he discovered on his travels could help explain just exactly who Anya O'Connell was—or is. "I don't even know what came over me when I changed Eldy."

Kel tucks a stray piece of hair behind my ear. "I don't know either, my Rose. But I do know that it was not chance that you fell into the Enchanted Vale. You belong here. Magic lives within you."

Farron comes up beside me. "You're just as incredible as the legends we love to read about. I wish we had time to discover all your secrets."

I offer him a soft smile. "Me too, but right now we have to focus on Ezryn. Has anyone seen him?"

"No," Keldarion says, a muscle feathering in his jaw. "I spoke with Kairyn. Ezryn is in solitary confinement, awaiting the trial in the morning. Guards are posted outside the chamber, but no one is in there with him. At least there will be no concern about someone encountering his beast."

"How can we just leave him there? He's all alone. How can he even be put on trial? He's the High Prince." Tears flow down my cheeks.

"Ezryn broke their sacred creed. The law states that power passes to the steward in such cases," Farron explains.

"I can't let this happen."

"But you must," Keldarion says simply, wiping my tears away. "And you know it, else you'd have already razed this whole keep to the ground. Because you know Ezryn. Know him in a way none other does. That is the truest form of love."

I swallow, my throat dry. I may not understand or agree with Ezryn's decision to go through with this, but he holds his honor in the highest regard. If I deny him the chance to seek true repentance... "I need to see him."

"We tried, Rosie," Farron says gently. "He's not allowed, and ... he doesn't want to see us."

Anger rises in my chest. "Doesn't want to see me? I'm his ma—" I cut myself off, realizing this is the first chance I've had to say it out loud. Say it in front of Farron and Keldarion.

"Your mate," Keldarion finishes, taking one of my hands in his. "I know."

Farron takes my other hand.

They don't need words; love flows freely through our bond between all of us.

Keldarion takes Farron's hand, so we stand in a circle. "You are my mate. Farron is yours, and now Ezryn is as well. I've told you both this before, but I will shelter you from this upcoming storm. When Ezryn returns to us, we will not let him go. The four of us belong together."

Keldarion's words sound like a vow.

There's a shuffle behind us, and as we turn, Dayton is awkwardly standing in the doorway.

Awkward isn't a word I often associate with the Prince of Summer, but that's how he looks now, hand clutching the back of his neck, cheeks flushed. How long was he waiting there? What words did he hear?

"Day." I step forward, but he just drops some more scrolls and books on the table before turning back to the door. "Don't go."

He shakes his head, donning a smile that doesn't quite reach his eyes. "No room for a beast among princes."

85

ROSALINA

The only light is my dim lantern, the only sound the drip of water down the cavernous walls.

The dungeons of Keep Hammergarden are more cave than castle. We're deep beneath the mountain now, and I wrap my shawl tighter around my body to fight off the chill.

I know Keldarion told me not to come, that Ezryn didn't even want to see us.

But I am his mate. As I lay awake in my bed, embraced by both Farron and Kel who slept on either side of me, there was nothing I could do but feel my bond screaming in my chest. I stared up at the ceiling, tears pouring down my cheeks in the dark.

It was Kel who made my mind up for me. One minute I was lying on the bed, the next he was lifting me in his arms, sneaking us toward the door so as not to wake Farron. "Take the stairs all the way down as far as you can go. Then follow your nose—the damp air will lead you to solitary confinement," he whispered as he set me down. Without my touch, he shifted into the icy white wolf.

Despite all our fights and secrets, Keldarion's faith in me is the one thing that never wavers.

I followed Kel's instructions. Now, two guards stand before a wooden door at the end of the cavernous hallway. I raise my chin in the air and refuse to let my voice shake. "I wish to look into the eyes of my mate before he faces his trial."

They look at each other.

"The High Princess Isidora and Prince Thalionor held a mate bond that was revered throughout Spring," I say. "I would expect servants of the realm to honor such a union."

One grunts. "Five minutes. Not a second longer."

Then he opens the door.

My heart pounds as I rush through the next hallway. Damp rock lies on either side, but at the very end, I see the shine of metal bars. Tears fill my eyes as my mate bond sings. He's close.

I run to the end of the hall, gripping the cell bars. "Ezryn?" There's nothing but darkness.

But there is sound: a deep, labored breathing.

I hold up my lantern and try to focus my enhanced sight into the shadows. Something shifts in the gloom.

A great animal raises its head, dark eyes shining yellow in the light of my lantern. White bones tangle in its fur, and crops of fungi grow around its ears and on its paws. In the corner of the cell, I spot his armor neatly piled, the underclothes folded.

"You shouldn't be here," the beast rumbles.

"I don't care what I should or shouldn't do." My voice is a snarl. "You are my mate. I'm not leaving you."

A whine sounds through the wolf's chest, and he lowers his head to his paws. "It is a great dishonor to be mated to me. I am sorry you must suffer such shame."

An angry cry rips out of me, and I shake the bars, as useless as that is. "I don't care what they call you or what they've said you've done. I will stand by you—now and forever."

The wolf stands and pads over to me. Then he collapses in front of the bars as if even that amount of movement was unbearable. There's no fight in his voice as he says, "I nearly killed you, Rosalina. It is proof of what I've known since I murdered my own mother. There is a darkness in me that cannot be purged."

"Then I will love you in the darkness," I say.

The wolf closes his eyes and for a second, a sense of peace washes over his features. "Your indomitable spirit is the only hope I have left."

"Ezryn," I whisper, "we can get through this. Your realm needs you. There's something terrible happening."

"I've destroyed everything," he whispers. "My parents trusted me to lead our people. I stole my mother from the Spring Realm. My father is dying. I've betrayed our creed, everything she stood for." His face scrunches up. "My parents' legacy lies with Kairyn. It is up to him now"

Profound sorrow grips me as I realize the surrender in Ezryn's eyes. He's been fighting for so long to prove to himself he's *good*— something I've known from the beginning. But he's never forgiven himself for his mother's death, and I don't know if he'll ever be able to forgive himself for hurting me.

"Do you really trust Kairyn to be fair in his judgment?" Nerves roil within me, thinking of the anger in Kairyn's voice the first day we saw him in the Hall of Vernalion.

"For the first time in our lives, I think we understand each other. He is a son of Spring—his honor will guide him. I will accept his ruling, whether it be punishment or ..." Ezryn's voice grows quiet. "Forgiveness."

I see now. He feels like he owes Kairyn for taking their mother away. Accepting judgment from his brother may be the only way for Ezryn to heal from this.

"You can't give up," I say. "We'll get through this trial. You'll come home to Castletree with me and Kel, and Day, and Farron and—"

The wolf shakes its head. "I only wish that my father lives to see the realm at peace. Then Mother can rest easily. Kairyn will give me the judgment I deserve."

A growl erupts from my throat. "And what about what I deserve? My mate safe and in my arms!"

The wolf shifts, sadly. A sob breaks free from my chest, and I push myself against the bars, reaching out to him. My fingers lace through the fur by his ears. The air sings with magic, and Ezryn shifts. My hands now clutch the side of his face, his fae body leaning against the bars before me.

He blinks at me, his dark eyes beautiful in the lamplight. I'll never tire of seeing this face. A smile cracks through my tears, and I stroke the points of his ears, tangle my hands in his hair.

He reaches through the bars and grabs my chin. "I will never leave you, Rosalina. No matter what happens to me, I'll always be a part of you now."

A voice echoes down the hallway: "Time's up!" The guards.

Ezryn flicks his gaze into the dark. "Now, go. If you linger any longer, they'll come looking for you, and they'll be surprised by what they find."

"Ezryn—" I begin, but he pulls away, body shifting back into the beast.

As I walk back through the dark hallways, I realize my last hope now lies with Kairyn. I pray that his own shattered heart still holds some mercy.

86

CASPIAN

Acurtain of briars around the bed. Yes, she would like that. I craft it, red petals interweaving in a flowing sheet. *Perfect.* In my mind, my thorns are not blighted purple things, but the bright green vines of a rosebush. I need to keep building this imaginary house bigger, reinforcing the windows, letting nothing of the outside world in. Taller walls, more vines, more roses—

Crack.

Pain radiates through my body. A substantial part of my pretend house shatters, bursting into flame. Glimpses of reality break through in fiery bursts of agony: the rusted manacles digging into my wrists, the decaying post I'm chained to, the ground where my bare feet can't find purchase on the blood-soaked stone. But I'm still standing. There's that, at least.

I heave in a breath, preparing for the next assault, trying to build up this barrier in my mind against the real world. More roses, more—

Crack.

The flail comes down across my back, spreading its barbed flame tips. I bite my teeth so hard, I think they'll break. I won't cry out. I won't give him that satisfaction.

My cheek scrapes against the wooden post. It stands like a sentinel in Nether Reach's square. Through the black edges of my vision, I see quite a crowd has gathered to witness the Prince of Thorns' punishment. There are chittering goblins and soldiers alike. There's even a cave troll or two in the back.

Can't blame them. I'd watch me get whipped, too.

My mother's not here, though. I think she left after the first fifty lashes.

"Decided to join us, pretty?" A voice sneers behind me.

I curse the delay of the next strike. It's easier to disappear in the rhythm of it, but the pause only amplifies the impact of the pain. Groaning, I glance over my shoulder. The Queen of the Below must be furious with me, as she assigned *him*.

No one remembers his real name, or they don't care to, but in the Tower of Nether Reach, he's known as Emberlash, a twisted deserter of the Autumn Realm with a disposition for fire. He's enchanted his barbed whip with flames.

It's stupidly effective at not just breaking apart the skin but searing through the muscle down to the bone. The pain jolts me fully back into reality, and I silence another cry. Stars, it feels like he's stripped my whole spine bare.

"Did you hear me, beautiful?" Emberlash jeers. He's filed his teeth into points, giving his words an airy hiss. "Ready to cry for mercy now?"

"Just woke up from a nap," I call, trying desperately to hide the hoarse quaver in my voice. "Barely felt a thing so far."

The fae gives an animalistic sort of snarl. Anyone who ventures to the Below has to be somewhat unbalanced, and Emberlash is no exception.

Perhaps to my own detriment.

With a swift, malicious swing, the flail cracks down upon my back. The barbs, wickedly sharp, tear through what's left of my flesh. Waves of heat engulf me, and it smells like burning. Seven realms, is that my own skin? *Don't cry out, don't cry out.*

I need to disappear deep into my mind. I built these retreats, these escapes, not just to hide from the pain, but to block out the whispers.

Not the goblins' jeering or Emberlash's taunts.

But the whispers within.

The Green Flame, slithering through me like a snake waiting to strike. *You could annihilate them all, crumble this tower, and never submit.*

If I used that magic.

I lost control of it once. I won't again.

It's what she wants. Sira wouldn't care if I destroyed this tower with green flames. No, she's hoping for it. Hoping for the day I get so fed up with these punishments, I give in to it.

But it'll take a lot more than this to break me.

So, I build the house of roses. I escape into it, because today, she's here.

Rosalina looks half made of flowers in my imagination. *You're here because of me,* she says.

My mother found out I lied and that I knew of her power all along. Now, like me, Sira knows exactly who Rosalina is.

And she isn't happy I kept that from her.

The whipping continues, and I feel my feet slipping. It's worse being held up only by the chains. She sentenced me to two hundred lashes, but Emberlash will keep me here until his arm gives out, or until I give him a scream or a beg. I've lost count, and surely there must be no more skin on my back.

I pull Rosalina down on the bed. I imagine kissing her. Because I *did* kiss her. A stupid, reckless, amazing kiss. A kiss to get me through what was to come. *She liked it.* I know she did.

My knees buckle and slam to the ground. I'm coughing up blood now. Taunts and shouts breach my barrier. The roses are turning to cursed thorns. They're dying. Reality crashes in.

Rosalina.

She kissed me in a way that makes me want to rethink everything. Because if Farron succeeds at what I asked him to do, would that shatter what's between us?

Stars, stars. Every sane part of me hopes so.

And all the other parts pray it doesn't.

Luckily, there's no one to listen to my prayers.

There's only a curtain of petals between me and oblivion. I think I'm choking on blood now. Gods, it's disgusting.

I don't pray, but all my hopes are in that princeling.

Fare.

I kind of wish he didn't hate me.

I would hate me too if I were him.

The roses rot, and Rosalina disappears. I'm left with the post and the manacles, the goblins and this pain. Damn, it hurts. A miserable begging cry waits on my lips, and a green coil rises within me. I don't know which one's going to win, only that either way, I lose.

"That's enough." A familiar voice cuts through the fragments of my mind. The Nightingale stands before Emberlash.

"The Prince of Thorns hasn't finished his punishment." He cracks his neck, looking down at her. The fae man's nearly three times her size, but she just raises her chin.

How long has she been watching? I don't understand why she would want it to stop. She should relish in this. I killed her Dreadknights.

"My mother ordered two hundred lashes. You've done more, by my count."

"Only one hundred seventy-five." He licks his lips. "And the Queen won't mind him taking a bit more, anyhow."

I don't know who's lying.

The Nightingale puts a hand on her hips, but a few of her prismatic thorns break through the stone. "Perhaps, but if she sides with me, I'm going to request to deliver your punishment myself. Would you like to find out how I'd do it?"

"Can't give lashes if you can't take them. You don't scare me, Princess."

"Oh, I wouldn't do something so barbaric as the whip," she trills, the hint of a laugh in her words. More thorns burst from the ground. "I'd wrap my thorns around each of your five appendages, and pull and pull and pull, just to see which one breaks off first."

"F-five?" Emberlash gulps, gaze flicking down.

The Nightingale steps forward, and the man staggers back. "I bet I know which small, scraggly part of you would snap first. Get out of my sight."

Emberlash coils his fiery whip and spits on the ground before slinking away.

I want to collapse; I want to fade into oblivion. But I can't. The hardest part is coming.

There's the click of a lock. My wrists are raw and cut from the rusted metal. The Nightingale's gloved hand is on my arm. "Stand if you can," she hisses at me. "Everyone is watching."

My voice cracks. "I can't—"

"Stand."

I know she's right, so I do it, vision blurring. Gently, she weaves a thin thorn into my palm, and I squeeze down on it, the sharp bite of pain helping me forget about my aching back for a moment.

They're all watching, this host of goblins and soldiers. They've seen me beaten before, of course, but Sira hasn't been this upset in a long time. I can't show them just how badly she's hurt me.

Casually, I run a hand through my sweat-soaked hair. "Nothing like a session from Emberlash to really get the blood flowing." I wink, gesturing to the bloody stone. "I'd recommend it anytime you need a boost."

The faces of the crowd are completely shocked. Awed that I'm standing, awed that I'm speaking. Lastly, I fix them with a glare, a dark look that says: that pain was nothing to me, and if they ever disobeyed, this would be a fraction of what I inflict on them.

"Well, sister dear, shall we take our leave?"

I couldn't summon briars right now if I tried. She knows it. The Nightingale fixes her own menacing glare on the crowd and prismatic thorns coil around us. Being oddly careful of my back, she drags us under.

THE MOMENT we push up through the ground and I recognize my own room, I cry out and collapse. Birdy's thorns don't let me fall, encircling my arms and placing me face down on my bed.

I writhe, screaming into my pillow, and try to reach around to touch my searing back.

"Don't." Birdy smacks my hand away.

"Is there even any skin left?" Through my blurred vision, I see her grimace, the quirk of her lip. My sister doesn't often get squeamish.

"Be grateful Mother forbids anyone from laying a hand on your face." She holds a bottle to my lips. "Drink."

It could be any one of her concoctions, but I drink anyway. I should feel more worried, figuring the last time I saw her, I annihilated her squadron.

But … that's not how it is between us.

Swallowing, the world fades away.

When I come back to myself, everything is hazy. My skin still throbs, but it's settled down to a dull ache. I crane my neck and see Birdy has laid thin ointment-laden strips of fabric across my back. She's kneeling over her bag of supplies, no longer dressed in her armor, but in a long black tunic and leggings, short hair tied up.

She looks so much younger like this.

"What time is it?" I ask, voice hoarse.

"Just past midnight." She comes and sits down on the floor by the side of my bed.

Mentally, I work out the timing of it all. "Only a few hours until Ezryn's trial, then." It was one of the last things I had learned before I was moved from detainment to the square. The Spring Prince had been witnessed without his helm and was to go on trial.

And, of course, there was the matter of his mate bond.

"You killed my Dreadknights."

I don't break her blue gaze. "I thought you'd be sadder about it. Not even a tear? I know you're able to pull out all manner of emotions at will."

Her stone face doesn't crack. "You destroyed them for what? For

Keldarion? For those princes you're obsessed with? Or was it for Rosalina? The Dreadknights were all I had, Cas."

Maybe she thought they were her path to freedom. I can't blame her for trying. I try, too. All the horrible things I've done—the trickery of my bargain with Farron, the goblin siege in Autumn—are only minor consequences compared to what will happen if I fail to escape the Below.

"The Dreadknights may have taken your orders," I say, "but they were loyal to Sira. What was the first lesson I taught you?"

"You can't trust anyone in the Below," she answers.

"You can't trust anyone in the Below," I repeat.

A question lingers between us, unsaid: *Can I trust you?*

I don't think either of us knows the answer to that. But I say what I can. "Birdy, they weren't all you have."

"What do you know about it? I had my Dreadknights and my thorns! That's it!" She rises, wiping her eyes with the heel of her palm. "You have your shadows and your thorns and whatever that green magic—"

"Trust me," I say, "you want nothing to do with that."

"And she ..." the Nightingale continues. "She has thorns and fire, and who knows what else? Not that she's any good with either. But these briars are *all* I have left now."

"How do you know, Birdy?"

Her face cracks, and she shakes her head. "Stop squirming." She lifts the edge of one of my bandages. "They're healing."

"Is Kairyn going to sentence the High Prince to death?"

The Nightingale stills. Says nothing.

"You don't know, do you?" I ask. "Have you even talked to your metal dog? Last I saw, he had his hands around your throat."

"Kairyn is conflicted. I never thought that idiot High Prince would actually make him steward. Kairyn *has* to realize it's not enough. It can't be enough."

"Maybe it's enough for him. The love and acceptance of a High Prince is a tantalizing thing."

"He could *be* a High Prince," Birdy hisses, pacing. "As the steward, it's his right to pass judgment, and their creed demands death for such crimes as Ezryn committed. Kairyn could inherit Spring's Blessing; he could get everything he's ever wanted."

I shift slightly. "Would any of that matter to Kairyn if Ezryn is too dead to witness it?"

Birdy lets out an enraged growl, knocking a whole row of books off my shelf. "He *can't* choose Ezryn over me!" Her eyes widen. "I mean our plan. Our vision for Spring, for the Enchanted Vale."

"We'll see."

She shakes her head and begins to forcefully tug on her armor. "Get better, Cas. Kairyn isn't my only plan in motion. All flowers rot, even roses. I will prove my worth to Mother."

"Wr—Wait." I push myself up on my forearms. "If you kill Rosalina, it will destroy you, too."

She pulls her mask over her face, thorns rising around her. "Don't worry, big brother. I died a long time ago."

The thorns carry her under, and I fall back down to the mattress. She'll try to go after Rosalina again. The only thing that keeps me from racing after her is a single thought: she's underestimated Rosalina.

The world has. And when the time comes, she'll glow so brightly, no one will be able to stop her.

87

DAYTON

Early morning light shines over the ramparts of Keep Hammergarden. A gentle wind blows, carrying the scent of cherry blossoms.

My family and I wait together as if at a funeral.

Kel, Farron, Rosalina, and I stand in a row, peering over the stone rampart wall that looks over the main gates of the keep. Down below, a wooden dais has been crafted overnight. A crowd has begun to gather. Their hushed whispers merge together to form a near-deafening roar.

We were all confined to the keep last night. For safeguarding, Kairyn called it. We all knew the truth of it. He didn't want any of us getting ideas about breaking Ezryn out of his own confinement. Not that I even have any magic right now. Farron drained it all to save Rosie, and I won't be able to replenish it until we return to Castletree.

Despite the guards roaming the keep, I know any one of us—Rosie included—could have broken Ez out. But Kel's words rang in my mind my whole sleepless night: *This is his will.*

Realms damn him, why does Ezryn have to be so bloody honorable?

At least those three had each other last night.

"The wait is killing me." Farron digs his hands into his hair. "Can't we bribe Kairyn to stop this? Threaten him? I'm not above well-executed coercion."

"This isn't about Kairyn, and you know it," Kel growls. The Sword of the Protector gleams on his back, poking out of its sheath. Rosie had thrown it in the lake to hide it from the Below, and thankfully we were able to retrieve it before returning to the keep.

Ezryn's storm had churned it up from the bottom of the lake, and Rosie had spotted it among the debris. "Ezryn would never forgive us if we removed his own agency to follow the oaths and traditions of his people."

Below, the gates creak open, and a hush falls over the crowd. Kairyn marches out, black cape flapping. His father trails behind, being carried on a litter by four Spring guards. Each step of Kairyn's heavy boots up the dais clangs through the air. I notice the crack in his mask has been patched with a line of gold.

The soldiers carefully place the litter down beside Kairyn. By the gods, Thalionor looks terrible. I can't even see his face, but it's evident by his posture: stiff hands clutching the armrests, head lolling on his chest. Yellow ooze drips from beneath the helm over his neck. I wouldn't be surprised if they put a helm on a corpse and called him Prince.

A sob sounds, and I look down the ramparts to see Marigold and Astrid. Marigold's leaning heavily on Astrid's shoulder as the younger fae rubs her back. I know Marigold has served Ezryn since he was a child; this can't be any easier for her than it is for us.

"Does the crowd seem odd to you?" Farron mutters, nudging Kel.

"What do you mean?"

Farron shakes his head. "I can't put my finger on it. But some of them appear ... vacant."

"Ezryn has been a beloved member of the noble house since his birth. They're probably in shock that he is to face trial," Kel answers.

Down below, Kairyn raises a hand. "Citizens of Florendel, I stand before you steward of Spring, son of Prince Thalionor and the late former High Princess Isidora, and brother to the current High Prince of Spring. It is with great sadness I share with you that the High Prince will face trial this morning for the gravest of sins, the ultimate betrayal of his people."

A gasp sounds, and my back teeth grind together. Hatred churns inside of me, staring at Kairyn. Kel says this isn't about him. That he's just doing what he has to, what the creed demands.

I call bullshit.

I've always known, ever since that little asshole used to tag around with us, that there was something wicked inside of him. Whether he was tormenting village kids or muttering remarks beneath his helm, I recognized it as more than sibling rivalry between him and Ez. He's always hated his older brother. Resented him.

"I bet Kai fucking planned this somehow," I growl. "Knew those guards would witness Ez's face."

Kel shakes his head. "Kairyn saved his life against the Nightingale's monster. Saved all our lives."

I pace behind them, hands itching for my swords. "I just can't fucking believe we're going to stand here, waiting and watching, as Ezryn's *life* is in that madman's hands! Ezryn's going to let this happen to himself—"

Kel slams a hand on my palm and holds me in an icy glare. "This is Ezryn's choice. You will respect it."

I sneer and throw his hand off me.

Farron steps forward, eyes shifting between the two of us. "Ezryn had the choice to publicly unhelm Kai years ago, when Ez defeated him in the Rite. Surely, Kairyn will show the same mercy."

"Or he'll kill him," I say.

A keening sound utters from up the rampart, and Rosalina doubles over, clutching her heart. It's the first sound I've heard her make all morning. Seven realms, I'm an idiot. Kel shoots me a nasty glare, then walks over to her and places a hand on her back.

If I'm handling this badly, how must she feel?

She's his mate.

She's Ezryn's fucking mate. Just like she's mates with Kel and Farron.

The thought sends me spiraling, and I whip away, digging my hands into the stone wall to keep from punching it.

Tears spring to my eyes. Rosalina is mates with every one of the High Princes.

Except for me.

What did I do? It couldn't be because I haven't loved her enough, because, fuck, I've loved her so much I've felt like it would break me. Why would the universe curse me like this? Curse me worse than spending each night as a beast?

Then a thought strikes me like a blade.

Maybe it was because I was never meant to be the High Prince of Summer. Keldarion, Ez, Farron … They were all the eldest or the only. Fated in the stars for their Blessings.

I received mine through blood and death.

Maybe she was meant for Damocles. Maybe she would have loved him, and he would have loved her. He should be the one still living now.

And I should be the one buried in the ground.

Footsteps sound on the stair, and Eldy walks up, a forlorn look on his face. Whatever Rosalina did to him yesterday has worn off, and he has resumed his fae form. More of her strange magic. We need to explore it, but right now, Ezryn takes priority.

"Any news?" Kel asks.

"I have finished preparing him," Eldy responds solemnly. "The trial is about to begin."

88

EZRYN

All my life, I have strived to bring honor to my people. To my realm. To my family. To myself.

Now, as I step out into the sunlight, all the eyes of the capital stare at me with shame.

Guards escort me and my hands are bound, but it is unnecessary. I would not shame myself further by trying to escape punishment. My face was witnessed by the soldiers I slayed, by the other High Princes, by my brother's guard. There could be no greater dishonor.

I wear the starlight silver armor that was specially crafted for me when I took the mantle of High Prince. The helm I bear is forged from the most precious metals. If this is to be my end, then I shall lay down my life with what pride remains.

The crowd parts as I walk from the keep toward the dais where my brother stands. A sensation flickers near my heart, a pulling and a pleading all at once. I look up at the ramparts.

Rosalina.

My mate…

Her expression is one of sheer anguish, tears glittering in the morning sun. I nearly killed her. My curse had almost broken. I had finally found my mate and she wanted to accept the bond with me …

But why? In what way did I deserve to love someone as pure as Rosalina? To *be* loved by her?

The beast roils within my chest, antsy and restless. He wanted to be rid of me.

I suppose I needed him more than he needs me.

I look down, unable to hold her gaze anymore. Not only have I shamed myself and my family, but I have brought great shame upon her as well. She is mated to a creedbreaker.

My only respite is that I know by accepting whatever punishment is bestowed, I will regain a sliver of honor. I once passed judgment on Kairyn, and now he will pass judgment on me. A cycle, like that of the seasons. It seems fitting.

I think, deep inside, I knew this day would come. I was destined to answer to him for taking our mother away.

A guard pushes on my back, urging me to ascend the stairs up to the top of the dais. My brother looms before me, his shadow long. I cannot bring myself to look up at my father. Perhaps a small mercy of his condition is that he is not lucid enough to understand the disgrace of his eldest son.

"Kneel," Kairyn says lowly.

I do, sinking to my knees at my brother's feet.

"Before me is the High Prince Ezryn," Kairyn booms. "He is here to face trial for the most grievous of evils. Our High Prince has broken the sacred creed, forsaken his oath to realm and citizen, and revealed his face outside of kin."

The crowd gasps, their horror giving way to sobs and cries of outrage. I stay still, though each breath is a struggle.

"Not only did Prince Ezryn reveal his face, he brutally murdered those who witnessed it and then desecrated one of our most sacred spaces," Kairyn continues. "As steward of Spring, I shall bestow judgment."

I bow my head. Many years ago, it was I in his position, publicly decrying him. I understand him and hold no hatred. Duty before blood. The realm before the heart.

"Do you deny the accusations, Prince Ezryn?" Kairyn asks.

Distantly, I note he is not using my full title. "I do not," I respond.

The crowd gasps again. My hands seize into fists as I feel the weight of their shock. That space beside my heart aches.

Kairyn steps toward me. "Then I will do what I must—"

"Wait!" a voice croaks. The sound is dusty, as if unearthed after being buried for centuries. My father rises to his feet.

"Sire!" a guard cries and rushes forward to steady him, but my father pushes him off.

"F-forgiveness," my father says. "L-let us have forgiveness—"

His words are cut off by Kairyn, who grabs him roughly by the shoulders and pushes him on to the chair atop the litter. "Sit, Father. You are ill. This betrayal has caused you too much distress already." He nods to the guards. "We shall return you to your chambers so you may rest."

"Wait..." I think my father says, but the guards lift his litter and carry him inside the keep.

Kairyn's heavy breath reverberates beneath his helm. The crowd has started murmuring now, repeating my father's word: Forgiveness.

Don't they understand? There has been no royal pardon ever granted in history. I would make no special request for myself.

Even in my father's most feeble state, the people are loyal to him. It is testament to his many long years serving beside the High Princess, for his leadership in battle and government. They must mourn who he used to be, as they mourn my mother. This dedication … They're extending it to me.

"Forgiveness for High Prince Ezryn!" one of them calls.

"Amnesty!"

"Show mercy, m'lord!"

And then one voice cries out above all the rest, and a body flings between me and Kairyn. Arms spread wide, hair blowing in the breeze, is my mate. "High Prince Ezryn removed his helm to save my life. I am his mate. It is written in both the stars and the creed that we are to witness all of one another," Rosalina breathes. "I was then set upon by those guards and he tried to protect me. It was an unfortunate accident, but High Prince Ezryn did not willingly forsake his creed. Your father, the rightful steward of Spring, has passed the judgment of forgiveness. Let his decision stand." Her body trembles, but I feel her resolution as strong as steel. "Please, Kairyn."

Kairyn looks around. He must feel it, as I do. He's lost the people. They're rallying behind me.

Could Spring possibly offer forgiveness to a creedbreaker? Could there be salvation?

Kairyn stands still before suddenly throwing back his head. "Well! The people would like to offer mercy to one who makes a mockery of our way. I see how it is." He shoves Rosalina to the side and snarls to her, "*I* am the rightful steward. Your *mate* named me so before you wandered into a river."

Rosalina glares at him but stands off to the side, arms crossed.

I notice now Kel, Dayton, and Farron have made their way close to the dais. What must they think of me, to see me in such shame?

"Very well then," Kairyn says, holding his arms out. "Who am I to speak against the wills of the realm? They beg for mercy. I shall grant it. Just tell the people one thing." Kairyn lowers down so we're helm to helm. The dark void where his eyes should be blazes with shadow. He says the words slowly, as if carving away at me with a serrated knife: "Who killed our mother?"

I take in a breath.

Kairyn rises to his feet, voice booming. "Answer it for your faithful citizens. Who murdered High Princess Isidora?"

My voice breaks. "I did."

"Louder!" Kairyn roars. "Let the realm hear the truth. Who murdered Isidora?"

"I did!" I cry, sinking inward.

"Ez, no!" Kel yells from the side of the dais.

My voice barely carries. "It was an accident. I didn't mean to—"

"But if it wasn't for you, our mother would still be here," Kairyn hisses.

The crowd is in an uproar now. Words of forgiveness have been replaced with that of *murderer*.

Ezryn, don't listen to him. It's Rosalina's voice crying out in my head. I want to hold on to it … But another voice screams louder.

Murderer, Kairyn's voice growls in my mind. *You murdered our mother.*

"He admits it!" Kairyn yells aloud. "And so, a sentence must be given."

Rosalina rushes forward, throwing her body in front of mine again. "It's not fair! He doesn't deserve this, and you know it, Kairyn. Leave him alone!"

But I do. I've deserved this for decades. The Enchantress thought she cursed me with my beast. Instead, she only gave me another way to kill, to wreak my malice upon the world.

This is my true penance.

I look to Keldarion. Perhaps it is the bonds woven through our love for Rosalina, or perhaps it is the centuries of brotherhood, but he understands. He steps upon the dais and grabs Rose around the waist. "Come on."

"No! No!" Rosalina screams, scraping at his arms like a wildcat.

"For Ezryn," Kel breathes.

She looks to me, and there's betrayal in her eyes. Not for the same reason my people are betrayed. Because I'm not fighting.

But this is how it has to be. I never took responsibility for our mother's death. I must now, and fate has deemed it be on this public stage. The world will know me as I have always known myself.

Kai leans down, knocking his helm against my own. "They all expect that I'll kill you, brother. The people. Our father. Your family." He looks down. "I suspect even you think that is my plan."

"Then do it."

"Isn't that the tragedy of it all?" There's a sadness in his voice. "It would be a mercy to kill you. It would rid me of so many insufferable problems. And yet, I find even now, I cannot do it. I cannot bring myself to end your life."

"I never wished to bring you sorrow, Kairyn."

"Yet that's all you've done. Mother and Father's favorite. The perfect son. The flawless leader. Then to take her away from me..." His voice cracks, and for a moment, I can picture the child's face behind the mask. "You should have killed me during the Rite. At least then my soul would have redemption."

"Is it too late for us?" I whisper. "Perhaps we can seek redemption together—"

Kairyn laughs, a joyless sound. "There is no place that will shelter me for the things I have done. I suppose we are one and the same, aren't we? Except you're on your knees, and I am on a throne."

"Kai—"

My brother stands and looks to the crowd. "For the murder of High Princess Isidora and the breaking of his creed, I depose Ezryn, son of Thalionor, of his title of High Prince. I order Spring's Blessing to be passed to the next in line." His breath sounds like rolling thunder. "Me."

"Are you crazy?" Farron cries from the side of the dais. "You haven't been prepared to take the Blessing! It could kill him! It could kill you!"

I force myself to my feet. "Brother, don't do this. Our magic is not used to being merged. It will be too much—"

"I'm not you," Kairyn says. "I will not bow to the magic as you did."

"Then kill me," I urge. "It will pass naturally. It is safer—"

Kairyn turns. "I already told you. I cannot do that. So, you will pass the Blessing to me. Now. Either I will get this power, or it will claim us both."

All hope drains from my body. I turn to Kel. "Take her away."

Kel's eyes blaze with ice. Rosalina is still clutched in his arms. "Ez, don't do this!"

"You can't trust him!" Dayton cries, slamming his fist on the wooden dais.

But there's nothing left.

I have received my sentence.

I have lost my honor.

I am not fit to be High Prince. By all rights, it must go to Kairyn.

A guard releases my bonds and I lay my hands on Kairyn's chest. "Protect our realm."

Kairyn only nods.

I have never been taught how to pass the incredible power of Spring on to another person, but there is an ancient knowledge that lurks within the magic. The Blessing itself seems to protest, clawing at the inside of my chest. But I force it outward. It doesn't belong to me anymore, shouldn't belong to me.

It needs to go to someone who can protect Spring.

My brother, for all his faults, will see this done. He has already safeguarded the mountain villages and proved himself a valuable leader to the acolytes. While the other High Princes may disapprove, they will offer their guidance. I pray my brother can fulfill the role of a great ruler for Spring that I was never able to embody.

The sheer weight of the magic swells within me, a torrent of raw power coursing through my veins. The air crackles with energy. A connection forges between us, our magic linking like chainmail. As I release the first surge of magic into Kairyn, a searing agony rips through my core. It is as if my very soul is being torn asunder.

I am unraveling, my essence being broken link by link and instead being attached to my brother's being.

The magic is a maelstrom, an uncontrollable force that threatens to consume me entirely. I cry out and my vision blurs. The world around me fades as I pour everything I am into him.

My brother's form begins to glow with an ethereal light. I am diminished. The wellspring of my own magic is empty, and I am hollow.

My vision comes back in specks of light. I'm on all fours, breath heavy. Sweat drips out of the bottom of my helm. When I look up, I see Kairyn, radiating like the sun itself.

"I have been reborn," he calls out. Two green vines crack through the dais, seizing my wrists to my side. Kairyn laughs.

I feel nothing. I know there should be sorrow. Regret. Despair. But I am nothing.

Though two things still linger quietly, hiding beneath my heart. A whimpering beast...

And her.

"It is done," Kairyn snarls. "I am the new High Prince of Spring."

Heavy feet thud beside me. Kel lays a hand on my shoulder. I shrink away from his touch. "You've gotten what you want, Kairyn. Let us take Ezryn now and leave you with your realm."

"Address me with my proper respects, *High Prince* Keldarion."

Kel takes a shaky breath. "High Prince Kairyn, we will remove Ezryn from your care now."

"A thoughtful idea, but one I cannot allow. For my brother's punishment is not yet complete." Kairyn pulls my head up by my helm. "My brother is hereby banished from the Spring Realm, never to return."

The crowd cries out. An aching emptiness shoots through my body. Banished ... from my home.

"He will see himself through the gates of Florendel to the outskirts of the city," Kairyn continues. He turns to Kel. "When he arrives there, you may do with him as you wish. I would recommend not taking him back to Castletree. I am part of that domain now, and everything within the Spring Wing—from its treasures to the staff— belongs to me."

Now, Dayton and Farron are on my other side. "Enough of your spectacle. We will see him out the gates," Dayton growls.

"That is not how things are done in Spring," Kairyn hisses. "Remove yourself from this dais before you dishonor your so-called *brother* anymore."

None of them move.

"Go," I whisper. Still, they do not move. "GO!"

Kel goes first, his eyes filled with pain as he looks back at me. Dayton and Farron follow.

I dare not look at Rosalina.

Kairyn places a hand on my shoulder. "You know what must happen now, big brother. The final punishment for a breaker of creed."

I close my eyes, my head suddenly so heavy.

"Guards!" Kairyn roars. "Remove his armor!"

There are hands all over me, stripping me of my breastplate, my greaves, my gloves. My beautiful armor is thrown aside across the dais, scuffing against the wood.

I kneel before my brother only in the long-sleeve black shirt and trousers. Ranger's cloth, nothing more.

And my helm, of course.

My brother places his hands on either side of my helmet. I look up at him and can almost see his eyes peering down at me, so full of resentment. Of sorrow.

"Spring," he says shakily, "you will now gaze upon the face of the leader who betrayed you. Observe his flesh and witness his shame. Creedbreaker. In the long histories, your name will be reviled. And all who love you shall behold how far you have fallen."

With those words, my brother rips off my helm.

89

ROSALINA

"N o!" I scream, but my voice is stolen by the crowd. They gasp, they sob. Others yell.

The High Prince has been unhelmed.

No, I think. *He's not the High Prince anymore.*

I look at Kairyn. Emotionless. Still. Radiating with power.

Maybe it was done in the name of their creed, but it was done with villainy. "You betrayed us," I snarl under my breath. Flames flicker on my fingertips. "I'm going to make you pay—"

Strong arms wrap around me, pinning me to an ice-cold chest. "Control your anger," Kel rumbles in my ear. "Now is not the time nor place. Ezryn must complete his punishment. Otherwise, it will all be for nothing."

My rage cracks, and a sob breaks out of me instead.

"I know," Kel whispers, his own voice raspy. "I know."

Ezryn kneels atop the dais, chin up. His face—his beautiful face I only discovered yesterday—is stoic, impassive. But I feel it through our mate bond: a shame and guilt like I've never experienced. The weight of it has me clutching at my chest. I want to run away and throw myself into the dirt, never to see the light of day again.

"One last thing." Kairyn's voice echoes hauntingly. He whips a slim knife from the folds of his black cape. "All who look upon you henceforth will know you as creedbreaker."

He grabs Ezryn's chin and jerks his head to the side.

Ezryn does not resist as Kairyn slides the knife along the tip of his pointed ear, arcing it in a curve. Cutting off the point, rounding it like a human's. A flick of his wrist and he's done. The tip of Ezryn's perfectly pointed ear falls to the dais in a wet slap. Blood drips down his face, down his neck.

I fall then, an unhuman scream wrenching itself from me. Shaking, I clutch Keldarion's leg and vomit on to the ground.

Another wet slap, and I know Kairyn has taken the tip of Ezryn's other ear. I need to stand. I need to be there for my mate.

"Help me," I croak.

Keldarion lifts me up, and I can tell by the tremor of his fingertips, the cold prickling in the air around us, he feels the same as I. But his tortured gaze confirms my own thoughts. *We must bear this for Ezryn.*

"You are no longer welcome in Spring," Kairyn calls out. "You are the Traitor Prince. The Matronslayer. Let it be known what your people think of betrayers as you make your final walk through the city."

Ezryn's deep brown eyes flash, but he says nothing. Blood drips along the sides of his face. He takes a step down the dais. Then another.

"Boo!" a citizen screams. "Matronslayer!"

"Shame!" another screams.

My throat tightens. "Be quiet. All of you."

But the voices are a chorus now, shouts of murder, of disgrace. They make way, parting before Ezryn with each step he takes.

I can't let him do this alone. I push off from Kel and run after him, shoving my way through the crowd. The other princes run right behind me.

My heart hammers as I try to keep my eyes on him amid the throng. He walks so stiffly, so proudly, shoulders back and head held high, blood dripping behind him. But inside, he's breaking.

"You have brought shame to Spring!" one fae man calls from the edge of the path. He whips back his arm and tosses. A rotten head of lettuce smashes against Ez's shoulder. Ez flinches, then keeps walking.

"I'll fucking cut his arm off," Dayton growls, but Farron places a hand against his chest.

"And if we interfere, what will happen to Ez then? This isn't our dominion, Day."

"Then I'll fucking cut Kairyn's head off," Dayton snarls back.

Farron gives a pained expression. "That's not what Ezryn wanted. He willingly passed on the Blessing. He truly believes Kairyn is the most fit to rule."

"Yeah, well, Ezryn's an idiot," Dayton mumbles, but doesn't make a move toward the citizen.

As much as my heart is breaking, I know Farron's right. This *is* Ezryn's will. He would never forgive us if we retaliated against his citizens or interfered.

So, all I can do is push my way through the crowd, staying near him as we walk solemnly between his parted people. Or those that used to be his people.

A hiss roils up from someone on a balcony. "Long live Princess Isidora!" she cries, then throws a small rock. It clips Ezryn in the brow. More blood oozes down his face. He doesn't look toward his assailant, but only keeps walking.

It's as if these few have emboldened the others. More heckles rise. A tomato smacks against Ezryn's chest, then a small clay pot cracks against his thigh. He buckles but keeps walking. A rotten stench roils up into the air as refuse flies into his path, landing on his shoulders, his arms, his hair.

Tears stream down my face. "Stop it," I whisper. "Please, stop it." I want to shield him, want to wipe away the blood and sweat and debris that mar his body. But there's nothing I can do. The thought makes me feel useless, weak. Feelings I never wanted to experience again.

"Move," Farron growls beside me, shoving people out of the way. Some move with indignant looks, others too focused on Ezryn to care. But this person is rooted to the spot, swaying, eyes wide and unblinking. Farron shoves them again, but they don't budge.

"Come on." Dayton grabs both mine and Farron's hands and pulls us forward, so we don't lose sight of Ezryn. Kel has already muscled his way far ahead.

"He hasn't got much further to go. It's almost over," Dayton says lowly, squeezing my hand.

I want to take solace in that fact, but I can't. Because I can feel the blood on my own face, the disgust and judgment of these people as if they're gazing at me.

"Have these plants always been here?" Farron mumbles.

"Now's not really the time, Fare," Dayton says, yanking us forward again.

The gates leading outside of the city lie straight ahead. Ezryn's steps are wobbly now, but we're almost there.

Farron pulls free of Dayton's grip. "No, look. These red flowers. They're the same as in the throne room. And they're all over the city."

"Matronslayer!" one of the soldiers guarding the gate snarls. He leans down and rips up a chunk of earth. "You will pay for what you did to our High Princess!" With a cry, he hurls the soil. It cracks against Ezryn's knee, and he falls.

I pitch forward, too, sobbing. The physical pain is nothing; my heart is ripping from my chest.

"Rosie." Dayton gathers me in his arms, then looks around. "Fare? Where did he go?"

Ezryn staggers up. His brow is coated with blood, one eye bruised from a rock. He takes a trembling step toward the gate.

"Shit, he's looking at those damned flowers," Dayton grumbles, peering over the crowd to find Farron. "I'm getting you outside of the city, then I'll grab him."

I can't even speak. My vision is blurred with tears. One step at a time. That's all I can manage. Once we're outside the city, we'll be together. It will be okay.

A wind courses down the streets and over the gathered people, carrying Kairyn's voice: "And so our city is rid of the Traitor Prince. Let us usher in a new dawn for Spring!"

With Kairyn's words, Ezryn takes his final steps out of the gate and leaves his home city behind.

Relief floods through my breast as I watch him step behind the huge doors. Kel is waiting at the entrance and wraps his arms around me and Dayton. "Farron?" he asks.

Dayton rolls his eyes. "Got distracted, as usual. I'll grab him once I see Ezryn's safe."

Kel nods, then slips us out of the doors as they slam shut.

We stand in the grassy, tree-covered forest outside of the city. The jeers of the crowd fade away, and finally, I feel like I can catch my breath.

Kel steps forward, looking around. "Ezryn?"

He's not in the small clearing. But there are so many trees, he must have just—

"Well, well, well, that was a moving little ceremony, wasn't it?" A woman's voice cuts through the quiet.

She steps out from behind one of the trees, her shimmering blue dagger held at Ezryn's throat.

The Nightingale.

Three helmed knights flank her. My heart seizes. Two of them carry divine weapons: one a lance, one a trident.

I've seen these weapons before at the top of Queen's Reach Monastery. Didn't the legend say they were only to be wielded by the Queen's chosen?

A mask shrouds the bottom half of her face, but her blue eyes flicker with mirth. "Keldarion, handsome, be a good dog and hand over your sword."

The ground goes out from under me. Sharp needles dig into my flesh as her brambles wrap tighter and tighter around me, digging into my skin.

The Nightingale's eyes smile up at me before she turns back to Kel and Dayton. "Or I'll pluck the life right out of your pretty little Rose."

90

ROSALINA

The Nightingale throws Ezryn to the ground and waltzes over to me. I squirm, suspended in her briars' hold, but each movement sends thorns digging into my skin. She runs her dagger along my collarbone and narrows her eyes at me, observing, judging. "Today is a good day."

Ezryn staggers to his feet, clothes ripped, ears bloody. Instead of addressing the Nightingale, he looks to the three knights. Their armor is fine, gleaming in dark jewel tones: one bronze, one turquoise, the other sapphire. "You are the Penta Conclave. Kairyn's men. This woman is a servant of the Below."

The knights stay silent.

Ezryn's eyes widen. "Those weapons you wield are sacred to the Queen. There's an enchantment on them. If you use them without bearing the Queen's token, a precious necklace gifted to the High Rulers, it will eat away at you, body and soul. Do not be swayed by this witch. It will destroy you!"

The Nightingale laughs and drifts away from me. Every movement is like a dance, rhythmic and flowing. "Witch? That's rich, coming from the creedbreaker." She stops in front of Ezryn. "But you're not just a traitor, are you? You're also a fool." She turns and reaches under the breastplate of the Bronze Knight who bears the lance, pulling out a necklace.

Farron's necklace.

Then she goes to the knight clad in turquoise, holding the trident. From him, she pulls out Dayton's seashell. Ezryn's mouth drops, shock shooting across his features.

Then she walks to the weaponless Sapphire Knight. Slowly, almost sensually, she reaches beneath his breastplate and holds up Keldarion's snowflake necklace. "My brother succeeded at one thing, at least. But I still need that sword, Kel. You're not really fit to wield something called the Sword of the Protector, are you?"

Kel bares his teeth but says nothing.

The Nightingale looks at Ezryn, covered in blood. "I mean, come on. Look at him."

I writhe against my binds. Warm blood drips from scratches on my wrists. I need to bring flame to my hands, to burn everything down, but my body feels weak from last night. "Stop this! Tell us what you want. We don't have to be enemies."

"What I want?" She pitches her voice up in a girlish way. "Ooh, let's see. I want the princes on their knees begging for their lives. I want your pretty head on a pike so I can admire your beauty until you rot and wither. And, ah, yes. I want Keldarion's *fucking* sword."

My breath hitches. She's completely unhinged. What did the Princes—what did I—ever do to her?

Ezryn shakes his head and looks at the knights imploringly. "You are Kairyn's most loyal men! Why did you betray him for service to the Below?"

The Nightingale lets out a growl. "It's getting annoying how ignorant you are." She storms over to Ezryn and glares. "Do you truly think your brother forgave you for banishing him to the monastery all those years ago? You should have killed him, given him an honorable death. Instead, you desired to hide him away. I gave Kairyn purpose. I gave him a home. I gave him power." Her eyes glimmer. "And you just gave him Spring's Blessing. I hope your honor was worth the Spring Realm."

For the first time since his unhelming, Ez breaks. His expression turns from fae to feral, lips pulled back, brow furrowed. "Liar!" He lunges for her, wrapping his hands around her throat and throwing her to the ground.

"I'll kill you!" he roars, his full weight atop the woman. Her eyes widen with fear.

There's the flash of metal and the Bronze Knight cracks his lance across Ezryn's body. He falls off her, toppling to the ground. The Sapphire Knight leaps on top of him, drawing his fist back and pummeling his face. The Turquoise Knight stomps hard on Ezryn's hand.

Beastly roars emit from Dayton and Kel as they rush forward. But it's too late. The Nightingale sits up, coughing, and glares at me.

The briars twist, digging deeper into my flesh, thorns breaking skin and rooting into muscle. Against my will, I scream.

"Another step, and I stick her like a pig," the Nightingale growls.

Kel and Dayton stop, gazes darting between me and Ezryn. Pain roars in my chest as the knights deliver blow after blow against him.

"Stop!" I cry out, desperately reaching for my magic, for anything, but it feels so far away. "Stop!"

I never thought such hatred could be conveyed in only the eyes, but somehow the Nightingale does it. She holds up her hand. The knights stop, then back away.

Ezryn is a bloody pulp, lying face down in the mud. His clothes are rags, his skin ribbons. His dark hair is so matted with blood, it's plastered to his face.

"Now, that is quite enough of that." The Nightingale massages her neck. "Accept it, Ezryn. Your brother has a vision for a new world. One where he is not just the spare, the monastery boy. In fact, that old necklace of yours now belongs to him. And with it, he wields the Hammer of Hope."

Ezryn says nothing. If it weren't for the bond within my chest, I would wonder if he still breathes.

I have to do something. The briars that bind me … Are they any different from Caspian's? His thorns always fell so easily under my command. Surely, I can do the same.

I close my eyes and reach out my consciousness, trying to send the tendrils of myself into her briars. My magic slams against a barrier. I push harder, grimacing, but it's like trying to shove a boulder. Mine and Caspian's magic lined up so perfectly, we could flow one into the other. But I'm running against a dam here.

Kel steps forward. "The Queen herself gave the Sword of the Protector to Winter. It has been passed down from High Ruler to High Ruler for centuries. You would not be so bold as to threaten the Queen's order."

The Nightingale laughs. "Oh, I would be so bold. And then some. But very well, Keldarion. If you are so certain this sword belongs to you, then wield it. Cut me down. Slay me, mighty hero."

"Careful, Kel," Dayton murmurs.

But Kel has never been careful. With a roar, he dashes forward, drawing the sword from its sheath.

Then he cries out. Electric pain floods through me and I buckle, only digging myself further into the thorns. Kel falls to the ground, the sword skittering over the dirt. He clutches his wrist. Lines of black magic surge from his palm up his forearm.

The Nightingale strides over and slams a heel down on the hilt. "Annoying, isn't it, not to have the Queen's token? Makes it quite challenging to wield the weapons. Unless you're like my dear knights here. They were never so concerned about their pretty faces, anyway."

As if responding to her words, the Bronze Knight and the Turquoise Knight lift their helms. I gasp.

Their faces are no longer fae, but something tormented, disfigured. Dark veins pulse beneath rotten skin, leading to eyes flooded red with blood. Chunks of bone jut out, gleaming in the morning light. It's as if their skin has become too tight, their teeth and eyes and bone bulging out.

"Horrible thing that happens when you wield these weapons without the token. But thankfully, we've got four of them now," the Nightingale says lightly.

Kel crawls toward her. "I don't care what happens to me. You can't take my sword."

An irritated hiss surges out of her throat. "I tire of your heroics! Enough. Don't you understand, Keldarion? *I am in control.*" A thorn shoots out from the briar patch and lands straight at my neck. Every gulp I take forces the needle right into my jugular. "Do as I say, or I will bleed her out right now. And do not doubt me when I say it will be my *fucking* pleasure."

"Kel, stop." Dayton holds his hands up. "Just do what she says."

The Nightingale waltzes up to Dayton. Runs a hand down his bare chest. "Smart boy. Where's your little Autumn friend? Not that it really matters. We have everything we need from him." She looks behind her at the Bronze Knight.

Dayton only growls.

The Nightingale snaps her fingers, and the Sapphire Knight walks forward, picking up the Sword of the Protector. It gleams beneath the dappled light. "We can now wield four out of five weapons! And it wasn't even that hard." Her piercing blue gaze levels on me. "Only one more."

"You have my sword. Now let Rosalina go," Kel says.

But I can feel her hatred like I feel the pierce of the briars. She'll never let me go. I will my heart to still, my mind to focus. Hers may be different than Caspian's, but I *can* control the briars. I just need a little time to unravel it.

The Nightingale crosses her arms. "Sometimes I play this game where I try to figure out which of you is the most stupid. It's truly a hard challenge. You all keep vying for the top prize. But I have to say, you are the winner today, Keldarion. And that says a lot, figuring your little Spring mutt willingly gave up his Blessing to the man who's been conspiring to steal his throne."

Ezryn has stopped twitching now. The blood around his head has formed a large pool. If he doesn't receive medical care soon, he'll die. Tears spring to my eyes, but I force my breath to steady. I have to figure this out.

"You sure have a lot to say, don't you, sweetheart?" Dayton jeers.

"Maybe you should keep a diary instead of boring us with your monologues."

Her piercing gaze levels on him. "Perhaps you should work on not being a slovenly parasite. Maybe then you could finally find a mate."

Dayton stumbles back.

"Too close to the heart?" Laughter sounds in her voice as she turns to her knights. "Bind them."

"We gave you what you wanted!" Kel roars.

"You have *no* idea what I want."

Dayton and Kel exchange looks as the Sapphire Knight unclips two steel manacles from his belt and strides towards them.

The Nightingale waves a slender hand through the air. "Resist and I'll kill her, so on and so forth."

The Sapphire Knight pushes Kel and Dayton to their knees, hands bound behind their back. His helm tilts toward Ezryn's body, bloody and broken. "What of the Spring Prince?"

"Leave him for the wolves. I got in enough trouble with Kairyn last time." She points to the Bronze and Sapphire Knight. "Deliver these two to Kairyn, with regards from his little bird. I'm going to the monastery." With bouncing steps, she walks over to me. I shudder, surging my magic through the briars, trying to get something to catch, to spark. "I want to have some fun with my new pet."

Then all I can hear are Dayton and Kel's screams as I'm whipped away beneath the earth by briars beyond my control.

PART FIVE
VENGEANCE

91

EZRYN

The darkness is retreating.

No ... No. I must hold on to the shadows.

Without it, the pain comes. The remembering.

There are voices drifting through the edges of my mind.

"Where's that salve?"

"I've got it. Here's the poultice, made just as you said."

"Good, good. Now, pass me the waterskin, dear. Thank you."

Light glimmers and ripples on the fringes of my vision. These voices are familiar.

"I think he's waking up."

"You're all right, chap. Bit of a tug on your brow as I stitch it. Don't move."

"Heart rate is stronger, isn't it?"

"His breathing, too."

"Hang in there, Prince Ezryn!"

Who ... Who could say my name without disgust? Who is left that can bear to look at me? Not my father or brother. Not my people. And after the shame I brought upon her, not my mate.

My mate.

Gone.

My eyes open.

Three blurry faces waver above me. I blink until they come into focus.

Eldy. Marigold. Astrid.

With my vision comes the rest: blaring pain in my skull, my ears, my shoulder, my leg, my ribs. Every piece of me aching and raw. The memories come next. Armored gloves and boots pounding at my bones. Divine weapons in the hands of thieves.

I should be dead.

I force myself to a sitting position. The three of them take to fussing: hands on my back, the clucking of tongues.

There's no time for this.

"You should stay lying down," Astrid says. "You were in rough shape when we found you."

I put a hand to my brow, feeling the sutures. Eldy has always had a steady hand with a needle and thread. Then I touch my ears.

The skin is rough and hot. Cauterized. Another healing trick of the majordomo.

My honor—my helm—wasn't enough for Kairyn. He had to mutilate me, too.

"How did you find me?" I ask, voice raw.

"We weren't going to stay in that city without you." Marigold crosses her arms. "Not with the boy-tyrant running the shop."

"Where are we?" I put my hand on Eldy's shoulder to hoist myself to my feet. Astrid gives a cry of alarm and immediately runs to my other side, helping to steady me.

My head clears a little as I look around. I don't recognize it—it's a barren wasteland. Dead grass wilts over dry soil. A waterfall roars, running into a black lake. And a bone-white willow tree stands sentinel in the middle of the grove...

"This is my doing," I whisper.

"Lie back down, dearie," Marigold says softly. "You've been through enough."

Eldy looks at his feet. "We didn't know where else to take you. All of Spring is under Kairyn's watch. And Prince Daytonales and Prince

Keldarion are being held captive. There is no word on the location of Prince Farron."

My voice is low, controlled. "Where. Is. She."

Their wary glances at one another are all I need to know.

They took her. The witch and the knights. *They took her from me.*

I push away from the group.

Marigold runs beside me. "Where do you think you're going?"

"To save her."

"Sire, you're still injured!"

Though my bones are bruised, my skin torn, I have breath in my lungs and my heart still beats. I don't even bother to look at them as I find my footing and stride forward. "You three have seen me well tended. You have my gratitude."

Now, it's Eldy who stands in my path. His eyes waver, a pained expression on his face. He was my father's most loyal advisor all these years, a mentor to me as I grew. He was always more family than servant. And now he stands before me in defiance. "Ezryn, you have no weapon."

"I will make do." I push past him.

His voice rings out true, honest: "You have no Blessing."

The reminder rips through my body like fingers plucking at the empty part of me.

Stupid, trusting fool, Kairyn laughs in my head. *You always had to be perfect, didn't you? The perfect son. The perfect leader. The perfect brother. Your self-righteous honor led you to giving up the one thing that may have been able to save her.*

Rosalina's face flashes in my mind: the look of horror as I marched out on to the dais. The defiance when she leapt before me and faced my brother.

When she first looked at me—truly looked at me—in the grove. For the first time in my life, I was seen. A sacred witness. My mate, our bond forged from the stars...

And they *have* her.

My steps thunder as I storm toward the willow tree. There's something cracking inside of me, all the barriers I built crumbling down.

I accepted when he broke his banishment.

I accepted his punishment on the dais.

I gave him the stewardship.

I gave him Spring's Blessing.

Because I believed it was what was best for the Spring Realm.

Because it was our way.

But Kairyn was working with the Below. Kairyn not only betrayed me, but our realm.

Both of us, traitors to our realm. I do not deserve mercy for what I've done.

Why should he?

I tried to save Spring. I tried to help my brother.

Now I will raze them to the ground if I have to.

Kill them all, Kairyn says.

I stand before the willow tree. This was where the first sacred blood was spilt. By my hand. My mother's blade shines from where it's embedded in the trunk.

I place my hands on the hilt.

There are voices behind me, shouting, asking me to slow. I ignore them. There's only one voice I'm listening to now.

Kill them all.

But it doesn't sound like Kairyn anymore. And distantly, I realize...

It was never his voice.

It was always mine.

I have always been the demon.

With all the strength left in me, I pull on the sword. A screaming sound tears from the trunk of the tree as the blade rips loose.

I hold it up, examining it in the light. Still sharp.

Kill them all.

For Rosalina, I will do it.

For Rosalina, I will do anything.

92

ROSALINA

A dull ache pounds in my head, and my mouth feels dry and cottony. I open my eyes and try to orient myself. Rainbow light filters in through stained glass in a rounded room. The High Tower of Castletree?

No. There aren't enough briars here, only a few scattered along the floor. Oily, iridescent ones. The Nightingale's thorns.

Slowly, my vision clears. I'm in the monastery's highest tower, the one Kairyn brought me to.

"Oh, so you finally decided to join us?" a sing-song voice chirps. "I thought you were out for good."

"Where are the princes?" I growl. I'm not restrained, just lying on a small wooden bench.

The Nightingale doesn't answer, busily rearranging some glass jars, chalices, and vases of flowers on a windowsill. She hums to herself, the sound muffled beneath her mask.

This is where they housed the Queen's weapons, but there's only one left: the rose gold bow.

In front of the elevator are two soldiers. The Queen's Guard, I heard them called last time I was here. Their faces are stoic, spears behind their backs.

And beside them is one of Kairyn's Penta Conclave. His turquoise armor gleams, and he wrings his hands on the hilt of a trident. A chain with a single seashell dangles from his neck.

"That belongs to Dayton, you fucking bastard!" I snarl, surging up. "What did you do to him?"

The Nightingale turns, sighing. With the flick of her wrist, briars ensnare me. I try again to take control of them. But it doesn't feel like before when she was blocking me.

No, I feel nothing at all.

I try my fire next, but there's not even a tiny whisper of magic.

It's like I'm human again.

"We have all the weapons, and almost all the Queen's tokens." The Nightingale smirks. "We're closer to our goal than ever."

Her eyes drift to the center of the room, where the bow sits.

You're not wielding all the weapons. The roses on the bow are so like the one on my necklace. But Caspian didn't hand over my moonstone rose with the rest of them. Is it a token, too?

It doesn't matter. I need to get out of here. I try to reach for my mate bonds, screaming out to them. *Kel! Ezryn! Farron!* But even my thoughts feel trapped inside.

The Nightingale gives another long laugh. She waves a near-empty glass chalice, a few drops of black liquid swishing within. "This marked a significant breakthrough for me, one of several I've experienced lately. Once this circulates in your bloodstream, it will eliminate all traces of magic, thorns, and mate bonds. Now, you're no better than an ordinary human."

No wonder she hadn't felt the need to chain me. "Where are the princes?"

"Is that all you're worried about?" She makes a mock pouting face. "Can't even be bothered to praise my wonderful accomplishments." She gestures to the windowsill with a flourish, displaying all her vials, glasses, and vases of flower buds.

"I don't care—" I begin, then stop. If she wants to tell me how she sapped my magic, then I'm all ears. A purple flower bud catches my eye. "You're the one who poisoned Ezryn and me by the willow tree."

She lightly strokes the purple flower. "I wish it were my own creation, but no. That little botanical beauty is a mix of Kairyn's magic and Quellos's twisted experiments. A flower with pollen capable of producing hallucinations crafted from your worst nightmares. You must agree, it was highly effective."

The memory of Ezryn's screams sends a shiver down my spine. Fucking Perth Quellos, working for the Below. He finally found a place to appreciate his despicable mind. I need to keep her talking. "Did Quellos figure out how to steal my magic, too?"

"Don't give that bald weakling all the credit. Sure, his little greenhouse of horrors may cultivate these beauties, but I brewed the potion." She picks up a black flower and brings it to her nose, covered by her mask. "Perfectly safe as is, but when I found just the right chemistry ... Your little spark of magic is nothing more than ash."

"You're using the beauty of Spring against its own people," I say.

"Spring was rotting anyway," she snarls back. She picks up the vase, tracing her hand over the bouquet of budding flowers. "Mother never appreciates my potions. Says I'm wasting my time. But look what Kairyn, Quellos, and I have done. Purple flowers for nightmares, black for magic suppression. But these beautiful red ones are the star of the show."

I blink my eyes. I've seen those flowers—they're everywhere around Florendel. They were even in my room. "What do they do?"

The Nightingale beams down at the red bud. "Once it blooms, it expels a pollen that turns one's mind into an empty space and links it to a host of my choosing."

No wonder water had been the cure both for my nightmares at Sylvanita Lake and when I was up the mountain. I needed to clear my nose of the poisoned pollen. I look around the room, searching for a carafe or jug. Maybe water could cure my magic suppression...

But no. She'd said the black flower had to be brewed in a potion and ingested. I'll need an antidote. And more information. "Who is the host?"

The Nightingale blinks at me, pride shining in her eyes. "This special bloom will turn one into a symbiont of High Prince Kairyn."

I gasp. He was the one who told the acolyte to stick them in my room... "Kairyn's been trying to kill me all along."

"Well, he doesn't have the balls to kill his brother," she says sharply. "But unhelming him and cutting up his ears was pretty good, wasn't it? And since you're still alive, I get to have you all to myself."

No, no, this isn't good. There has to be a way to stop all this. Has to be something that can get me out of here. "That's it, then? You didn't grow a flower with nice magic at all?" I say in as snarky a tone as I can manage. "What about the yellow flower?"

The Nightingale plucks it from the bouquet and laughs. "Oh, this is as far from nice as you can get. It's not used for a quick puff of pollen or in a potion. You grind the petals for this one, you see. Put it in food or tea. Can't even taste it. And slowly, bit by bit, your mind weakens. Your muscles, too. Turns you feeble. You think you're getting sick, but truly you're becoming ... better." A crazed gleam flashes in her eye. "It can turn a simple rat into a monstrous beast of vine and teeth. Or a fae into a ... Well, we're not sure yet. But we'll see soon enough."

"You're the monster," I spit.

"So Mother likes to tell me."

Fear sends my whole body shaking. "Where are the princes?"

She sets down the vase. "Alive, if that's what you're so concerned about. I've left Ezryn to wander and die in whatever shameful way he sees fit, an idiotic requirement of his brother."

"Kairyn is a fucking traitor!" I spit.

She whirls to me, glaring. The briars tighten, thorns pricking into my flesh. "And he's the only reason that mate of yours is still alive. You should thank him. If it were up to me, the former High Prince of Spring would be dead."

I match her glare, refusing to show my pain. She sighs and releases the hold slightly. "The High Princes of Summer and Winter are being held in Keep Hammergarden. Or are you actually asking about my brother? Wouldn't that be interesting if you were? In which case, yes, he's alive. Mostly."

Panic rears through me and my mind screams, *Caspian! Caspian?* But there's nothing. "Where is he?"

"He was a very bad boy," she purrs. "Letting all those princes and you escape, lying to Mother."

"He saved your stupid life, and he took the blame for that rat monster you set free."

"Then he's forgotten every lesson he taught me about surviving in the Below," she says. "It's your fault. You're making my brother soft."

"Like I have any influence over the Prince of Thorns."

"You really have no idea, do you?" Her gaze narrows to slits resembling a cat's. She doesn't look much like Caspian, but her mannerisms, the tilt of her head, even the cadence of her speech are eerily similar. "Well, he's being punished. Don't worry. Painful as it is, he's used to it."

Horrors pass through my mind at what Sira could be inflicting on him in the Below. But she wouldn't kill him, would she? Not her own son.

"Mother is very interested in you, *Lady of Castletree*. My brother made me promise to keep all your secrets from Mother, but who knows? Maybe I'll tell her. He left me without my Dreadknights after all. Though I am curious—do you know why you can create the thorns?"

I stare at her. The way she worded it, like *she* knows, and I don't understand at all. Caspian knows, too. His words from his birthday party when I questioned him on the shared power come back to me: *'Gift or legacy, the magic is the same, wouldn't you agree?'* He'd flashed a golden bracelet inlaid with roses. "How can you control the briars?"

She tilts her head. "The same reason as you."

Her thorns fall away, and I rub at my arms, scratched up and down. "What do you want with me?"

"Kairyn said you wore a moonstone rose necklace, but all Cas retrieved from you was this." From beneath her armor, she pulls out a golden leaf necklace, the one I was gifted from Farron's father.

"That belongs to me," I snarl.

She shakes her head, tucking it away. "It is pretty, even if it's not magical. The only thing I care about is the location of the moonstone. The one that belonged to your mother."

They'll just try to take it from you again, Caspian had told me. He was right. Though I'm certainly not going to tell her that. *Lie.* I have to lie to her.

She storms closer. "You had it the night of the jubilee. Where is it now?"

"Maybe I wouldn't have lost it if you hadn't set a giant rat on me!" I hiss, the anger coming easily.

She straightens. "Lost it? Hmm, well, there are ways to find magical artifacts. Or it could just be a piece of junk. You'll never know though."

"I am mate to the High Prince of Autumn and Winter. Holding me here will—"

"Without the necklace, you're of no further use to me," she interrupts. "But Mother is curious about you, especially after your thorny display in the Below. And because Caspian tried so hard to hide it from her. Do you know why he's so interested in *you?*"

"I don't know," I lie.

"No matter." The Nightingale turns back to her potions. "Mother wants me to deliver you to her in the Below."

My gaze shifts out the window over the top of Mount Lumidor to Florendel. The Nightingale thinks I'm useless without my magic. But she doesn't know I made it to the Enchanted Vale as a human. I fought goblins and protected the princes and ran through a battlefield as a human. It's something I'm quite well-versed at.

And this human will escape and find her princes.

"If I'm wanted in the Below, why take me here?"

She whirls. "Because I'm preparing myself to tell Mother you perished from your wounds before I could deliver you."

"But I'm not hurt."

Then, the Turquoise Knight stabs me with his trident.

93

KELDARION

T hat bastard has my fucking sword. The Sword of the Protector sits sheathed on the back of one of Kairyn's Penta Conclave, the icy hilt gleaming in the sun. It's strange to have despised a thing for so long, now to yearn for it with every fiber of my being. It had always been within arm's reach, yet I never took it up.

No, Caspian had to hand it to me. Then he took my token, and servants of the Below stole my sword. Was it all part of his plan? I don't know. Stars know where he is now.

"What more does this tyrant have to say?" Dayton growls, chained beside me. They shackled both our wrists and ankles with Spring steel, then forced a vile potion down our lips. With that, the last traces of my magic disappeared. I can't even feel my bond with Rosalina.

But we will be reunited again. She's strong. It will take more than the Nightingale to break her.

I turn my attention back to Dayton, following the Summer Prince's gaze. Kairyn's seen fit to lead us back out to the dais in the public courtyard, once again gathering the people of Florendel. Vases of large red flowers, not yet bloomed, decorate everything from the courtyard to the nearby houses.

Kairyn has also dragged out his father, Thalionor. This elderly prince, slumped in his chair, tended by acolytes, is nothing like my memories of the strong and powerful leader.

Two of Kairyn's Penta Conclave flank him. One wields my Sword of the Protector, the other the Lance of Valor. Our necklaces are preventing the further decay of these knights.

A great crowd has gathered. They speak in hushed tones, murmuring about seeing two High Princes chained.

"Word will spread," I whisper to Dayton. "Our realms and Autumn will learn of the treachery and send reinforcements. He cannot possibly think he can hold us."

Dayton nods, still desperately scanning the audience. It's late morning now. I can only hope Kairyn will send us to our cells before nightfall. I can't summon my wolf willingly with this damned potion in my veins, but I'm certain the Enchantress's curse will overpower it. Perhaps we do want him to continue his speech until dusk.

So what if the people of Spring see us change into beasts? It matters not if it gets me closer to saving Rosalina. And Ezryn...

Where is he now? Powerless, weaponless, alone. *He's looking for Rose.* I know it within my heart. *He's looking for our mate.*

"People of Spring!" Kairyn calls out, silencing the crowd with the boom of his voice. "We have witnessed a great tragedy today. My brother's betrayal, the prince who swore to protect you."

"The only betrayal was yours," Dayton grumbles under his breath.

"But we of Spring are forged of fire and iron will!"

A cheer arises, and I see the desperation in the people's faces. The panicked need for reassurance that everything will be okay. But some faces in the crowd are completely blank, no emotion at all.

Kairyn paces on the dais. "From this tragedy, I will craft us a stronger, better future. We will usher in a new era for Spring. A glorious beginning of goblin and fae!"

My blood runs cold. "What?"

Down the street, the massive gates of Florendel open wide, unveiling hundreds of goblin ranks, marching in well-organized formations. Spring guards on horseback accompany them on both sides.

A chant rises from the goblins, like the steely bang of a drum: "Kairyn. Kairyn. Kairyn."

"This is fucking madness," Dayton growls, voice nearly lost to the chant and the rising cries of the crowd.

Some citizens stand shocked, barely able to move out of the way of the approaching army. Others begin vocalizing their protest. Fae swarm toward the dais.

"You're mad," I snarl at the new High Prince. "Your people will never accept this."

They may have reluctantly accepted Ezryn's banishment, but to work with the monsters that raided their towns and villages for hundreds of years? Kairyn has truly turned against reason.

In answer, Kairyn spreads his arms to the side, palms to the sky. Magic crackles. I swing my head from side to side, watching as every red bud that decorates the rooftops, the lampposts, the awnings, bursts into bloom. Their pollen catches in the wind and swirls through the crowd.

The uproar dies. I gaze in terror as a fae, fist clenched with anger, quietly lowers their hand, eyes growing distant. They step back to make room for the approaching goblins.

"People of Spring," Kairyn continues, "only together can we topple our true enemy. The High Princes who have hidden in the castle while the rest of us have suffered!"

"I expected you to aid us in battling the forces of the Below," I bellow, "not to align with them!"

Dayton's eyes widen, and he surges forward with such a force, a small crack appears in his metal shackles. "Farron!"

I look through the crowd. Sure enough, there he is. But Farron's joined the growing chant. A chant both the goblins and the people of Spring now cry out: "Kairyn! Kairyn! Kairyn!"

"It's the plants. Once someone gets a whiff of that pollen, they're under Kairyn's control," I growl. Farron must have inhaled some when we were following Ezryn through the streets.

Dayton lets out a pained breath. Golden hair falls across his blue eyes. "Fare..."

The goblins now stand among the fae, their cheer growing loud enough to shake the dais. A swirl of pollen hovers above Dayton's head. "Don't breathe—" I start when I feel a peculiar sweetness on my tongue. My mind drains to that strange space between sleep and awake. And my mouth moves not of my own accord.

"Kairyn," I chant. "Kairyn! Kairyn!"

94

EZRYN

There's a strangeness to my movement. Everything feels too loose, too free. I've spent my life bound beneath metal. But I've been stripped, piece by piece. Uncoiled.

My fingers tighten on the hilt of my mother's sword. In its reflection gleams the tall point of the monastery. That's where she is.

"Sire." Eldy hovers a shaky hand above my shoulder, then removes it. "The Queen's Army that remain are loyal to Kairyn, and they've been trained since birth. They will not let you pass. And without the Blessing—"

"There is no magic left within me." Some fae have minor magic, but Kairyn drained even that. "I don't need magic to get what I want."

Eldy's lip quivers, eyes darting to the monastery, then back to me. "It's not just the soldiers that live there, but also the Golden Acolytes. Their loyalties may be questionable but the Spring Realm royalty has always protected them. As their prince—"

I push past him and take the first step toward the monastery. "I'm not a prince of Spring. Not anymore."

95

ROSALINA

T he trident draws out of my stomach, soaked in blood, red as a rose. And for a moment, I don't quite believe it to be my own. Because I don't feel any pain.

There's only shock.

The Nightingale truly means to kill me.

I stumble back. There's a three-pronged gash through my dress, the tattered ends dripping.

Her laugh echoes through the small room, breaking whatever spell I'm under. The pain comes sharp and biting, like my skin is on fire. Two of the Queen's Army stand before the elevator. I'll find another way, then. I cry out, staggering across the chamber, throwing open the door. And come face to face with two lines of armored men and women.

More of the traitorous Queen's Army.

"Don't bother running," the Nightingale trills. "Our army has this tower completely occupied."

My desperation intensifies as I scrutinize my helpless, blood-covered hands. The realization strikes: magic resides within me, but it's imprisoned by that detestable flower.

There's a yank on my hair as she tugs me back, then slams me against a wall. With a menacing touch, she runs the tip of her dagger along my arm, leaving behind a slender, crimson trail.

Tears stream from my eyes. Helpless. That's what she's made me. "Please," I sob. "Think of what your mother will do if she finds out." If I stay here, I die. As little as I wish to see Sira again, if she takes me to the Below then perhaps...

Caspian, help me. Please, help me.

"Shut up! You don't know a thing about my mother!" The Nightingale pushes the dagger into my flesh, tearing through muscle.

I cry out, writhing as white-hot flashes of pain course through me. My knees give way, and she allows me to crumple to the floor.

"You think I can't handle my own mother?" The Nightingale delivers a swift kick to my gut, and I curl over. With no air to scream, all I can do is heave, trying desperately to force breath into my useless lungs. "What would you know, anyway? You don't even have a mother."

She backs away, snarling, and flies a fist into the wall before pacing the room. The other blurry shapes—the Turquoise Knight and the two guards—keep their gazes locked on me.

Slowly, I push myself up to all fours. My body screams in protest, blood dripping down in a steady stream. If I don't bind this soon, I'm going to faint.

"There's no way out for you. Why do you bother getting up?" she chides.

"Because I have something to fight for. I have someone to fight for."

Through the pulses of pain, I think of them. Kel, Ezryn, Dayton, and Farron. I think of Castletree and my friends. My father. Even the Prince of Thorns. Then the Enchanted Vale, a place I finally belong. And that is worth fighting for.

Tears stream down my face. Worth dying for.

The Nightingale kneels before me, snatching my jaw and bringing the dagger to my throat. "Why am I toying with you? A cat with a mouse. You're not worth it." She studies me like someone might study their reflection in a mirror. Her hands shake.

"W-what are you fighting for?" I whisper. "Tell me that, at least. Will my death help you with it?"

Her blue eyes widen. That color … Something painful clenches in my chest.

"Your death will quell the nightmares," she says softly. "Your death will finally bring me peace."

The cool metal presses harder against my throat, but I don't close my eyes. I keep them locked on her. "I hope it brings you that, at least."

Tears brim in her eyes and her hand shakes on the knife. "He's *not* right. I can do this—"

She drops the dagger. And then we're staring at each other.

A clatter sounds to the side of the room.

The Nightingale stands swiftly, dropping me to the floor. The elevator doors open, revealing a member of the Queen's Army. They're covered in blood. She exchanges hushed whispers with him, then turns.

"You, with me." She gestures for the Turquoise Knight to follow her, then turns to the two guards. "Don't let her escape. And don't touch her until I return."

Then she enters the elevator and descends.

I clamber back, grateful for this brief respite. Quickly, I tear the ends of my dress and tie them in a knot around my waist, staunching the blood flow.

My mind feels hazy with terror and from that magic suppression potion. I turn to her makeshift station. She wouldn't have an antidote here, would she? And if she did, how would I know which one it is? I'd just as likely poison myself as find the cure. Water helped me before with the other flowers, but I don't see any in this room. Besides, water cleared the pollen from my nose, but the Nightingale forced me to ingest her poison.

I can't get out through the door, not with the host of soldiers outside. The window? Throw myself out? Could I transform into a bird like Eldy? But if I can't even reach my elemental magic, I doubt I could reach that unknown power.

Last, my gaze shifts to the bow in the center of the room. Everyone who touches it burns up instantly, not the slow rot like the other weapons. That's what Kairyn had told me. What was the name of this again?

The Bow of Rad—

Large hands grab me by my bloody arm and yank. One of the guards starts dragging me across the floor.

"The Nightingale said not to touch her," his counterpart voices.

The one who grabbed me slams me down on a slab of stone that used to display one of the weapons. My ears ring with the force. His hands press so firmly on to my shoulders, I can barely move.

"I'm not going to kill her." He tilts his head. His armor is filthy, covered in dirt and grime. He turns to me, smiling. "I've already broken one vow of honor."

"What?" Ice fills my blood. "P-please. No."

The other guard stares at us, me on my back, his companion above me. He does nothing.

"You're pretty, even covered in blood." The guard licks his cracked lips and tilts his head so strands of sticky hair fall across his brow. "Can't wait to see it smeared across your pink skin."

In a burst of anger, I scream and kick out my legs. Connecting with his armor, I feel my knees bruising but don't stop. It makes little difference in his hold. Then I snarl and spit, sending a gob of saliva smack on his cheek.

He sneers, but it's the other guard who yells, "You fucking cunt!" Blinding pain explodes across my face as he hits me.

I choke, vision going blurry, the warm stream of blood running from my nose. Two sets of hands cover me. Disgusting, groping hands. I hear clinks of armor falling to the ground. The tearing fabric of my dress, and rough fingers digging into my legs.

And I scream again. A scream filled with so much terror, I barely recognize it as my own voice.

96

EZRYN

I push open the large metal doors to the monastery. One of the Queen's Army stands there, wearing leather armor with a spear slung across his back. He opens his mouth to speak, but I don't let the words fall.

I drag the sword across his neck, pushing myself inside the building as he chokes on his own blood. The entrance hall has three more soldiers. Their weapons aren't even drawn.

Giving a disappointed shake of my head, I launch at them, striking two across the back of their knees. I quickly dodge the one who finally draws his spear. He stumbles, off balance from the miss, and I push between the gap of his armor, piercing his kidney.

He drops.

There's the creaking of metal, and the elevator shoots up, carrying a bleeding soldier. His wavering gaze meets mine. He's only delayed the inevitable. I'm not surprised, nor disappointed. I'll start at the bottom and tear apart every inch of this damned place until I get her back.

Regardless, I wouldn't have used the elevator.

She is here, but the bond is weak, like a part of her is not answering my call. Every floor must be checked. Every level must be purged.

I take my first step up the monastery stairs, sword still slick with blood. There is no point cleaning it now.

Voices shout, and four more of the spear-wielding Queen's Army charge down the stairwell. There's confidence in their faces. They think having the high ground will give them the advantage, that I will be frail without my magic.

They're wrong.

The chant of their charge turns to a scream as I lunge at the first, the stairway only wide enough for one abreast. I throw him over my shoulder, and he clatters down the stairs, neck snapping at an odd angle.

The one behind stands horrified for a single second, but I am unbothered. Guts spill from his stomach with his jaw still dropped. The third turns to flee, and the kill is easy enough through his back.

The next level is a long hall, much of the same, waiting soldiers. But these men have heard the screams from below. And fear makes them sloppy.

I'm barely breathing hard as I walk up to the next floor.

This one is a narrow walkway with a single wooden door. Muffled voices sound behind it, cries of terror. Sword tight in my palm, I shove through.

Acolytes huddle among brooms and dusters. One, no more than a child, clutches a young fae woman, eyes closed as if to anticipate a strike. "Leave," I say. They tremble, like shivering blades of grass. "Now!"

Scrambling, they stagger down the stairs, over the blood and carnage.

I don't look back.

Queen's Army swarm the staircase of the next level, and the room beyond it. These soldiers know who I am. The word has spread, and the hiss of *matronslayer*, of *creedbreaker*, rings in the air. Rings in the air until their throats are slit.

I ascend with only superficial wounds. Glimpsing out a window, I'd say I'm more than halfway up.

The Queen's Army may have been trained to fight since birth, but none of them have seen combat. Have any of them taken a life before? Do they understand the precise force required on a blade to penetrate a man's flesh? Have they ever made a wrong move and caused the tip to become wedged between two ribs?

Level after level, they fall to my sword, my mind focused on only this task. I do not feel the ache of my muscles or the labor of my breath. The acolytes I let pass, but the soldiers will never drop their weapons. Not those corrupted by Kairyn. *How exactly did you sway their loyalty, brother?*

Bodies litter each floor, blood dripping down the black stairs like a river.

Did Kairyn think he weakened me after taking away the Blessing? No, he freed me.

I shoved my magic away after the death of our mother, learned to fight without it. The sword is the only weapon I need. I do not even need the beast.

Though he is no different from me. Tearing goblins with tooth and claw is surprisingly similar to butchering fae with steel.

Almost at the top of the monastery, the bond in my chest is as blurry as ever. But of course, this is where they would take her.

The corridor is wide, and I know she's beyond the door. Rosalina is so close.

But it's filled with soldiers of the Queen's Army. And Kairyn's left his best for last. Plated armor covers their chests and legs, helmets protecting their skulls. Each of them is armed with shield and spear.

"We've been given orders to take you alive, if you surrender completely." One steps forward, torchlight flickering on his helm. I wonder what his expression is beyond it, hidden beneath the shadows.

He can see mine clearly now. They all can. And based on the spears quivering in their hands, they know I'm not about to surrender.

I twirl my sword through the large standing sconce, letting the flames lick at the metal. "You don't think I climbed all those stairs just to get on my knees now, do you?"

Kairyn's left his best guards here. To protect his little bird and her prize. But he knew I'd come for her.

Coward Kairyn couldn't even kill me yourself. Had to get an army to do it.

Or try to.

"Then we have no choice," the soldier says. Twenty to one. Good odds.

Or it should be.

There's the sound of jangling metal as they affirm my decision, but I leave my blade in the flame, leave it there until the last possible moment, letting it bathe in the heat.

Wind brushes the side of my wounded ear as the soldier arcs his spear down. I lurch forward and drive the red-hot sword through his armor. It's as smooth as if it were his bare flesh. Pulling it out, he clatters to the ground, a heap of useless metal.

The others close in, but I swing my blade in a wide sweep, sparks flying as it cuts into steel.

A spear pierces me in the shoulder. I turn, sword stabbing the gap in the soldier's armor between head and chest. Then I duck out of the way, pulling the spear from me and using it to cut through another approaching soldier.

One by one, they fall beneath me. Two left, and my blade is still plenty hot.

Shaking, one of the soldiers charges. I cut clean through the steel, and he falls at my feet.

"You are an evil, vile creature," the last one yells, spear quaking. "This blood you spill will stain you forever."

His own sprays the ground next. And it's eerily quiet, besides his raspy breathing.

I stand above him.

"Monster. You're a monster," he gurgles.

"No." I drive the sword through his breastplate. "I'm a beast."

97

ROSALINA

No, no, no. *Please, no.* Not this. Desperately, I fight against the hold of the guard, kicking as he tries to force my knees apart. But he's *so* strong. I've lost so much blood, my mind is hazy. The other guard who hit me drops his pants. I thrash, throat raw with screaming.

The other one has grabbed my arms, but it's the slight turn of his head I notice first. The low surprised murmur under his breath.

A man steps into the room, no armor, face sprayed with blood. But his eyes are on fire. And they're on me. He drops his sword.

Ezryn. My lips form the word I can't speak. My mind desperately tries to call to him through the muddled bond.

He moves before the soldiers even let me go. He grabs the one above me by the neck and drags him to the side of the center stone tablet that still holds the bow. He slams the man's head down hard. Hard enough to break the skull. Hard enough to spray blood and brain matter. Hard enough to kill him in a single blow.

But he doesn't stop with one hit. He smashes the guard's head down again and again and again and again, until there's nothing but broken flesh beneath his fingers.

The guard who hit me lets me go, stumbling over one of the Nightingale's iridescent brambles, then vomits over himself.

Ezryn drops the mutilated guard to the ground and retrieves his sword. His eyes are ablaze with a terrible fury.

There's the screech of metal, and I whirl to the elevator. The Nightingale and the trident-wielding knight step out.

Her gaze shifts from the guard with his pants around his ankles to me splayed on the stone tablet. She draws a dagger from her hip and throws with deadly precision.

"Ezryn! Look out!" I scream, scrambling up, desperately shoving my dress down.

But the dagger wasn't aimed at him. It strikes the guard in the skull. He drops. The Nightingale waltzes over to retrieve her blade. "Disgusting creatures, men. Aren't they?" She shakes her head. "Regrettable. But I promise to make your death quick."

She draws another dagger and throws. Silver flashes, and Ezryn steps in front of me and knocks it away with his sword.

"Going to try and kill me too?" She sniffs, hand on her hip. "Half this monastery is already dead. You saw to that."

I pull myself up, gripping the back of Ezryn's shirt, needing that contact with him.

The Nightingale makes a clicking sound, as if considering. "Kai won't be happy about me killing you. But nothing will keep me from my vengeance. Even you, Prince of Blood."

With a wave of the Nightingale's hand, the Turquoise Knight charges. He hurtles his trident at Ezryn, who intercepts the attack, blocking and pushing his adversary to the side.

But it leaves me wide open for the Nightingale. She tilts her head, and her hood shifts slightly. Poking out from beneath her pointed ear is the white petal of a flower. A stardrop.

Odd. I wouldn't think she'd wear anything that isn't completely practical. She walks toward me, unbothered.

Desperately, I grasp the spear of one of the fallen soldiers and run at her. I toss it. She sidesteps out of the way easily. But the move brought me right beside her.

"Did you really think that would do anything?" she asks.

"No, but this will." I shoot my hand beneath her hood and snatch the white flower. Then stuff the whole thing in my mouth.

Because I've seen this flower before. Seen it pinned in the armor of Kairyn and his Penta Conclave. Seen the acolytes who work in the keep wear them behind their ears. Even Eldy wore one for a time.

This is the antidote.

That's why Kairyn's minions are always wearing them. He didn't want to chance one of his loyal followers being corrupted by any of this poisoned magic.

The white bloom negates the magic. At least smelling it does. When I walked up the mountain in a haze, passing a patch of them cleared my head slightly.

But I can't just smell this; the poison she gave me is in my system.

I gulp the petals down. *Either this will kill me or…*

"Stop!" the Nightingale snarls, drawing a slim blade and striking it toward me.

Or it will save us.

The Nightingale is too late.

My magic is back.

I feel for her iridescent thorns scattered throughout the room. She's not expecting my attack, and I easily make them my own, bringing them up as a shield around me. Her blade embeds in the briar, giving me a precious moment to think.

A quick glance shows me Ezryn is holding his own against the Turquoise Knight, despite the divine weapon.

I need to get to him. Then I can try to use the Nightingale's vines to carry us out of here.

A briar snags me around the ankle, and I fall.

"If you want to play with thorns," the Nightingale snarls, "you're going to get pricked."

"Likewise." I shoot out my hands, taking control of two briars. They writhe up, slashing across her stomach.

Ezryn lets out a grunt as the prongs of the trident rake against his shoulder. He twists, slamming his blade against the knight. The turquoise armor shimmers in the dim light as Ezryn's blade rebounds harmlessly off the breastplate. Gritting his teeth, Ezryn dances back.

The Turquoise Knight laughs, then twirls his trident until the whole thing glows and the smell of sea water infuses the room.

I need to concentrate on my own fight, but I can't take my eyes off Ez. I pull at the briars holding my ankle, tearing them loose, and scramble away from the approaching Nightingale.

With a huge force, the Turquoise Knight shoots forward and smashes Ezryn on the side of the head with the trident's shaft. He staggers backward, grabbing the bow's pedestal to steady himself.

"Careful! Don't touch it!" I scream.

Ezryn gazes up at the radiant weapon and hastily pulls his hand back.

The Nightingale drops her dagger and barrels down on me, fingernails like claws over my face, tearing at my hair. "Magic isn't enough to save you. You're not special. You're soft! Weak!"

I grab her wrists, eyes wide as Ezryn leaps away from the trident's pronged jab. The knight is too strong. Without the Blessing, he won't be able to—

Ezryn rolls, then stands before the pedestal, the bow's light silhouetting him in an ethereal glow. The Turquoise Knight gives a half-laugh, half-bellow, then charges, bloody points of the trident aimed straight for Ezryn's chest.

But my mate falls to the ground, whipping his leg out, tripping the goliath knight. In a crash of turquoise armor, the knight stumbles, the trident falling from his grasp. His bare hands reach out to steady himself—

Grasping on to the Bow of Radiance.

Blinding light envelops the Turquoise Knight, and his body convulses. A harrowing scream pierces the chamber. His armor cracks, then caves in on itself, becoming a puckered shell. The helmet flies off and rolls across the floor, landing right in front of the Nightingale. Left behind is a lifeless husk, and Ezryn, breath heavy as he stands victorious.

The Nightingale falls away from me and picks up the helmet. Her lip twitches. "Oh, you shall pay for that."

Thorns burst through the stone, striking Ezryn, and lifting him into the air. His silver sword slips from his fingers.

"Ezryn!" I call out, holding out my hands, trying to take control of her thorns.

"Not today!" The Nightingale glares at me, and I'm hit by a wave of her power. "These are *my* thorns. Make your own if you want to play."

I can't! I try to concentrate, but I don't know what I'm even reaching for. She's right. This is her magic. And I can't get in if she won't let me.

Anger rises through my chest, and flames erupt from my fingers. With a flick of her wrist, a large, oily briar slams into me, and I clatter against the stone table in the middle of the room. My ears ring, my vision blurry. Colors from the stained glass swirl over my arm, painting a wavering rainbow across my skin.

Ezryn struggles in the grip of the thorns.

"Oh, Prince of Blood," she purrs, "a tower of soldiers, one member of the Penta Conclave, and it was all for naught. Because you were never going to get past me."

Ezryn snarls, eyes blazing.

"There's only one thing left to decide." Her blue eyes flick to me. "Which one of you to kill first?"

I stagger to all fours. I need to help him. But how? I can't take control of her thorns. My magic is back—but it's nowhere near as powerful as hers. Though my whole body shakes from my wounds, adrenaline keeps me conscious. Adrenaline and spite.

"Oh, don't look so glum, Princess." She smirks. "Just make those little golden roses. Or was that another fairytale like the Enchantress and her beasts of the Briar?"

"That was no story," I say.

The air crackles with magic as Ezryn changes, one moment a man, the next a great black wolf. His jaws widen, and he swipes a massive paw at the Nightingale. She leaps back but isn't quick enough as he strikes her across the arm.

"I'm not so easily disposed of as your goblins, beast!" The monastery shakes with her rage. The stained-glass window behind her shatters, spraying crystal into the air. Thorns break through stone, covering the entire room.

It's like we're at Castletree, with its briars and beasts.

Her iridescent thorns ensnare the massive black wolf. Tears stream down my cheeks to see the wolf struggle and whine, huge thorns digging into his flesh. My fingers curl into a fist, a light flickering over the top of my knuckles.

Light from the Bow of Radiance that glimmers beside me. The weapon of the Queen.

You have everything you need right here. Caspian's words drift into my mind, and I place my hand over my heart, mirroring his movement.

Slowly, I stand, eyes on the glowing bow.

The Nightingale cocks her head. "That weapon doesn't belong to you, *human.*"

Except it does. It isn't the magic of thorns I wield, but that of roses, like the Queen planted in this realm. The magic of change, of object to element, or fae to animal. And the magic of realms.

Twenty-five years ago, my mother left. Twenty-five years ago, the Enchantress came to Castletree.

Or the disguised Queen returned to Castletree.

Words and images play through the hushed corridors of my memory; moments insignificant on their own now converging into a tapestry as clear as the one that hangs here in the monastery.

The Queen was fascinated with humans.

This magic inside of me is no mere coincidence.

It is my legacy.

You welcomed me home, Cas. You called me Princess because you knew. You always knew who I was.

I reach for the bow.

"Rosalina, no!" Ezryn calls.

"Touch that without the Queen's token, and it'll burn you up!" the Nightingale hisses.

"I don't need her token," I snarl and grab the bow. "I have her blood."

Power rushes through me, lighting me from within. The bow ripples and changes, golden vines growing along the staff. And as I hold it, my skin lights, glowing white-gold.

The Nightingale freezes, horror erupting over her features. Shock and reverence ripple in the wolf's eyes.

A string of glimmering gold appears as I draw my hand back, and an arrow of starlight rests on my sight. This may be a magic bow, but the aim is all my own.

And I aim at the Nightingale's heart.

"You don't need the token," she says, eyes widening. "Give me that bow."

I'm half-tempted to, just so I can watch her burn up.

I adjust my aim, and the arrow flies into the thorns. They writhe in golden light before shivering away in black dust. The wolf falls to the ground.

"Leave," I say, drawing another arrow and pointing it at her.

"Why would you spare my life?" she growls, almost cowering beneath the light of the bow.

For Caspian and the affection he holds for her. For another reason, I can't name. For the simple fact that I do not wish more blood on my hands. In answer, I only draw the arrow back further.

She hisses, then a tangle of new thorns start to rise. This I allow. Just enough to swallow her up and take her back to the Below.

The moment she's gone, all the energy leaves my body, and the bow drops. I fall.

Arms catch me, and I tumble against Ezryn's bare skin. We collapse together to the ground.

"Ez," I say weakly.

"I've got you," he murmurs against my hair. "I've got you, my Queen."

98

ROSALINA

Ezryn holds me fiercely. Shaking, I run my fingers up his bare arms, then clutch his face. The face that is new and familiar all at once. Dried blood splatters his cheeks, his nose, his neck.

It covers me, too.

My skin feels different, different even than when I transformed into fae. The glow hasn't entirely faded. I place my hands over my belly, where the prongs of the trident had gouged my skin.

It's healed.

I look up. Ezryn keeps me rooted with the deep brown of his eyes. My racing heart still refuses to settle beneath my breast. "How did you know I was here?"

A large hand gently cups my cheek. "I'll always find you."

Our bond alights between us, warm and welcoming. "How did you get to me?"

"There is nothing—*nothing*—that could keep me from you. No blood nor blade nor judgment cast upon me. I would tear my bones from the grips of death and offer a thousand more in my stead if it means you await me at the end of it all."

A desperate urgency simmers within me. A fire not yet put out. As if he can sense it as well, he passionately presses his lips against mine, fists curl in my hair. I clamber over him. He's still naked from his transformation from the wolf. We fall to the floor, stone covered with blood, bodies, and thorns.

"Nothing will take you from me," he growls. A darkness shines over his eyes as he makes quick work of my tattered dress. I need his hands over me, need them to replace every unwanted touch.

My fingernails rake across his chest, following the dark line of hair until it dips beneath the V of his hip bones. I grasp his cock before positioning it near my entrance and letting him slide inside. The sound that comes out of me is animalistic.

"Rosalina." He rises, keeping me in his lap, teeth scraping along my collarbone to my neck. He bites the sensitive skin, and I cry out, pushing down harder, moving frantically on his length.

Our mouths collide, messy, wet. I bite his lip, and the heat in me grows and grows and grows.

There is a fire in me that cannot be put out.

Ezryn spins us, gently laying my head on the ground. But that's the only gentle thing about it. His hands grip my hips, lifting them, as he sinks into me to the root.

We don't need words, our unspoken passion alive between us. This is completely visceral. He kisses me as we begin to move, long, powerful strokes. A wild, unfettered claiming.

The pulse of our bodies is rhythmic. The pleasure of my mate blocks out everything else. This is all I need right now. Him.

Without slowing his pace, he reaches between my legs and rubs my clit. A broken, guttural sound escapes me, and I claw at his hair. I need him closer, closer, closer.

"Ezryn, I'm ... Oh god, I'm—"

He clasps his hand over my mouth, and I bite down on his palm. He's not finished with me.

He drives deeper, harder, hands sweeping from my face, over my breasts, finally gripping my hips. His fingertips dig into my flesh as he slams into me again and again and again. I lose all sense of myself, becoming nothing but a wild thing. Tears streaming down my cheeks, I clutch him with everything I am.

Needing to become his. Needing to scream out the fear, the confusion, the power that radiates through me.

His head tilts, powerful muscles in his neck straining, dark brown hair wild. And I cannot hold back this wave anymore. I feel his crest within me.

My inner muscles clench tightly, then ripple in a wave of blazing heat against his pounding cock.

"Rosalina." He groans my name long and loud as he feels me pulse around him. Then he slams hard, releasing himself. I gasp, feeling his warmth fill me deep.

His weight collapses over me. I wrap my arms around him, vowing to never let him go.

I DIDN'T WANT to put on my tattered gown, so I opted instead for an undershift from one of the robes we found in a closet. Ezryn, his own clothes tattered, wears the white long-sleeve shirt and dark gray pants of the acolytes.

"How are your injuries?" he asks.

"I'll be all right, the bow healed me," I whisper. Before he can pull away, I cup his face in my hands. His ears are raw and red, the points jagged flesh. But there's nothing to be done about that now. "You are my mate, and I *love* you. We have bonded again. But your curse didn't break."

He's silent for a moment. It had almost broken at Sylvanita Lake. The rush of magic, the unfettered power of the High Prince of Spring … It had been too close to the memory of when he received his Blessing. My heart aches, imagining the pain and grief he must have felt.

But now that he's passed on his Blessing, he shouldn't have to worry about that supercharging of power.

Yet, his curse did not break.

Ezryn turns away. "I do not deserve to have my curse broken."

Perhaps it's not just the Enchantress's magic that must be satisfied.

My mother's magic, I think.

A chill wraps around me like a cloak as I turn to the Bow of Radiance lying on the ground. Papa had always painted my mother as compassionate. So why would she curse the princes and put the Enchanted Vale at risk? And the biggest question of all: *Where are you now?* Why didn't she return to me and Papa?

I sling the bow on my back. Ezryn stands beside the body of the Turquoise Knight, the token of the Summer Prince in his hand. He walks to me and places it around my neck. "For safekeeping until we return it to Dayton."

I press my hand over the shell, nodding. My eyes glisten, thinking of the other princes. "Can you feel them, too? Kel and Farron?" I ask.

"I can. They're alive."

The thought comforts me. I turn to the trident on the ground. "We can't leave this here."

"No. We cannot permit the enemy to possess these weapons."

"Going to be heavy for me to carry around," I say. But as my fingers graze the trident, it changes to a beam of light and streaks into the necklace.

Ezryn kneels beside me. "The tokens and the weapons are intertwined. During wartimes, this ensured the Queen's chosen always had a way to protect themselves."

"But Kel always kept the Sword of the Protector under his bed." A pretty stupid hiding spot, figuring my drunk ass and a bunch of goblins were able to find it.

Ezryn takes a deep breath. "The sword represented a lot of things to Kel. Things he wasn't ready to carry with him at all times."

I nod and rise to my feet. "We need to find the others."

We make our way to the elevator. It rattles and begins its descent. "Keep your eyes on the mountains."

I swallow in a dry throat, keeping my eyes fixed on the mountain range beyond. But even with my back turned, it does not block out the smell. *Prince of Blood.* That's what the Nightingale had called him. Just how many died so he could save me?

I would do the same to save him. To save any of them.

And as the elevator clangs to a stop at the bottom of the monastery, I know I may have to.

99

DAYTON

"Dayton! Day, please wake up."

An image swirls before me, and I'm not at all surprised by it. Loose brown hair, that heart-shaped face. "Rosie?"

"Please, we don't have a lot of time," Rosie says. And her eyes blaze like blue flames. "Take a deep breath."

I do as she says, mind clearing. *Rosie's eyes aren't blue.*

There's a hand on my face, a rough one.

"There you are," she says. Not Rosalina, but Wrenley. A cloak of blue covers her white and gold acolyte robes.

"W-what?"

She places a finger to her lips. Slowly, I take in my surroundings. In a cage of steel, looking out at the Hall of Vernalion, the throne room of Keep Hammergarden. It's eerily silent besides the deep breaths of Prince Thalionor, who is slumped in a chair next to the throne. The steward is looking rough, body shaking.

Kel stands in a cage beside us, completely still, eyes vacant.

Stars, had I just been like that?

"It's the red flowers," Wrenley speaks lowly. "They help others see the High Prince's reasoning."

"Turns them into mindless husks, you mean," I snarl under my breath. "How did you escape it?"

She touches her pointed ear where a white flower sits, and I mimic the movement, realizing she's placed one behind my ear.

"Kairyn told us all to wear these when we left the monastery," she says. "We thought it was a symbol, but I realized the pollen of the red flowers does not affect us. And if you chew a petal, it will restore your magic."

I do as she says, though no magic returns to me. I'm still on empty until I get home to Castletree. She shakily pulls a key ring off her belt. "Got these off a sleeping guard."

The lock clicks open and she grabs my hand, leading me behind one of the stone pillars. "Some of the acolytes are fleeing the monastery, fleeing Florendel. But I couldn't leave without you."

A hollowness tightens in my chest. "You're trembling."

Her hands squeeze into my shirt, and tears pool over her blue eyes. "It's just … I was at the monastery and … and *he* came."

She falls against me, and I instinctually wrap my arms around her. "Who came? Kairyn?"

"No." Her voice is soft, near empty. "Ezryn."

"Why would he…" Then I remember, that's where the Nightingale said she was taking Rosie.

"I don't know. Rage from his banishment, from losing his magic?" Her lip quivers. "He killed them all—every last one in his path. It was a slaughter. Everyone, even the women and the children. I barely escaped."

"No." I shake my head. "Ezryn wouldn't do that. He…" My voice trails off. There's always been a darkness in the Prince of Spring, one I've glimpsed in the feral rage of his beast. But losing his creed, his magic. What if something happened to Rosalina? "He wouldn't." But my voice has lost its conviction.

Fear is still plain on her face, and there's dried blood on her cheek. "We have to go. Quickly, before they return."

"I'm not leaving without Kel."

She keeps a firm grasp on my arm. "I don't have another flower. He could become dangerous if we move him."

I stare at the cage, the blank-faced Winter Prince inside.

"Kairyn won't kill him," Wrenley pleads. "He's too important."

"No." I yank my arm away. "I'm not being parted from any more of my family."

Taking the flower from behind my ear, I rip it down the middle. I place it under his nose, then stuff a petal between his lips. "Come on, big guy, wake up."

Wrenley grips the back of my shirt in earnest. "There's movement down the hall. We have to go. Leave him!"

I hear it too, the clatter of armor, that deep, commanding voice. The new High Prince of Spring returns.

"Breathe, Kel," I growl, practically shoving the flower under his nose. "Start the lock."

With shaking hands, she does. I don't want to put the girl in more danger, especially after she's been through so much, but I'll be damned if I lose someone else today.

The voices grow louder. Kel blinks, gasping, and the milky film fades from his eyes. Wrenley opens the door, and I grab Kel as he topples forward.

"There's no time to explain. Come on." I hoist his arm over my shoulder, and we stumble from the cage.

"This way, behind the tapestry. The servant's exit," Wrenley says.

We enter the small stone passage as the doors to the throne room open. Wanting no more to look on the wretched new High Prince of Spring than I would like to shove my dick through hot coals, I let the tapestry fall behind us.

Wrenley leads us through the twisting corridors until we exit in a small alley outside of the keep. By the sun, it's early afternoon. I rapidly explain the flowers to Keldarion.

"It's how he's getting away with this." Kel gestures to the main road where goblins march next to the citizens of Spring.

"The whole bloody capital is infested with these flowers," I say.

"What of Rosalina? Have you seen her?" Keldarion asks.

"No, I woke up two moments before you. But I think Ez is in trouble," I murmur, leaving out the murderous details until we get confirmation. "The Nightingale took Rosie. She mentioned something about going to Queen's Reach."

Kel absently massages his chest. "Yes, she's in Spring. I can feel her."

"We need to go. There's a hidden way out of the city," Wrenley says desperately.

"I can't leave Florendel," I say. "Not without Fare. He's in the crowd. We just need to get him one of these pretty white flowers."

"I'll follow my bond to Rosalina," Keldarion says. "Find Farron and we'll meet in the field of flowers outside Florendel."

I nod. "From there we can take the Equinox Pass through the mountains to Summer. My sister will aid us."

Keldarion grabs my forearm and shakes. "I will see you there, brother."

"Bring her back," I say and watch him walk away. "Now, to find that little Autumn leaf."

"It's too dangerous. We need to escape," Wrenley says. "He could be *anywhere*,"

"Then I'll look *everywhere*," I snap. "Either we all leave this capital or none of us do."

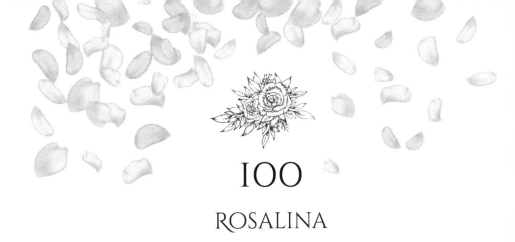

IOO

ROSALINA

We're rounding a rocky bend along the mountain when I see him and immediately take off into a run. "Kel!"

His pace increases, jog turning into a sprint, white hair blowing. Further down the mountain, I observe the distinct shapes of Astrid, Marigold, and Eldy. They came looking for me.

Tears well in my eyes, and suddenly Kel is before me. Damn, he's fast.

"Rosalina." He gathers me in his arms and lifts me.

I bury my face into his neck. "I'm so glad you're all right."

There's a presence behind me, and Kel places me down. "Ez."

Ezryn stands perfectly still, and Kel's gaze is intense. I realize this is the first time Keldarion has had a true moment to look at his best friend's face. Really look at him.

He steps close, placing a hand on Ezryn's cheek, and though Ezryn stiffens beneath his touch, he does not push him away.

"Ezryn," I say lightly, "the staff are coming. Do you wish to cover your face?"

Ezryn withdraws, brows lowering. "The creed means nothing to me now."

The words are final, and they leave a hollow place in me. "Dayton and Farron?" I ask Kel.

"That acolyte woman that's always milling about came and set Dayton and I free. The two of them are searching the city for Farron. He's alive, but under hypnosis from the flowers."

Wrenley, then. She really does care about Dayton. I chew my bottom lip. "Yes, the Nightingale explained all of her flowers. I see you've found the white ones." Tucked behind Kel's ear are a few white petals. I gesture to the small cloth bag around my shoulders. "We gathered some from the top of the monastery, just in case."

"Good," Keldarion says. "We're to meet them in the field of flowers outside Florendel. From there, we'll take the road to Summer, seeing as our tokens are missing."

I place my hand on my neck. "I have Dayton's."

Kel nods. "That will help."

If only I could summon my own thorns, but that power seems beyond my reach. I've done it three times before: in the Below, fighting Lucas, and saving Dayton, but I can't seem to find the key to keeping it.

"Did you see my father?" Ezryn asks.

His voice is so raspy and brittle, like he barely remembers how to speak. Like he only knows how to exist in the moments of pure adrenaline: in battle or fucking me on a blood-covered floor.

We need to get somewhere safe, I think, *then he can rest. Then he can recover.*

"He's in the Hall of Vernalion," Keldarion answers. "Ezryn, he does not look well."

"I can't abandon him to my brother."

"Then we don't leave Spring without him," I say.

"It'll be dangerous to go into a city full of goblins and infiltrate the keep," Keldarion raises a dark brow.

I put my hands on my hips. "You already know I'm not going to be left behind."

His rough hand cups my face, gliding along my ears. "That I do, Rose."

"M'lady!" a high voice calls from below, and I see Astrid, Marigold, and Eldy making their way up the hill.

I rush to meet them, embracing in a tangle of hugs. "I'm so glad to see you all!"

"I was able to send your letter before the trial," Astrid says. "Autumn will take good care of your father. I know it."

I give a sigh of relief. If I can't be with Papa right now, then there's no one better to look after him than Farron's family. "Thank you."

Eldy turns his attention to Ezryn. "Sire, I serve you completely. Creedbreaker or not, an infestation has taken over Florendel. I will not rest until you have reclaimed your rightful place."

Ezryn's fists tighten at his side. "I'm not a prince," he growls. "And I'm in no need of servants."

Eldy puts a hand on Ezryn's shoulder. "Then what about a friend?"

Ezryn walks away.

Keldarion grabs my arm and pulls me close, gaze fixed on Ezryn. "He's not right. What happened up there?"

"Something broke in him when he found out Kairyn was working for the Below," I whisper back. "He thought he was doing what was best for the realm, and it would offer him the redemption he's always needed. To find out it all meant nothing …"

"Ezryn has been holding in his emotions for years. Something has broken loose."

I hold tight to my mate's arm. "Kel, he tore apart the monastery to get to me. What if that part of him breaks again?"

"Then I'll stop him." Keldarion tugs me closer and kisses the top of my head. "We'll put him back together, Rose. It's our job to take care of Ez now." I let out a breath and step toward Eldy, taking the bow off my back. "Ezryn may reject his princedom, but I am a princess." A new confidence rises in my voice. "And I would be glad to have you in my service, Eldor of the Spring Realm."

"That bow…" Keldarion whispers.

"I believe," I say, running my fingers along the golden grip, light shimmering beneath my touch, "that my mother was the Queen."

"Your Majesty!" Eldy drops to his knees, gray hair failing.

Astrid and Marigold stare at me with matching wide eyes, then sink to the ground.

Keldarion looks between Ezryn and me, a smile on his face. "Princess."

"Did you know?" I ask breathlessly.

He shakes his head. "No, though I'm not surprised. You've always been the strongest of us all."

"I wish there was a way I could get you all safely to Castletree," I tell Astrid, Marigold, and Eldy. "There's no way to know what will happen to us when we venture into Florendel. If something goes wrong, someone will need to warn the rest of the staff about what happened in Spring, and that Kairyn could show up at anytime."

"Well, there is one thing I could try," Eldy says. He closes his eyes, concentration turning inward. A spark of magic surges in the air, and suddenly, the man is replaced by a small wren.

"You can still do it?" I gasp.

"Yes, mistress," the little bird peeps.

"Castletree is not far, as the crow flies," Keldarion says. "He could make it before nightfall."

I turn to Astrid and Marigold. "It will be safer there than here. There's no one better to lead the staff than you two. Will you join him?"

Astrid grasps both my hands. "From the moment Prince Ezryn put me in your service, Princess Rosalina, I have known there is something special about you. You showed me kindness even when you had no reason to. You have fought bravely for us. Beyond it all, you have become my friend. I trust you."

"Might as well try, girlie." Marigold smirks. "I won't have that birdbrain flying across the Briar with no one to watch his tail feathers."

I close my eyes, concentrating on the feel of Astrid's hands in mine. When I turned Eldy into a bird, it had been instinctual, a last-ditch effort at survival. But this is slower, more focused.

Magic rises in me like a tide, prickling along my skin. I let it fill me until there is no more room, then I open a stream from my fingers to Astrid, letting it flow from me to her.

Something shocks me, and I grip her hands tighter, like the bite of a snake.

There is already magic in her.

Powerful magic.

But it's magic I know to my bone. Like being taught a brand-new language in a single second. This is my mother's curse woven into her very being.

I understand it would be unwise to try to break it this way. Instead, I let my own magic pass through the cracks, settle in the empty spaces. Not a lot, just enough for one transformation of her own.

And once I find the spaces, it's surprisingly easy. I see the shape of my mother's magic, the artifacts of change.

This is just adding one more layer.

Sweat pools on my brow and upper lip. *Almost there ...* I push one last flood of power into Astrid and feel a bright sparkle. Light flashes beyond my closed lids.

With a gasp, I open my eyes to see a pale white bird fluttering before me.

"You did it!" Astrid chirps happily.

My face lights up with a smile as I swiftly turn to Marigold. A strange sense of sadness fills me as I feel her curse still inside. A torment that could be no more if we had broken Ezryn's curse.

Marigold's change happens quicker, and soon she becomes a larger wren, flapping golden wings beside the other two.

"When you get to Castletree, instruct the staff to start fortifications," I say. "Harvest whatever food you can from the gardens, board the windows, and begin sorting the weapons."

"Of course, Princess," Astrid says. "But why?"

Keldarion places an arm around my waist. "Rosalina is right. What Kairyn began cannot go unanswered. War is coming to the Enchanted Vale."

IOI

KELDARION

"What in the seven realms is that?" I murmur, hunched behind Ezryn as he guides us through the secret mountain passage beneath Keep Hammergarden. Rosalina trails closely behind me, her bow a perfect fit for her hand. *Princess.*

But she wasn't the first person to call herself that. *What do you know about her, Cas?*

"That is my brother's project," Ezryn whispers, drawing me from my thoughts.

A formidable airship stands silent and foreboding. Its dark wood exterior exudes an aura of menacing elegance. The smoky black sails, resembling the outstretched wings of a colossal bat, rest folded, casting a looming presence in the dimly lit chamber.

"Stick tight to the walls," Ezryn commands. "Almost there."

I know this cavernous path is one of the few ways into the keep without going through the city itself, but now I'm wishing we took our chances above ground. The cavern is swarming with goblins and Queen's Army. Thankfully, they all seem focused on the ship, pulling ropes and loading crates into the hull.

I managed to escape the city originally by blending in with the dazed citizens, but there's no way Ezryn will make it past any of the guards. Not only do his ears now mark him as the banished prince, but his eyes ... There's something alight within him that I don't think he could quell if he wanted to.

We stay in the shadows and creep behind a line of rocks before Ezryn finds the hidden doorway. His agile fingers detect the right notch in the rock, and it opens, revealing a staircase.

It's strange to see his expression as he works; it almost seems more emotionless than his helmet.

"We get my father and come back out this way. No distractions," he orders.

Rose nods. "Right. Dayton and Farron are waiting."

I take the first step on to the stairs, holding my hand back for Rosalina. Her touch gives me strength. As much as I would rather she be anywhere but here, I know there's nowhere entirely safe in the Enchanted Vale.

Despite all my fighting, all my denial, I know the truth of it now.

We are safest when we are together.

Ezryn closes the door, and we proceed up the stairs. He looks strange, in the white and gold acolyte clothes, the flower behind his wounded ears. The same flower Rosalina and I wear to protect us. The stairs lead to a low ceiling with a hatch. I push it open and poke my head out to a dark room. Carefully, I lift myself up, then reach down for Rosalina. Her bow gives off a soft light.

"I've been here before," she says, looking around. "The first time Ezryn confronted his brother, Dayton, Astrid, Marigold, Eldy, and I hid in here to watch. See? You can look out at the throne room here." She pulls me over to a mesh covering, thin enough to see through.

Sure enough, the entire throne room spreads before us. It's covered in plants: huge vases and pots filled with blooming red flowers and creeping green vines. At least there's no one here, save for—

"My father," Ezryn breathes.

Prince Thalionor sits in a wooden chair beside the throne. I stifle a jolt. We saw him only earlier today, and his health seemed grim, but now...

He wavers back and forth, fingers scratching along the metal helms that make up the throne. His armor is ill-fitting, the breastplate askew, one shoulder pauldron hanging off. It's as if the old fae has increased in size. Long, greasy gray hair pokes out from beneath his helm. Yellow pus dribbles from beneath it as well, spilling over his gorget.

I keep my voice low, steady. "We must be careful. He's surely being watched—"

Before the words have even left my mouth, Ezryn has torn open the door and sprinted into the throne room.

"Damn fae princes," Rose growls before taking off after him.

I swallow my frustration, then follow.

Ezryn's footsteps ring through the hall as he bounds toward Prince Thalionor. "Father!" He grabs his shoulders, urging him to stand.

"Argh!" the old fae cries, lunging forward. His long fingernails catch on Ezryn's ragged shirt and scrape down his chest.

Ez pulls back. "Father, it's me. Your son. You must come with us. Do you understand?"

A croaking sound emits from Thalionor's throat. He shudders, thudding back against his chair.

"I wouldn't provoke him if I were you."

The voice seems to originate from each corner of the throne room. Heavy steps thud in a rhythm. My whole body stiffens, and I turn around to the double-doors leading into the Hall of Vernalion.

Kairyn walks in, flanked by two knights in shining armor: one in sapphire, the other in bronze.

A growl forces out of me. It's the Sapphire Knight with my sword. *My sword.*

Kairyn claps his hands together slowly. The hall booms with the sound. "Look at you, Ezryn. Ever the perfect son. You could have escaped with your life. But instead, you had to come back for our dear father." He touches a wooden shape at his neck: Ezryn's necklace. A glimmering light appears, shining right by his hand before materializing into a massive war hammer. It's so huge, it looks like it would take two hands to wield, yet Kairyn holds it effortlessly. "Perhaps I don't understand your dedication because Father never even *looked* at me while you were around."

"I won't let you get away with this, Kairyn," Ezryn says, standing. "You have taken my throne, my Blessing, my dignity. But I will not forsake Father to your torment."

Kairyn stops and stares at the ground. His voice grows louder, raged. "I have *tried* to save your life. Again and again and *again*, I've fought for you to live. And this is how you repay me? Constantly coming back, straight into the web? I can't do it anymore." Kairyn looks up. "This time, I have to kill you."

I step in front of Ezryn, channeling bolts of magic into my hands. They glimmer with an icy sheen. "Try."

Kairyn throws his head back and laughs. "Isn't that so beautiful? Keldarion here to save you. Again. He was always the brother you really wanted, wasn't he, Ez? I was such a disappointment to you. To Father. To Mother."

In a sudden movement, Kairyn draws back the massive war hammer and slams it down on the floor. A fissure cracks up the hall, stopping right before us.

The dark space where Kairyn's eyes would be flashes. "Are you proud of me now, brother?"

Tension roils in the room. I know where this is going. "Rose, your bow can end this fight quickly," I whisper. "Ezryn, we must provide coverage and protection for her. When you have the shot, Rose, you take it—"

But I don't get to finish.

Ezryn takes one step forward. Then another. Then drags his sword along the floor. The screech of metal tears through the throne room.

"Enough talking." His voice is low, steps thundering. "I'm taking back what is mine."

"The Blessing?" Kairyn snarls. "You wouldn't—"

Ezryn releases a roar that seems to shake the very hall and charges.

102

DAYTON

Never thought I'd see the day when goblins roamed the streets of Florendel. Cloaks up and eyes forward, Wrenley and I escape their notice by pretending to be hypnotized citizens.

The goblins all seem to have their wits, the pollen of those freaky red flowers only affecting the fae. Despite Kairyn's efforts to plant them in every corner of the city, they still haven't reached everyone.

Wrenley had to damn-near hold me back when a baker ran out of his shop, trying to hit a goblin over the head with a rolling pin. Spring guards loyal to Kairyn, followed by a host of snickering monsters, hauled him away to gods know where.

I wanted to help him, but I won't be any good to Fare if I get myself captured.

We round another narrow street, and Wrenley curls into my side. I have to praise her bravery. She stayed to help me instead of fleeing.

If it hadn't been for her, then … *Rosie and Ezryn would have come for us.* But I don't even know if they're okay.

My heart stutters as I look into a pair of golden, if slightly glazed, eyes. "Fare." He's wandering around like a specter.

"Keep moving," Wrenley hisses under her breath. "We'll draw attention otherwise."

We're in the market, but no one's buying. No one's selling. Vendors man their stalls, picking up and putting down wares in a rhythmic pattern.

"How is Kairyn going to rule a city of ghosts?" I growl.

"He must have a plan," Wrenley says. "I don't think the effects of the pollen will last forever. By the time it wears off—"

"He'll have the soldiers and goblins in place. His new reign will be absolute." I give a heavy sigh. "It'll make it almost impossible for the people to fight back."

"He's smarter than you think."

I whirl, pushing her against the wall. "If I didn't know better, I'd say you were still loyal to him. That sounded an awful lot like a compliment."

Her face scrunches up in a frown. "I know him well from the monastery. Which is why I'm telling you not to underestimate him."

I release her before any of the goblins see my outburst. She saved my life. And now she's helping me save Fare.

"Okay," I say. "Time to get my boy."

"We'll have to break his daze. The stardrop works, or water, if there's enough to clear the airways."

"I could throw him in that fountain." I point to one in the center of the square.

"There are goblins everywhere," she says. "They'll notice you doing that."

"Don't worry." I give her a wink. "I always have a plan. And you're going to help me with this one."

Grabbing her hand, I drag her to the nearby fountain. We sit along the edge. A few other dazed Spring folks rest around us, so it's easy enough to blend in. In the center of the fountain, water sprays out from a cluster of stone butterflies.

"What are you doing?" Wrenley hisses under her breath.

"I had the great idea of sending a wave of water over everyone." I lean in close so as not to be heard, my mouth a breath away from her ear. "The only problem is all of my magic got drained saving my girl. Until I refresh at Castletree, I'm dry as a bone."

"Your girl?" Wrenley says softly. "I thought she was Prince Farron's mate."

I swallow in a tight throat. She's not wrong. "So, you're going to cause the uproar with this water."

Her eyes widen. "I-I don't have any magic. I couldn't."

Her fingers tremble in my hand, and I realize I haven't let go. But she hasn't let me go, either. Her skin is more calloused than Rosalina's, hand smaller than Farron's, and yet ... I can't deny there is something comforting about having someone to hold in this moment. Having a connection to one person in a place so dangerous. "Your father is from the Summer Realm, right? All children of Summer share a connection to the sea." Slowly, I draw both our hands into the fountain. "Can you feel it?"

She grimaces. "Feels like water."

The fountain is cold, mountain water. It's not *Summer*, with the salt and cresting waves. But every moment we hesitate, Fare gets further and further away. I can't lose him.

Rosie wouldn't have any trouble seeing the similarity between salt and fresh water. No, she shifts effortlessly between all of us. She appeared just as at home here in Spring as she did in the Autumn Realm. But I can't keep thinking about Rosalina. I need to focus on Wrenley.

"Magic flows through all of the Enchanted Vale, as do rivers and lakes and seas. You are connected to it."

She shakes her head, a look of sadness in her eyes. "Not like that."

"Try thinking of a memory around water. Do the Golden Acolytes have any hymns about a lake?" Her glare has me chuckling softly. "Humor me, Wren."

"My brother taught me to swim," she whispers. "The river was so cold I used to spit and snarl every time he brought me to the edge. But once I got in, I always had fun. He'd throw colorful stones and make me dive to get them."

"My brothers taught me to swim, too," I say. "Though their idea of fun was tossing me in the surf and seeing how long it took me to come to the surface. Joke was on them. I could hold my breath under water a whole minute longer than Damocles."

It's so rare to think of Damocles and Decimus like that. To have a memory that isn't tainted by blood. Even though there's no magic within me, there's a tiny part that sparks, thinking of those waves, the beach and sand.

Keeping my eyes closed, I swirl our hands in the water. "Feel it flow between your fingers. Mold it in your mind, let it take shape. Then, Wrenley, let it go."

A huge geyser of water explodes from the fountain, covering us and the nearby citizens in its wave. Screams and disorder erupt.

"You did it!" I cry, hoping my voice is lost in the uproar.

There's a smile on Wrenley's face, one I've never seen on her before, but for some reason it's familiar. A laugh bubbles out of her. "I can't believe I did that. How did I *do* that?"

"Judging by the size of that wave, there's more than a *little* magic in you."

Her wet hair falls across her brow, and there's such a look of bewildered joy on her face, I almost hate to interrupt it in any way. Unfortunately, her smile doesn't fit in with the dazed look most Spring citizens bear.

"Come on," I grip her arm, helping her stand. "Let's find Farron."

The crowd is in chaos. Fae shriek as the water breaks their hypnosis. Goblins and soldiers attempt to intervene.

I see Fare in the crowd and snag his arm. Unfortunately, he escaped the water and is still dazed as fuck.

"This way!" Wrenley waves to me from an alley, and I drag Fare toward her.

In the brief safety of the shadows, I spin him around, heart clenching. "Baby, you fucking idiot. You were curious and got too close to those flowers, huh? Damn you." I kiss him. But it's like kissing a statue.

"That's not going to work." Wrenley tears the flower from her hair in half and shoves it under his nose.

Farron takes a huge gasp, then blinks his large eyes. "D-Day? What's—"

"I thought I smelled High Prince."

We whirl to see two goblins at the entrance to the alley, armed with short swords and shields.

Farron immediately steps in front of me, flames dancing on his fingertips.

"Your magic will only draw more," Wrenley says. "We have to run."

"They've got us backed into a corner, sweetheart," I say. No magic, no swords. I'm just thinking of how I can convince the gobbos to engage with me in a fistfight when something whooshes in front of my face.

A crossbow bolt lodges in the head of the first goblin. The second only has time to look up before a bolt strikes him through the eye.

Tilla is hunched on a rooftop, crossbow in hand, dark hair blowing wildly in the wind. She quickly slings it over her shoulder, then throws a rope down at us. "This way."

Farron scales the wall first, and I gesture for Wrenley to go next.

"I don't know if I can." Her fingers shake as she touches the rope, glancing nervously at the dead goblins, their black blood seeping into the cobblestone. "I'm not brave like you."

"What are you talking about?" I touch her shoulder. "You *saved* me and Keldarion. Plus, you worked for Kairyn. If that's not brave, I don't know what is. Now link your hands around my neck. I'll pull you up."

She nods determinedly, and we quickly scale the wall.

"Tilla!" I open my arms for a hug. "Never thought I'd be happy to see you."

Her lip curls into a sneer and she sidesteps. "Can't say I've yet to feel the same, Summer Prince. Follow me."

We jump from rooftop to rooftop, quick as shadows. From up here it's easy to see just how bad Florendel is. Goblins, Spring guards, and members of the Queen's Army patrol every corner. Fae wander in a daze, and those that don't are carted away.

Tilla silently motions toward a rock wall along the base of the mountain at the edge of the city. When she presses her palm against the stone, the rock shimmers. She passes through.

An illusion.

We enter to a wave of thick heat, dark red walls, and on to a narrow bridge overlooking the Draconhold Forge.

There are no workers, and no store of swords or metal like last time we were here. "A little on the empty side," I say lowly.

Tilla looks over her shoulder. "Kairyn's forces stormed the place immediately after Ezryn's banishment. They took everything: the weapons, the metal. Killed anyone who tried to stop them."

A growl rumbles in my chest. We pass over the bridge and into another narrow tunnel.

"I've been trying to help those who were unaffected escape the city," Tilla continues. "And help free those that are. Water and that white flower are the only ways to do it. Either clear the pollen from the airways or neutralize it. We're gathering in the mountain tunnels."

"Where will you go?" Wrenley asks.

"I don't know. The idea of abandoning my city kills me, but there's no way to fight this."

Farron and I exchange a glance. *Go to Castletree.* That should be the answer. Why else did the Queen make it so large and vast? Why else create a road from each capital to the castle? But now those roads are overrun with briars and goblins. And even if the people were to make it there, what would they find? Thorny halls and cursed nights? The new High Prince?

We have failed our people.

We have failed our people so greatly.

"Send them to Summer," I say quickly. "I'll help you guide them."

Tilla gives me an almost pitying expression. "There's something you need to see."

She guides us around another corner until I feel a trickle of fresh air. There's a small, curved opening in the rock.

She nods for me to proceed.

Outside, I can peer beyond the walls of Keep Hammergarden, past the Meadowmere Forest and the field of flowers where I'm meant to meet Kel. I can even see the start of the Equinox Passage that cuts through the mountains between Spring and Summer. But right before it are rows and rows of troops. They fly the flag of Spring, but it isn't only Kairyn's soldiers or the Queen's Army camped. There are leagues of goblins, forces of the Below.

Kairyn's been preparing this for a long time, and based on their direction, he isn't just planning to overtake Spring.

No.

His next target is the Summer Realm.

103

ROSALINA

Kairyn raises the Hammer of Hope just in time to block Ezryn's sword.

Kel steps in front of me. "Lift your bow, Rose."

I do as he says, my hands shaky on the grip.

The Sapphire and Bronze Knight immediately charge at Ez, defending their master.

"Get back! He's mine," Kairyn screams, pulling his hammer away from Ez's blade before swinging it down again. Ez jumps back, avoiding the attack, then charges.

The knights stagger backward before setting their sights on Kel and me. Kel holds his hands together; an icy blue light radiates between them. "All right then. You two are mine."

The knights run. My heart bursts in my chest as I raise the bow. I know what to do. I did it before at the tower. If I can't do this, they'll kill my mate.

A glowing arrow appears as I pull back the string. But the knights are too close to Ezryn. He and Kairyn fly across the Hall of Vernalion, moving too fast for me to track. If I miss—

"Now, Rose!" Kel yells.

I close my eyes and cry out, releasing the string. My first thought is how ashamed Dayton would be of me: *Always keep your eyes open.* The second is I've gone too wide. My radiant arrow smashes against the far side of the throne room, stone exploding with the impact. The knights exchange a single glance behind before resuming their charge.

Then they're upon us. Kel lunges forward, hands moving with such speed, I can barely follow. He has no weapon, but he *is* a weapon. A line of dagger-sharp icicles shoot up from the ground, snaring the Bronze Knight. Then a spray of ice knives dance toward the Sapphire Knight but his sword smashes through them, and they fall to the floor.

A lance cracks over the icicles, and the Bronze Knight attacks on Kel's right side. He blocks with a quickly made ice shield, but it shatters instantly. Then he's dodging the Sword of the Protector, sliding underneath, sending a blustering icy wind to throw the knights off balance. Left, right, left, right, Kel blocks one attack only to dodge another.

I raise the bow again. "Come on, come on, come on." But everyone's moving so fast. I'd only just mastered a still target. How am I supposed to get one that's running and dodging and getting thrown down by a burst of ice?

At the back of the throne room, Ez and Kai move in sync, each blow of the sword or hammer blocked by the other. Every movement of Ezryn's is fused with rage and agony. They're locked too close together, I could never hit Kairyn without the radial blast damaging Ez.

Kel needs my help. Even lacking his sword, he's holding up for now. A blast of freezing air shoots out, staggering the Bronze Knight for a moment. Kel turns his attention to the other one.

Now. I don't think. I draw up my bow, pull back my string, breathe out. Release.

A radiant arrow flies through the air and lands short, just at the Bronze Knight's feet. But the arrow creates a blast of light, sending the Bronze Knight flying and slamming against a stone pillar.

I refrain from doing a little jump of joy. But it would have been undeserved, anyway; the knight staggers up, helm thrown off, revealing the sickening, sunken face. His bulging eyes train on me.

Oh, fuck.

Kel's pressing down against the Sapphire Knight, a crafted ice pike versus the Sword of the Protector. Cracks form in his enchanted weapon. I turn and run, finding cover behind a pillar. Holding my bow tight to my chest, I try to steady my breath.

I peer out from the shelter of the pillar. Huge fissures have formed in the ground from the crack of Kairyn's massive hammer. Somehow, Ez is able to dodge each blow, his sword fighting to find an opening. I pull back, preparing to look the other way at Kel.

As soon as I move, I'm faced with the hideous visage of the Bronze Knight. His gaping eyes and snapping teeth appear right in front of me. I scream, falling backward. The knight raises his lance above his head, then shoves it down.

I roll. The pointed end digs deep into the stone where I'd been lying. I roll again, able to leap to my feet as he yanks the lance from the ground. With a cry, I smash his chest plate with my bow. The armor crackles and melts, revealing marred skin below. Maybe if I can touch his skin, he'll explode like the Turquoise Knight did in the monastery—

But there's no time to contemplate. The knight looks down at his melted chest plate then up at me and grins. I run.

Kel's walking backward toward the throne, sending up huge blocks of ice between him and the Sapphire Knight. Each time, the Sapphire Knight draws back the Sword of the Protector and smashes the ice to shards. Kel's ice makes the sword glow a brilliant white-blue. The Sapphire Knight twists the blade in his hand, admiring this. Then he drives the blade through the air. Black ice daggers shoot up from the ground, heading for Kel.

I draw my bow and fire. My arrow slams into the black ice spikes, creating a blast of water and light. I run to Kel, and he pulls me tight against him.

The Bronze and Sapphire Knight look at each other, then walk in unison toward us.

A gurgling noise comes from behind me, Ezryn's father writhing beside the throne. He's scratching at his helmet, his neck. Vines have curled up around his hands. His armor has popped off in places, and the skin beneath is speckled with pus-filled blisters. *What's happening to him?*

I look up at Kel. "We don't need to kill these guys. We just have to get Ez and his dad and escape."

Kel growls lowly, "Getting Ezryn is the hard part."

Right now, Ezryn's being pushed back by the huge swings of Kai's hammer. Kairyn is clad in heavy black armor and wields the Blessing of Spring. Ezryn has nothing. This isn't a fight we can win.

I suck in a breath. "I have an idea."

The Bronze and Sapphire Knight are almost upon us. "Let's hear it, Darling," Kel says.

"You get those two against the back wall," I say and dart off. "And I'll get Ez toward us."

Without questioning, Kel leaps forward and throws out his hands. A winter's gale erupts from his palms, a storm with ice shards and winds freezing cold. The knights stumble, then fall, hurtling through the throne room before smacking against the stone. Kel roars, his face a pained grimace from the immense power.

I focus all my attention on Ezryn. On my mate, who seems so far away from me, even though he's only across the room. *Ezryn. Come back to me.*

He turns. Stares. Ducks under the swing of the hammer.

Come back to me! Now!

A confused expression crosses his face, but he disengages from his brother. Then he runs toward us.

I draw my bow. Wait one second. Two. Ezryn reaches the midpoint of the Hall of Vernalion, with Kel and me at the front, and Kairyn and his knights still at the back. Then I look at the huge fissure Kairyn created with his hammer. And release.

Light bursts through the throne room, near blinding. Stone erupts in a massive shower. Chunks smash against my shoulders, my chest. Dust fills the air.

But when it clears, a gaping hole leading to the cavern below lies between us and them.

I cough, searching the dusty air for my mates. Kel staggers forward, grabbing my arm. He points to Ez, face down in the rubble. We hurry over and each grab an arm.

Ez shakes his head, looking disoriented.

"Hurry," Kel says. "Let's retrieve your father and go."

Something clears in Ez's eyes. Or comes alive. He tears free from our grip and looks back across the fissure where his brother paces like an angry lion.

"So, you're going to run," Kairyn calls. "Run, run away. I feel it in my chest. Spring's Blessing is relieved to finally have a worthy vessel."

"Don't do it. Don't let him tempt you," Kel says lowly.

I can sense the emotions as if they were my own: Ezryn's rage, his shame. Kairyn symbolizes the catalyst of so many profound losses—his honor, his realm, his magic. And there's only one way to reclaim it.

Kill his brother.

There's nothing we can say.

Ezryn leaps across the fissure.

104

EZRYN

I don't even bother to look how far the fissure stretches before I leap. I will make it, or I will die.

I will kill my brother, or I will die.

My bones rattle as I land on the other side. Kairyn steps back, shocked I would attempt the jump. Then he raises his hammer. "Let us end this, then."

He swings, but not at me. The war hammer collides with one of the stone pillars. Cracks shoot up the side. He yells, swinging his hammer again. The pillar groans, falling forward, crashing across the fissure. A bridge. He waves a hand toward Kel and Rose. "Kill them!"

His knights do not hesitate. They vault on to the fallen pillar and carefully traverse to the other end.

Rage like I've never known surges through my body. Kairyn has taken *everything* from me. I have been humiliated, disgraced, disregarded by my own people. My name has been marred in history.

Because I trusted him.

Trusted my *family*.

And worse than all of that, his actions nearly killed Rosalina. I won't let him hurt anyone ever again.

I will cover myself with blood so he cannot shed another drop.

He blocks my first swing with his hammer. I swirl around him, going for his back. I'm too quick for him to block this, but his armor is made of finest metal. My sword *pings* against it. My own body feels too buoyant in nothing but fabric rags. But I must use it to my advantage.

Kairyn yells, swinging the hammer in a great arc. I throw myself forward, rolling across rubble, then leap up. I drive the point of my mother's sword into the gap between his shoulder and breastplate. He roars and staggers back. It is not a killing blow, but that hammer cannot be light to wield.

Kairyn runs a gloved hand along the wound, pulls his fingers back bloody. "There it is. Took long enough to come out. Must have been hard to hide all this time."

"Is this what you wanted?" I roar. "To corrupt me?"

"You did that yourself."

No, no. He did this to me. He made me this way…

Kairyn paces, dragging the hammer behind him. "It's always been inside you. The rage. The jealousy. The hatred. You were the one who removed your helmet. You were the one who desecrated the grove. You killed our mother."

"No!" I lunge, barreling the sword down. He blocks it with a gauntlet, grunting.

"No? Look at you. You don't care what it takes, what you have to sacrifice, as long as you can kill me." The owl helm twitches. "You'd even sacrifice your mate."

Across the fissure, Rose and Kel are back-to-back, pinned against the side of the throne by the two members of the Penta Conclave. Kel's holding them off with ice shields, but each one he creates is weaker than the last. Rose has her bow drawn, but she can't use it so close. Fear is etched across her face.

I stumble away from Kairyn. I left them alone … Those I love most in this world.

"We're not so different, brother," Kairyn says. "Maybe we both never reached our true potential. There's a world outside of this one. A place where men like us do not need to hide our natures. Where we do not need to be ashamed." He holds out his hand. "Come with me.

Be *my* steward. You and I possess the power to rule more than Spring. We can take down my new masters. Then the entire Vale will be at our control."

Slowly, I turn to look at him. "I'm nothing like you."

His breathing grows ragged. "You'll see it soon enough. We are both forsaken."

Using all the power left within me, I dodge around Kairyn and leap to the pillar. My steps are steady as I race across the narrow beam, landing on solid ground before the throne.

With a yell, I raise my sword, about to charge the knights—

When my feet whip out from under me.

"How dare you turn against me when you are faced with death?" The roar sounds from all around. I'm flung up in the air, a mossy green vine holding my leg. Kairyn moves beneath me, swampy tendrils of earth encircling his body and floating him over the fissure.

Magic crackles. *Spring's Blessing.*

"You have always hated me. Admit it! Tell the truth!" he booms. The vines snap, and I'm slammed down to the stone. The wind rushes from my chest.

I try to hack at the vine holding my leg, but I'm whipped up before I can make a move. Another snap, and I'm blasted against a different pillar. Something cracks in my ribs. I'm not sure I'll get my breath back this time.

"What did I ever do but admire you? Were you so desperate for Mother and Father's love you could not bear if they gave any to me? Did you stop them from loving me?"

Crash. I'm hurtled against the ground. My sword flies out of my grip and clatters away.

Images and light swirl before my eyes. The throne room fades, replaced by green. Then Kairyn's standing above me.

Mossy plants coil one over another, growing underneath my back, then arching up, forming a dome around the two of us. He's barricaded us in our own chamber of mulch and moss.

Warm wetness drips down my face. I start to pull myself up—

Kairyn stands over me, then drops the hammer on to my chest.

What breath I had left flies out in a gasp. Pain staggers through my ribcage, my spine. The crushing pressure is like no agony I've ever known.

"And now we have come to this." The owl helm quirks to the side. "The end."

I want to tell him it doesn't have to be like this. But it's not only the weight on my chest that stops me.

It's also because I know the Ezryn that would offer him forgiveness died.

The Ezryn who believed in mercy died.

So it does have to be like this. Me. Or him.

Then Kairyn moves strangely. He puts his hands on either side of his helm and lifts.

My brother shakes his head, his long black hair falling free. Dark eyes peer back at me.

I remember them.

I remember them, lit up as he ran through Meadowmere, chasing fireflies. I remember them looking up at me as we flipped through picture books in our shared bedroom. I remember them staring at me with both fear and admiration as I donned my first helm and never saw his face with my naked eyes again.

Until now.

Kairyn's lip trembles and his voice cracks. "You would choose death rather than stand by my side?"

I fight against the breathlessness in my chest, the great weight. "It would not be to stand by you, brother, but to kneel before you. And that is something I cannot do, not with what you have done."

A hardness falls across his features. "Then you will die."

I close my eyes. For some reason, it brings me peace to have seen my brother's face one last time. I only hope Kel and Rose can find a way out of this. That there will be peace for them.

My Petal. I'm so sorry.

Kairyn grips the hilt of the hammer. Even the smallest bit of extra pressure on my chest sends me gasping. "Look at me as I end your life."

He pushes down.

My first rib breaks with a *snap*. I can't even scream, all the wind ripped from my lungs. Kairyn's face is soft as he pushes down and down. "It's okay," he murmurs as he kills me. "Look at me. Shush, shush. Look at me. It's okay."

My chest is caving in. Agony ripples out from my ribs to my fingertips, my legs, my skull. Kairyn's face fades in bursts of blackness.

I know it now for good.

I'm going to die.

And I hope she knows … I hope she knows how much I loved her.

There's the sound of plant fibers shredding, and something flashes in my peripheral vision. I fight through the darkness to see it.

Another similar sound and flash occur on my opposite side. I turn my head.

A thorn. Dark purple.

Another thorned vine erupts out of the ground, then another, tearing open the dome. Kairyn releases the hammer and quickly puts his helm back on, looking around. "What's going on?"

I recognize these thorns. They feel like home.

A huge briar spurts up, cracking through the stone ground, and slams into Kairyn. He flies backward, hitting the floor hard. Then it's as if a whole briar appears, tearing down Kairyn's dome. One of the thorned vines wraps around the hilt of the hammer and pulls.

I gasp in a rattling breath, relief flooding through me at the release of pressure. I force myself up. At least one rib is broken, maybe two, a couple more bruised.

I turn to the huge bramble bush. And floating above it, held aloft by thorned vines, is Caspian.

His arms are crossed, a smirk on his face.

He looks horrible. His skin is ghastly pale. A black goo oozes out from his nose and mouth. And though his eyes are bruised and lined with dark circles, there's a defiant look there that I've never seen him without.

Caspian. The Prince of Thorns. My enemy.

Saved my life.

The thorned vines float Caspian to the ground. He walks over to me, hips swaying side to side as if he were attending the fanciest dinner party. "Why, Ezryn, I adore the new look. You're certainly not hideous. What a treat."

I look from him to my brother, lying in a pile of rubble, to Kel and Rose still fending off the knights.

Then a gurgled cry emits from the throne. My father falls, tumbling down the steps.

I turn my back to Caspian without a second thought, racing to my father as fast as my injured body will carry me. He lies face down at the base of the stairs, convulsing.

I fall to my knees beside him and look back at Caspian. "I don't understand why you did what you did, but … Thank you. Can you get us out of here?"

Caspian isn't looking at me, or even Kel or Rosalina. He's looking at my father.

"Caspian!" I cry.

"Ezryn," he says, voice low and gravelly. "You need to step away—"

I shake my head, turning back to my father. His whole body seizes. He needs help. He needs a healer. He needs—

A thorned vine shoots out from Caspian's hand.

And stabs straight into my father's heart.

105

ROSALINA

Everything is happening too fast: the spray of Keldarion's ice shield as he barely holds the sword and lance at bay, the thorns carving through the ground, Caspian appearing—Caspian! Caspian! Caspian!—and Ezryn's cry, something born of both rage and sorrow, as the Prince of Thorns drives a sharpened vine through Thalionor's heart.

Ezryn clutches his father's lifeless body, mouth agape. Strangled cries escape him as he shakes the old fae. He places his hand over the gaping wound, spewing heart's blood, but even I can see Thalionor is already gone.

Across the throne room, I notice Kairyn staggering up.

How could you? I gasp in my mind, eyes on Caspian. He wavers. I've never seen him like this. So weak. So sick.

Caspian begins to cough. They're so strong, his whole body wracks. A trail of sludge ejects from his mouth on to the floor. The purple thorns start to wither and die.

I retreat behind Keldarion, heart pounding. The knights haven't stopped their relentless attack, and Kel is barely holding them off. Caspian is so weak. He just killed Prince Thalionor. And Ez…

Ez drops his father's body. Stands. Walks a few steps, back stiff, to where his sword lies. Picks it up. Turns to face Caspian.

"You killed my father," he says lowly. "Now, your death belongs to me."

Caspian sighs. "I thought that might be the case."

Stop! I scream in my mind, but neither of them turn to me.

A great shadow engulfs us, bringing the smell of swamp and mulch. Plants slither from the pillars, the ground, the ceiling, and rally to Kairyn. They wrap around his limbs and chest; he grows five feet, then ten as more and more plants form giant legs, lifting him into the air. Moss and vines cover his arms, creating two long whips.

Kairyn lurches his massive, botanical body back and bellows, a sound like felling trees.

"You will all pay!" he cries, then whips one of his large plant arms forward, knocking away the Sapphire and Bronze Knights. Then he wraps Kel and me in his vines, squeezing us so tight, I lose the grip on my bow. It clatters to the ground. We're flung upward, far above the throne.

With his other arm, he does the same to Ez and Cas, wrapping them together and lifting them high into the air. The musty aroma of decaying vegetation clouds my nose.

"Each one of you has been nothing but a relentless weed since I first met you," Kairyn growls. "I pluck you out, and yet you keep coming back."

The vines wrap tighter around us, and I cry out. Kel struggles to break free, but his hands are pinned.

"Especially *you.*" Kairyn pulls his arm in, bringing Caspian closer. "Do you truly have no loyalty? Not even to your sister?"

Caspian licks his lips, smearing black all over them. "If anyone appreciates a little chaos, it's my Birdy."

Kairyn lets loose another enraged howl. "I will get my vengeance!"

My bones creak as the vines tighten. Kel grits his teeth beside me, blue eyes flashing with pain.

Across from us, Caspian and Ezryn are squeezed tighter and tighter. They cry out, fighting against the hold.

It can't end like this. I won't meet my end alongside Keldarion when we've barely even had a start. I won't lose Ezryn when he needs me most to find him. Won't go before I tell Dayton what he means to me, or let Farron know how I've healed because of his love.

I look across at Caspian. And I won't give up on him.

I close my eyes.

"Rose," Kel grunts. "I'm so sorry. For everything. For hiding the truth. I thought I was protecting you, but instead I only—"

"Kel," I say seriously. "You have no idea how long I've waited for this apology. And I still intend to hear the whole thing. With you on your knees, preferably. But for right now, *shut up.*"

Because what I'm looking for isn't outside, with my mates or my bow.

It's inside.

It's who I am, who I've always been. The blood that runs through my veins. An eternal love I've carried since my birth.

My mother's magic may have made Castletree, and our home may be fading. But her magic also flows through me.

This time it's not an eruption of fire. No force or power surging through me. It is a release.

I bloom.

Human daughter of George and Anya O'Connell. Fae daughter of Queen Aurelia—the Enchantress who cursed the High Princes.

I don't need Caspian's briars or the Nightingale's.

It lives in me.

I am the Golden Rose.

My magic blossoms out of me like a wind through a field of flowers. Golden briars crack through the stone, spreading across the throne room. Roses bloom along them, glittering with hope. My thorns shoot toward Kairyn, tearing at his limbs of mulch and moss.

"What is this? Get off of me!" he cries. His control slackens on the vines surrounding us.

My thorns are like an extension of me; they respond to my intentions and do my direct bidding. Thrusting my hand upward, a briar shoots skyward, tearing through the vines that ensnare us. Kel and I tumble to the ground, but he wraps me in his arms, absorbing the brunt of the fall.

He sits up with a shake of his head. "You're right. My apology can wait."

I stand and run, my thorns weaving beside me like sea monsters dipping in and out of the waves. With an upward thrust of my hand, my vines rip open the constraints around Ez and Caspian.

But before they tumble to the floor, I ensnare them with my own golden thorns.

"Let me go!" Ezryn screams.

But Caspian only smirks. "Clever girl."

I shoot a hand out to the side, and my thorns engulf Keldarion. "What are you doing, Rose?" he yells.

Then I slam my palms downward. The vines descend through the earth, taking Kel, Ez, and Caspian with them. My thorns know the path because my heart knows the path.

It will always lead me home to Castletree.

I step backward to see the Sapphire Knight and the Bronze Knight running toward me.

"It's been fun," I say, my golden thorns wrapping around my legs. My turn to go home.

I'm fully embraced by brambles. *To Castletree,* I tell them. I feel the rush as I'm pulled downward—

SLAM!

Pain shoots through me like a crack of lightning. I fall to the hard ground, my thorns withering.

SLAM!

Another burst of pain. I blink my eyes rapidly, trying to make sense. And then I see it.

Kairyn, his massive hammer raised, pounding my roses again and again. His divine weapon glows with light.

With his huge, gloved hands, he plucks one of my roses. It twists in his palm, losing its glimmer. Evolving into an entirely separate plant.

His heavy boots thud over to me. I clutch the stones, trying to pull myself away, but he grabs my shoulder, pushing me on to my back. He hovers over me, his helm like a descending bird of prey.

"I may have lost them, but you're all that truly matters." He looks down at the ground, helm lit up with a radiant gleam. "You and this bow."

Then the new High Prince of Spring shoves his deadly flower under my nose. I inhale the sickly sweet scent. My mind turns to fog. At least Keldarion, Ezryn, and Caspian are safe.

106

FARRON

Type cave tunnels beneath Florendel are vast and intricate, warm from the blazing fires of the forges and the deep molten rock. We're lucky enough to avoid any guards or goblins.

When Tilla finally opens the door that leads to a small path outside the city, the blaring sun cuts into my aching head. It must be late afternoon now. It was just past dawn when everything went hazy—I remember checking one of the strange red flowers as we followed Ezryn out of the city, and then suddenly Day was right in front of me. *He came for me.*

"Thank you, Tilla," Dayton says as we step out into the light. "I don't know what we would have done without you."

"What are old friends for?" She gives a wry smile. "Now to figure out where to take our people."

I stroke my chin. "Why not lead the refugees to Winter? It's a longer trek than Summer, but you'll avoid that army."

"That's a dangerous path," Wrenley says quietly, "and narrow. If Spring were to come after you, you'd be ambushed and trapped between mountains and ice."

"We could make it through the mountain passages before Kairyn realizes we're gone," Tilla says. "Besides, his forces are currently concentrated on Summer."

Dayton's face turns grim. I know the image of the army making camp before the passage to his realm must be fresh in his mind. I squeeze his hand. "We're faster than any army. We'll make it to Summer before them and warn your sister. From there, I'll take a horse and get to Autumn. Our people will not let Summer stand alone."

He nods. I absently reach up to touch my necklace, but it's not there, of course. We're escaping Keep Hammergarden with only the clothes on our back and my small rucksack of items. Luckily, within it is the book Caspian wanted. I have a feeling I'm going to need it before the end to fulfill my promise to the Prince of Thorns. The promise to find a way to make him human.

Dayton puts a hand on Tilla's shoulder. "We'll be meeting with Keldarion soon. I'll tell him to catch you on the road and lead you to Winter."

Tilla nods. "I appreciate it. Most of us can hold our own, but we have elders, children, and injured. I won't leave anymore behind."

"You've changed, Tilla," Dayton says quietly. "Or maybe I was always wrong about you."

She's silent for a moment, trying to gauge if the Summer Prince is being serious for once. But I know he is.

"For a long time, I was wrong about myself," Tilla says. "And I think, Daytonales, you might know what I mean. You've changed as well."

In parting, Tilla hands us a bag of supplies: rations, water skins, and a few daggers. We thank her and quietly pick a path away from the city wall, keeping to the treeline until finally the field of flowers comes into view. Wrenley insisted on coming with us instead of escaping with Tilla and the others.

The sun gleams off the seashells on Day's neck. For a second, it's almost like he hasn't lost his token. "Can't believe you managed to keep most of your necklace," I say.

A flush colors his cheeks. "I can't keep all of you, Fare, but I can keep this."

My heart stutters. *But what if I want to keep all of you?*

"Do you think they've arrived yet?" Dayton asks, pulling Wrenley up a large boulder.

I reach deep within my bond, searching for Rosalina. She's in Spring, but it leads backward, not forward. Earlier, I had felt huge flashes of her emotions. Fear. Sadness. Power. Everything in me screams to run to her, but that would only draw more attention to us when we need to escape. I must trust her other mates to return her to me. I shake my head. "Not yet, but Kel and Ezryn are with her. I can feel them."

At the mention of Ezryn, Wrenley stiffens and quickly scampers forward. Strange.

Dayton hauls me up the last bit of the hill until the field lies before us.

"We made it," Wrenley sighs, chestnut waves catching in the wind. "And the flowers are welcoming us. Look! It's good luck to see the Lights of Fate."

Far from us, floating among the blooms, are the tiny blue orbs of the will-o'-wisps. If one fell on Rosie's breast now, she'd have three mate bonds: one to me, Kel, and Ezryn. My insides grow tight, and I avoid Dayton's gaze.

"Come on," Dayton says. "There's cover by that cluster of trees over there. We can watch for their arrival."

I nod and follow him.

A slicing pain cuts across my body, and I fall to my knees, a scream tearing from my throat. It feels like a fire is consuming me with desperation and loss. "Rosalina!"

Dayton is over me in a moment, hand on my back. "Fare? What's wrong? What's happening?"

I clutch at my heart as if it could keep it together in my chest. My gaze shoots toward Florendel. "It's Rosie. She's in pain. I can't feel Kel and Ez anymore. She's alone."

107

KELDARION

Golden vines and roses flutter around me, and I land with a crash among the familiar briars of Castletree's entrance hall. Caspian and Ezryn lie in a similar heap beside me, but I know instantly she's not here.

Roaring, I launch toward Castletree's door. Pressing in the knob, I switch the dial to that of Spring and pull.

The door doesn't open.

But of course. The new High Prince has not connected to Castletree's magic. The way is closed. I curse. Fine, I'll figure out a different way—

My thoughts trail off as a strange sensation prickles along the back of my neck, like shadows leaching over my body.

I whirl. Caspian kneels on the ground, barely able to hold himself up, black sludge dripping down his face. And Ezryn—Ezryn, my best friend, my brother—stands above him, sword poised to strike.

Time seems to slow. I meet Caspian's gaze, and there is only surrender there. A goodbye.

An end to it all.

Dusky rays shine in from the open window. Funny how the briars all curve around the sill to let the sun in. A light that's glinting off his dark eyes now.

I flick my fingers and a blade of ice forms in my palm, and it's my own sort of surrender. A surrender to the choice I was always going to make.

108

EZRYN

This moment has played out in my mind a thousand times. At last, I will slice through the darkness and purge the rot from the ground. I didn't know which emotion would course through my veins when the time came, but with the Prince of Thorns helpless before me, there is a sense of pure freedom.

This is justice for his torment of Keldarion, his betrayal of the Vale and it will free Rosalina. It is a gift I will give all of us. He doesn't move, but only closes his eyes as my sword arcs toward his neck.

Steel rings out across the castle, and a shudder ripples through my body as my blade clashes with another. Keldarion stands before me, white hair shrouding his face, but I see his eyes clear enough, full of wild desperation.

Snarling, I push on his blade of ice. "Let me do this for you, brother. Let me free you and our mate of your twisted bargain. Let me *help* you." And with every ounce of strength I have, I push down harder and harder on the sword, willing it to break. Willing *him* to break.

He does not.

"No," Keldarion says in a low growl. Feet braced on the ground as he pushes back against me with a power that would destroy any ordinary man.

But he doesn't look behind, doesn't see Caspian's gaze cut into mine. A knowing, scheming smirk. Whatever surrender had been there was just another act. *He knew Kel would save him.*

Snarling, I sever the duel and stagger back. "Ignorant! You are willingly oblivious to his ways and his trickery as you ever were. Stand down, Keldarion. This needs to end."

Keldarion shakes his head, a look of familiar sorrow and torment. "I can't."

"He *killed* my father. He laid siege on Autumn. And he holds your magic at bay. You can never truly be with Rosalina while blood still runs in his veins." I pace, looking for an opening between him and Caspian. "You would have me carve a path through you to exact my vengeance?"

Keldarion looks down at his sword and then back at me. "You will do what you must, as will I."

There has been so much fury in my blood, the feeling of deep sorrow is almost welcome. It clears my mind. Makes my objective clear. I had believed without my creed I would be lost.

But the opposite is true.

It has freed me to see the world as it truly is. To see people as they truly are.

And I will do whatever I need to in order to set her free.

I lower my sword. "Though there is no strike of a blade, you have cut through our brotherhood. It is no more."

"Ezryn..." Keldarion steps toward me.

"You have made your choice, High Prince of Winter, and I have made mine." I look past him to Caspian, withering on the floor. "And to you, Prince of Thorns, I leave you a promise. Your death is marked by me. I will claim it. Next time, I will not be merciful to whoever stands in my way."

"Wait," Keldarion calls. "What about Rosalina?"

"I will rescue her on my own." I turn toward the main door, toward the Briar. "Goodbye, Keldarion. You will not see me at Castletree again."

109

KELDARION

The slam of the door echoes through Castletree. Many times, I have watched Ezryn leave. Many times, I have wondered if he would ever return.

But he always came back.

This time he won't.

Even the air above me seems too heavy a weight. I collapse to my knees with a resounding thud, ice sword clattering out of my hands and shattering.

A profound sense of loss fills me. For my brother, for Rosalina, to be so truly trapped in this weak and dying shell of Castletree.

There's a light tug on the front of my shirt as Caspian pulls himself up before me. His eyes narrow and he studies me before wiping his mouth with the sleeve of his tunic.

"Kel," he says lowly.

I don't reply. Can't.

"Keldarion," he purrs, and his hands rest upon my neck. He leans against me, blinking up with those enormous, violet eyes.

A smile tugs at the edges of his full lips as he draws even closer, then presses those lips against my own.

It's been decades since he's kissed me, and yet it's as if time has simply melted away. The softness of his hair as I grip the back of his neck, the fierce urgency of his hands clutching my shoulders, and the passionate dance of our bodies pressed close together—every sensation, every touch ignites a blaze of longing that defies the long years that have passed.

He kisses me like he did the night we first made the bargain, full of desperation with the whispers of dark promise. The bargain that still digs into my wrist because I cannot banish my love for him.

That love that has cost me my brother, my realm, but maybe not Rosalina.

"Do not fret, Kel," Caspian laughs darkly as he pulls away, lips moving to my ear. "No one will take your mate from you but me."

110

DAYTON

I wish I knew what damned cosmic entity I pissed off, because we really can't catch a break.

"Come on, Fare," I say, holding his shaking body. Sweat beads on his forehead, and his fingers clutch the ground. "Where is she?"

His head whips up, auburn hair wild, and takes off running across the flower field. Stems snap beneath our feet, the bobbing blue lights fluttering away.

"Where is he going?" Wrenley yells, cloak blowing in the wind.

"I don't know," I call back.

A rumble shakes the ground, and I swear I see the entire mountain range move. Fluorescent green smoke billows from beyond the walls of Florendel. Then a massive dark shape emerges from the clouds.

"Is that a fucking…"

"It's a flying ship." Wrenley gazes up, eyes wide.

The black sails and hull cut through the air. The windows gleam with that same strange green magic that infected Farron's realm. The magic Caspian used to save our asses.

Farron raises a shaky finger skyward. "There," he rasps. "She's *there*."

I grab his shoulder and spin him around as the shadow of the ship passes above us. "We'll get her, Farron. That ship is heading to Summer. I won't let anyone harm my realm, and I won't let anyone harm her. You know me, Fare. You know this."

"I love you," he whispers. "And so does Rosie."

He gives me a weak smile and leans in toward me. But then pauses, his features suddenly lit up by a bright golden light, casting his hair copper. The light ... It's coming from my chest, glowing like the goddamn sun itself.

The light of a mate bond.

Slowly, I turn, following the line of light, so bright and true, to see its origin.

Wrenley stands in the middle of the field of flowers, brown hair blowing around her face. One of the will-o'-wisps is spread across her chest, causing her bond to awaken the light that leads her directly to her mate.

And like an arrow of gold, it strikes me in the chest.

"Dayton," Wrenley says, "we're mates."

III

ROSALINA

My mouth is bone-dry, joints sore. A dull ache pounds in my temple. Dusky red light filters in through my blurry vision.

I blink my eyes, trying to force myself to focus. Last thing I remember…

I sent Keldarion, Ez, and Caspian to Castletree. I have no idea where Dayton and Farron are. As for myself—

Kairyn took me.

Shaking my head, I look around. My arms are bound in two huge steel manacles. They're chained to a pole. I'm in a small wooden room, dark except for a window letting in the fading red light.

My legs shake, but I force myself to stand and peer outside.

Sky as far as I can see, with clouds drifting past at an incredible speed.

I'm *flying*.

This must be Kairyn's ship. Where is he taking me?

My stomach lurches as I peer over the side. A sparkling ocean lies beneath us, waves crashing upon cliffs of white rock. I recognize the sandstone from a fateful night months ago.

The Summer Realm.

I can feel it creeping up: the panic, the terror. But I close my eyes and force a few deep breaths. More than ever, I need to be strong.

They've taken my bow. But they can never take my heart.

Beyond anything else, I know I will escape. My friends are counting on me. I will not forsake the people of Castletree to the chains of their curse or abandon my father to the desolation of a daughter lost.

Somewhere, across the realms, my mother is out there. I will find her, wherever she is.

The Enchanted Vale is not only my home, it's my legacy. I won't let it fall.

And more than anything, I know I will tear this ship apart, obliterate Kairyn's entire army with thorns and curses, and uproot the Below itself to return to my princes.

Spring may be lost, but not my hope.

It's time the Enchanted Vale had a queen again.

112

QUEEN AURELIA

The boy is coming. I know the near silent tread of his footsteps well.

His screams were particularly loud this time. I can always hear them as they rise through cracks in the pit. But today they filled my whole cell with the agonizing sound.

Does she know the sound carries to me? Is it another part of my torment, or just one of the multitude of horrors in the Below?

He doesn't look at me—he hardly ever does—but simply sits down against the wall of green crystal that serves as the border of my prison. His dark hair is spread against the flat, sheer gem. A few drops of blood splatter from the wounds on his back. He's shirtless. It would be too painful to wear a shirt until he heals.

I kneel, waiting for him to speak. A wave of dizziness overtakes me, and I grasp the wall to steady myself, fingers clutching some of the multitude of green crystals growing along the rock wall.

The crystals she uses to slowly drain away my power, drop by drop. All at once would ruin her plan, after all.

"He's fallen ill," the boy says dryly.

My heart clenches. I don't let it show on my face. "What?"

"Your husband."

"How?"

He turns slightly, just to display that he's rolling his eyes. "Oh, maybe that's what happens when you bind someone's life force to a dying tree."

"Create more thorns!" I snap.

"That won't help. They keep the structure intact, but they don't give the magic back. The Briar has already given what life it can. My thorns are cursed. I knew even as a child when you gave me this stupid power."

He waves his wrist, the golden rose bracelet dangling.

"They've helped Castletree."

"Not for much longer. And if Castletree dies, so does your husband." He turns to face me, and I try not to gape at the full extent of his wounds. Even with his magic, they will take a long time to heal. "Why would you do that, anyway?"

"I couldn't watch him die," I explain.

"Why not just make him fae?" he whispers.

"That isn't within my power." We've had this conversation before. The boy is obviously in a mood. I'm sure he'll circle back soon enough to what he really wants from me. What he's always after.

"You're the bloody *Queen*," he snarls. "You made yourself human."

"Castletree is the source of all magic in the Vale. It's eternal. So should he be," I murmur. "Besides, I didn't make myself *human*. I— never mind. I suppose we're both fools when it comes to magic and love."

The boy clutches his wrist, covering his frosted bargain bracelet. I dare him with my glare to ask his request again. One I couldn't fulfill even if his mother hadn't imprisoned me.

I could change fae into animal, myself into a beast, but I cannot make myself human any more than I can make him human.

I catch sight of something in the bag Caspian dropped beside him. Poking out is a leather notebook, the edges sprayed with blood, as if he was clutching it when…

When he was punished.

"The flail this time?" I muse.

"She let Shrowgar do it," he mutters bitterly. "He really doesn't like me."

The book has fallen open, and I strain to read the neatly written words.

Things that make me smile.

1. *Dancing to beautiful music*
2. *Fine clothing*
3. *Competitive board games*
4. ~~*Annoying*~~ *Keldarion*
5. *Rosalina, Rosalina, Rosalina*

The last line is written in a different script, finer and more elegant. I place my finger against the crystal as if I could trace the letters. He toes the book shut and raises a brow at me. "You're always so nosey."

I stand and cross my arms, catching my reflection in the crystal: matted hair and a threadbare dress, feet bare. No wonder this man—no more than a child to my ancient eyes—doesn't respect me for who I am. "There really is no entertainment of any sort down here. How about you offer the goblins a fiddle and start a merry band for me?"

He chuckles lightly, dark waves falling in his eyes.

I swallow, throat dry. "Did she ... Did she give that to you?"

"Yes."

He tilts his head, and hanging around his neck is a moonstone rose.

"And my necklace," I ask slowly. "Did she give you that?"

With blood-stained fingertips, he gently touches the stone. "No. I stole it for safekeeping."

"Caspian," I say, hating the vulnerability in my voice. But his visits are so infrequent, and I need to know. "Please tell me. Are ... are my daughters alive?"

He stares at me. Questions like this increase the risk of him coming here. Then he gives a long sigh. "Try as the world might, your youngest always manages to flutter away. And Rose ... Well, she found your bow."

The thought fills me with pride and fear. I can't help but picture her eternally as the bundle in the cradle by the firelight, chestnut curls, and rounded ears. If she wields the Bow of Radiance ... The look on the boy's face is one of utter agony.

"What aren't you telling me? Why were you punished?"

"They have her. Servants of the Below have her."

My blood turns to ice, and it takes all my remaining strength to stay standing.

"I failed..." He blinks wildly, surprised. Failure is not something that happens often to him. "I'm not powerful enough."

"Maybe not on your own."

He stands. "Don't start that again. I'm not working with you. I don't work with anyone. And I won't betray my mother."

I press my palm against the crystal barrier. "I know all you have done for my daughters. All you have done for Castletree and the realms—"

Anger twists deep into his features. "I didn't do that for you or for the realms or your dumb tree. You should have cursed me when you cursed the rest of them."

"Regardless, there's one thing I know. One thing I'm certain of."

He looks up, reluctantly placing his palm against mine.

I offer him a sad smile. "I know you will never let any harm come to Rosalina. Caspian, you have always been a worthy mate for my daughter."

Thank you so much for reading Forged by Malice! We hope you enjoyed your third adventure in the Enchanted Vale.

Reviews help others find our book. They are vital to indie authors like us. If you could take a moment to leave a review on Amazon and Goodreads, it would mean the world to us!

You can leave a review on Amazon here:

You can leave a review on Goodreads here:

THE ENCHANTMENT CONTINUES IN...

BROKEN BY DAYLIGHT

Beasts of the Briar Book 4
September 10th 2024

Acknowledgments

Wow, here we are, at the end of Rosalina's third adventure! It certainly the darkest story yet, and we must admit we had the time of our lives writing it. If you're feeling a little heartbroken, please take solace in knowing our princes and Rosie are quite resilient, and they will be back wreaking havoc in Book 4!

If you're cursing our names right now, let us give you a few more to add to the list, for this book could not be possible without the incredible love, support, and patience of those listed below.

Firstly, thank you to Susan Velazquez Colmant, super woman and agent extraordinaire. You must be a fae in disguise because you can work magic. We could not imagine a better champion for our stories. Thank you for helping us craft the Spring Realm into the magical world it is.

To the rest of the JABberwocky team, with special regards to Christina and Valentina, thank you for always having our back. We are so lucky to get to work with such a wonderful team.

To Stevie Finegan, wonder woman and agent extraordinaire. Working with you has been such a dream, and we are so grateful to have you on our side!

To our new favorite person in the entire world, our editor, Ajebowale Roberts. Meeting you has changed our lives! There is no one we trust

Rosie with more than you, and we are so excited to keep creating magic with you. Thank you for loving Rosie and her beasts as much as us.

To Harper Voyager and Magpie: magic-makers, wonder-workers, and spell-weavers. You have fostered the most superb community of book lovers. We are so proud and appreciative to be a part of your team. Thank you for representing our stories in such a beautiful way.

To our guinea pigs, test subjects, but most importantly, our friends, who have helped us shape Ezryn's journey into something we are so proud of: Anne, Beate, Camille, Carlie, Jamie, Katie, Kaylee, Khepri, Lindsay, Natasha, Olivia, Renee, Sarah, Tatjana, Taylor C., and Taylor G. Thank you for laughing and crying with us. We love you so much.

A huge, bottom of the heart, enthusiastic thank you to the bookish community. We write the words, but you make the magic. Your enthusiasm has literally made these two girls' dreams come true. Thank you, thank you, thank you. A huge shout-out to Elena, Hailey, Lindsay, and Stacey – dear friends who we're so lucky to have met through this community.

Lastly, a huge thank you to the friends and family who have been there for us during both the lowest lows and the highest highs. To Mom and Dad for always believing in us and for cheering us on at every stage. To our aunts for their endless love and enthusiasm. And to Graeme, my own Spring storm.

See you in Summer, beloved readers.

Elizabeth & Helen

ALSO BY ELIZABETH HELEN

Beasts of the Briar

Bonded by Thorns

Woven by Gold

Forged by Malice

Broken by Daylight

Novella

Prince of the Arena

About the Authors

Elizabeth Helen is the combined pen-name of sister writing duo, Elizabeth and Helen. Elizabeth and Helen write fantasy romance and love creating enchanting adventures for their characters. When they're not writing, you can find them snuggling their cats, exploring their rainforest home, or rolling the dice for a game of Dungeons & Dragons. You can connect with them on TikTok, Instagram, or Facebook.

Facebook Readers' Group

Join our Facebook Readers' Group to interact with like-minded bookish people, get behind-the-scenes info on the creation of our books, receive sneak peeks for Book 4, and chat all about the Enchanted Vale and the fae princes!
facebook.com/groups/elizabethhelen

AuthorEizabethHelen.com

f facebook.com/elizabethhelenauthor
instagram.com/author.elizabeth.helen
tiktok.com/@authorelizabethhelen
amazon.com/author/elizabethhelen
goodreads.com/elizabeth_helen

BONUS STORY

PRINCE OF THE ARENA

Before the curse, Farron travels to the Summer Realm to watch Dayton compete in the Solstice Games.

Read this Dayton and Farron spicy and sweet bonus chapter exclusive to newsletter subscribers.

ElizabethHelen.SubStack.com

PLAYLIST

Spoilers ahead!
Scan the code with the Spotify app.

The Force Theme x Main Theme | Samuel Kim *(Prologue)*
Let The Light In |Lana Del Rey, Father John Misty *("I'm your mate, Daytonales")*
"You don't dream in cryo..." | James Horner *(Ezryn enters the Hall of Vernalion)*
Khazad-dûm | Bear McCreary *(Draconhold Forge)*
The Storm | Alan Menken *(Dayton rescues the acolyte)*
Memories of Mother | Bear McCreary *(Legends atop the monastery)*
Vanessa's Trick | Alan Menken *(The Nightingale brews her potions)*
Tomorrow I'll Leave Blaviken For Good | Sonya Belousova *(Dreaming of Kel)*
Morally Grey | April Jai *(A late-night visitor)*
The Mother We Share | CHVRCHES *(Caspian and Birdy)*
Butterflies| Tom Odell, AURORA *(Tales of Lancelot and Guinevere)*
I Know Places | Taylor Swift *(Four times the fun in a flower petal)*
Double Trouble (Team Rocket) | Pokémon *(The villains plot their dark deeds)*
Immigrant Song | Led Zeppelin *(A frosted thorn rescue)*
The Christening | James Newton Howard *(Sira emerges)*
my tears ricochet | Taylor Swift *(The bargain)*
If I Can't Love Her | Terrence Mann *(Kel in his feels: the sequel)*
Visions of Gideon | Sufjan Stevens *(Dayton is ready)*
Once Upon A December | Alala *(Up the mountain)*
Across the Stars | John Williams *(Ezryn removes his helmet)*
Work Song | Hozier *(Begging for Ezryn)*
Blood upon the Snow | Hozier, Bear McCreary *(Keldarion soothes the storm)*
I'm So Sorry (Anakin's Betrayal) | Samuel Kim *(Ezryn on trial)*
Shutting down Grace's lab | James Horner *(Leaving Florendel behind)*
Nampat | Bear McCreary *(A new age of goblin and fae)*
A Friend | Ludwig Göransson *(Prince of Blood)*
Blinded By The Light | Neil Acree *(The Queen's daughter)*
Take Me to Church | Hozier *(Claiming)*
Duel of the Fates | John William *(Brother v. Brother)*
Pass Through Fire | Neal Acree *(The Golden Rose)*

PLAYLIST

I Stand Alone | Steve Perry *(Ezryn sets off on his own)*
His Dark Materials | Baltic House Orchestra *(Kiss of a dark promise)*
Eric's Decision | Alan Menken *(The Lonely Lover has a mate)*
One Day | Hans Zimmer *(It's time the Enchanted Vale had a queen again)*
Main Title: Prologue | Alan Menken *(Prisoner of the Below)*

Made in the USA
Columbia, SC
06 May 2024

35328912R00355